Strong, ha...
These me...

AT HI...

HER BOSS
THE HERO

Three exciting, dramatic romances from
favourite authors: Alison Roberts,
Anne Fraser and Molly Evans

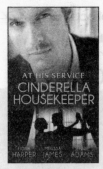

At His Service
CINDERELLA HOUSEKEEPER

FIONA HARPER • MELISSA JAMES • JENNIE ADAMS

Available in
July 2012

At His Service
HIS 9-5 SECRETARY

HELEN BROOKS • MICHELLE CELMER • JENNIE ADAMS

Available in
August 2012

At His Service
FLIRTING WITH THE BOSS

REBECCA WINTERS • ALLY BLAKE • BARBARA HANNAY

Available in
September 2012

At His Service
HER BOSS THE HERO

ALISON ROBERTS • ANNE FRASER • MOLLY EVANS

Available in
October 2012

At His Service
MILLIONAIRE'S MISTRESS

CATHY WILLIAMS • ANNE OLIVER • KELLY HUNTER

Available in
November 2012

At His Service
NANNY NEEDED

DIXIE COLTER • MELISSA JAMES • TERESA HILL

Available in
December 2012

AT HIS SERVICE:
HER BOSS
THE HERO

ALISON
ROBERTS

ANNE
FRASER

MOLLY
EVANS

Mills & Boon, an imprint of Harlequin (UK) Limited, Eton House, 18-24 Paradise Road, Richmond, Surrey TW9 1SR

AT HIS SERVICE: HER BOSS THE HERO
© Harlequin Enterprises II B.V./S.à.r.l. 2012

One Night With Her Boss © Alison Roberts 2009
Her Very Special Boss © Anne Fraser 2008
The Surgeon's Marriage Proposal © Molly Evans 2007

ISBN: 978 0 263 90224 2

026-1012

Harlequin (UK) policy is to use papers that are natural, renewable and recyclable products and made from wood grown in sustainable forests. The logging and manufacturing processes conform to the legal environmental regulations of the country of origin.

Printed and bound in Spain
by Blackprint CPI, Barcelona

One Night
With Her Boss

ALISON
ROBERTS

Alison Roberts lives in Christchurch, New Zealand. She began her working career as a primary school teacher, but now juggles available working hours between writing and active duty as an ambulance officer. Throwing in a large dose of parenting, housework, gardening and pet-minding keeps life busy, and teenage daughter Becky is responsible for an increasing number of days spent on equestrian pursuits. Finding time for everything can be a challenge, but the rewards make the effort more than worthwhile.

CHAPTER ONE

'I WON'T do it.'

'Won't do what? Hey, wait up, Tama!'

Tama James covered his head with a determined shove of his helmet. He scowled at his partner, Josh, as he swung himself into the rescue helicopter waiting for them on the tarmac, its rotors already turning.

'I just won't do it and that's *that*.'

'Nice attitude, mate.' The chopper pilot, Steve, grinned at Tama. 'I'll just radio ahead and let the cops know so they can tell that poor blighter in the car that's rolled off the hill, shall I?'

'I'm not talking about the job.' Tama snapped his safety belt on.

Josh clicked his microphone into place. 'He's talking about whatever just went down in the station manager's office. You should've seen his face when he came out of that meeting.'

Steve requested clearance, got the helicopter airborne and quickly turned onto a flight path that would lead them to the accident site—their fifth and hopefully last callout for the day.

'What aren't you going to do, then?' he asked a couple of minutes later.

Tama made a growling sound that was magnified by the communication channel built into their helmets.

'Babysitting,' he said disgustedly.

'I don't get it.' Josh sounded puzzled. 'Weren't you having a meeting with the boss and Trev Elliot?'

'Sir Trevor?' Steve whistled. 'Doesn't he *own* the finance company that funds this rescue service?'

'Yes on both counts,' Tama responded gloomily.

'So what's that got to do with babysitting?'

'Sir Trevor has a *daughter*.' Tama made the word sound like an unfortunate encumbrance. 'One who's decided she likes the idea of joining our service.'

'And?'

'And we're not that far from Broken Hills.' Tama clicked the mouse on his laptop. 'I'll check the GPS co-ordinates for the incident.'

'Not required,' Steve told him. 'I can see beacons.' He banked the helicopter into another turn. 'Police, fire service and ambulance are already on site, they just can't bring the victim up from the vehicle.'

They circled over the scene. A car had left the road and lay, upside down, several hundred metres from any kind of level surface. It was good for the helicopter crew that there were no trees on the hillside but the car must have been travelling at a good speed by the time it had hit the rocky outcrop, which wasn't so good for the occupant. Emergency service personnel had scrambled down the hillside but it was obvious that conditions were tricky.

Tama pushed thought of Sir Trevor's daughter from his head.

'Definitely a winch job,' he announced. 'No way anyone could carry a stretcher up that hill.'

'And we're well over thirty minutes' drive from the nearest hospital.' Josh was also peering downwards as they hovered. 'Nappy or stretcher for the winch?'

'Let's find out.' Tama changed radio channels to put him in touch with the ground ambulance crew. 'Update on status and injuries?' he requested.

'Open fracture of the femur. Chest and abdo injuries.'

'Status?'

'Two. His breathing's painful, though. A few broken ribs at least. BP's down. Moderate blood loss—he wasn't found for a while. We've got fluids up, pain relief on board and a traction splint in place.'

'Excellent. We'll be with you asap.' He didn't need to confer with Josh to decide that a stretcher was necessary. It might be a lot quicker and easier to pick someone up with a nappy harness but this victim's injuries were too severe to make that an option.

Steve had widened his circle as Tama was talking. 'We can put down here and empty the back,' he said. 'The less weight the better with the way this wind's picking up.'

Emergency-vehicle beacons twinkled from a distance as the light faded and Steve put the helicopter down on a nearby hill. Tama and Josh worked swiftly to remove the fitted stretcher, seats and any equipment not needed for the initial stages of this rescue mission. The more weight on board, the higher the risk of being caught in a downdraft. Dropping a hundred feet or more when you had a patient on a stretcher and a crew member dangling from the aircraft would be a disaster.

The task completed, Tama checked his gear and winch harness and climbed into his new position in the back of the chopper, ready for Josh to winch him down to the accident scene. Thanks to treatment already given by paramedics, there was no need to ready the trauma pack for deployment.

'Ninety seconds,' Steve commended as they lifted off again. 'Not bad!'

Tama's quick glance and raised eyebrow at Josh was a shorthand 'thumbs-up' signal. They were a slick team all right, and a lot of that efficiency came from a combination of experience and physical strength.

Neither of which Trevor Elliot's daughter would possess.

The mental tug back to that extraordinary interview was not only annoying, it refused to get entirely banished and niggled away in the back of Tama's mind.

'Turning downwind,' Steve announced.

'Roger. Secure aft.' Josh had checked the winch was operational. He was ready for the job. More than ready. Tama could almost see an aura of adrenaline around his colleague.

'I have the target.' He glanced at Tama and, satisfied his crewmate was as ready as he was, he turned to the winch control panel. 'Checking winch power.'

On this final run, there shouldn't have been any time at all to think outside the protocol. He'd done this a hundred times or more. Stepping into an arctic blast of air. Bracing himself. Leaning out—knowing how much space there was between his back and the ground below.

'Clear skids,' Josh confirmed. 'Clear to boom out.'

'Clear.'

Tama relaxed into his harness as the weight was taken and he got lowered to just below the skids.

The lightweight stretcher between his legs obscured his vision of what lay below. For now, he was totally dependent on Josh and Steve for his position and safety.

His own adrenaline levels kicked up several notches. He turned inwards to summon the calm strength that never failed him. This was no job for anyone who couldn't face the fear and do it anyway.

He wouldn't go as far as to say it was no job for a woman but she'd have to be an exceptional specimen.

Trevor Elliot's daughter?

A princess whose bra size probably exceeded her IQ?

Not a snowball's chance in hell.

Dusk was a favourite time for fitness enthusiasts to hit the circuit built into the outskirts of Hagley Park in Christchurch.

Swinging from the rungs of a horizontal ladder—her feet well off the ground—was a slim woman with a determined expression on her face and curly blonde hair that was tied back in a ponytail damp with perspiration.

'Give it a break, Mikki.' A man stood to one side of the structure, bent forward, with his hands on his thighs as he tried to catch his breath. 'This is embarrassing.'

Mikki hung on the last rung for a moment. She grinned down at her running companion and then refocussed, sucking in a breath and then expelling it as she pulled her body upwards. Once…twice… The burn in muscles in her arms and shoulders increased to real pain. Once more for luck and then she dropped to the ground, bending her knees to cushion the impact.

'Ready, slug?'

The man groaned but caught up with Mikki's steady jog as she continued along the track, past runners going in the opposite direction, cyclists heading home from work and the slower obstacles of people walking their dogs.

'There's no stopping you, is there?'

Mikki had taken another detour a few minutes later, to use fat stumps of wood as stepping blocks.

'Not today, that's for sure. I'm so excited!'

'Yeah…I noticed.'

'We can do our stretches now.'

'Hallelujah!'

They shared the massive trunk of an ancient oak tree for support. Mikki bent one leg up behind her and held it to stretch her quads.

'I still can't believe it, John. They're going to let me have a go at joining air rescue. Choppers!'

'So you've said. More than once.' The admonition was tempered with a fond tone. 'Good luck. Not that you'll need it.'

'I don't know about that.' Mikki swapped to her other leg. 'The pre-requisite physical assessment is tough enough to wipe out well over half the people who apply and I've never even *heard* of a female that's made it through.'

'If anyone can, you can.' John was stretching his Achilles tendon now. 'Damn shame it means you have to shift north, though. We'll miss you.'

'I'll miss you guys, too, but this is…this is huge for me, John. This is what I've wanted ever since… Good grief, do you know I started dreaming about this when I was sixteen? Twelve years ago!' Mikki couldn't stop the grin spreading across her face. 'And I've made it. Isn't it *great*?'

'You really want to give up being an emergency department doctor to work as a paramedic? In helicopters?'

'I would have gone straight into the ambulance service instead of medical school, you know, but Dad wouldn't hear of it. He wasn't exactly happy when I told him I wanted to join Médecins Sans Frontières either. He's going to hit the roof when he finds out the kind of front-line training I'm going to do for the next few months.'

'Will he try to stop you?'

'I don't think so.' Mikki put a hand on her shoulder and pulled her elbow to extend the stretch. 'I reckon I've finally convinced him how important my career is to me. He can't wrap me in cotton wool for ever.'

'From what I've heard, your dad can do anything he likes. Hey, doesn't his company practically own air rescue services up north?'

'One of them funds the service, yes.' A frown appeared on Mikki's face. 'And I'll make sure that isn't public knowledge. I've earned the right to try out for this team. God knows, I've trained hard enough and applied often enough. If anyone suggests it's come from strings being pulled, I'll give them a black eye.'

John laughed. 'Yeah…right!'

'I'm serious.' Mikki straightened to her full height which was, unfortunately, only five feet two. 'I'm going to do this, John, and I'm going to do it all by myself. Just watch this space!'

* * *

The messroom of the air rescue base lay between the manager's office, where the walls were covered in maps and communication equipment occupied the space between desk and filing cabinets, and a hangar that housed two state-of-the-art, MBB-Kawasaki BK-117 helicopters. Referred to as simply 'the mess', its title was appropriate.

At one end of the large space was an entertainment area with a wide-screen television and comfortable armchairs big enough to sleep in. At the other end, a small kitchen provided facilities for snacks and meals. As usual, the bench space was cluttered with unwashed mugs, milk cartons that hadn't made it back to the fridge and leftover fast-food containers. The laminated surface of the dining table was virtually invisible thanks to the wealth of emergency medicine journals, memos, magazines and a well spread-out daily newspaper.

Two men were standing on the same side of the table, leaning forward as they perused the front page of the newspaper. A good third of that page was taken up with a photograph that could well win some photography award for the year.

Taken with a high-powered zoom lens from the roadside, the photographer seemed almost level with the chopper and virtually close enough to touch it. Steve was clearly intent on the control panel of the craft. Josh was perched in the side door with both feet on the lower skid, his safety harness pulled tight as he leaned out to take hold of the harness cradling the stretcher.

Tama's position was elegant. One hand held the pole at the rear of the side hatch, pushing his body and the stretcher holding their patient away from the skids as he positioned the burden. Josh was about to take hold of the head end of the stretcher to guide it into the back of the helicopter.

For some reason, Tama had glanced up as the photograph was taken. Maybe he had been checking the carabina linking the stretcher harness strop to the winch. His expression was serious enough to convey the drama of the moment.

It was also easily recognisable.

Josh dug his colleague in the ribs with his elbow. 'You're famous now, mate. The chicks will be queuing up.'

'Are you suggesting they don't already?'

Josh snorted but then grinned. 'At least it's put you in a better mood today.'

'Nah.' Tama straightened and turned towards the bench. 'I'm in a really bad mood, actually.'

'Why?'

'Apparently Princess Mikayla arrives today. Got any red carpet handy?' Tama opened a cupboard to reveal an empty shelf. With a grimace, he picked up a dirty mug and stepped to the sink.

'Why?' Josh repeated. 'We're not due for any prerequisite challenges for ages. Isn't four the minimum number of applicants before we even schedule a course?'

'This one's special.' Tama wrinkled his nose as he emptied long abandoned coffee down the plughole. He turned on the hot tap. 'I have to babysit from the get-go. Make sure she doesn't break a single, precious fingernail.'

'If she's worried about her nails, she won't get far with the pre-requisite.'

'No.' Tama searched for a teaspoon at the bottom of the sink and sounded far more cheerful. 'And that way, my friend, lies the light at the end of this tunnel.'

'You mean, she can't do the physical assessment until we get enough applicants?'

'Nah. I'm going to do it with her. I'll be the assessor *and* the competition.'

Josh looked thoughtful. 'You're not planning to make this assessment impossible to pass by any chance, are you?'

'Of course not.' Tama's expression was innocent. 'It's a tough enough call as it stands.'

'You're not kidding. The ten circuits of those steep grandstand stairs in less than ten minutes just about did me in.'

'Then there's the forty push-ups and forty sit-ups.'

'The hundred-metre swim and treading water for ten minutes.'

'And don't forget the twenty-kilo pack run.' Tama grinned at Josh. 'Hey, I'll just be doing my job. Won't be my problem if she's not up to scratch.'

Josh shook his head in warning. 'Don't go out of your way to put the boss's nose out of joint, will you? We'll all catch the flak if you do.'

Tama spooned coffee granules into his clean mug. 'The way I see it, I'll be saving us all a hell of a lot of time and trouble if her highness doesn't make the grade for any further training.'

Josh sighed. 'So what you're really saying is that you're planning to break her and dump her in one easy move.'

Tama merely raised his eyebrow with a 'neither confirm nor deny' expression. Then he turned on his most charming smile. 'Want a coffee, mate?'

The newspaper cutting was in the back pocket of a rather snug pair of jeans and knowing it was there was making Mikayla Elliot uncharacteristically flustered.

She hadn't expected to find that her assigned mentor was none other than the hero who had been splashed over the front page of today's paper.

The image had been impressive enough. That look of ferocious concentration combined with a calm confidence on the face of a man at the pinnacle of a career that had always been a fantasy job for Mikki. It was the whole image that had prompted her to cut the picture out like some starstruck teenager, however. The aircraft, the crew, the patient and—as a blurry backdrop—a wrecked vehicle in hostile terrain.

But it had only been one man's face that had been visible in the picture and that man was now standing right in front of her. As large as life.

No…larger. Tama James towered over Mikki by at least twelve inches and he was probably twice her body weight.

With no helmet, the slightly too long dark curls of his hair made a luxuriantly soft-looking frame for his face. The dark olive skin and almost black eyes suggested he was a good part Maori and that impression was heightened by the fact that he wasn't wearing overalls and just below the sleeve of his black T-shirt his upper arm was encircled by an ethnic tattoo that looked like a series of waves between intricate borders.

What would he think if he knew that a picture of himself was currently nestled against Mikki's right buttock?

The level of disdain she thought she could detect in those dark eyes would go through the roof, that's what.

'Sorry?' Wondering how secure that scrap of folded paper was in her pocket had actually made Mikki miss something Tama was saying.

His look remained level. His face deadpan. As though he had expected nothing less than an inability to concentrate from what he saw in front of him.

Mikki wished she had tied her shoulder-length hair back. Worn something a lot less figure-hugging than the jeans and top she had on beneath her jacket. She wished she was six inches taller and a good deal heavier.

Standing near Tama made her feel weirdly…fragile. Like a doll. Was it because of his size and the aura of power he exuded or was it simply a reflection of what *he* was seeing?

'I just asked about your level of fitness.'

'Oh…' Mikki cleared her throat. It wasn't easy to hold eye contact with this man but, dammit, she had to find and hang onto some self-confidence somehow. 'It's OK, I guess.'

'It'll need to be.' The other man in this incredibly messy boys' zone the station manager had brought her to was grinning. At least Josh was friendly. Or was he?

'The assessment's a bit of a killer,' he added. 'You might want to have a few days in the gym to get ready for it. You should probably—'

Tama quelled his partner's advice with just a look. 'My only free day off is tomorrow.' He turned his gaze back to Mikki. 'You up for it?'

Mikki stared back. She could see a gleam in his eyes and it wasn't the kind of gleam she was accustomed to seeing in the eyes of men. This was…smug, that's what it was.

He didn't think she had a chance of making the grade.

He thought she was wasting his time.

Any remnants of her smile faded.

'You bet,' she told Tama. 'Just tell me where and when.'

CHAPTER TWO

JUST a couple of hours. Maybe not sweet but at least short.

'Sorry. You certainly gave it your best shot and I have to say I'm a lot more impressed than I expected to be, but there's a good reason this pre-requisite is tough.'

Tama twisted the shower control and turned to eye his face in the bathroom mirror while the water heated up. Just as well he lived alone at the moment, the way he was talking aloud to himself like this.

Rehearsing.

He picked up a razor but then took a second glance in the mirror. A day's worth of stubble might not be a bad look for today. Rugged.

A man who cared about things more important than appearances.

A man who meant business.

Tama abandoned the razor, using the mirror to try and perfect a sympathetic smile that was less of a smirk.

'You can always try again some time. When you feel ready.'

The smile was quite genuine as he stepped into the

shower. It was well worth giving up half of one of his precious free days to rid himself of the irritating burden Princess Mikayla represented.

There was no smile on his face an hour later, however.

The vast sports stadium on the outskirts of the city had more than a few fitness freaks intent on an early workout but the areas Tama needed were deserted. Maybe that was why the appearance of Mikayla Elliot seemed dramatic.

He was sitting on one of the lower tiers of steep seating at one end of an Olympic-sized diving pool. Directly opposite the double doors that led to the women's changing area. Had she really needed to push both doors to announce her entrance?

And how could someone as tiny as this little princess appear to have such shapely legs? He'd noticed it yesterday in those tight jeans she'd been wearing. You'd think that Lycra bike shorts would have cut them off and made them look stumpy but, no…she may be small but she was perfectly proportioned.

At least the baggy T-shirt she had on right now was covering those intriguingly compact breasts that yesterday's top had accentuated. Sad, really. If he'd met this woman under any other circumstances he would have found her more than passably attractive, but anything other than a very brief professional encounter was definitely not on the cards. Tama doubted that Mikki would want to speak to him again after this morning.

His nod of approval was in recognition of the sensible trainers she had on her feet and the way she had scraped back that silly cloud of blonde curls that begged for a tiara rather than a flying helmet. Her hair was tight in a band high on the back of her head and the length had been tightly plaited.

Mikki's face looked just as pinched as she walked towards Tama with no hint of hesitation in her step. She dropped a bag on a seat below him, extracted a water bottle and towel and then smiled up at him, albeit a trifle grimly.

'OK. What's first?'

'See that staircase on the other side of these seats?' The almost vertical one. Big steps. Twenty of them.

'Yep.'

'You run up, along the front of the top row of seats and down the steps on the other side. Along the front by the pool and then up again.'

'Cool.' She was warming up. Bouncing slowly onto her toes and down again to wake up her Achilles tendons. Stretching her shoulders at the same time and taking deep breaths to pre-oxygenate herself. Looking disconcertingly ready to fire herself into the task like a bullet from a gun.

The enthusiasm might be commendable but it was irritating. Did she really think she could do this? Most guys, including Tama, found it a challenging workout. She'd last five circuits, tops.

'The goal is ten circuits in under ten minutes,' he told her.

She eyed a chunky sports watch she was wearing and pushed a button, presumably putting it into stopwatch mode. Then she eyed the grandstand, her gaze travelling as though memorising the route and assessing the timeframes needed.

She wasn't stupid, then. Anyone else might have earned a mental tick for being able to look at the big picture before tackling the first stage. In this case, Tama wasn't prepared to concede any points.

'Plus...' He eased himself to his feet. 'You're not doing it by yourself.'

'What?' The plait on the back of Mikki's head swung as she looked over her shoulder. 'Someone else is coming?'

'No.'

Dammit! The way she stayed silent in the face of confusion, a tiny frown puckering her forehead as she waited for clarification, was also commendable. She wasn't about to jump to erroneous conclusions. And that look would extract the necessary information from anyone. There was an air of authority about this pint-sized princess. She was used to ruling her subjects. Tama hid a grin. He wasn't one of them.

'I'm doing it with you.' He stripped off the hooded jacket he was wearing. He knew the black singlet top did nothing to conceal the kind of physical condition he kept himself in but intimidation was a legitimate tool, wasn't it? He owed it to any candidate to make sure they gave their best performance.

The flicker he saw in Mikki's eyes as they widened was certainly gratifying.

'I thought you were doing the assessment.'

'Correct.' Tama deliberately flexed his upper body muscles in a slow stretch. 'It's quite possible to do both.'

'Right.'

She looked disconcerted. Used to being the focus of attention rather than a team member? A mental cross this time instead of a tick. Good. Tama held her gaze.

'Normally we don't run an assessment unless we've got at least four people ready to try out for the team.'

'So why am I doing it by myself?'

Tama's smile was one-sided. 'I guess you're special.' He twisted his body, elbows raised, partly to stretch but more to avoid eye contact. It would be unprofessional to mention her father and strings being pulled and, besides, if he got started, he might go too far. Might tell her what it was like to be one of twelve children—included but never really belonging. Fighting for any of the good things life had to offer. Struggling to get the kind of chances people like her had handed to them on silver platters.

A careful breath and he was under control. 'It helps to have someone else sharing the suffering,' he said more lightly. 'And it can make a difference, having a bit of competition. We're often pushed to or even beyond physical limits in this job.'

A single nod. 'You've done this before, of course.'

'Many times.' Tama conceded the advantage. 'But this is an initial evaluation, not a race. I don't expect you to have the kind of fitness level we maintain once we're in the job.' He didn't expect her to have much at all, did he?

She hadn't broken the eye contact. 'And you've been in the job how long?'

'Coming up to ten years.'

'And you do this kind of training how often?'

'We get reassessed every six months.'

She finally looked away, towards the cliff face of concrete steps. Then she stripped off the T-shirt to reveal a singlet top that clung just as tightly as Tama's did. He had to drag his eyes away from the faint outline of her ribs and the firm, perfect curves of her breasts. The size of good oranges, he decided.

Nice. His gaze flicked back involuntarily as he caught the movement a deep breath engendered. Fortunately, Mikki didn't notice his line of vision. She was looking at the steps.

'Ready when you are.'

If anything was going to kill her, this was.

The first five circuits had been OK. No more daunting that her usual park sessions, really, but then the punishing regime began to bite.

At least the man beside her was panting as hard as she was and his face was set in fierce lines of concentration.

Six circuits. Seven. Mikki knew she was slowing down but a glance at her stopwatch showed she had four minutes left. She dug deep. Visualised herself wearing the bright orange overalls of a helicopter crew member. Told herself they were climbing a mountain to get to a seriously injured patient.

Eight circuits. Nine. It hurt to suck in a breath now and she would probably be able to collect several hundred mils of fluid if she wrung out her hair and clothing. A sheen of sweat glistened on the rippling muscles ahead of her. Mikki watched the bulge of Tama's quads as he climbed step after step. She tried to force her own legs to match his rhythm.

She came very close to calling it quits on the upward leg of the last circuit. Halfway up and each step was so hard all Mikki wanted to do was melt into a puddle of overextended body parts. Preferably lose consciousness until life seemed worth living once more.

Just a few more steps, she reminded herself fuzzily. Then the straight bit and down the other side and you've made it. *He'll* be watching. He'll be impressed.

And that was enough to be able to do what seemed impossible. To keep pushing. To arrive at the end of this first test only a few seconds behind her assessor.

Did it matter that she flopped to the ground to sit on her bottom with her knees raised, her arms crossed on top of them and her head using them as a pillow? It must have been nearly a minute before Mikki had recovered enough for the roaring in her head to cease and she could raise it to see the expression on Tama's face.

Admiration.

Grudging maybe, but unmistakable.

Yes!

Mikki managed a smile. 'What's next, then?'

He actually grinned. 'No stopping you, is there, princess?'

It was a big ask to catch totally inadequate breath and glare at the same time but Mikki gave it a good shot.

'Princess?'

He had the grace to look…what, guilty? How odd.

'I work with blokes. We're into nicknames.'

Mikki digested the comment. He didn't want a woman on the team—was that what he had against her? Fair enough. She could overcome that kind of prejudice if she was given the opportunity.

'What's yours, then?'

'My what?'

'Nickname.'

'Don't have one.' Tama raised his face from the towel he was holding and frowned. 'Actually, I'd never noticed. I'm just me, I guess.'

Yeah...

Mikki copied his example, mopping perspiration from her face and neck. Drinking water and flexing muscles ready for the next challenge. Her gaze kept straying, however. Peeking. Taking in the fairly well-exposed and absolutely ripped body of her companion. His height and the width of his shoulders. Good grief, Tama James could probably pick her up with one hand and tuck her under his arm.

And why did that thought create an odd ache that had absolutely nothing to do with the strenuous physical activity her body had just been subjected to?

OK, he was attractive.

More than attractive. His face, with such strong features and eyes as dark as sin, would have made any female take a second glance. Factor in the 'just got out of bed' stubble, that glorious olive skin and that tattoo and you got a package that was so far out of any realm Mikki had experienced it was hardly surprising she was intrigued.

Plus, he was a hero in her dream career. Top of the ladder. There was automatic respect and admiration in place.

'You're staring.' The tone was accusing.

'Sorry.' At least her face was probably red enough to cover a blush. 'I've never worked with anyone who has, um, a tattoo like yours, that's all.'

'You're not working with me,' Tama said coolly. 'Yet. You ready for the next bit?'

'You mean I passed the last one?' The reminder that she couldn't consider herself a colleague needled Mikki. She couldn't resist making him remember how she'd kept up with his own efforts. Or had he slowed down for her benefit?

He was avoiding her gaze. 'All good so far,' he said calmly. 'Heaps to get through yet, though.'

Mikki smiled. 'Bring it on.'

Dammit, but this small, blonde bombshell was like the bloody battery bunny. She just went on and on. Through the press-ups and the sit-ups that Tama did at a speed that made his whole body burn. She seemed to enjoy the cooling-off the hundred-metre swim provided and treading water for ten minutes looked like a rest period.

If he couldn't crack her with the pack run, there was no way out of this babysitting lark.

Curiously, the notion of sending the princess packing was not nearly as appealing as it had been first thing this morning.

'Tell me why,' Tama ordered as he handed her the small backpack with a twenty-kilogram weight inside. 'Why do you want to join a helicopter team?'

'Preparation. I want to add the skills to my CV.'

'To what end?'

'MSF. Mèdecins San Frontiéres.'

'I know what it is.' Tama shook the incredulous expression from his face. 'I've thought about it myself.' He slid his arms through his pack straps. 'You're talking global hotspots. Third-world conditions. *War* zones.'

'Think I'm not up to it?'

Man, there was a bit of fire in there! Tama liked that. Sparks kept things hot.

'Didn't say that. Just curious as to why you'd want to.'

'Maybe I'm an adrenaline junkie.'

'*Are* you?' Thrill seekers who might take unnecessary risks and endanger other team members were not welcome on Tama's watch.

Mikki shook her head dismissively. 'I know the value of staying alive, if that's what you're getting at. I was in a major car crash when I was sixteen. Got a good look at what it would be like not to survive and I don't plan on repeating the experience.'

Tama nodded acknowledgement. He was tempted to ask more but that would be hardly professional, would it? He had no excuse to stray onto personal ground.

Yet.

'Having said that,' Mikki continued, 'I'm not exactly a shrinking violet either, and when I heard that MSF were short of doctors, I put my hand up.'

Tama's thoughts had been veering towards sympathy for Sir Trevor Elliot who probably had good reason to be concerned about his daughter's safety. They slammed to a halt.

'You're a *doctor*?'

'What did you think I was?'

Tama's mouth opened and then closed. Opened again. Preconceptions were exploding somewhere in the back of his mind, pretty dresses and low IQs among them. 'They…ah…said you worked in an emergency department, that's all. I…ah…'

'Assumed I was a nurse? A phlebotomist? Desk clerk?' Mikki gave an incredulous huff and turned away. 'Let's get this over with, shall we? I've got a manicure booked for later today.'

* * *

She had to reach out and touch it just to convince herself it was real and not part of a dream.

It was hanging at the end of a row of hooks. A bright orange set of long-sleeved overalls with horizontal fluorescent strips below the elbows and knees and the official air rescue insignia on the front.

'Had to be specially ordered in,' Josh told her. 'Smallest size they've ever been asked for.'

'They were quick. It's only been three days since I passed the pre-requisite.' Mikki stole a glance at the lead member of her mentor crew but Tama was looking at his partner.

'What was it they asked? If we had a mouse joining the crew?'

'Hey…Mickey Mouse!'

Oh…no! Surely that awful nickname that she thought she'd left behind at primary school wasn't about to resurface?

'Mouse,' Tama echoed thoughtfully. 'Hmm. Small and very…'

Mikki gave him a look. If he dared suggest she was scared of anything, he was going to regret it.

His lips curved. For the first time Mikki saw genuine amusement in his face and it came alive, with sparks of real mischief in the dark depths of his eyes. And, boy, he knew exactly what he was doing here. Did he have the intelligence to recognise limits?

'And smart,' he said innocently. 'Perfect.' His smile took on a wicked edge that warned Mikki he wasn't conceding victory quite yet. She followed his gaze as it travelled to where her hand was unconsciously stroking the fabric of her shiny new overalls.

'Just like your nails,' he added. 'Good job.'

Mikki drew in a breath. Some limits might need neon signs.

'Just for the record,' she informed him, 'I do not get manicures. My hair colour is natural and I have no intention of ever getting a boob job. Satisfied?'

His eyes widened a fraction but there was a flash of something other than feigned submission as he held his hands up, palms outward. Either he approved of her standing up for herself or he thought there was nothing wrong with the size of her breasts.

Mikki looked away. Tama might not be satisfied but *she* was. Enough to call a private truce. She'd let them get away with calling her 'Mouse' if that's what it took to join this team.

It still seemed like a dream but those overalls were real. She bit back a grin as she finally stopped touching them. It should be enough that she was wearing the black pants and T-shirt with the base insignia. That she had the heavy black boots with steel-capped toes on her feet already.

'What happens today?' Mikki queried.

'Depends,' Tama responded unhelpfully.

'On?'

'Callouts,' Josh supplied. He gave his partner an unreadable look but Mikki suspected a friendly reprimand was included. 'If it's quiet, Tama's going to start your basic training.'

'Cool.'

'Yeah.' Tama didn't seem to be sharing her enthusiasm, however. 'There's a lot to get through.'

'Such as?'

'Procedures. How to use the paging system. Map reading. Basic chopper safety. Gear...'

Josh groaned. 'Speaking of gear, I've got to get on with the stockroom check and clean up. It's a mess thanks to how busy we've been. Want to swap, Tama? I could train Mouse.'

Mikki's gaze flew to catch Tama's.

Those undercurrents in her pre-requisite assessment had been unmistakable. He hadn't thought she was a suitable candidate. He'd almost given the impression of experiencing physical pain when he'd had to tell her she'd passed and would be allowed to join the team for further training.

And then he'd gone. Just turned on his heel and left. It had been the station manager, Andy, who'd called her later to congratulate her and provide the information needed for the next stage, which had included arrangements for her uniform and other necessities.

Now Tama had the opportunity to step back. To give away the mentorship he'd been assigned. Was it permissible? Would he want to? Her gaze remained riveted on Tama's and it was the paramedic who finally broke the eye contact.

'Nah,' he drawled. Had the decision been a close call? 'I hate that paperwork that goes with a stocktake. I'll keep the mouse.'

Mikki had to stop an outward rush of breath. Had she been holding it? Why?

Because Tama was the senior crew member here, in every way, that's why. Josh was a nice guy and probably extremely competent but Tama's aura of confidence and ability and sheer...*power* was palpable.

This was the man Mikki wanted to work with despite whatever he might think of her.

And she wanted to work with him as closely as possible.

CHAPTER THREE

HE SHOULD have been more careful about what he wished for.

Things had started well enough. After a brief tour of the base, issuing Mikki with a pager and explaining how it worked, Tama had taken her into the hangar. One of the helicopters was already outside, with Steve busy checking it, which left plenty of space for them to stand back and admire the back-up aircraft.

'New Zealand was the first place in the world where a helicopter was used for rescue work, back in 1970.'

'Really?' Mikki stepped closer. 'I didn't know that.'

'It was only used for beach rescues for a long time. It wasn't till 1983 that we started to use them for general rescues.'

Mikki nodded. She seemed to be soaking up the information and Tama found himself unexpectedly enjoying his role. He dismissed the reaction and took a quick glance at his watch. And that was when he started wishing that his pager would go off and give him an excuse to escape Mikki's company for a while.

'It's got an eight- to twelve-seat capacity if it's not

used for medical evacuation but our stretchers and gear take up a lot of seating room. We're set up to carry seven people and a stretcher or four people and two stretchers.'

'What's the range?'

'Five-forty kilometres, depending on weight and weather and so on. We've got auxiliary tanks that extend that quite a bit. Its maximum speed is 278 kilometres an hour and it has a ceiling of ten thousand feet.' She wasn't really interested in the chopper's technical data, was she?

'So how far can we go on a job?'

'We'. It still rankled that she was here. That Tama would have to spend so much time and effort allowing her to gain a qualification that she intended to take elsewhere. If she wasn't Trevor Elliot's daughter, this would not be a happening thing, would it? And 'we' would not be going on any jobs for as long as Tama could keep a lid on this situation. He'd like to go on one, though, right about now. It wasn't going to stay this quiet all day, was it?

'Operations are normally kept within a 160-kilometre range of base, allowing forty-five minutes each way for travelling and thirty minutes at the rescue scene.'

Tama cleared his throat. He needed to get on with the training tasks assigned for the day. If it was going to stay quiet, then the sooner they got through them, the sooner he could get on with the backlog of journals he wanted to catch up on in his downtime.

'How much do you know about helicopter safety?'

'A bit. I worked in the ED of a hospital that had a helipad on the roof. I know not to approach or leave without pilot clearance and to stay in his line of vision.

And not to go near when the engine is starting up or running down because the rotors change height.'

'There's a few other considerations when we're out in the field. If you get blinded by dust or something, you have to stop and crouch or sit down. One of us will assist you. If you're carrying any gear, keep it horizontal and below waist level.'

They moved to the rear of the helicopter where the clamshell doors were open.

Mikki looked impressed. 'There's a lot of gear in there.'

'We've got a full set of what you'd expect in a well-equipped ambulance. Full resus gear, including 12-lead ECG monitoring, defibrillator with pacing capability. Suction, traction splints, scoop stretcher, IV gear, fluids, drugs. Usual stuff. Everything we need for initial stabilisation is in this kit.' Tama touched the large, soft pack strapped near the back of the machine against a folded scoop stretcher and the lightweight stretcher used for winching. 'Come and meet our pilot, Steve. He should be finished whatever he's doing outside now.'

He was. And he seemed delighted to meet Mikki. Proud to show off his sleek aircraft.

'Jump in,' he invited. 'See what it feels like from the inside. Ever been up in one of these?'

'No. Lots of small planes but never a chopper.'

Small planes. Tama almost snorted. Gulfstream jets more likely.

'I've got my private pilot's licence,' Mikki added casually, as she climbed into the copilot's seat. 'And I've done a bit of gliding.'

'Phew! You'll be flying one of these yourself next.'

Steve's gaze was openly admiring and it irritated the hell out of Tama.

'I'll do that,' he growled, moving past Steve before he could show Mikki how the safety belts worked. 'Don't let us interrupt your pre-flight stuff. We could get a job any minute, eh?'

He wished! It just wasn't comfortable having this woman within the close confines of a helicopter, which became more noticeable when they moved into the back so she could see the various seating options and how all the gear fitted. Unbearably so when Tama helped Mikki put on and adjust a seating harness.

It was inevitable that he was close enough to discover that her hair smelt of...what, strawberries? Something summery and fresh, anyway. As fresh as the puff of her breath he could feel on his neck as he leaned in. And there was no way he could avoid brushing her body with his hands on more than one occasion.

This was why he didn't like the idea of having a female crew member. It was distracting.

Alarmingly so, in this case. She didn't simply have the usual kind of feminine attractions that any man was programmed to take notice of, she had kept up with him under gruelling physical challenges that would have destroyed a lot of men. She was intelligent. And she had a pilot's licence as well? *Sheesh!*

Why wouldn't that damn pager go off? Tama wished harder and his wish came true. The pager beeped stridently and when Mikki had silenced hers, she looked up at Tama and her face was glowing.

'A job!' Her gaze held a plea that would have melted virtually any man. 'Will I be able to come, too?'

'No,' Tama snapped as he read the message on the pager. That was not part of the wish.

'Why not?' It wasn't Mikki asking. Steve walked past the open hatch on his way to the pilot's seat. 'We've got the room.'

Tama quelled him with a look that warned his colleague not to interfere. 'It might be a winch job,' he informed Mikki. 'You've had no training and you'd just get in the way. We'd end up dumping you in a paddock somewhere, along with all the other non-essential weight.'

The excitement drained from her face and a hint of colour crept into her cheeks. Mikki dropped her gaze instantly, presumably thinking she could disguise her disappointment, and her tone was light as she unclipped the harness.

'That's cool. There's plenty I can do here, I expect.'

Dammit. Did she have to be so reasonable? Tama strode into the mess room to pull on his overalls. Josh was a step ahead of him.

'Just a prang,' he told Tama. 'Roadside. Easy landing.'

'No winching, then?' Mikki was watching Josh but Tama saw the way her gaze slid towards the peg that her own overalls were hanging on.

'Not this time.'

Now Tama could feel Mikki's gaze on him. A silent query this time but one that would need a different explanation to cover his refusal. He could come up with several.

Like not knowing where gear was, for example, when it might be needed in a hurry. Say…a suction kit. Having to take the time to make sure she was following protocols regarding crew safety when his attention would be better spent on the patient. She might argue, of course, but that would be good. He'd rather see her angry than disappointed. He doubted very much that he would see any expression of defeat, however.

Did he want to?

Yes. No.

This was confusing. Having Mikki here was distracting *and* confusing and Tama didn't like it one little bit. The only saving grace was that it was temporary. And the sooner she got her damned qualification, the sooner she would be out of his place of work *and* his life.

She was still staring at him.

'Fine.' Tama kept his gaze on the zip he was pulling closed. 'You can come. But you'll have to do exactly what you're told, *when* you're told. Got it?'

'Got it.' Mikki was already halfway into her overalls. 'Hey, Tama?'

'What?' Both the tone and the eye contact were reluctant.

Her smile was almost shy. 'Thanks.'

His only response was a grunt as he jammed his helmet over his head. What was it about this princess? How could just a smile—and not even a real one at that—stir some odd sensation in his gut?

He couldn't identify the sensation but it made him feel…bigger somehow. Important. Powerful, even.

Confusing, that's what it was all right.

And Tama James did not like feeling confused.

This was *so* exciting!

Mikki would have hugged herself with the sheer thrill of it all but imagine if Tama saw that? He'd already caught her stroking her new overalls like some dreamy bride mooning over her confection of a frock.

She kept herself very, very still in her seat, thankful no one could see what was happening inside. The way her heart lifted to her mouth to mirror the helicopter rising into the air and then beat a tattoo against her ribs as they took off into a clear, blue sky. The way her stomach swooped and clenched when they hit some turbulence.

Don't be sick, she begged silently. *Please!*

'You all right?' Tama was giving her a suspicious look. Had he guessed her inner turmoil and the very real possibility that her stomach might not cope?

'I'm good,' Mikki assured him. And she was. She *had* to be!

'It's about a twenty-minute ride,' Tama said, still watching her. 'There's two vehicles involved and the fire service is only arriving on scene now so we might arrive to find people still trapped.'

Mikki nodded. Her head felt heavy with the unfamiliar helmet and her nod was probably over-eager. She became still again. This was her first opportunity to show Tama what she was capable of professionally and she was determined not to mess it up.

'Take a look around in the back here.'

They had their helmet radios on a different channel to the one Josh and Steve were using as they discussed navigation. Tama's voice, inside the helmet, was so clear and close it was disturbingly intimate. As though he had his mouth right beside her ear, his lips close enough to touch her skin.

And that gave Mikki a shiver to add to the strange physical sensations this ride was already clocking up.

'We haven't had a chance to go through the gear in here.' Tama's voice continued to caress her ear. 'Might be a good idea if you at least knew where the basics were.'

She was ready for the weight of the helmet this time. Her nod was carefully controlled.

'You can talk, you know,' Tama said drily. 'You've got a mike as well as earphones in there.'

'OK.'

'See where the portable oxygen is?'

'Yes.'

'There's adult and child masks, acute and nebuliser, plus a non-rebreather in the pouch.'

'What's in that big pack?'

'It's called a Thomas pack. It's got pretty well everything and it's what we take from the chopper for a job like this. Blood-pressure cuffs and a stethoscope, chest decompression sets, intubation gear, bag mask unit, IV gear, fluids and drugs. We'll go through it properly when we're back at base.'

Mikki had a sudden inkling of what this was like from Tama's viewpoint. She was being allowed out on a job before she really had any idea about resources and protocols. Before he had any idea what her level of skill was. He was probably thinking—quite rightly—that she could be a hindrance rather than any help.

Mikki took a deep breath and tried to quell her rush of nerves but they came back with a vengeance when they slowly circled the scene and came in to land. The view from up high was spectacular but getting the big picture with such clarity made this all seem almost overwhelming.

Traffic was backed up for miles in both directions,

with police cars blocking the road well away from the
accident site, so that even before Mikki could glimpse
what they were heading for, she already had the impression it was major.

More police cars. Fire engines and two ambulances
and so many people made up the inner circle and
there—in its centre—were two horribly mangled vehicles. A car and a small truck. Mikki could see someone
lying on the ground and another sitting with ambulance
officers in attendance. And, judging by the cluster of
rescue workers, someone else was still trapped in the
car.

Multiple patients, potentially critically injured, but it
shouldn't be throwing her into this kind of a spin. She
dealt with the aftermath of MVAs all the time in
Emergency and she was good at it. They often had more
than one victim arrive from a single incident.

But this was very, very different.

These people hadn't already been triaged and stabilised by competent paramedics. Removed from a scene
of carnage to arrive neatly packaged on a stretcher into
a department that was well prepared with equipment and
personnel. This was frontline stuff with an emotional
element Mikki hadn't expected, thanks to seeing the
lines of traffic and the scope of the rescue effort and
being there—in real time—to imagine the shock of
having one's life so unexpectedly thrown into chaos.

You know what to do, Mikki reminded herself as the
helicopter touched down in a paddock beside the road,
far enough away for the rotor wash not to create havoc.
It's basic. Airway, breathing, circulation. Assess each
one and deal with it if it's not adequate before moving

on to the next. It may be more difficult and messier out here in the field but the priorities were the same.

And this was exactly where she wanted to be, wasn't it? Frontline. Dealing with all the complications any kind of environment could create. Relying on her own skills and resources that would be far less than those an emergency department could offer. She wasn't being thrown into this alone, in any case. She was with someone who was the top of their field. She was here to learn.

Confidence was available after all. She had Tama by her side. Mikki gathered all she could find as she followed him towards the car. Josh peeled off, after a brief, almost non-verbal communication with his senior partner, to go to the ambulance officers attending the people already out of the vehicles. Two more ambulance officers were right beside the car. The rear door had been cut away and a woman perched on the back seat, holding the driver's head in a position that would keep his airway open and protect his neck.

Another straightened from where the front door had also been cut away.

'He's unresponsive,' the paramedic informed Tama. 'They've only just pulled the truck clear and got these doors off for us so I haven't even completed my assessment, sorry.'

Tama leaned in. 'Hey, mate,' he called. 'Can you hear me? Can you open your eyes?' His fingers were on the man's wrist, and then his neck. 'Carotid pulse,' he said aloud. 'No radial. BP's well down.'

'He's bleeding heavily,' the paramedic noted. 'His leg's trapped under the dash.'

A fireman moved in from the crumpled bonnet of the

car. 'We're about to do a dash roll. You'll be able to get him out then.'

Mikki had to move as a thick hose was pulled past her feet, a piece of equipment attached to its end that looked like a modified pneumatic drill. She was trying to concentrate on the continuing communication between Tama and the road-based paramedic but this was no emergency department handover.

The pneumatic gear the fire service were using was loud enough to mean people had to shout to communicate and everyone seemed to have urgent tasks that other people were being ordered to carry out. The woman on the ground a short distance away was screaming and a new, approaching siren added to the cacophony.

It smelt of hot metal and petrol and blood and everything looked deformed and sharp. Dangerous.

'Can you move?' A fireman requested curtly. He was holding the heavy-looking cutting gear. 'I need to get in here.'

'Give us a minute,' Tama ordered. 'I want to get an IV in and some oxygen on before we do anything more.' He slid the Thomas pack off his back and, magically, enough clear space opened beside him to allow the pack to be opened out. 'Mikki? You want to get the IV in?'

'Sure.'

She hoped she sounded sure. An eagerness to show Tama what she could do—*please* him, even—bubbled inside her, and he'd handed her what should be an easy way to begin. Apart from having to step around the crumpled driver's door on the ground, access wasn't a problem. The paramedic unhooked a pair of shears from his belt and cut through the jersey and shirt covering her patient's arm. Mikki slid a tourniquet on and pulled it tight.

Tama leaned past to slip an oxygen mask over the man's face, then he hooked the stethoscope hanging around his neck into his ears and leaned in to listen to the man's chest. The paramedic was waiting his turn to get close, a stiff neck collar in his hands.

'Chest and neck injuries,' Tama informed Mikki succinctly. 'I'm not happy with his airway but an OP will have to do until we get him out. BP's well down so I want to get fluids started stat.'

Mikki just nodded, concentrating on gaining access to a forearm vein with the wide-bore cannula she held. It wasn't easy. Their patient was a very large man and she was having to go on touch rather than a visual target. To her relief, blood flowed into the chamber instantly. She advanced the needle a little further, slid the cannula home and withdrew the mechanism.

'Got a luer plug?'

'Here.' The paramedic had a dressing and tape ready to secure the line as well and then a giving set and bag of fluids appeared with commendable swiftness, but if Mikki had expected any praise for succeeding in her task, she would have been disappointed. Not that there was time to think of it because things were moving very rapidly now.

Josh joined them.

'Truck driver's only got minor injuries and the female passenger from the car is stable. They're both being transported by road. Where are we here?'

They were at the point of being able to move their patient. Mikki stood back, letting the more experienced and stronger men put on an impressive display of peeling back crumpled metal and then using a body splint and backboard to turn and slide the victim free with minimal disruption to his spinal alignment.

The unconscious driver was on a stretcher within a very short period of time, moved clear of the wreckage, but securing him in the helicopter was still some way off, it appeared. The man's breathing was deteriorating and Tama clearly wanted to try and stabilise his condition prior to transport. He opened pockets of the Thomas pack and took out a large, tightly rolled package.

Mikki was using the stethoscope as Tama untied the package and opened it up to reveal an intubation kit. She nodded her agreement.

'He's got some bleeding going on in his trachea,' she said. 'And I don't like this swelling in his neck. If we don't secure his airway now, we might lose it completely.'

'Absolutely.' Tama was holding up a pair of gloves that looked far too small for his hands. 'Go for it, Doc.'

Mikki couldn't help her jaw dropping in astonishment.

Technically, she had higher qualifications than either of the paramedic air rescue crew. She had intubated dozens of people in emergency departments and Theatre but these guys had the huge advantage of experience in working under precisely these conditions.

Rescue crews were still busy around them. It was noisy and dirty and…foreign. And this was an obese patient who could be difficult to intubate even under ideal circumstances. Tama was throwing her in the deep end here but she had breezed through that cannulation, hadn't she?

She could do this, too.

Except it was harder than she had feared. With blood

in the airway and bright sunlight negating the effect of the laryngoscope's light, it was impossible.

'I can't see a thing,' Mikki had to admit.

'Here. I'll shade you.' Tama loomed close over Mikki and the man's head, blocking the light from falling directly on them.

Mikki still couldn't visualise the vocal cords. It was hard to keep a note of desperation from her voice.

'I need suction.'

'It's here.' Tama managed to slip the handle of the suction unit inside their patient's mouth without dislodging the laryngoscope Mikki held in place. She reached for an ET tube.

'Here goes,' she muttered hopefully.

Her first attempt failed.

'Oxygen saturation is dropping.' Josh was right beside her. 'I'll bag mask him for a sec.'

Mikki sat back on her heels, looking for a replacement tube in the kit. She caught Tama's steady gaze. 'Maybe you should do this,' she suggested. Or Josh could. Except that Josh was now responding to a signal from a fire officer. It looked as though one of the rescue workers had injured himself.

'Have another go,' Tama directed.

So she did and again it proved impossible.

'The trachea's swelling,' she said in despair. 'I can't get this past the cords even with a guide wire.'

'I'll have a go.'

They swapped places. Tama handed her the bag-mask unit and she held the mask over the man's face, squeezing the bag to try and get a high concentration of oxygen into the man's lungs. She could feel it becoming more difficult as the airway closed further. Tama was pulling on gloves. As he picked up the laryngoscope, Mikki could hear the deterioration in the man's breathing. A nasty stridor that suggested they might be about to lose this challenge.

Tama positioned himself and the patient's head. He inserted the laryngoscope.

'Give me some cricoid pressure,' he instructed seconds later.

Mikki pressed on an Adam's apple that was actually hard to locate in an already thick neck that had severe swelling going on as well. If things were this hard from the outside, what hope did Tama have of slipping a tube through the airway internally?

Very little, but he managed. Almost instantly, he slipped the tube into place and then straightened to secure it and attach the bag mask to the end of the tube. Mikki picked up the unit as Tama placed his stethoscope on the chest. She squeezed the bag as he listened for lung sounds and then placed the disc below the ribs to exclude air going into the epigastrium.

'We're in,' he announced calmly. 'Let's get this guy on board and get moving.'

The packing up and preparation for take off were practised and smooth. Josh returned and again Mikki was left on the outskirts of the routine, simply watching.

No wonder. She had messed up, hadn't she? Failed on the first real medical challenge that had been thrown her way.

She was a liability. Tama hadn't wanted her on his crew in the first place and now he had good reason to resent her inclusion.

No wonder he was so focussed on his patient he didn't spare her even a glance on the homeward journey. No surprise she wasn't asked to assist in any medical capacity either. These guys had it sorted. Intensive monitoring, another IV line, fluids going in under pressure, a badly broken leg dressed and splinted.

She was just a passenger. An unwanted one. Present but not included, and it stirred memories Mikki had thought long buried.

They came in to land on the hospital helipad with their patient still stable and breathing well. The two paramedics were clearly satisfied with the way the job had gone. Tama seemed to have forgotten the debacle with intubation but Mikki couldn't. She had to bite her lip and blink away a very unexpected prickle in her eyes that suggested the possibility of tears.

She was about to *cry*?

No way!

Mikki clenched her jaw tight as she climbed out of the helicopter to follow the stretcher. She wasn't going to let it matter that Tama didn't want her. That she had played into his hands by begging to go on a job and then demonstrating a very uncharacteristic lack of ability.

He'd give her another chance.

He *had* to.

CHAPTER FOUR

'HAPPY?'

'Yeah...sure,' Tama replied.

Josh quirked an eyebrow. 'You should be. You don't have to carry on with the incredibly boring stocktake.'

This was true. If it remained quiet on station he could carry on with Mikki's training. She needed to learn how to load and unload the stretchers. How to secure sliding doors and all the medical gear and what to check before telling the pilot that 'all was secure in the rear'.

'Do you know how many individual components we have in IV gear alone?'

'No.' And Tama didn't know why he wasn't as happy as he claimed to be either.

'Fourteen,' Josh said in disgust. 'Five different gauges of cannula, wipes, luer plugs, giving sets, Tegaderm, tape...'

Tama pushed open the door of the men's changing room, barely registering the list. Mikki wasn't in the kitchen end of the messroom and it was well past time they had some lunch. Where was she?

'Then there's four sizes of syringes and six sizes of

needles on top of that,' Josh continued, 'and I have to count every single one of them.' He, too, looked around the room. 'Where's the mouse?'

'Dunno.'

'She was kind of quiet when we got to the hospital. If the job had been a bit much for her, I would have expected her to feel happy to be on familiar turf, even if it wasn't an ED she's worked in. She didn't look happy, though, did she?'

'No.'

'Maybe she doesn't like it as much as she thought she would. She looked pretty excited when we headed off.'

'Yeah.' That glow had been well and truly snuffed out, hadn't it? And Tama knew why. Having been called to check that fire officer, Josh hadn't seen Tama take over the intubation of that difficult patient. He had no idea how tense it had been. How lucky Tama had been to succeed on his first try and how it must have made Mikki feel like she'd messed up and shown herself to be less than competent.

The wind had been taken out of the royal sails all right. Tama had demonstrated his own prowess at her expense. He should be pleased with himself. Experiencing the kind of satisfaction that had once been a dream—to prove that someone like him was just as good, if not better, than someone like her. He should be *happy*, dammit!

'Coffee?'

'Sure.' Maybe she was still in the tiny bathroom area kept for visitors that was now deemed the female locker room. That would be it. She probably needed to touch up her mascara or nail polish or something after working rough.

I don't do manicures.

Josh turned from where he was fossicking in the fridge. 'And how about I nuke the leftover chow mein we put in the freezer last week?'

Tama nodded. He wasn't bothered about what they ate. He was more bothered by how clearly he could hear Mikki's words echoing in his head. She wasn't into nail polish. Her hair colour was natural and she liked the size of her breasts. So *there*!

Tama could feel a corner of his mouth pulling sideways. Spirit like that was something he could approve of. Like the way she had punished herself keeping up with him during those pre-requisite challenges. She had been so determined to make the grade, hadn't she? To prove she was up to the job.

Had that spirit been snuffed out, along with the glow?

OK, the glow had been irritating but that was partly because he understood it. Not that he'd ever let it show on *his* face like that. At least, he hoped he hadn't, but he knew what it was like to get a shot at something you wanted badly enough to get so excited about. And he also knew what it was like to want something that badly and have it all turn to custard. To blame yourself for whatever was going wrong. He hoped Mikki wasn't into beating herself up too thoroughly. While it might be good to have tarnished the glow a little, crushing that spirit entirely would not only be unnecessary, it could lead to repercussions. What if the boss learned that the princess was unhappy? Who would be held accountable? Him, that's who.

Josh was pushing buttons on the microwave and Tama should have been looking forward to the food, not standing here, worrying about the mental state of an extra crew member.

The faint growling sound he emitted did not come from his empty stomach.

Josh looked over his shoulder. 'What's up?'

'Just need a bit a fresh air. Be back in a minute. Don't eat it all.'

Patting his pocket as he strode through the hangar on his way outside was automatic. Remembering that he'd packed in smoking a long time ago didn't help alleviate the odd tension. Neither did spotting Mikki.

She'd hung her overalls back on the peg and she was just standing there, her back towards Tama. She probably had no idea how the slump of her shoulders was advertising her state of mind as clearly as her expressions did.

Tama's need for a bit of solitude went head to head with the knowledge that he could—and should—do something to debrief their new recruit. She hadn't seen him, however. He could slip out the back door and find a quiet spot in the sun for a minute or two.

There would be plenty of time later for some reassurance and encouragement, but Tama had hesitated and then he was lost. With a sigh, he gave in to the pull that led him away from the back door.

'What *do* you think you're doing?'

Mikki jumped.

Oh, God! What had she done wrong *now*?

This day had started with such promise and excitement and now it was going from bad to worse, but she wasn't about to let Tama know how crushed she was feeling. She really didn't want to give him the satisfaction of having his doubts affirmed.

No. She knew that when the going got tough, that was when the tough had to get going. Mikki straightened her shoulders and lifted her chin before she turned to face Tama. She held his gaze and waited for whatever reprimand was coming. Ready to fight back, if necessary.

Her resolve to hold that eye contact wavered with the horrible thought that Tama could see way too much. There was something about those dark eyes that made her feel curiously defenceless. Whatever he saw, however, didn't seem to displease him because his mouth pulled to one side in a half-smile that was distinctly disconcerting. People didn't usually smile at you when they were about to tear you to shreds.

'We tend to leave our overalls on for the rest of the shift after the first callout,' he said. 'You never know what's coming next.'

'We'. He'd said 'we' as though he considered her to be one of the crew. Mikki took a careful inward breath and dampened the flash of hope that tiny word had created. Was he patronising her in some way? Did he really expect her to believe he didn't consider her an incompetent encumbrance after this morning's efforts?

Employing the benefit of the doubt would have been the wise thing to do but insecurity was deeprooted. She did do her best to sound offhand, to try and pretend it didn't matter. 'I thought you might prefer to leave me behind next time.'

'Why?'

'Well…' He *knew*, dammit. She could see it in his

eyes. Did he expect her to describe her inability to perform a lifesaving procedure? Spell it out in excruciating detail? Mikki could feel heat creeping up from her neck and heading towards her cheeks. 'I didn't exactly—'

'You did great,' Tama interrupted, sounding as casual as Mikki had been striving for. As though it was no big deal. 'It was a pretty full-on scene for your first callout.'

He was smiling with both sides of his mouth now and it connected to his eyes in a way that made them... warmer. It gave the impression he was being genuine but kindness seemed too much to expect. Inappropriate, somehow. Mikki could feel herself frowning as she tried to remember what had seemed so important a moment ago.

'I'd like to have done a better job with that intubation.'

The big man actually shrugged. 'We got there in the end.'

'*You* got there.'

'I got lucky.' Unexpectedly, Tama's eyes danced for a heartbeat. 'Plus, I knew it was a pig of a job. I went down two sizes in the ET tube.'

Mikki shut her eyes for a moment, both as a distraction from that disconcerting twinkle and to berate herself. Why hadn't she thought of that for her second attempt? With all the swelling and bleeding going on, it made perfect sense to downsize from what a patient of that build would normally need.

'Nice job with that IV,' Tama added. 'We could have lost that guy if we hadn't got fluids started soon enough. Tip someone into irreversible shock and it doesn't matter what fancy techniques you throw in later. They're still going to go into multi-organ failure and die.'

Mikki couldn't help staring. He *was* being nice to her. But why? If she had done outstandingly well the first time they had worked together in the field she might have understood. He hadn't been thrilled to have her on the team but if she had proved herself a valuable addition then at least acceptance, if not respect, might have been reasonable, but she hadn't done outstandingly well. Anyone could put in an IV.

Tama was still talking about it. 'Bit different for you, to say the least. You don't have someone trapped in awkward positions in ED and a dozen impatient firemen breathing down your neck.'

Her mind was racing at a million miles an hour. Tama was being kind. Glossing over something he could have used to her disadvantage, even to the point of refusing to take her on missions for the foreseeable future. Instead, he was glossing over the failure and focussing on what she had achieved. It came across a bit like someone patting a child on the head and telling them they'd done well just because you could see they'd done their best.

Was it because he was responsible for training her and that schedule had a certain number of boxes to get ticked? And the sooner they were done, the sooner Tama's involvement would be over? Maybe he didn't care about the quality of his trainee's work as much as getting his sentence as a mentor done and dusted.

Still…Mikki dredged up a smile and turned to unhook her overalls from the peg. This was the second chance she wanted, wasn't it? She couldn't afford to be over-sensitive about the motives for which it was being offered.

'Get changed fast,' Tama advised finally. 'Lunch is getting cold.'

So that was that. The incident had been discussed and was to be forgotten. Mikki had been on her first callout and was that much closer to becoming an accepted crew member.

Her spirits lifted even further when her training continued after a short meal break. Mikki practised loading and unloading gear from the back of the helicopter. Hooking straps into place and checking they were secure. Easing the foot end of the stretcher into slots where it could be locked into place.

Tama was an excellent teacher. He demonstrated the task to show her what the expected skills were and then he repeated the action slowly, pausing to explain exactly what he was doing and why. Then he showed her again, at normal speed, with just a few key words to remind her of what needed to happen.

'Unclip here. Slide. Lift. Use your legs, not your back.'

Mikki did her best but had to growl in frustration when it came to the stretcher.

'My legs are too short. I can't reach properly.'

'Bend from the hips to give yourself a longer stretch. Bring one knee up and support yourself on the floor. The knees of the overalls are padded so it's safe to kneel even at an accident site.'

'Hey!' Mikki could reach and push far more easily. She flipped the locking mechanism over the stretcher handle. 'That worked.' She beamed.

Tama was watching with what appeared to be an equal measure of satisfaction. With her performance or his advice?

'Your legs reach the ground,' he said blandly. 'Just the right length if you ask me.'

It was just a moment in time. A couple of heartbeats, but it was long enough to feel *too* long. As though something was being said that had nothing at all to do with the task in hand.

Or was she being over-sensitive again? Reading more into the interaction with her mentor because there was something about him that was so dangerously attractive?

Mikki dragged an unwilling line of vision away. Seeking distraction. She found it way above Tama's head.

'What's that?'

'What?' Tama turned his head.

'That…platform thing with the ladder.' She pointed to the far corner of the hangar's roof.

'It's a simulator. For winch training. That's a skid and that pole thing that's folded in at the moment is a boom.'

'So you can hang from that? In a harness?'

'You have to do some groundwork first. Learn how to use the harnesses and work with carabiners and what hand signals mean and so on. *Then* we start using the simulator.'

Mikki's upward gaze was rapt. 'Cool!'

'Don't get too excited.' His tone was a warning. 'Not everybody gets to do winch training and it'll be a while before I'm ready to make a decision as to whether or not *you're* a suitable candidate. Months, probably.'

Mikki just nodded. She didn't want to catch Tama's gaze and read a reminder that she hadn't particularly impressed him with her skills so far. The silence that fell could have become awkward but the hangar door opened in the nick of time to admit the station manager, Andy.

'HUET tomorrow,' he informed Tama.

'What? That's not supposed to be on the agenda until next month.'

'They brought it forward. Did you not see last week's memo? The gear's needed somewhere else next month. There's no need to sound quite so unenthusiastic either. You knew it was coming.'

'Yeah…but not tomorrow! We're on duty.'

'Relief crew's coming in. They're doing their training the following day. No excuses,' Andy ordered. 'You know how important this is, Tama, and you know it doesn't happen very often. We go when we're told.' He smiled at Mikki. 'You get to do it, too,' he said. 'You're lucky. This only happens once every couple of years. We have to get the gear flown in from Australia for this and it's a big deal. Great opportunity for you.'

Mikki had no idea what he was talking about but the enthusiasm was contagious. She returned the smile. 'That's great!'

'Tell Tama that,' Andy ordered, heading back to his office.

'You have no idea what he's talking about, do you?' Tama asked drily.

'No.' Mikki caught her bottom lip between her teeth. 'Hewy?'

'H.U.E.T.,' Tama spelt out. 'Stands for Helicopter Underwater Escape Training.'

'Oh…'

'There's a morning of theory in the classroom and then we get to go out to that sports complex where you did the pre-requisite. There'll be a crane beside the diving pool and it has a cage that's designed to replicate the fuselage and seating of a helicopter.'

Mikki could actually feel the sinking sensation in her heart. 'And it goes in the pool?' As if it hadn't been a big enough ask, running up and down the steps beside that pool.

'Yep.'

'With people inside?'

'Yep.'

'Wearing clothes? And helmets? In harnesses and safety belts?'

'Oh, yeah.'

'And we have to escape and get to the surface so we don't drown.'

'More than once. We get to do it vertical a couple of times and then it goes in vertical and gets flipped on one side. And while it's not compulsory, if you really want to get the most out of the training…' Tama's gaze was a steady challenge '…you can get turned completely upside down with or without blackout goggles.'

Good grief! This sounded like a lot more than she had bargained for in her training. The fear that might come from dangling from a winch line paled in comparison. Her heart skipped a beat and picked up speed but showing Tama how nervous the prospect made her feel was not an option.

She grinned. 'Talk about being thrown in the deep end!'

Tama didn't return the smile. 'This is serious,' he told her. 'And dangerous. You won't be forced to participate.'

'Sounds like an opportunity I'd be stupid to miss.' Mikki lifted her chin. 'I'll give it a go. Do we take turns?'

'No. It's crew training. We'll all be in the crate together.'

Tama's expression was controlled to the point of appearing empty but Mikki had no trouble interpreting what was going on behind those dark eyes. A female crew member who panicked and made the training even more dangerous for anyone else would be more than a liability.

She would be history.

Mikki swallowed hard, aware of goose-bumps rising on her arms. She had wanted a second chance to prove herself to this man. This may be bigger and scarier than any situation she would have preferred and it might not showcase any medical skills but this was it.

And, dammit, she was going to show Tama James what she was made of.

They were almost done.

A bedraggled knot of people—Tama, Josh, Steve and Mikki—stood on the side of the diving pool. They were wearing float suits, which were like their overalls with the addition of a special lining, but enough water had seeped in over the last hour to chill them and they all shivered occasionally as they listened to the man in charge of this practical session of their HUET.

'You've done well,' he was saying. 'I'm impressed, guys. Especially with you, Mikki, given that you've only just started working with choppers.'

'Th-thanks.' The attempt to suppress a shiver failed but Mikki was smiling as she pushed back the sopping length of her braid that was still sending a trickle of water to drip off the pads of her life jacket.

Her dive mask was pushed to the top of her head and it made her face seem smaller. Her features were as delicate and perfectly proportioned as the rest of her body, Tama realised. He also had the thought that from any kind of a distance you would have considered this to be a child playing dressup. He was close enough to see the mature and steely determination in those blue eyes, however, and so far she had lived up to whatever standard she had deemed necessary.

Mikki had exceeded his expectations, that was for sure.

She'd sat quietly, strapped into the seat, as they'd been lowered into the pool for the first time. She had remembered to hold her breath until the bubbles had cleared and that had been the only occasion she had fumbled at all with releasing her harness. She'd stayed admirably calm on the next try, managing to open the door herself when she had a turn on that side of the 'fuselage'.

Even having the crate rotated on their last attempt hadn't fazed her, but the real test was coming. Now, when they were cold and feeling the kind of exhaustion that came after bodies were pushed to keep releasing high levels of adrenaline. The instructor was thinking ahead as well.

'This one's the biggie,' he warned. 'Upside down. You've got to hold your breath, release your harness, find the door and orient yourself before you swim to the surface.' He was looking at Mikki. 'This isn't compulsory, any more than the blackout goggles are. It's your call.'

Would she do it? Tama wouldn't blame her if she declined. She'd proved herself already as far as he was concerned. Outstandingly quick in the classroom and gutsy as hell so far in the practical.

'Mikki?' The instructor had moved so that he towered over the shortest member of the crew. 'You've probably done enough for your first HUET. Want to call it quits for the day and get warm and dry?'

Mikki didn't hesitate. 'No,' she said.

Tama exchanged a meaningful glance with Josh and mirrored the raised eyebrows but hid his grin.

Go, the mouse!

'I want to do it,' Mikki added firmly. 'I'd rather find out how tough it is in a controlled environment than in some lake or out at sea.'

It was ridiculous to feel so proud of her. Puzzling, in fact. Tama knew he was frowning as he spoke up.

'I don't want Mikki by the door. We need someone who's confident of opening it fast.'

'You want that spot?'

'Sure. I'll have some goggles, too, thanks.'

'Right. Let's get into this, guys. I reckon you'll all be pretty keen to get this over and done with.'

He wasn't wrong.

Tama had done this before but he still felt a flutter of nerves with the lurch as the crate was swung up and then over the deep pool. Maybe those nerves were there *because* he had done it before. From knowing how easily panic could claw at you and how hard it could be to fight it taking hold. How incredibly disorienting it was to be upside down underwater.

His senses were heightened by wearing the blackout goggles. He could hear the shouts of people poolside, operating the machinery or just watching in fascination. He could smell the chlorine and feel the chafe of wet clothing and the heaviness of his boots.

And he could sense Mikki strapped into the seat beside his position near the door. Steve and Josh were in the front seats of this skeletal 'helicopter'. It was just Tama and Mikki here at the back and he was even more aware of how tiny she was. Fragile? Not on your life. Vulnerable? Quite possibly. Wasn't everybody in some circumstances?

Slowly, the crate was turned until they were upside down. Hanging in their harnesses with blood rushing to their heads and effort needed to stop limbs dangling inconveniently. For a moment, Tama regretted opting for the blackout goggles. With the next lurch that signified their descent came a real flash of concern for Mikki. He wanted to be able to see her to gauge how she was coping with hanging like this. Whether she had any idea at all that this was about to get one hell of a lot harder.

Right…*now*…as their heads reached water level and the downward momentum continued.

Tama remembered to keep his mouth shut and hold his breath. He may not be able to see the bubbles escaping but he could hear them and feel them. It was like being immersed in a huge effervescent drink. He waited until it was quiet and still. And in that moment of quiet, with everything totally black came something like a faint wash of panic. Not for himself. For the princess.

Because, despite the short length of their acquaintanceship, Tama knew perfectly well that Mikayla Elliot did not have a princess mentality, no matter what her background was. She was tiny but, man, she was tough. Currently a lone female in a male world. An ultimately feminine one at that. Her size gave her the pathos of the runt of the litter. Her career choice made her a maverick.

They had that in common, didn't they? Never mind that her sheer guts had earned his genuine respect. He had the feeling there were more surprises in store with this woman and he didn't want to miss out on any of them. Most of all, right now he didn't want anything bad to happen to her.

With more haste than he would otherwise have employed, Tama used one hand to unclip his harness and with the other hand he reached for the door control and unlocked it. He shoved the door open. Now he should pull himself through it, turn the right way up and kick for the surface before his lungs started to really complain about the lack of fresh oxygen.

He couldn't do it. With no vision, he couldn't be sure that Mikki had freed herself from her harness. She'd had that momentary fumble on the first try, hadn't she? The rocking of the crate and sounds he could hear all seemed to be generated from the space Steve and Josh were occupying.

Those sounds diminished rapidly. Within seconds, Tama instinctively knew it was just himself and Mikki left in this crate, under metres of water. He could imagine Josh and Steve breaking the surface and climbing from the pool. Joining the spectators to watch and wait for the remaining crew members. How long before they started to feel anxious? For alarm to become apparent? For someone to jump in and rescue Mikki?

Keeping one hand on the doorframe to keep himself oriented, Tama pushed back and then extended his other arm.

Feeling for Mikki. Ready to unclip her harness and haul her to safety if necessary.

It didn't matter a damn if she needed assistance to complete this assignment. It's what he would do for any crew member if this was for real, wasn't it?

And, dammit, Mikki was part of *his* crew now.

* * *

The hand touched her just as panic threatened to turn Mikki's brain to mush and make her cry out for help, even with the background knowledge that the action would speed up the process of drowning.

She reached out with her hand and found it grasped securely. With her other hand she finally managed to unclip her harness and wriggle free.

Tama was pulling her forward.

To safety.

Her lungs hurt. She couldn't tell which way was up and if Tama hadn't had hold of her hand she could have been in real trouble. His upward kick as she cleared the crate was strong enough to propel them both towards the surface but it took a fraction too long. Mikki's lungs gave up the struggle to hold her breath a fraction too early. She took some water in with that first frantic gulp of air and began coughing and spluttering.

'You OK, Mouse?'

Tama had his arms right around her and it took a moment for Mikki to realise she was clinging to his neck as he trod water out in the middle of the dive pool. She tried to answer but couldn't speak yet. She tried to move but Tama's hold tightened.

'Be still,' he advised calmly. 'Get your breath back.'

There was something so gentle in that command to 'be still' that Mikki found herself transfixed. Almost hypnotised.

Their heads were so close.

Close enough to kiss.

Where had *that* come from? Involuntarily, Mikki's gaze dropped to Tama's mouth and desire hit somewhere deep in her belly with the kick of a mule. He had the most *kissable* mouth she'd ever seen. Lips that looked so soft but had such firm lines. Lines that were currently crooked with one side pulled up into a hint of a smile.

Mikki's gaze shot up to find Tama watching her very steadily. His gaze dropped to *her* mouth.

Oh…Lord! Had he guessed what she'd been thinking about? And the way he was looking back at her now… was it possible he'd been thinking the same thing?

Yes.

If they'd been alone, Mikki would swear he would have kissed her at that moment. And she would have wanted him to. But they were far from alone and re-membering that finally made Mikki aware of the sounds around them. The spectators' noise level was increas-ing. They were clapping.

Cheering, even.

The realisation of what she had just achieved hit home. She had confronted real danger and won. That flood of adrenaline and pure excitement came from winning the challenge, didn't it? Cheating death.

The sheer thrill of being alive. Of feeling so alive that every cell in your body seemed to be humming. It had nothing to do with the feel of Tama's arms around her body or that tiny fantasy she'd just experienced about kissing him.

OK, maybe it had a little bit to do with that. Physical attraction was another way of making your body feel alive, but it was just the icing on the cake that had led Mikki on this career path. The pursuit of this thrill.

Mikki was still holding Tama's gaze and…and it was like looking into a mirror.

He understood.

Here was someone else who recognised that thrill. Not reckless enough to chase it for its own sake but who could appreciate its benefits. Knew it was the most excitement life had to offer. Maybe he also shared the knowledge that, while physical attraction and fulfilment could be an added thrill, it could never be allowed to get in the way of experiencing the best.

Tama's eyes widened and there was a flash of something more than surprise as he clearly recognised the reflection. He let her go so they could both swim to the side of the pool but the knowledge of a real connection was still there and Mikki knew it wasn't something that was going to be broken easily.

CHAPTER FIVE

THE face behind the Perspex window of the helicopter got smaller.

It was too high now to be sure of where he was looking, but the downward tilt of Tama's head suggested that he was still watching Mikki, well after the hand he'd raised to return her wave had been lowered.

The way she was still watching him as the wash from the rotors faded and she was able to push back the wayward curls that had been teased from their restraint.

The way they had both been watching each other for the last two days. Stealing extra glances whenever there was a chance of them being undetected.

Awareness, that's what it was.

They were on new ground now. A foundation of mutual respect. Not that Mikki had had an opportunity to prove much in the way of her clinical skills because every job in the last two days had been a potential winch situation and she'd been left behind on station.

There'd been plenty of downtime as well, however, and Mikki had used it well. Just before this mission had been dropped on the crew, she had been demonstrating the hand signals she'd learned while they'd lounged in the armchairs of the messroom. She stood between the men and the huge television where a replay of a recent rugby game was on.

'Wind direction,' she announced, holding both arms extended to one side. 'I face the helicopter and point my arms towards the landing zone with the wind at my back.'

'Excellent,' Josh told her. Mikki acknowledged the praise with a quick smile as she moved into a new position.

'Move forward,' she said, using both arms in front and together with a pulling motion. 'Or move back.' With palms at right angles to her wrists, she pushed the air in front of her.

It was while she was demonstrating the 'do not land' signal of each arm straight out horizontally and then swung overhead that Mikki shifted her gaze from the approving smile still on Josh's face to notice that Tama's gaze was not following the movement of her hands.

He was staring at her *chest*!

It should have made Mikki angry. It would have if she'd been demonstrating something to anyone else and had noticed a completely inappropriate focus that could be deemed sexist. Demeaning, in fact.

What was disturbing about this was that her reaction was nothing like anger. It felt like having fuel poured over a spark she seemed incapable of extinguishing. A tickle of desire that was so pleasurable it was addictive.

And growing.

This new foundation was not simply a matter of the respect she'd earned during the HUET. It was coloured by the connection they'd discovered.

An awareness that was only a hair's breadth from be-

ing an irresistible attraction. Made all the more irresistible by the thought that someone like Tama could find
someone like *her* interesting. Heady stuff. A drug that
was tempting Mikki to go back to it again and again. To
test its effect. To see if she would become resistant.

She would have expected Tama to have dismissed it
by now but, instead, it seemed to be growing. Feeding
on itself. An appetite that could become an addiction
because it was apparently being fed from both sides by
stolen glances and an appreciation of the information
they were gathering.

'Shut down,' Mikki ordered briskly, making a 'cut-
throat' gesture with her right hand.

Tama's gaze flew up and Mikki could see that she had
startled him out of whatever direction his thoughts had
been travelling. She could also see the faint query in his
eyes and then a twinkle that blatantly said he knew he'd
been busted and didn't care.

Damn it! That sheer confidence in combination with
that mischievous twinkle was just adding power to a
magnetic pull. One that Mikki simply had to resist. This
man was her mentor, for heaven's sake. She was here
to gather the skills she needed for the next step in a carefully planned career. A fling—however thrilling it might
be—was not an option. It would either distract her from
what she needed to learn or it would end in tears and
possibly ruin the only chance she was going to get to
have this training. Definitely ruin the opportunity she
had of learning from the best in the field.

But did she even have grounds to worry? Tama James
had to be the most career-focussed man she'd ever met.
More passionately involved with his work than many

registrars she'd worked with who were consumed by ambition to make a consultant's position in the shortest possible time.

No way would he risk his job, and doing something as inappropriate as having a sexual relationship with his pupil would definitely land him in very hot water.

'Clear to start engine.' Mikki raised her right arm and drew circles in the air above her head. She extended her arms sideways. 'Clear to lift.' Then she raised them high with her thumbs clear of her fists. 'Take off,' she instructed.

And, right on cue, the pagers sounded and both men jumped up from their chairs.

Josh gave Mikki a suspicious glance. 'That was spooky. You got a hot line to Control or something?'

'Feminine intuition,' she responded. 'One of the benefits of having a chick on the crew.'

'One of many, I'm sure,' Tama murmured as he walked past, but Mikki didn't dare meet his gaze.

Going any further down that conversational path would be blatant flirting. Playing the dangerous game of exploring the edges of an existing attraction was one thing. Encouraging it would be insane. The rules of this game were quite clear. If awareness and attraction were building blocks, they could do what children who weren't friends could do. Check out the shapes and colours of the blocks. Shift them around a little and make pleasing shapes. Parallel play.

What they could *not* do was play together. To make anything that would undoubtedly lead to joining more than building blocks.

'I hope this isn't going to be another winch job,' she

said casually as she followed the men into the office where they would get details of the mission and do the initial map work.

But it was and again Mikki was left on station to keep herself busy. Not that there was any shortage of options. The stack of articles Tama had copied for her sat on a coffee-table near where he'd been sitting, and Mikki picked up one of the few she hadn't read yet titled 'Air Medical Transport of the Cardiovascular Patient'.

She sat down with every intention of absorbing what she needed to know concerning aspects such as the risk of patient deterioration due to a decrease in barometric pressure with rising altitude.

Was it her imagination that the soft cushions of this chair were still warm from their previous occupant? That there was a faint, musky, very masculine scent surrounding her?

Whatever. It was enough to make Mikki pull her feet up and curl deeper into the chair, oblivious to the faint smile curving her lips.

'Cardiac reserve,' she muttered aloud, her tone resigned. 'The ability of the heart to increase output in response to increased demands.'

For the first time, as he watched the figure on the ground get smaller and smaller, Tama felt a pang of disappointment that Mikki had been left behind.

Had it really only been last week when he'd been wishing so fervently for a mission that would enable escape from her company?

Josh seemed to be reading his mind as Steve banked the helicopter and their forward speed increased.

'Damn shame the mouse couldn't come.'

'It's an injured tramper. We're not likely to find a close landing space in that kind of bush.'

'Get her winch trained, then,' Steve suggested. 'I'll bet she's keen.'

'It's way too early to even think about that,' Tama growled.

His colleagues were silent for a moment. Wondering why he was in a bad mood perhaps? And who was he trying to convince, anyway? Them or himself?

'She's capable enough,' Josh said. 'Look at the way she threw herself into the HUET. Amazing!'

Tama simply grunted. They could think what they liked about his mood. He wasn't about to admit his total agreement. Not out loud, that's for sure. No reason not to let his mind play along those lines, though.

The princess was amazing all right and not just for the physical courage she had displayed during the underwater escape training.

She hadn't whinged once about being left behind on mission after mission. She'd been using her time constructively to devour the pile of written material Tama had actually intended to daunt her. All those heavy articles on the conditions they could be expected to transport and considerations that came with treating complications at high altitude and in a confined space.

Josh broke into his thoughts. 'You know, it could be useful to have a doc who's winch trained.'

'Why?'

'There's stuff she'd be qualified to do that we can't.'

The disturbing notion that Dr Elliot could end up being better at this job than he was hadn't occurred to Tama.

'Like what?' he snapped.

'Oh, I dunno. Amputations?'

'We can take on-line direction for treatment that's out of our protocols if it's a last resort.'

'Yeah, but how much time does it take to find a doctor who can talk us through something like that? And what about, say, a thoracotomy?'

'Cracking a chest in the field? Are you kidding? Just how likely do you think it would be for someone to survive that?'

'They do it in ED.'

'Almost never. And they generally have a cardiothoracic surgeon to do the procedure and a theatre to tidy up in afterwards.' Tama knew he was being dismissive. Probably sounding more and more grumpy, but he didn't like the idea of Mikki ending up better than him. To have something he'd worked for so damn hard handed to her on a plate—like everything else in her life.

'Hey, I'm just saying.' Josh shook his head, abandoning the conversation. 'I reckon the mouse would be good to have around, that's all. She's really into the whole helicopter scene.' He grinned at Tama. 'She's got the hand signals down pat, you have to admit that.'

'Yeah.'

Tama turned his head to stare down at the ground. They were approaching the rugged, bush-covered hills that lay between the city and the coastline. Somewhere down there lay an injured tramper who was probably hypothermic by now because it had taken his friend a good few hours to walk out and call for help.

That's what he should be thinking about. Not replaying the mental footage of Mikki standing in front of them, her face a mixture of satisfaction and an eagerness to impress, moving her body like some football team's head cheerleader.

It wasn't just the hand signals she'd mastered, though, was it?

She'd also learned the layout of the back of the helicopter by now and could find anything in the Thomas pack in no time flat. It had been fun testing her yesterday.

'Find a large trauma dressing.

'Where are the spare batteries?'

It could have been a game judging by the smile with which Mikki produced whatever she was asked to find.

'Magill forceps.

'Chest decompression kit.

'Sharps container.'

She got fast enough to need more of a challenge.

'A tourniquet, 16-gauge cannula, wipe, luer plug and tegaderm. Set up a running line of 0.9 per cent saline while I'm pretending to get the IV access.'

Not a peep came out of Mikki about why it might have been more appropriate for *her* to be the one putting a line in while Tama assisted by setting up fluids.

Unlike Josh, she'd never suggested it could be worthwhile accelerating her training because she could do more in the field than he was authorised to do.

In fact, not once since she'd set foot on their station had she pulled rank in any way. She hadn't used her superior qualifications, any limitations that would have been perfectly reasonable given her gender, or any status associated with who her father happened to be.

He'd been expecting her to, he realised now. Ready to fight back. He wouldn't have been at all surprised if the boss had called him in for a quiet word because Mikki had said something to her father and he wanted to make sure his daughter got everything she wanted.

Had she not said anything? How often did she talk to her father? Did she know that Tama knew who he was? His colleagues had agreed with him right from the start that Mikki was to be treated like any other trainee and it would be better not to even mention her family connections so maybe she didn't realise they knew.

Were they both keeping that knowledge as a kind of ace up their sleeves? Would Mikki use hers first? Tama had to admit he was impressed that she hadn't let anything slip. But, then, that admiration that had started so grudgingly had taken on a life of its own, hadn't it?

Hell, even if this woman had resembled a potato in her physical appearance, Tama would have been impressed by now.

And she didn't look anything like a potato.

She looked…amazing.

Tama sighed aloud. There it was, in a nutshell. He was attracted to her…big-time.

Josh had overheard the sigh. 'Getting bored, mate? We're almost there.'

'Never bored,' Tama's smile at his friend was a kind of apology for his distraction. 'Bring it on!'

OK. He was attracted to Mikki, but did it matter? He wasn't going to act on it. The very idea was ludicrous. She was here to learn. From him. That put him in the position of being her superior. Her teacher. Ethically, he would be on dodgy ground if he let any kind of relationship interfere with that.

And he didn't do relationships. Especially not with

someone like Mikki. She was so not his type it was
almost funny. Relationships meant you got close to
someone, and if Mikki knew his background she'd look
down on him. She wouldn't be able to help herself. Just
part of her social programming.

No. Tama liked where he was. He liked the respect—
admiration, even—he could read in Mikki's face. His
past was his own so it was good that there was a very
large barrier that would prevent him acting on his attraction. He didn't need to think of getting that close.

Hey…nobody got that close so why the hell was he
even thinking about it?

Because Mikki had got under his skin, that's why. Far
enough to make him miss her when she wasn't around.
There was no harm in appreciating the woman, though,
was there? Playing a little?

Admitting the attraction was a release in a way. He
knew what he was up against and he could handle it.
From here on in, it was not going to distract him from
the important things, like doing his job. This job, for
instance. They were circling the area the GPS navigation system had identified. Any minute now and they
would be into the rescue effort. Everything was good.

And if the next job meant that they had the mouse
along to play, so be it. Tama could handle that, too.

The strident sound of the pagers came within minutes
of the helicopter touching down but Tama appeared to
be taking the details of the call with good humour.

Mikki was watching him.

She'd watched the helicopter land and Tama and Josh
climb out, laughing and talking as they'd made their way

back inside. It had been so good to see them. Because she'd spent two hours studying and had had enough?

Yes, but that didn't explain the way her heart tripped when she saw the now familiar shape of Tama heading her way. Her excitement wasn't just about having stimulating company on station or the prospect of a new job that would include her in the action.

She had missed Tama's presence. Missed the way he filled a room and gave even the air she breathed an extra dimension. He was larger than life, that was the problem. More so than any man she'd ever met. Some of that aura radiated and it was almost like the kind of adrenaline rush you got from facing a major challenge and succeeding.

It made her feel…bigger, somehow. Taller and braver and…special.

Tama wasn't looking at her right now as he talked to the dispatcher and scribbled down the co-ordinates he was being given. His head was bent and Mikki indulged herself for a second longer, her eyes feasting on the way tiny curls spiralled against the soft-looking skin at the nape of his neck. A vulnerable spot on a man who seemed anything but vulnerable. It made Mikki want to touch it. To touch *him*. She dragged her gaze away as Tama turned to hand the scrap of paper with numbers on it to Josh, who moved towards the wall maps.

'Roger,' he said finally. 'We'll get airborne as soon as we've refuelled.'

'Another job?' The question was redundant. Stupid, in fact, but Mikki couldn't help asking it. Knowing that Tama would look in her direction when he answered. Wanting him to notice her.

The smile was a bonus she hadn't expected. 'Tractor rollover,' he told her. 'Forty-two-year-old farmer.'

'Is he trapped?'

'No, and the ground was reasonably soft by the sound of things, but he's got chest injuries and the local ambulance crew is concerned about his breathing.'

'How far?'

Josh was using his finger to trace lines on one of the large wall maps. 'Here. Fifteen- to twenty-minute flight, tops.'

'And it's not a winch job.' Tama actually sounded quite cheerful about the fact. 'You good to go, Mouse?'

'Absolutely.'

Finally. The frustration of the last few days evaporated and Mikki was left with a sense that the enforced time on station had actually been a blessing in disguise. She was familiar with the gear and the protocols. Far more at ease with these men. Confident, even.

It felt so right to be keeping step with Tama despite having to take much longer strides to stay by his side. Perfectly normal to climb into her seat, fasten her safety straps—lap belt first and then shoulder straps—and then glance up to be rewarded with an approving nod. This time, she actually felt like part of the team and that impression only strengthened when they arrived at the scene.

'This is John.' The local ambulance officer introduced them to their patient. 'He lost control of the tractor on that hill and it rolled. He was caught under it and then thrown clear when it rolled again.'

The tractor was lying on its side, half in a ditch, close to where the ambulance was parked.

'Steering...wheel...' John groaned. 'Got...me...'

'Don't try and talk, mate.' Tama had his hand on John's wrist, both to assess his pulse and convey reassurance through touch. 'We're going to look after you and get you to hospital, OK?'

John gave a single nod and then closed his eyes.

'I couldn't get a line in.' The ambulance officer sounded apologetic as he noticed Josh pulling supplies from the pack. 'His blood pressure was well down by the time I arrived. He's pretty flat.'

'You single-crewed?' Tama asked.

'Yes.' The ambulance officer was obviously relieved to have a crew with higher qualifications to take over. 'His airway was clear when I got here and there were no obvious signs of any neck injury. Breathing seemed OK, too. He said it hurt but his oxygen saturation was ninety-eight per cent.'

'Down to ninety-five now.' Josh dropped a tourniquet beside John's arm and handed a stethoscope to Mikki as though it was part of a practised team routine.

Mikki fitted the earpieces.

'What's his blood pressure now?' she queried.

'It's been a few minutes since I took it. It was eighty-five over sixty.'

'Narrow pulse pressure,' Tama commented. 'We're just going to have a look at your chest, John.'

The farmer didn't open his eyes. He seemed to be concentrating on drawing breath. Rapid, shallow breaths that looked laboured.

'Flail chest,' Mikki noted, as Tama pulled aside the woollen shirt and cut John's singlet with a pair of shears he pulled from a pouch on his overalls.

She watched for a moment longer, assessing the

section of rib cage that was being sucked in the opposite direction to the rest of his ribs. There were multiple fractures there and the list of potential damage that might accompany them was long.

'Have a listen,' Tama invited, moving to make room for Mikki to crouch closer to their patient. 'I'm going to check his belly.'

The injured part of the chest was on the left side. Low enough to make an internal injury to the spleen a distinct possibility, along with bleeding that could well be contributing to low blood pressure.

Josh was attempting to gain IV access and Tama's hands were palpating John's abdomen but Mikki focussed on what she was hearing with her stethoscope. Or not hearing.

'Breath sounds well down on the left side,' she reported. 'And heart sounds are muffled.'

'I can't find a vein,' Josh said. 'You want to try, Tama?'

'In a sec.' Tama was holding Mikki's gaze. 'What are you thinking?'

There was respect in that gaze. A willingness to let her make decisions about treating a man who was critically injured. Mikki didn't want control, however. She wanted teamwork.

'Narrow pulse pressure,' she said, instead of offering a diagnosis. 'Tachycardia. His jugular veins are distended, see?'

Tama glanced at the bulging veins in John's neck and nodded curtly. 'Tamponade?'

Mikki tapped the chest wall. 'Could be a tension pneumothorax. Or a combination of both.'

'Chest decompression or a pericardiocentesis?'

Mikki touched John's neck. 'No tracheal deviation.' Her gaze travelled to a face partially covered by an oxygen mask. 'He's going blue. What's the oxygen saturation now?'

'Ninety per cent.'

'John? Can you hear me?' Mikki rubbed his collarbone. 'Can you open your eyes?'

There was no response.

The farmer was in shock and deteriorating fast. If air was entering the chest outside the lungs because of trauma to the ribs, it could be compressing his heart and lung and would be fatal if that air wasn't removed. If he was bleeding around his heart as a result of the crush injury, that vital organ would cease to function and he would die very quickly.

'What would you do first?' she asked Tama.

'Your call,' he responded quietly. He wasn't testing her. She could see that he was weighing up exactly the same considerations she was. If one procedure didn't help, they would have to try another anyway. What was paramount was making a decision and getting on with it.

'Pericardiocentesis,' Mikki decided swiftly. 'Followed by a chest decompression if it's needed.'

'You happy to do it?'

Mikki nodded. 'I'd like a monitor on.'

There was a narrow space around the heart where blood could create enough pressure to stop it functioning. A space that was easy to miss with the point of a needle. Not going far enough would mean not removing the blood. Going too far would mean pushing a needle into cardiac tissue and potentially creating further complications.

Tama put the leads of the monitor on. Josh pulled out

the kit she needed. Mikki put on a fresh pair on gloves and didn't allow her thoughts to go anywhere near the idea of failure, even though this was technically a lot more difficult than an intubation.

'Keep an eye on the trace, please,' she asked Tama. 'I'm going in slowly and I want to know if you see any changes in rhythm.'

Their patient was unconscious. He didn't feel the needle entering his chest just under his breastbone. Mikki angled the needle at forty-five degrees, aiming for the left shoulder blade. She pulled back on the plunger as she kept advancing the needle.

'Ectopic,' Tama warned, his voice very close behind her. 'Ventricular.'

Mikki slowed. She was close. She pulled back on the plunger as she kept advancing the needle, a millimetre at a time.

'Bingo,' she said softly, seconds later. It was easy to draw back the plunger now. The syringe filled with blood. 'Twenty mils should be enough to make a difference if the tamponade's the main culprit.'

They all watched for a minute to see John's respiratory efforts improving and his blood pressure creeping up.

Another minute and he began to regain consciousness. Less than five minutes later they had intravenous access established, fluids running and their patient stable enough to transport. The short flight to the hospital was a busy time of reassessment, monitoring and further treatment and it wasn't until well after the handover to emergency department staff that Mikki discovered how impressed her colleagues were.

'He would've died if you hadn't been there,' Josh told her. 'That was awesome, Mikki Mouse.'

'It's an effective procedure when it's needed.' Mikki tried to sound modest. 'But it's not that different to a chest decompression for pneumothorax. I'm surprised you don't have it in your procedures.'

'It's coming in.' Tama's voice had a curiously rough edge as though the words were hard to get out. 'I wouldn't mind getting a head start on it, though.'

'I'll run through it with you on a manikin any time you like.'

'Cool.'

Josh wanted to discuss the case as they flew back to base. To go over the signs and symptoms and talk more about the lifesaving procedure, but Tama was curiously quiet. Mikki caught him watching her with an oddly assessing gaze.

Had she passed muster this time, perhaps?

She got the impression she had and the sheer joy that gave her was startling enough to make her want to sit quietly and savour it. She let Josh continue talking and just made the right noises when needed. Even after they landed and climbed out of the helicopter, Josh was still talking.

'Man, I'm starving,' he announced. 'Did we have lunch?' He didn't wait for Tama's response. 'So long ago it doesn't count, anyway. I'm going to make a mountain of toast.'

He set off towards the messroom.

Steve was still busy shutting down the helicopter.

Mikki was suddenly alone in the hangar with Tama and, without looking, she knew he was staring at her.

She ducked her head. 'I'm pretty hungry myself. I'll go and help Josh with that toast.'

'No.' The single word stopped her in her tracks. 'Wait a sec. I...want to talk to you.'

Mikki turned. That odd note was in his voice again. As though he was saying something he would rather not be saying but felt compelled to.

There was certainly something compelling about his gaze. Mikki couldn't look away.

Tama looked as though he was seeing her for the first time.

She could see respect.

Acceptance.

And something more.

Something that made her toes curl and her blood tingle.

It was Tama who broke the eye contact. Slowly. Deliberately. He cleared his throat and stared fixedly above her head. Mikki didn't follow his line of vision. She wanted to watch his face when he said whatever was important enough to make him look like this.

'I know you're keen,' he said gruffly. 'But I have to be seen to be careful about following the rules, you know?'

Keen? Mikki focussed on Tama's face, her mind one step ahead of him.

Dear Lord, he'd noticed the way she'd been watching him. The attraction wasn't mutual, as she'd thought, and he was about to tell her he couldn't teach someone who fancied him.

'But I've changed my mind,' Tama continued. 'If you really are that keen, we can...you know...do something about it. The boss doesn't need to find out.'

The flush of colour entering Mikki's cheeks got rapidly hotter. Was he offering her *sex*?

'How 'bout it?' Tama finally looked down and caught her transfixed gaze.

'Ah...' Mikki couldn't think of a thing to say. Talk about direct! 'Yes, please' might be equally direct and honest, but it lacked a certain something.

Tama lowered his voice to a sexy rumble. 'You want to, don't you?'

Oh...*help*! There was no denying that. And Tama was doing that thing with his lips again. That quirky half-smile that went with the twinkle Mikki was coming to recognise. Pure mischief. She sucked in a breath.

'I guess I could...'

Her hesitation was all too plain.

'I know it's more than a bit out of order. Way too soon and all that, but you know what?' The twinkle gained intensity. 'I reckon you'll do OK.'

Mikki's jaw dropped. 'Oh...' Maybe she hadn't measured up as well as she'd imagined.

Her reaction didn't seem to be what Tama had expected. He frowned. 'So...you want to start now?'

'Now?' Mikki squeaked. *'Here?'*

'Where else?' Tama was looking over her head again. 'It's the only place I know of that's got a winch simulator.'

CHAPTER SIX

'WINCH training? *Already?*'

'I'd barely started before we had our days off. I should be able to get into it properly this week. I'm lucky, Dad. Usually you have to wait *months* to get this sort of training.'

Mikki heard a deep sigh that travelled remarkably well, considering her father was currently on the other side of the world.

'I'm perfectly safe, Dad,' she said patiently. 'So far all I've been allowed to do is learn safety stuff and terminology and how to wear the harness and hook carabiners on and off things. My feet haven't left the ground and when they do, it'll only be in the hangar.'

'At the rate you're going, you'll be dangling out of a helicopter on a bit of string in no time.'

Mikki laughed. 'It's a wire capable of holding a ton of weight, as you well know. I'll bet you've done more research than I have about what's involved with helicopter crew training.'

Her father chuckled. 'Knowledge is power, you know.

I believe you've got bush and snow terrain survival training coming up as well. Do you know when?'

'No idea. I would imagine they wait for a group of trainees before that kind of operation. I'll have to ask Tama.'

'Tama,' her father repeated thoughtfully. 'Hmm...'

Mikki's mouth went suddenly dry. Could there be some kind of telepathic link being beamed by satellite? Surely there hadn't been any clue in her own tone or recent conversations to reveal how often that name echoed in her own head. Along with images that could stir up some rather disturbing physical effects. Good grief, what if her father knew that she had thought Tama was offering her sex instead of winch training?

That she might have been incapable of declining such an offer?

Or maybe there was another link. An equally disturbing one for some unidentifiable reason.

'You don't know him, do you, Dad?'

'No, of course not.' The response was lightning fast. 'Why would I?'

'You've been known to attend the odd fundraising function to do with helicopter rescue. Especially when you're handing over those big cheques. You just *sounded* like you'd heard the name before.'

'It's an unusual name, that's all.'

'He's part Maori.'

'And he's the senior crew member on your shift, yes?'

'Yes. And if I don't impress the pants off him, I won't get the qualification I want.'

'*What* did you say?'

Mikki groaned. 'Just an expression, Dad.'

'Hmm. Well, you're a big girl now. It's none of my business. What's he like, this Tama fellow, anyway?'

Unconsciously, Mikki licked her lips. This was like having a plate of comfort food put in front of you when you were cold and tired and hungry. An opportunity for her mind to feast on a whole smorgasbord of Tama's attributes.

Tall. Strong. Fierce. With the single-mindedness and determination of a warrior but with a thread of sensitivity that spoke of an equal ability to be gentle.

A streak of mischief that made dark eyes gleam and a smile that would melt the heart of any woman.

Someone who lived for challenge. For the thrill of revelling in how good it was to be alive and was prepared to do whatever it took to keep others alive.

A soulmate.

'He's the best,' she told her father simply. 'I couldn't have wished for a better teacher.'

Her father sighed again. 'You sound happy, anyway.'

'I *am* happy, Dad. I've never been happier. This is exactly what I've wanted to be doing for longer than I can remember.'

'Do you think there's any chance you'll get this danger-chasing business out of your system one of these days? Find a nice bloke and settle down, even? Preferably with someone who doesn't share your passion of leaping out of helicopters and saving lives?'

'I can pretty well guarantee that a nice bloke who's interested in a picket fence and a bunch of kids will not be leaping out of any helicopters.'

Someone like Tama 'settling down'? As if!

Her falling for someone who wanted the secure, ordinary life her father was thinking of?

Again, it was unlikely enough to be amusing.

'You're not even sixty, Dad. It's a bit young to be pining for grandchildren.'

The silence on the other end of the line made Mikki give herself a mental kick. Her father needed no reminder of how small his family was. Or how pining for someone had almost destroyed him in the years following her mother's death. Of the breeding ground for the over-protectiveness they still wrangled over.

Mikki caught a breath and made herself smile to ensure she sounded cheerful.

'I'll have to get to work soon, Dad. You haven't told me how it's going in New York. When do you have to get on a plane again? It's Zurich next, isn't it?'

The stack of materials was large and awkward to hold but Mikki's arms enclosed it willingly.

'You photocopied all this on your days off? And found all these videos and DVDs? Thank you *so* much!'

'No big deal.' Tama shrugged off the gratitude. He'd owed her one and he wasn't about to admit why. 'Some of it's as boring as hell, mind you. One of those videos is a lecture on the components and capabilities of winching gear. Way too many facts and figures to be interesting.'

'I'm interested,' Mikki assured him.

She was, too. Possibly in more than the kind of materials needed for her training. He'd been testing her the other day, hadn't he? Teasing her by not being specific about what he was offering. Playing with fire to find out whether she might be interested in *him*.

She'd been confused to start with, of course, but Tama had seen the signs of a response she probably hadn't known she'd been showing. The way her pupils had dilated, her breath quickening as her lips had parted slightly.

So damn hot, he'd had to step back before he could get burned. To stop the game before it had ended in tears. And then he knew he kind of owed her an apology and he wasn't quite sure how to offer it. He'd spent quite a lot of time on his days off thinking about it and by last night he'd come up with a perfect penance. He'd get all the resources she needed to make her training state of the art and he'd be there, every step of the way, to ensure her success.

'There's some good stuff in there as well. Practical demos on one of the DVDs. They've even filmed some real cases.'

'Fantastic. If you show me how to use the DVD player, I'll get into it the first time I get left on station.'

'What makes you think you'll be left behind?'

'If last shift was anything to go by, I'll have more than enough time to absorb this lot.'

'You're tempting fate, you know.'

'Ha!' Mikki shook her head, carrying her bundle of articles and audiovisual recordings towards the mess-room. 'You'll see.'

But it was Mikki who was proved wrong.

There were four missions that day and not one of them required the use of a winch.

They transferred a critically ill teenage girl from a rural hospital to an intensive care unit in the city, and Tama was struck by the rapport Mikki gained instantly with their patient. He watched the way she held the girl's hand during the flight and how their eye contact seemed to reassure and calm a terrified teenager.

The second job was time-consuming because they had to wait when it took longer than expected for a ski-rescue team to bring in a man who had collided with a tree and received head injuries. The injury had made their patient combative and Mikki was the target for some fairly colourful verbal abuse.

'Get her away from me. I don't want some female ambulance driver looking after me.'

'She's a doctor,' Tama told the man. 'She's more highly qualified than any of us.'

'I don't care. She's a woman. You can't trust any of them.'

Tama had seen resignation in Mikki's gaze as she'd stepped back. Concern for the man but acknowledgement that being assertive could distress him further and worsen his condition.

And he'd seen something else. Tama couldn't be sure what he'd read exactly in Mikki's eyes and face but he knew, beyond a shadow of a doubt, that their patient's impression was absolutely wrong.

Mikki could be trusted with anything. She was one hundred per cent genuine.

They went to an isolated farm where a three-week-old baby had contracted an infection and was in respiratory distress, and this time Tama could really appreciate Mikki's skills. Tama watched the confident, deft movements of hands that were half the size of his own as they located and managed to cannulate a tiny vein that looked like a thread.

Josh was watching just as closely and was clearly equally impressed with the feat, but Tama hoped his mind wasn't stepping in the same direction as his own. Just for a moment or two he couldn't help imagining how soft and sure the touch of those fingers would be. How it might be to experience that touch on his own skin.

Just the kind of distracting thought that would have annoyed the hell out of him a couple of weeks ago, but he could handle it now. Could enjoy the sensation and then put it aside—ready to help set up the monitoring equipment this baby badly needed.

Maybe he was getting used to dealing with a misplaced libido. Or maybe it was a combination of the confidence he had that he could deal with it added to the respect he was gaining for his pupil.

That respect went up a notch on the final job of the day. A car had gone off a coastal road and it could easily have been a winching job but the tide was out and beside the rocks was a stretch of firm sand that made an ideal place to land. The car was upside down and the single occupant was sprawled, face down, half on the back seat and half on the roof that was now the vehicle's floor. Totally out of reach.

'We'll have to wait for the fire service to cut access,' Tama decreed, but Mikki wasn't having any of it.

'I could fit through the window.'

'No way! Too dangerous.'

'Not if we knock the rest of the glass out. The car's stable enough, isn't it?'

'I guess.' The crumpled wreck was perfectly stable, wedged between two giant boulders. Tama was curiously reluctant to allow Mikki to squeeze into the tiny gap of a windowframe, however.

'Ignition's off. Fire danger should be low and it's an old car. There won't be any undeployed airbags. Not in the back, anyway.'

Tama turned to the chief fire officer, who was now standing beside him. 'It'll take us a few minutes to set up for cutting.'

'At least let me get in to make sure his airway's open,' Mikki pleaded.

The fire officer grinned. 'Keen, isn't she?'

'Yeah.' And suddenly Tama was proud of how brave Mikki was. Could appreciate her diminutive size. 'OK, go for it, Mouse. We'll pass in whatever you need.'

By the time they freed the victim, he was set to go, with a neck collar in place, oxygen on and IV fluids running.

She was good.

So good it no longer seemed premature to take her a step further in her training. Winch work, for sure, as soon as they could fit it in. Tama was going to sit down and have a good look at his calendar tonight as well. A clear day or two and he would start the preparations needed to give Mikki her survival training.

Why did frustration seem to be an inherent part of this job?

Was it just that Mikki wanted too much, too soon?

Last shift she'd been frustrated because she'd been left behind on station and had had to use her time to study. This shift the opposite was happening. Three busy days so far and she'd gone on every mission because not one of them had needed winching.

And it was frustrating because she wanted to soak in

all the background information Tama had provided for her on winching. She'd had her evenings, of course, but it wasn't the same as being able to fire questions at Tama as they occurred to her. Something as practical as playing with the simulator was as far away as it had ever been.

Mikki knew perfectly well that hindsight would make her appreciate this full-on spell. Already, she could see that both Tama and Josh had come to trust her judgement and recognise her strengths. They simply handed her the IV gear now and her opinion on every case was always sought. They had gelled together as a team even before the milestone of their tenth mission together that had been clocked up late yesterday.

But today was the last of their four-day shift and Mikki didn't want a stretch of days off when she was no closer to her new goal of being winch capable, so she was striding into the hanger with a purposeful step, a little earlier than usual, intent on persuading Tama to start her practical training.

The hangar was dimly lit with the new day just gathering strength, but the light was not dim enough to hide the two figures who were standing near the helicopter.

Both Tama and the station manager, Andy, were watching her with a focus that was unsettling, to say the least.

'Something wrong?' Mikki queried, by way of a greeting.

'Yeah.' Tama's scowl deepened. 'Josh won't be in to work today.'

'He's sick?'

'Not exactly.'

'He was out running last night,' Andy told her. 'This

idiot took a corner too fast, went off the road, through a fence and into the park Josh was running in.'

'Oh, my God,' Mikki breathed. 'He got *hit*?'

'Leg broken in three places,' Tama said gloomily. 'Femur, tib and fib, and his foot got squashed. He was in surgery for three hours.'

'He'll be in hospital for weeks,' Andy added. 'Off work for months.'

Mikki stood still, absorbing the bad news. Josh was a part of her team now. A friend. He'd been Tama's partner for a long time, too, and part of her concern and sympathy had to go to her mentor who would, no doubt, have to work with someone he didn't know nearly as well for quite some time.

Tama seemed to read and accept her mixed response. 'At least it wasn't his head,' he said quietly. 'He'll come right.'

Mikki nodded. 'Is he allowed visitors yet?'

'We'll go and annoy him every time we're at the hospital.'

'But...' A new concern emerged. 'What's going to happen today? With the crew, I mean?' Would a stranger be ready to accept her as a third crew member? Make her an integral part of the team the way Tama and Josh had?

'I was going to call in a replacement,' Andy said. 'But it was looking like we might have to stand you guys down. Then I thought of my old mate, Alistair.'

'Ex-helicopter crew,' Tama put in. 'Before my time.'

'Yes. He's retired from helicopter work,' Andy continued, 'but his qualifications are still current. He's got a website design business now that's quite portable. He's happy to hang out on station and be available for any winch jobs. Only operating the winch, mind you.' Andy chuckled. 'He says he's over dangling. He can still do his normal work on station. It's a fairly unusual arrangement but I've managed to clear it.'

'For any jobs that don't require winching,' Tama finished, 'I've told Andy that I'm more than happy to crew with you.'

Andy was frowning. 'It's kind of a big ask this soon in your training, Mikki. I said we'd have to see how you felt about it.'

'I...I'm happy if Tama's happy,' Mikki said slowly. She caught Tama's gaze, knowing that her questions would be written on her face.

You really want this? You trust me to be your partner?
The dark eyes were steady on hers. Warm.
Yes, they said. *You can do this. We can do this.*
'I'm happy,' was all Tama said.

Andy gave a nod. 'Let's see how it goes, then.' He smiled at Mikki. 'Tama tells me he wants to accelerate your training to include winching, but don't go getting any ideas that you'll be allowed to do anything in the near future.' He was looking at Tama. 'Safety first, remember?'

Tama cleared his throat. 'How could I forget?' he muttered. Then he smiled at Mikki. 'No time like the present, is there? Good thing you got to work early, Mouse.'

It was and it wasn't.

One frustration faded only to be replaced by a new one.

An unexpectedly fierce and potentially problematic one.

It started with Tama's first words when Andy had gone back to his office.

'Let's get a nappy on you, then,' he said.

'The harness, I hope.' Mikki hoped the light response would hide something more than embarrassment at the terminology. The very idea of Tama touching her in places that a nappy would cover was more than enough to send a flood of colour to her cheeks.

'We use a nappy harness by preference.' Tama was sorting through a box of gear in the corner of the hangar. 'Much more dangerous winching someone in a stretcher. Get a good spin or something going and it can be hard to control. Here.' He was holding out a collection of straps and fasteners. 'We'll pretend you're the patient. I'll just put my harness on first.'

The moment his hands touched Mikki's waist to put her harness in place she knew she was in trouble. She actually had to close her eyes as he reached for the wide strap that went between her legs and his hands brushed the insides of her thighs.

'Don't mind me.' She could hear the grin in his voice.

She tried to smile back. To appear as nonchalant as Tama sounded, but her heart was hammering and her lips felt frozen.

She knew this sensation. Kind of. She'd only ever experienced a pale imitation of this, however. Lust, pure and simple.

She *didn't* mind. Far, far from it.

She wanted more.

Heaven help her, but she wanted that touch on her thighs without the barrier of clothing, and she wanted it as fiercely as she had ever wanted anything in her life.

'Now I clip your harness to mine,' Tama was saying. 'Like this. And I tell you to put your arms around my neck.'

He was holding her steady. The way he would be holding a patient so that they could both be winched up to a hovering helicopter.

So close Mikki could feel the whole, hard length of Tama's body.

Could feel a strange, humming sensation that went through the layers of clothing and then skin and muscle to settle in her bones with a liquid warmth so exquisite Mikki had to bite her lip to prevent the escape of a soft, appreciative sigh.

Tama stood very still. Silent. For just a heartbeat too long.

Long enough for the undercurrents to be shining like neon lamps.

There was no way out of this unless Mikki could pull back far enough to see Tama's face and then say something. *Anything.* A stupid question about the carabiners linking their harnesses would do the trick. Something that sounded professional enough to diffuse this tension.

Mikki managed the first part of the plan but then the words failed to form and she found herself staring into Tama's eyes and the tension rocketed up. They were so close.

Way too close. When Tama's gaze dropped from her eyes to her lips, she knew he was thinking about kissing her. It was like that moment in the diving pool, with the major difference that they were alone here. No audience. Nobody would know.

No way could Mikki produce a single word now.

Neither could she move enough to even take a new breath. She didn't want to break the spell.

She *wanted* Tama to kiss her.

Any resolutions about avoiding the pull of an attraction that could cost her this career opportunity were relentlessly crushed. There was no way she could resist this man. If he wanted her, she was here. A more than willing partner.

And he did want her. She knew it. Maybe it had always been a matter of 'when', not 'if', and the moment had arrived.

How long had they been like that? Staring at each other? Not long enough for Mikki to feel a desperate need for a new supply of oxygen but it was long enough to feel like for ever.

Long enough to provide a background where the slamming of a side hangar door had all the effect of a gunshot.

Steve had arrived for work and, as the sound of the metal door closing faded away, their pagers sounded.

It hung between them.

That almost kiss.

Like a strand of something solid. A connection Mikki could feel with varying degrees of intensity from that moment on.

So strong to begin with as she climbed into the helicopter with the adrenaline rush of her first callout, having been promoted to second crew member but fading as they arrived at a medical centre an hour's drive from the city where an eleven-year-old was suffering a life threatening asthma attack.

She would not have expected to notice it with the full on effort of keeping this child alive until they reached the hospital. The aggressive drug therapy they instigated was still not enough and in mid-flight the panicked child went into respiratory arrest.

The back of a helicopter had never seemed so cramped or their supplies so awkwardly packed and hard to access. Mikki was at the head of the stretcher, with her arms around their seated patient, her hands on his small rib cage, helping the exhausted boy in his efforts to expel air. Tama was doing his best to secure a second IV line. They both felt the exact moment the child gave up the struggle to breathe and for just a heartbeat the two medics made eye contact with each other.

The boy needed intubation and Mikki couldn't stop herself remembering her failure in a situation that had been this urgent. The first time she had been under Tama's critical evaluation for her clinical skills. They would have to swap positions if Tama was to do this intubation and it would take time they didn't have if they wanted to save this child.

And there was that connection again. Not remotely sexual. It was deeper. Stronger.

It told Mikki that she didn't need to move. That he trusted her. That he was here and would assist but this was something she could do. That she needed to do.

He was right on both counts. Five minutes before they landed on the rooftop helipad of the biggest hospital in town, Mikki had secured the tube that would keep the boy's airway open and she was carefully ventilating him to avoid damaging lungs that were still far

from being able to function normally. The paediatric
team, including an anaesthetist, was waiting for them
in the emergency department and Mikki watched as
they adjusted settings on the machine that would take
over his breathing, put monitoring lines in place and
arranged transfer to the paediatric intensive care unit.

Tama stood beside her and when the admitting team
finally nodded their satisfaction at the stability of their
patient's condition, Tama looked down and smiled at
Mikki and she could feel the strength of that connection
all over again.

'Shall we go and visit Josh before we head back
to station?'

'Of course.' Concern for their colleague came back
in a rush and Mikki realised what an emotional roller-
coaster this day was presenting. No wonder she was
feeling a little strange.

Vulnerable.

And no wonder the relief of seeing a smile on Josh's
face brought tears to her eyes.

'Hey, I'm not dead, Mouse.'

'You could have been. Thank God the wheel went
over your foot and not your head.'

'He would have been fine in that case,' Tama growled.
'Not much to damage at that end, is there, mate?'

Laughter chased away the threat of the silly, feminine
tears and then something new got thrown into the emotional cauldron of Mikki's day.

Pride.

'You should've seen Mouse on this last run,' Tama
told his partner. 'Intubating a kid in respiratory arrest.
Mid-air. Have to say, if she wasn't heading for war-torn

countries in a few months, your job might not be there to come back to.'

'Hey, I can do a threesome. You wouldn't get rid of me that easily.'

The nurse who had come in to check Josh's IV and the attached self-administered pain relief looked up and grinned.

'Threesome, huh?' She raised an eyebrow at Mikki. 'Lucky you.'

'Yeah.' Mikki returned the grin, still bursting with pride from Tama's praise. Feeling closer to both these men than she ever had to any work colleagues.

She loved this job.

She loved them.

For the first time in her life she was exactly where she wanted to be.

She belonged.

And then she made the mistake of catching Tama's gaze, and that strand of connection was like liquid fire. There was nothing professional about this non-verbal communication. It was purely sexual. There would be no 'threesome', his look told her. This was between the two of them.

The temperature of the room seemed to be rising steadily but Josh was now busy flirting with his nurse and apparently didn't notice.

'I might not get in to see you tomorrow,' Tama told Josh a few minutes later as they prepared to leave. 'Depends on Mouse, of course.'

'What does?' Mikki asked.

'I checked my calendar last night,' Tama said casually. 'And the long-range weather forecast today. If you're keen, we could get dropped on the top of a mountain tomorrow and get your survival training out of the way.'

'So soon?' Mikki wasn't sure she was ready. 'I was expecting to have to wait until there was a group for that.'

Josh was clearly getting a good effect from his pain relief medication. He was grinning broadly. 'You're special,' he told Mikki. 'Tama wants to give you the royal treatment.'

'Oi!' Tama's tone held a distinct reprimand. 'It's your fault my diary's clear, mate. We were supposed to be driving up north so you could be at your mum's birthday party, remember?'

Josh groaned. 'Mum's on her way here instead. She's going to sit in the corner of my room and probably knit me a giant sock to go over my leg. You can't leave me alone listening to those needles clacking, Tama. I'll go crazy.'

Tama grinned. 'So would I. Your mum never gives up trying to tell me it's time I settled down and started making babies. Think I'd rather be making a snow cave with the mouse, thanks.'

Mikki tried to ignore the reference to making babies. 'A snow cave?' she echoed. No. She couldn't ignore it after all. 'We'd be spending the night on the top of a mountain?'

'And another one out in the bush.'

'You could wait,' Josh grumbled. 'I'd like to come as well. Could do with a refresher.'

'Can't wait *that* long,' Tama said decisively. 'What about you, Mouse?'

He wasn't looking at Mikki but the innuendo was blatant.

Dropped into the wilderness and forced to spend

their days and nights together, there was absolutely no doubt that the tension simmering between them would have to be addressed.

Tama was creating this opportunity so did it mean he wanted something to happen? If she didn't want that, now was the time to say so. To make some kind of excuse. A prior engagement that would make it impossible to spend the next couple of days alone with Tama. It might be the sensible thing to do.

Carefully, Mikki took a deep breath. She looked at Josh rather than Tama. 'Sorry, mate, but I can't turn down an offer like that, can I? We'll tell you all about it as soon as we get back.'

Tama was right behind her as she stepped out of the room.

'We'll see about that,' he murmured. 'There may be some aspects of your survival training that you might not want to share with everybody.'

CHAPTER SEVEN

SHE could share *this* with everybody.

If she could find the right words.

Words that could convey the sense of desolation she felt seeing Steve taking the helicopter back to base, leaving Tama and herself standing on a snow-covered slope.

The tiny dot of the aircraft faded into the endless blue sky and Mikki had the weird sensation of looking down from even higher than the helicopter had been. Seeing herself and her sole companion fading to black dots on a pristine white background. Insignificant and then invisible as her mind's eye saw the towering peaks of the mountains behind them, the tussock-covered high country below and then mile after mile—as far as the eye could see—of bush-covered land.

Wilderness. The blanket of greenery might give the impression of soft lines but beneath that canopy was a harsh landscape of steep slopes punctuated by baby rivers that tumbled into ravines. Dense bush that would be impenetrable in many places. Slippery tussock sprouting through puddles of icy snow, and where they were right now knee-deep snow, the chill of which

Mikki could feel pressing on her leather boots like a solid weight.

The silence, when the final chop of the helicopter's rotors had faded to nothing, was as awe-inspiring as the scenery. So deep it seemed almost sacrilege to break it. Not that Tama was sharing Mikki's reverence.

'Nice, huh?' He took a deep breath of the cold air. 'You don't get a view like this every day.'

'No.' Mikki was still trying to take it in. To push back a fear she hadn't expected to be so strong.

'You OK?'

'Yes.' No. What did they think they were doing, putting themselves into such a hostile environment voluntarily? This was crazy!

Mikki finally dragged her gaze from the mind-boggling vastness around them. She turned and found it a comfort to see the figure of another human body, especially one as big and solid as Tama. She raised her gaze and there was a pair of dark eyes behind ski goggles staring back. Lips that showed above the black wool of a balaclava were curved into a smile.

'You just need to trust me, princess,' he said. 'Can you do that?'

She had no choice.

They may have spent yesterday evening sorting supplies and clothing and going over basic survival techniques, but there was no way Mikki could be doing this on her own.

She had to trust Tama.

With her life.

Strangely, it was easy to take that step. The fear she had been so aware of ebbed sharply because the trust was genuine. A part of that connection that was so much stronger than simply attraction.

She didn't even mind him calling her 'princess' because she knew there was respect in their bond. Instead of being demeaning, the title was more like an endearment and *that* notion reminded Mikki that there was more on the agenda here than just her survival training.

Excitement replaced fear. A delicious tingle of anticipation.

'Of course I can,' she told Tama. 'I'm assuming you're keen to get off this mountain alive.'

'You bet.'

'And I'm guessing you've done this before.'

'Once or twice.'

'In this particular location?'

'Absolutely.' Tama looked around them, taking a long moment to stare at the mountain peaks. 'I love it up here,' he added. 'We're on top the world. Free.'

Mikki was looking at him rather than the mountains. Listening to a note in his voice she hadn't heard before. A tone that reverberated and gave her the odd urge to touch him. A moment later she realised why. It had been a piece of personal information, hadn't it?

In all the interaction she'd had so far with this man, nothing as personal as a passion for anything other than his work had been apparent. It was like having a drink offered when she hadn't realised how thirsty she was. A tiny taste and Mikki wanted more. A lot more. She wanted to know what else he loved. *Who* he loved. What did he need to feel 'free' from?

'You're staring at me again.'

'Again?'

'You do it a lot.'

'Do I?' It was time to change the subject. 'I'm just waiting for words of wisdom to spill from your lips, that's all. What's first? Do we get to build a snow cave?'

'No.' Tama seemed to be collecting himself. Focussing on what they were there to do. 'We're going to make a mound rather than a cave. Caves are best for a larger group. A mound is all two of us will need for a night.'

Just the two of them. In close quarters. *All* night. Was it just a lower level of oxygen at this high altitude that was making Mikki notice a slight dizziness?

'The first thing we do is STOP,' Tama said firmly.

'Stop what?' Mikki asked nervously. Her wayward thoughts, maybe?

'S.T.O.P.,' he spelt out. 'It stands for Stop, Think, Observe and Plan. What if Steve hadn't just flown off into the sunset? What if he was lying dead in the mangled helicopter we just crawled out of? And what did we wait for before escaping the wreckage?'

They had been over important considerations of surviving a crash last night.

'We waited until all movement had stopped,' Mikki responded obediently. 'We didn't want to get sliced to bits by rotors that were still in the process of shearing off.'

'Good. What should we do now?'

'Wait until the risk of fire has gone and go back to check that the emergency locator beacon is activated and see if the radio works.'

'And?'

'And we try and retrieve the survival pack, if we didn't already bring it out with us.'

'Right.' Tama was well into teaching mode now. 'Our

ELB isn't working for whatever reason and neither is the radio. What now?'

'We try our cellphones.'

'No coverage here.'

'We should stay close to the wreck, which is going to be a lot more visible than we are. We could try and signal a passing aircraft by using mirrors or flares or making a fire.'

'You *were* paying attention.' Tama nodded approvingly, which sent a ridiculously warm glow through Mikki. 'What else should you be thinking about?'

'Any immediate threats to our safety. The dangers of hypothermia and dehydration.'

'What do we need?'

'Shelter. Water. Fire, if possible.' Mikki was enjoying the challenge. 'I think we need to build a shelter close to the wreck, try and keep warm and conserve energy. And if we're not found by morning, we should try and walk out.'

'Sounds like a plan.' Tama raised an eyebrow. 'What have you left out?'

'The patient? If we'd had a patient on board and got them out we wouldn't be able to go anywhere.'

Tama shook his head. 'Keep thinking. Remember STOP.'

'I'm up to P. Oh-h.' Mikki rolled her eyes. 'I haven't observed much, have I?'

'What should we look at?'

'The weather. Terrain. Materials that might be useful.'

'Cool. We know the weather's OK but if this was for real, what might we be looking for?'

'Wind direction and speed. Say, a nor'westerly that

means bad weather's on the way. Strong winds and rain could increase avalanche risk.' Mikki had begun moving her feet without realising it because they were getting cold enough to be painful.

Tama noticed. 'We'll start moving,' he decided. 'You can tell me about the terrain and where any danger areas for avalanche might be if you spot them.'

'Don't we need to plan our route first?'

'We'll talk about that, too.' Tama picked up the small backpack that contained their survival kit. 'I've done this before and our route is carefully planned to give us practice in the skills we need. Follow my steps to start with and watch how I'm kicking the snow to pack it down and then testing it before I put any weight down.' He grinned. 'Should keep us from falling into a crevasse, hopefully. You'll get a turn at keeping us alive later.'

Mikki picked up her pack that held water and dehydrated food and followed Tama. Yes, they would talk about what she was here to learn but it was inevitable that they would talk about other things, wasn't it?

Personal things that might allow her an insight into this intriguing man.

For the next two hours, anyone observing them would have considered themselves simply watching an intense teaching session. Mikki learned how to walk safely on a snow-covered slope. How to examine the terrain around, above and below them and how to describe a col and a gully and a buttress.

She learned how to spot changes in the snow that might indicate a hazard and how to estimate distances and plan a route that might eventually lead to safety. She spent some time choosing the place to build their shelter for the night and then they started the task that Tama said would take them another couple of hours.

The undercurrent—of being completely isolated with that simmering, as yet unexplored, physical attraction between her and Tama was just that. An unacknowledged undercurrent that was there with every burst of conversation and every shared glance. A pleasant sensation that suggested they were both going with the flow rather than fighting it.

A new depth was being added to their relationship, Mikki realised. Amidst the energy that came from a skilled teacher interacting with a willing student she could sense more than Tama's passion for his subject. There was a palpable pride in what he did. Who he was. Real patience in leading her to teach herself what she needed to know and a genuine interest in her success.

In *her*?

They took turns with the small shovel from Tama's pack to heap snow into a large mound. Tama took over when the height was above Mikki's head level. He made the task look easy and didn't even get particularly out of breath while he talked at the same time. He told her the story of a plane-crash victim who survived against huge odds and walked out of the bush a week later, mid-winter, in nothing more than a pair of shorts and a T-shirt.

'Sometimes,' he concluded, 'I think survival is more about sheer bloody-mindedness and refusing to give up than all the fancy stuff we can teach. Have you got that kind of determination, Mikki?'

He'd called her 'Mikki'. Not 'princess' or 'Mouse'. This was new. And it was a personal question. Was

Tama feeling the same kind of curiosity about her that she was about him?

'I guess,' she responded carefully. 'I'm here, aren't I? Given how over-protective my dad is, it's taken a fair bit of determination to get this far.'

Tama seemed to be shovelling harder. 'We need to get a good dome shape to this,' he said. 'That way we can maintain an arch shape when we hollow it out. That makes the roof self-supporting and it won't drip on us.' He threw another shovelful of snow upwards. 'Why is your father so over-protective?'

'My mother died just before my tenth birthday. Dad absolutely adored her and her death very nearly destroyed him. For a while, he pushed me away totally but…when he found he was able to love again, he went a bit too far the other way. Wanted to wrap me up in cotton wool and make sure he didn't lose someone else, I suppose.'

'You're an only child?'

'Yes. Mum was diagnosed with breast cancer at the same appointment she found out she was pregnant with me.'

The movement of the shovel ceased. 'Wow. That must have been tough. Did she put off treatment?'

'Yes.' Mikki had to turn and pretend she was admiring the scenery again. Boy, Tama knew how to get straight to the heart of a painful subject, didn't he? Had she really wanted to start treading on personal ground like this?

The silence continued. Respectful. Waiting.

'I didn't know that until after she died,' Mikki said finally. 'Some well-meaning friend was trying to find a way to help Dad with his depression and I overheard her talking to another friend. She thought he might be blaming himself because he allowed her to continue with the pregnancy instead of starting chemo.'

Another silence fell in which Mikki could feel Tama staring at her.

'So you blamed yourself instead.'

Mikki turned swiftly. 'Why did you say that?'

'It's what kids do.' It was too hard to see Tama's eyes behind the ski goggles from this distance but she could see sympathy in every line of his face. 'Their world gets tipped upside down and someone they love gets ripped away from them. We're egocentric creatures at the best of times and when you're too young to know any better, or there's no one around who knows or cares how you feel and you don't get told it's not true, it's inevitable you end up thinking it's your fault.'

The words were heartfelt. So heartfelt it was Mikki's turn to stare intently at Tama.

She had to clear her throat to break the new silence. 'What did you blame yourself for, Tama?'

Tama dug the shovel into the snow forcefully and heaved the load upwards, grateful for a physically demanding task.

Dammit. That had been unbelievably careless. But how had Mikki picked up that he was talking about himself so easily? It was like she could see the part of him he'd been able to keep so well hidden for so many years.

'I'm just saying,' he muttered. 'That's what kids are like.'

He needed to direct the conversation back to safe

ground. Why had he asked such a personal question in the first place? He knew perfectly well what level of determination this pint-sized woman possessed.

This had been a mistake. He'd got carried away back there when they'd been visiting Josh. Pushed the boundaries of the game thanks to the temptation that nurse's comment had provoked. A threesome? No way. But the idea of being alone—just him and Mikki—had been irresistible. And so easy to arrange with no suspicions being raised.

But it had been a mistake. He needed to back off and get this excursion onto purely professional grounds.

'We can start digging the tunnel now.' Tama stepped away from the impressively large mound of snow. 'We start out here and go down about a metre. We won't come up until we're well under the edge of the mound and then we'll start hollowing out from the middle. I'll shovel it behind me and you can scoop it up and get rid of it.'

The task was not difficult but it was time-consuming and they had to rest at intervals to conserve energy.

Verbal interaction was minimal because Mikki was out of sight and busy behind him. When there was an opportunity to say something, Tama kept right away from anything personal. He had a wealth of stories he could tell about how people dealt with survival in the wilderness. Plus any number of useful tips.

'Don't ever carry a butane lighter with your survival kit,' he warned Mikki. 'Too damn dangerous. Have an airtight, melt-proof container and keep waterproof matches or magnesium fire-starters in it.

'Use your watch for a compass. Keep it flat and point

the hour hand at the sun. Half the distance between the hour hand and twelve o'clock is due south.

'You can make a decent fishing hook by bending a syringe needle. I'll show you tomorrow when we get near the river.'

It worked for a while, even though it felt forced at best and a bit ridiculous at times. It wasn't so easy to control his thoughts while he was alone in the centre of the mound, carving out the space they would share for the night. He kept thinking about the kind of darkness her words had skimmed. A darkness he could understand only too well.

Was that where her astonishing strength of character came from? That period of heading into adolescence, not only missing the person she needed most. But carrying the burden of guilt that her very existence might have contributed to her mother's death?

He gave up trying to squash his curiosity when he emerged to share a drink of water and a muesli bar from Mikki's pack.

'At least your dad didn't blame you,' he found himself saying out of the blue. 'Or he wouldn't have been so over-protective.'

'That came later,' Mikki said. 'After the car accident when I was sixteen.'

Ah, yes. That accident. He'd been curious about that when she'd mentioned it the day of that physical assessment. It had been so easy to stay away from stepping onto personal ground back then. Not so easy now.

'You were hurt?' The mental image of Mikki lying badly injured in the kind of scenes he often attended was disturbing enough to give him a kick in the gut.

'Amazingly, no, but the other three teenagers in the

car were hurt. One of them died. I was the front-seat passenger and…I got lucky, I guess.'

'They were your friends?'

'Yeah…' She didn't sound sure.

'A boyfriend was one of them?'

'No.' Mikki's tone told him it was time to stop prying. Clearly, she didn't want to talk about it.

That was fine. Good, even. They could really get away from this personal stuff. He could dismiss his curiosity about those intervening years. The ones between her mother's death and the accident that had made her father so over-protective. Had he not cared much until then? Been so focussed on a sick wife and then too broken-hearted to really notice his kid? She must have been incredibly lonely if that had been the case. Not that he was going to ask but he didn't like the idea of her being a lonely child any more than being injured.

Mikki broke into his thoughts. 'What about you?' she asked. 'Were you an only child?'

Maybe they couldn't stay away from this personal stuff after all. He'd brought this on himself, though, hadn't he?

'Yes and no,' Tama answered reluctantly. He pushed the top of his water bottle shut with a snap, shoved it back into the pack and turned to climb back into the tunnel. Then he caught Mikki watching him and sighed inwardly.

'Yeah, OK. It's just not something I tell people.' *Ever.* So why did it feel like the time to break that ironclad rule? Because Mikki had experienced something that might give her insight into how it had really been? There was something there. A connection. A kind of force that pulled the words from his mouth. 'Yes, I was an only child. I didn't have a dad that I knew about. I got sent to live with my uncle and aunt and eleven cousins.'

Tama ducked his head into the tunnel. He'd said enough. Too much.

Mikki's voice floated into the tunnel with him. 'How old were you?'

'About six,' Tama growled. He wriggled further into the mound. This conversation was over.

Mikki crouched at the neck of the tunnel, ready to scoop the snow that came towards her and spread it away from the opening.

She had barely heard Tama's muttered response to her question but it resonated in her head as loudly as if he'd shouted it.

He'd been six. A small child.

For whatever reason, his mother had given him up and sent him to live with relatives. To be one of a huge family where one more mouth to feed probably hadn't been noticed. *He* might not have been noticed.

Just like her, he'd lost his mother.

And he'd blamed himself, hadn't he? That was why those words had been so heartfelt.

As a little boy, Tama had felt unloved and possibly very lonely, and he'd believed it was his own fault. That somehow, unknowingly, he'd done something so wrong he'd had to be severely punished.

Mikki's heart ached. For Tama. For herself. For the children they had been and for what had been taken from them. No wonder she felt so drawn to this man. Was it the similarity of their pasts that attracted them both to this kind of work? This unique combination of risking yourself to care for others?

Was the reason she felt Tama was a soulmate as simple as that?

Maybe.

Except that there was another factor in this attraction.

A very physical one.

The inside of the snow mound had a wide platform against one side and a narrower one against the other.

'We sleep there,' Tama explained, pointing to the wider platform. 'And we cook on this one.'

'Cook?'

'Didn't I tell you I can cook?' Tama was using a tiny bright light that was remarkably effective in the confines of this small space. 'Watch this.'

He produced a tiny primus stove from his pack and a small, lightweight, aluminium pan. Mikki found the water and the packages of dehydrated food he requested and then did as instructed and watched, increasingly aware of how intimate this situation was.

Here they were, in a tiny cocoon, so isolated that the rest of the world might as well have ceased to exist.

Just herself and Tama. In a space small enough to be warmed by the combination of their body heat and the small stove. When an absolutely delicious smell began to emanate from the pan, it felt—ridiculously—like home.

Mikki cast an anxious glance upwards a moment later, however.

'Won't the heat from the flames melt the roof?'

'A bit, but it won't drip on us. That's the beauty of

making a good arch shape. It won't cave in either, so don't worry.'

Mikki smiled. 'I'm so hungry I don't care. It would be worth it.'

They both had a spoon and they took turns eating the hot mixture of pasta, meat and vegetables. A muesli bar stuffed with chocolate chips was dessert.

'Still hungry?' Tama asked as Mikki washed down her last mouthful with a swig of water.

'No. And I'm heaps warmer. I feel great.'

The warmth from Tama's approving gaze made her feel even better. Mikki liked it that they didn't need to wear the goggles in here. She loved being able to see Tama's eyes. To try and read his expressions. She just wished she knew more of what was going on behind those dark eyes. Maybe she was still hungry. Just not for food.

'I'm warm, too,' Tama said. 'Amazingly effective shelter, isn't it? Put your gloves back on, though. We don't want to risk frostbite while we sleep.'

Mikki pulled on woollen gloves and then her waterproof, thermal mittens as Tama opened a small package that contained a foil sheet. He spread it on the sleeping platform as she pulled her woollen hat on more securely and made sure her anorak was zipped up. She stepped into the sleeping bag Tama handed her from the pack and pulled it up to her waist.

'I'm going to turn off the light,' Tama warned. 'Come and make yourself comfortable on the bed.'

A bed they were about to share. Mikki's mouth felt dry and she had to lick her lips. Did Tama feel this sudden tension? Should she try and make it go away by making a joke?

'Hey.' She grinned, hopping a step closer. 'I'm not sure we know each other well enough to sleep together yet.'

The only response to her remark was to be plunged into total darkness as Tama flicked off the light. Then, out of the darkness and silence, came Tama's voice. A low rumble that made Mikki's toes curl inside her heavy boots.

'We know each other just fine,' he said.

CHAPTER EIGHT

'YOU'RE perfectly safe.'

Tama sat down on the snow platform and then lay down, his head going behind Mikki's back as she stayed sitting on the edge. His tone was amused.

'We'd be risking hypothermia taking any of our clothes off. Lie down, Mouse. You must be tired.'

She was and she did. Cautiously. It was hard to share this space without touching the body of the large man lying beside her, but they were so padded up in their multiple layers of protective clothing, it didn't really matter.

It shouldn't matter anyway. But, then, she shouldn't be able to sense the heat from his body like this. To feel his touch through all those layers as clearly as if he was touching her skin.

Mikki moved a moment later, uncomfortably aware of the pressure of Tama's hip against hers.

'Be still,' Tama murmured.

Mikki froze instantly. The words transported her back to that day in the diving pool when he'd just pulled her from the helicopter 'wreck' and she was taking that long-awaited breath of air. She could see his face so close to her own. Could feel that first rush of desire to touch his lips with her own.

Oh, *help*! Her cringe was almost a wriggle.

'What's up?' Tama asked. 'You cold?'

'Nope. I'm good.'

'Could've fooled me.'

'This is just a bit…weird.'

It was automatic to turn her head towards the person she was talking to. Not that she could see Tama. This was a darkness like nothing she had ever experienced. She wouldn't be able to see her hand if she held it close enough to touch her nose.

Funny how it heightened other senses. She could feel Tama's breath on her face. *Smell* him. A musky, masculine scent she could almost taste.

'Scared, huh?'

Mikki hesitated. 'Yes.' The admission was reluctant because she wouldn't be surprised if Tama thought less of her for it, but it was the truth. There was a real element of fear still lurking. If Tama hadn't been here beside her, she would be terrified.

'You should be,' Tama said quietly. 'Any intelligent person would be in a situation like this.' He was shifting his weight now. Putting his arm around Mikki and pulling her closer. 'You're OK,' he said. 'I'm here.'

Mikki absorbed the reassurance. Allowed herself to sink into the circle of his arm and let the side of her body mould itself to his. Maybe she didn't need to be so afraid of their environment but she still didn't feel safe being this close to Tama.

'It still feels weird,' she said into the new silence.

'Why?' Tama chuckled and the puff of breath was warm. 'You don't make a habit of sleeping with men in holes in the snow?'

The teasing diffused the tension. 'I don't make a habit of sleeping with men at all.'

'Whoa!' She could hear Tama suck in his breath. 'You a virgin, princess?'

'No.' For some obscure reason it felt like an insult. As though she might not be attractive enough to have had the opportunity. Or too uptight to consider sex before marriage acceptable. 'And don't call me that.'

'Why not?'

'I don't like it.'

'Hmm.' Tama sounded interested now. 'What else don't you like? Apart from sleeping with men, that is.'

Mikki wanted to hit him. 'I didn't say I didn't *like* sleeping with men. I said I didn't make a *habit* of it.'

'Good. Delighted to hear it.'

He sounded delighted. Why? What business was it of his, anyway?

'What about you?' Mikki countered.

'I *never* sleep with men.'

Mikki snorted. 'Very funny.'

'And you're the first woman I've slept with in…oh, ages.'

'Yeah, weeks, I bet. And you're not *sleeping* with me.'

'Not yet,' Tama conceded graciously. 'But I will.'

Mikki held her breath unconsciously. There was such promise in those few words but did he mean slumber or sex?

'You're not breathing,' Tama said softly.

'Yes, I am.' Mikki let her breath out with a whoosh. 'See?'

'Just as well. I was just starting to think I might need to resuscitate you.'

Mouth-to-mouth resuscitation? Mikki swallowed. She hadn't imagined that tone of disappointment beneath the light banter. Was he looking for an excuse to kiss her? Desire kicked in and her heart missed a beat and sped up. It felt so obvious she was afraid Tama would be able to feel it as well. She tried to slow her heart rate by slowing her breathing. But that made it very quiet.

'Uh-oh,' Tama murmured. 'You're doing it again.'

He was so close Mikki could feel the words as much as hear them, and the distance closed as he spoke so that by the time he spoke the last word it simply morphed into a kiss. The talking finished but his lips kept moving on top of hers. Gently. And then more firmly.

It was a conversation all of its own with all the nuances that speech could contain with the tiny variations of pressure and position. Despite the deafening level of sound desire was trying to make, Mikki could 'hear' the underlying communication.

I like you. I'm interested.

Me, too.

I like this. Do you?

Yes. Oh…yes!

The kiss went on. And on. Desire was tightly reined in, which made it possible for this conversation to seem relaxed. A pleasure in itself that was not necessarily leading to anything else.

As naturally as the verbal communication had become non-verbal, the process was reversed.

'Nice,' Tama murmured as he drew back slowly. 'Very nice.'

'Mmm.' Mikki ran her tongue over her lower lip. It still tingled. It still tasted of Tama. 'Nice' was far too pale a word.

'You're still safe,' Tama told her. 'I don't do relationships.'

'Oh?' The statement should have been reassuring. Where did that frisson of disappointment come from?

'No.' The affirmation was definite.

'How old are you?'

'Thirty-six.'

'And you've never had a relationship?'

'Define "relationship".'

'Um…' Mikki had to think. 'If you see someone more than a couple of times it becomes a relationship because you have the expectation of seeing them again. You *want* to see them again.'

'Does it involve sex?'

'At some point, if it's an adult relationship, then sex is involved. That's what makes it a relationship rather than just a friendship.'

'OK. In that case, I take it back. I've had heaps of relationships.'

'If you go into it knowing that it's short term, it's not a *real* relationship,' Mikki continued as she thought aloud. 'It becomes real when you start caring about that person. When you have the expectation that it's going to continue and lead to something else.'

'Like marriage and mortgages?'

'I guess.'

'Then no. I was right. I've never had a real relationship

and I don't intend to. Any hint that a woman wants that stuff and I'm outta there. Not my scene. How 'bout you?'

'It's not something I can see in my immediate future,' Mikki said confidently. 'But I wouldn't say "never". Maybe, one day, when I meet the right person, I'll change my mind.'

'Really?'

'Sure. Why not?'

'Because you've seen what it can do to someone.'

'What do you mean?'

'You said it nearly destroyed your father when your mother died. He must have loved her very much. They must have had the best kind of relationship.'

'They did. And, yes, he adored her.'

'And it was nearly the end of the world for him when he lost her. It must have been unbearable. I've seen that happen, too. Why put yourself at risk like that?'

'Because…' Mikki was getting an insight into herself through Tama that she'd never considered. Was she the same? Had she run from any relationship that looked like it was getting serious because she didn't want to risk the fallout if things went wrong? 'It must be worth it. It's that "better to have loved and lost" theory.'

'I don't buy into it,' Tama said dismissively. 'There's other good stuff to be found in life. Like this…'

He was kissing her again. And this time it felt even more natural than the first time. His taste was familiar and…wonderful. His warmth seeped into every cell in Mikki's body and the movement of his lips sent impulses that brought her whole body alive. Made it tingle with energy and contentment and desire all at the same time.

And then his tongue touched hers and Mikki lost any

ability to analyse how she felt. The world had already been banished to this tiny space and now her awareness shrank much further. She just existed in that point of contact between herself and Tama. A white-hot flame that flickered and grew and consumed everything else. Including oxygen. Mikki finally had to pull back to drag in a breath of air.

'This isn't good.'

'What?' Tama sounded astonished. 'I thought it was pretty fantastic myself. Best kiss I've had in...oh, ages.'

Mikki suppressed a smile. 'I meant it's not a good idea. We can't have sex, Tama.'

'No. That would require a little less in the way of clothing than we currently have and it would be silly to risk dying of hypothermia.'

'I meant not at all.'

'We're only kissing.'

'And kissing is generally the first step on a path that leads to a lot more.' It would be too disappointing to get more of Tama's kisses and know they were leading to nothing more. Better to pull the plug right now. 'What happens when we're not sleeping on top of a mountain? Tomorrow, say, or next week?'

'Do you want a lot more, Mouse?'

'No.' *Yes.*

'You sure about that?' Tama's lips were teasing hers again.

'We *can't.*' Mikki was desperately trying to remember why it was such a bad idea. Oh, yes... 'It would be... completely inappropriate.'

'Would it?'

'Yes. Of course it would. You must see that.'

'Help me out here. We're both adults, aren't we?'

'Y-yes.'

'And we're both single. At least, I'm single. How 'bout you?'

'Of course I'm single. I wouldn't be kissing you if I wasn't.'

'I also get the impression that neither of us is into those long-term, *real* relationships you were talking about. Not yet, in your case, anyway.' A hint of alarm crept into his voice. 'You don't see me as husband material do you?'

Mikki almost laughed. 'No way! And I'm certainly not looking. Settling down anywhere—with *anyone*— is the last thing I want right now. I've got way too much to do with my life first.'

'So there you go. We're the same, you and me.' Tama's grip on Mikki tightened by way of emphasis. 'We want the same things. So why not sex? I think…' Tama's lips touched Mikki's again and his tongue stroked hers for just a heartbeat. 'I think it would be very, *very* good.'

Mikki had absolutely no doubts about that.

'You're my teacher.' She forced the words out in a rush. 'I'm with you because I need to learn stuff.'

'Agreed.' She could hear Tama smiling. 'So the curriculum has some extras. I'm sure there's some things I could teach you in bed, princess.'

Oh, *Lord*! Mikki had absolutely no doubts about *that* either.

'I'm dependent on you for a qualification I really want to get, Tama. That makes it inappropriate. Unethical. If anyone knew, you'd get into big trouble. I'd probably end up having to leave without the qualifications I need to get me into MSF.'

'What if it didn't? What if nobody knew about it except us?'

'It's way too risky. What if it turned to custard and you took your revenge by failing me?'

'It wouldn't.'

'Why not?'

'Because we're not talking *real* here, that's why not. We're talking sexual attraction. At least, that's what it is for me. I know it's inappropriate and I've tried to ignore it, but it doesn't seem to be going away. Quite the opposite.' He sighed, an eloquent admission of defeat, and when he spoke again, his voice was husky. 'I want you.' His lips were close to Mikki's again and she felt his words right through her body. 'And I think…' He paused to brush her lips very softly. 'I think you might feel the same way.'

'Mmm.' The sound was strangled. Embarrassingly close to a moan, really.

'So maybe we should just get it out of our systems. Deal with it. Unresolved sexual tension could lead to frustration that might interfere more with your training than your imagined fallout that's not going to happen because we're not going to have a *real* relationship. We can't, can we? You're not even going to be around for long enough.'

'That's true. A couple of months at the most, if you do your job properly.'

'So there you go. We're talking a few weeks. We don't even need to think that far ahead. This could be a one-off situation. A kind of debrief. A way of defusing tension.'

'A one-off?' Mikki didn't like that idea. It was too casual. Cheap.

'Theoretically. I guess what I'm saying here is that we shouldn't take it too seriously. We know what we want and there's no real reason why we shouldn't go there and then take it one step at a time. See what happens. I reckon we could make it work.'

'And nobody would find out?'

'Not from me, they wouldn't.'

'And you wouldn't let it interfere with work? With my training?'

'That would be unethical. I'm not an unethical person, Mikki, I promise you that.'

He'd used her name again.

And he'd made a promise she knew instinctively she could trust. Just like she was trusting him to get her through this survival training.

'Think about it,' Tama said. He let his breath out in a sigh and pulled her even closer. 'Right now, we should sleep. We've got a big day tomorrow.'

Think about it, he'd said.

He'd meant for Mikki to think about it, but in the bright light of the new day, it was all Tama could think about himself. He'd dreamt about it, with his arm holding Mikki's body against his while he'd slept.

He'd wanted to kiss her the moment he'd opened his eyes to find her still snuggled against him. He'd wanted to breathe warmth into her body in case she was as chilled and stiff as he felt.

Instead, he'd made breakfast. Hot porridge and strong coffee. And he'd talked about the programme for the second day of training. How they would leave the snow and head for a river crossing and into the bush. How she would learn to make a shelter from brushwood and a fire from scratch.

He didn't mention a thing about that intimate conversation in the dark. The ball was in Mikki's court and it would be her choice whether she picked it up or not. However badly Tama wanted it, he wasn't going to influence her decision. If she was going to come to him, she had to want to.

If this was going to work, she had to want him as badly as he wanted her. And the ground rules had to be sacrosanct.

He hadn't said a word.

All day.

Either he'd lost interest or he was leaving the decision entirely up to her.

Mikki thought about those kisses and knew he wouldn't have lost interest any more than she had. She liked it that he wasn't putting any pressure on her. That he was giving her the choice. But it also made her feel curiously shy.

To come right out and say that, yes, she'd given it some thought and decided it was a great idea seemed way too brazen. She couldn't think of a way to say it with just the right degree of lightness so she ended up saying nothing about it at all. Just like Tama.

She listened to her mentor and asked questions about what he was teaching her, and she followed him and did everything she was instructed to do.

They worked their way carefully down a slope with

patches of icy snow between clumps of tussock. They chose a safe crossing place for the baby river and Mikki crossed her arms and held hands with Tama to give them greater weight and stability as they negotiated the shallow but fast-moving water.

They pushed their way into the bush and Mikki learned about which plants were edible and which were poisonous. They discussed the effects of Giardia parasites and how to treat water to make it safe to drink.

As promised, Tama showed her how to make a fishing hook and line when they came across the larger river they would follow downstream, but they didn't try their luck fishing for long.

'We've got enough food for tonight and there's a fair way to walk yet. You tired?'

'A bit,' Mikki admitted. 'It'll be nice to stop.' She was tired of walking with wet and squelchy boots and she was tired of trying to interpret every glance or touch from Tama to gauge what he might be thinking. Whether what had happened between them last night was on his mind as much as it was on hers.

But even when they stopped walking, she couldn't find a way of steering the conversation to anything really personal. It was far easier to stick with the teaching session and learn how to gather brushwood and join it together to make a shelter. How to find small twigs for kindling and then to light the fire by using a magnesium fire-starter.

'Shave pieces off one side with your pocket knife,' Tama instructed. 'And then you make a spark using that piece of flint embedded in the other side.'

Hot food, as daylight faded, was again very welcome.

The warmth from the fire was wonderful but Mikki eyed the narrow space beneath the shelter she had constructed dubiously.

'It's still going to be cold tonight, isn't it?'

'Yep. Usually is, outside like this.'

Too cold to take their clothes off, then. Mikki's nod was resigned but her heart rate picked up. If she was going to say anything, this was her chance. She swallowed. Then she cleared her throat. 'It would be silly to risk hypothermia.'

'It would.' But Tama was smiling. He was reading the direction of her thoughts easily and his smile was enough to give her a lot more courage.

'Shame,' she murmured.

They sat in silence for a minute.

'There *is* a hut,' Tama said.

'What?'

'I told you this route was carefully chosen. There's a hut about half a mile away. We needed one available as a precaution, in case someone got injured on a training exercise or the weather turned nasty. It's got a clearing beside it which is where the chopper's going to pick us up first thing in the morning.'

'So why are we out here instead of in a nice, warm hut?'

'Because it's part of the training. You needed to learn to make a shelter.'

'I've done that.'

Tama glanced over his shoulder. 'So you have.'

'If we happened to be near the clearing a little earlier than expected, no one would need to know why, would they?'

'No.'

'But…' Mikki felt embarrassed now. 'It still wouldn't be a good idea to…you know…'

'Have sex?' Tama supplied helpfully.

'Mmm.'

'Why not? We wouldn't be risking discovery. Or hypothermia.'

'We might be risking something else.'

'We've agreed on the ground rules. It's not going to interfere with your training and it's not going to get messed up by one of us being stupid enough to think it's real.'

'That's not what I meant. I'm talking about…' Mikki closed her eyes. This was horribly clinical. 'You know. Safe sex.'

'Oh-h. Not a problem.'

Mikki's eyes snapped open. 'You're telling me you carry condoms on a survival training exercise?'

Tama's grin was unrepentant. 'I'm a good Boy Scout. Always prepared. But, no, I don't *always* carry them. This time I did.'

Mikki opened her mouth, ready to express outrage at the implied expectation, but then she shut it again. She thought back to that moment in Josh's room. That silent acknowledgement that had passed between them of the attraction and the opportunity that being alone together would provide.

She stood up. 'Seeing as you're such a good Boy Scout,' she said, with a very womanly smile. 'You'll know what to do to make this fire safe to leave, won't you?'

They held hands as they stumbled along a rough track that led to a primitive but sturdy wooden hut. There was a pot-belly stove opposite the door that made the interior deliciously warm in a very short period of time. They both took off their outer, waterproof garments and their balaclavas and gloves and boots.

Leaving the door of the stove open provided a warm, glowing light. Enough to illuminate the narrow bunk beds built into both sides of the hut. Mikki looked at the width of the beds. She looked at the size of Tama and then she looked at the door.

'There's no chance anyone else will want to use this hut tonight, is there?'

'If they did, they would have been here before nightfall, and that was quite a while ago now.'

'Good.'

Mikki pulled a mattress off a bunk and put it on the floor in front of where Tama was stoking up the stove. She added a second mattress beside it and the whole floor area was virtually covered.

It was such an obvious move that Mikki felt embarrassed having completed it. She couldn't look at Tama because the courage she'd found to let him know what she wanted had deserted her. Setting up bedding like this made her feel suddenly and horribly...cheap.

It took only a small step for Tama to be close enough to touch her. He put his forefinger under her chin and used just enough pressure to make her lift her face and look up at him.

She saw understanding in his gaze. Reassurance. And then he smiled that gorgeous crooked smile and bent his head to claim her lips with his own.

* * *

They shouldn't be doing this.

Tama knew that, despite the arguments to the contrary he'd presented to Mikki last night.

He also knew he couldn't have continued resisting the temptation without repercussions. He'd been honest when he'd said that sexual frustration could interfere with their professional relationship more than any aftermath was likely to.

Mikki held her arms up like a child as he helped her undress by pulling the tight thermal top from her body, but there was nothing childlike about the way she dropped her arms around his neck and then stood on tiptoe to offer him her mouth.

Tama let his lips savour hers while his hands unclipped her bra and then slid slowly forward to trace her ribs and find…

Oh, *God*! He might have denied it so well he'd believed it but he'd been wanting to touch these small, perfect breasts since he'd first clapped eyes on them by the diving pool that day. He'd known how they would fit his hands. How firm and round they would feel. He hadn't imagined what it would do to him to feel the tiny, hard nub of an aroused nipple on them, though. With a groan he had to abandon the sweetness of Mikki's mouth and bend lower to explore with his tongue the place he'd just sensitised with his fingers.

Any thoughts of how wrong some might see this as being went up in smoke along with the crackle of the logs in the pot-belly stove. Thoughts like he might be abusing a position of power. Using Mikki simply for his own pleasure.

No. The sounds she was making as he slipped his hands inside her pants to help her undress further made it quite clear that Mikki was getting just as much pleasure from this as he was.

Maybe she was using *him*.

Tama stripped off his own clothes and, for a long moment, he looked at Mikki. Standing naked in the glow from the fire. She was tiny and vulnerable and…the most beautiful woman he'd ever seen. He would have to be so careful not to hurt her.

'You're lovely, Mikki,' he said quietly. 'Just…perfect.'

She raised her gaze from where she had been returning the visual exploration.

'You're not so bad yourself.'

Striving to sound casual might have worked except for that tell-tale wobble in her voice that spoke of barely restrained passion. Her gaze was steady, however. Mikki knew what she was doing there and she knew what she wanted.

Whatever the motivation for this, it was mutual. They both wanted it badly and if you wanted something enough you made sure it worked. Who had he been trying to kid by suggesting that this was going to be a one-off experience?

Tama drew Mikki close. Skin to skin. He kissed her until her legs were as wobbly as her voice had been and then he let his own knees bend, controlling their fall until they were cushioned on the mattresses and Mikki was lying beneath him. Reaching for him. Ready to take him to the place he most wanted to be.

Tama made sure he took Mikki with him to that place but later, much later, as he finally eased far enough away to find the clothing and sleeping bags they would need for the rest of the night, he had to seek reassurance.

'OK, babe?'

'I'm good.'

'What do you reckon?' Tama tried to keep the question light—as though a negative response would be perfectly acceptable. As though he wasn't already planning a way of getting more of the paradise he'd just discovered. 'We got it out of our systems?'

There was a short silence.

'No,' Mikki said decisively. 'Not quite yet.'

CHAPTER NINE

TAMA JAMES was clearly a man of his word.

He'd said nobody would find out and even when they went to visit his best friend together the day after they returned, he didn't do or say anything that could have raised suspicion from Josh.

'How was it?' Josh asked Mikki. 'Did you find it hard? Scary? Exciting?'

'All of the above,' she responded, careful not to look in Tama's direction.

'Did she pass?' Josh asked Tama.

'I reckon.'

Mikki stole a glance but Tama wasn't looking her way either.

'I survived two nights in the wild with Tama,' she told Josh with a grin. 'I reckon I can survive anything.'

'So true.' Josh nodded. 'Hey, I passed my consultant's visit this morning. Neurology in my foot's fine. They're talking about letting me out by the end of next week. I told Mum I'd go home for a week or two to recuperate. It was the only way I could stop her setting up camp in this room.'

'By the end of next week,' Mikki said, 'I might pass my winch training.'

'Whoa!' Tama was looking at her for the first time since they'd arrived for this visit. Sternly. 'Don't go jumping the gun, princess. It's me that gets to decide that stuff.'

'So decide,' Josh said. 'I told you ages ago that Mikki was ready to start winch training.'

Mikki nodded. 'I could get frustrated,' she said demurely. 'It wouldn't be good for our professional relationship.'

Tama was glaring at her now but it was a cover-up. Mikki could detect a lurking twinkle. 'We'll see,' was all he said.

Nobody at work guessed anything either.

It helped that Alistair was on station as the replacement crew member. Because he was new to the station and the crew, it bumped up Mikki's position from being the latest addition. A degree of familiarity and an enjoyment of her colleague's company was perfectly acceptable, and no eyebrows were raised if they let something slip about being together out of hours because Mikki took up a casual membership at the gym complex Tama used. The same one where she'd done her physical prerequisite. Friendly rivalry over fitness regimes became part of the daily conversation on station.

'So who won last night?' Alistair would ask.

'Me,' Mikki might say. 'I was half a length ahead when we finished twenty lengths of the pool.'

And she could smile at Tama. Take just a moment to bask in the eye contact. To hug the knowledge that there had been no winners or losers later that night. That while their physical competition in the gym was fierce, in bed there was gentleness. A desire to give pleasure that seemed limitless so far in its ability to grow and deliver. While they'd only had a single night together in Tama's apartment that first week back, they'd had two nights this week and she knew they were both wondering how long they would have to wait for their next out-of-hours encounter. How many nights together in a week would they be having by the end of the month?

The idea that they would get this attraction out of their systems by acting on it had become a private joke. An excuse to spend more and more time together. And it was working. Just like Tama had promised it could. As long as Mikki didn't let herself get in too deep. As long as she didn't make the mistake of thinking it meant more than it did.

She was safe enough. She'd never fallen in love to the extent that being with a man was more important than the goals she had set herself in life, and Tama had made it very clear how he felt on the subject, so it simply wasn't going to happen. And if things started to look like they were getting out of hand, the limited timeframe they had available was the best insurance policy either of them could have asked for.

No one questioned how much time Tama and Mikki spent together during any downtime on station because it was all professional. Tama had given in to Mikki's relentless pressure and had begun her winch training in earnest, and winch training was time-consuming.

For Mikki, it was easy to keep it professional because there was so much to learn and it was all so exciting. By the end of the second week back after the survival training, she had completed all her on-ground training. She could describe, identify and explain the use of all the components and pieces of equipment to be used and do all the safety checks. She could demonstrate knowledge of the winch and its operation. She had absorbed all the written and audiovisual material available and had learned the protocols and the vocabulary for communication. On the last day, when the shift ended and there was no danger of being called out, she was ready to do her ten-metre work in the safety of the hangar.

The station manager had given his approval.

'But be careful,' he told Tama. A look passed between Andy and Tama that Mikki couldn't read. 'Keep it super-safe.'

'Of course.'

'Don't do anything you don't feel confident about,' Andy told Mikki. 'You don't need to rush this. You could leave it a while yet, you know. Why don't you take the copilot seat for any winch missions that come up from now on. You'd get practical demonstrations that'd be a good learning experience and you wouldn't get left behind on station.'

'I want to do this,' Mikki assured him.

'She's getting frustrated,' Tama added.

'Oh.' Andy looked from Mikki to Tama and back again. 'I guess we can't have that, can we?'

Steve insisted on staying late to help.

'I'm the pilot,' he said. 'I have a vested interest in making my crewman winch proficient.'

'OK,' Tama nodded. 'I'll operate the winch and Steve can pretend to be the pilot.'

'Hey! I *am* the pilot.'

But Tama's attention was on Mikki. 'We'll run this as if it was for real. There'll be a standard winch patter between me and Steve, even though he'll be on the floor 'cos there's no room for him on the platform.'

Mikki climbed the metal rungs a little more slowly than Tama. Maybe she wasn't quite as confident as she'd made out to Andy.

Steve got into the spirit of the training exercise with enthusiasm.

'Target sighted,' he called. 'What's the target, Tama?'

'Train wreck,' Tama said. 'Carriages all squished into a narrow ravine. No chance of ground access.'

'Cool. Some nice dodgy flying through the mountains. Love it. Target sighted,' he repeated. 'Turning downwind.'

'Roger.' Tama was positioned by the winch machinery. 'I have the target. Checking winch power.'

Mikki was checking her harness. For the fourth time. She looked down from the platform. Ten metres onto concrete was still a long way off the floor. She looked up to find the encouragement she needed in Tama's quick glance. He thought she was ready and she was. She wanted this. She'd look pathetic if she backed out now that Tama had finally agreed to let her go to the next level.

'Clear to open door,' Steve called.

'Roger. Door back and locked. Bringing hook inboard. Hooking onto Mikki.'

The clunk of the carabiners fastening made Mikki's mouth dry out instantly but she didn't look down at the floor again. She checked that her pit pin was secure and then removed her seat belt. Then she kept her gaze on Tama.

'Moving Mikki to door.'

The patter was familiar because Mikki had learned and practised it already. Tama asked for permission to put Mikki onto the skids and she could feel the narrow, metal strip beneath her feet as she stood, still facing Tama in what would be the interior of the helicopter if this was for real.

Then all her weight was taken by the winch. Later in her training, she knew she would get equipment she might need, like the Thomas pack or a stretcher attached at this point to hang between her legs, but this time she only needed to think about herself.

She listened to the patter between Tama and Steve where permission was sought and gained to boom her out so that she hung just below the skids and then to winch her down to ground level. It was time to look down now and carefully estimate the distance.

'Minus eight,' Mikki called. 'Minus six…four, three, two…' And then her feet touched the floor of the hangar. Her hands shook just a little as she unhooked herself. She extended her right arm, with her hand palm upwards and gave a 'thumbs-up' signal to Tama to tell him to retract the hook.

He was smiling down at her. By the time they'd reversed the procedure and Mikki was safely back on the platform, he was grinning broadly.

Steve gave a cheer and he probably thought nothing of the fact that Tama gave Mikki a fierce hug. Just as well he didn't hear the words murmured in her ear.

'That's my girl,' Tama said. 'I'm proud of you, princess.'

Even better that Steve could have no idea of the effect of both Tama's touch and his pride in her. Mikki couldn't wait to do it again. To do more and to do it well enough to earn more of Tama's approval.

By the following week she could handle equipment as well as herself, and the ten-metre training had become routine. Nerves kicked in the day they had a false alarm call and got permission to use the air time to do Mikki's thirty-metre training from the helicopter, but again she passed the challenge with flying colours.

'We've only got your deployments in bush terrain to cover now,' Tama told her at the end of that week. 'Then you'll almost be ready for a real job.'

'Why not now?' Mikki asked. 'If it was a straight-forward winch away from trees? I feel ready.'

'You're not ready,' Tama told her. 'Not yet. I'll tell you when.'

Apparently she was still not ready the following week and by then Mikki was really starting to feel frustrated. She could understand why she wasn't allowed to be winched around trees or boats or anything complicated but occasionally a job was straightforward. Like the car at the bottom of a steep gully or the tramper who'd broken his leg on a small, offshore island.

'I could do it,' Mikki pleaded.

'No,' Tama said. 'Not yet.'

'I've been in touch with MSF personnel,' Mikki told him. 'They're interviewing for a new intake in London in just over a month. I want to be there. *With* my qualification.'

But Tama wasn't about to bend. 'Make the most of being able to come on the missions with us as an observer. Watch and learn.'

She couldn't argue about simply watching the job

that came in later that morning. A badly injured crew-man on a fishing vessel that was well out to sea. This job was dangerous and, of course, it would be Tama that would be winched down to the ship.

Mikki sat up front beside Steve.

'Bit different, this, isn't it?' he said once they were heading out to sea.

'Every job's different. It's part of what I love about doing this. You never know where you'll be going next or what you're going to find when you get there, but it's always exciting.'

Rather like her relationship with Tama. It was still working perfectly. Because they both knew it couldn't last? The completion of Mikki's training was almost in sight. Or it would be as soon as Tama allowed her to do some genuine winch work. She already had the paper-work ready to make her application to MSF. An appli-cation she intended to hand in at the interview in London. All it needed was the addition of her certifica-tion that she was qualified for helicopter work.

It was the perfect recipe for making the most of what they had and Mikki, at least, was still blown away by the most intense physical relationship she had ever ex-perienced. The sex was like what she'd just said to Steve about helicopter work. She never knew quite what to expect in the way of location or content, but it was always, *always* exciting.

Like the day when their hunger for each other had built during their hours of working together to such a degree the passion had taken over the moment the door of Tama's flat had slammed behind them. They hadn't even got any further than the narrow hallway.

Mikki could still feel the power of that encounter now—weeks later. She could feel the wall behind her back and Tama's hands on her body. His strength as he cupped her bottom and carried her weight as she clung, with her hands around his neck and her legs around his waist. The relentless journey he took them both on until they reached an unforgettable climax.

Mikki stole a glance at Steve but he was busy checking GPS co-ordinates and looking out for a sighting of their target. As she should also be doing. Tama was in the back with Alistair. Out of sight.

But not yet out of mind.

As an antidote for the desire she had conjured up, Mikki deliberately tried to banish the memory of the wildest sex she'd ever had by remembering something as different as possible. An ordinary bed. Slow, careful sex where every touch was a caress.

No. That wasn't helping. Desire still curled strongly within her.

What about the night they'd both been too tired to do anything but fall asleep together, Tama having one arm beneath her head and the other draped carelessly over her midriff.

No. In its own way, just as memorable. She had fallen asleep feeling so…safe.

She would miss Tama when she left, that was for sure, but it was something she was going to have to deal with. Knowing all along that that point was coming would surely make it easier. Less stressful, anyway.

'Target sighted,' came from one of the men in the back of the helicopter. 'Nine o'clock.'

'Roger.' The helicopter banked as Steve changed direction. 'Target in sight,' he said a moment later. He changed channels on the radio to put him in contact with Control. 'Patch me through to the skipper,' he ordered.

Mikki was impressed with the way Steve kept two lines of communication open then, one with the skipper of the fishing vessel and the other with his crew. He instructed the skipper to turn downwind and keep his speed up enough to be able to control his steering in the ocean swell.

'Turning base leg,' he told Alistair. 'Clear to open door.'

'Roger. Door back and locked. Deploying Hi Line.'

'Roger. Skipper?' Steve raised his voice and spoke slowly and clearly. 'The line is on its way down. Catch it, but do not attach it to any part of your vessel. I repeat. Do *not* attach the line to anything.'

'Roger.' The skipper's voice had a marked foreign accent. 'I hear you loud and clear.'

The Hi Line was an extra connection, held by people on the boat and attached to Tama's harness at the other end. He would be winched down far enough away from the danger of becoming entangled in the mast or aerials of the vessel and then he would be pulled in sideways by the Hi Line being retracted.

'Moving Tama to door,' Alistair said. 'Clear skids.'

'Clear skids.'

Mikki turned so that she could watch. She saw Tama hanging below the skids and then beginning his descent. She looked further down and could see the bristling spikes of the mast and aerials on the boat, along with containers and fishing tackle and all sorts of other obstructions. She could also see the pitch and roll of the vessel as it negotiated a fairly heavy sea.

Tama's voice was calm as he counted off his descent. 'Minus fifteen… Minus ten… Minus five…'

Maybe it was that calmness that was Mikki's undoing. Did he not see how dangerous this was? What if the lines got caught on a projection of some kind? Or the fishing crew hadn't understood directions and had wound the Hi Line around some solid object? What if the boat suddenly rolled or changed its pitch just as he was touching down on the deck? He could break his legs or his back.

He could be *killed*.

And Mikki would never see that quirky, one-sided smile again. Or the twinkle of mischief in those dark eyes. She would never taste the sweetness of his kisses or feel the touch of his hands on her body. She would never feel the swell of her heart that came from the particular pride of doing something that impressed him.

Fear blindsided her like a blast of icy air and Mikki felt chilled to the bone.

So unexpected. And disturbing. It should have been banished by seeing Tama arrive safely on the deck where he unhooked himself and his gear and then moved to crouch beside the injured man, but it still lurked. Unwelcome and unsettling.

Was it going to be like this when she left on the next stage of her career and wouldn't be seeing Tama again?

Was this what it was like to be in love with someone? To care about them so much that the thought of losing them was terrifying?

No.

She wasn't in love with Tama. However good this not-quite-real relationship was, she knew with absolute certainty that it was a one-off experience in her life. All the more thrilling because of the hero-worship aspect she'd been carrying from the first moment she'd met him. A bit embarrassing now to remember that she'd had that photograph of him folded up in the back pocket of her jeans.

Besides, when she left she'd know he was still alive. It would be her choice to leave his company, not something that was being ripped from her by fate. They could stay in touch by email perhaps. Even see each other again one day. Maybe part of that fear in watching Tama's descent had been because she knew she might be doing it herself before very long. She had taken apprehension for her own safety, blown it out of proportion and transferred it to Tama.

The patient had his crushed hand and badly broken arm dressed and splinted and pain relief administered, and then he was made secure in the nappy harness and preparations were made to bring him up to the aircraft.

No, Mikki repeated silently with more confidence. Tama was an amazing man but totally the wrong person for any woman to fall in love with. It would be more than stupid to fall for someone who'd made it very clear he would never return such emotions.

Mikki had grown out of being stupid a very long time ago.

Something wasn't right.

Maybe he was just tired. Nerve endings frayed after that big job this afternoon. Exciting but dangerous stuff, winching onto boats on the open sea. There was often a downside to that kind of adrenaline rush.

That could explain why Tama was sitting here, his

lunch only half-eaten and his coffee getting cold, feeling like he was missing something.

Something important.

Looking up, he could see Mikki sitting at the other end of the table with a pile of paperwork in front of her. He knew she was studying for the written paper she would need to sit soon. Not that she needed to. Tama could bet his pupil was going to get a hundred per cent of the answers correct. She would really put the pressure on to finish her practical training then, wouldn't she?

Did she have any idea how dangerous it could be? He had been thinking about it on his way down to the ship that morning. Feeling grateful that it was him doing this and that he didn't have to worry about Mikki getting something wrong. Getting herself tangled in obstacles or timing her landing on a pitching deck incorrectly. Smashing herself on an unforgiving metal surface.

Was that why he was dragging his feet about letting her go to the next stage of her winching training? Would he feel the same way about it if she wasn't sharing his bed as well as his work environment?

An unsettling thought that made him a little more uneasy.

It was no surprise that Mikki sensed the observation she was under and flicked her gaze up from the printed papers in front of her. For a moment they simply held the eye contact—a silent and intimate communication they'd become expert in over the last... Good grief—it was nearly a month since that astonishing night up on the mountain. Getting close to a record as far as Tama's involvement with women went.

No wonder he was nervous!

Mikki smiled at him. The kind of smile he had come to watch for. He loved seeing that she was happy. Happy to be where she was and doing what she was doing. Happy to be close to *him*. Tama smiled back but inside that feeling that something wasn't right grew bigger. It sat like a heavy weight in his gut.

'You're staring at me,' Mikki said.

'Am I?' Tama shrugged.

'Yeah.' Mikki's smile widened. 'Ask me a question.'

'What about?'

'What do you think?' Mikki rolled her eyes and then tapped the papers on the table.

Of course. What a stupid question. Mikki was focussed on only one thing in her life. Getting her damn qualification so she could disappear off to the other side of the world and get on with all the dangerous adventures she was so keen to experience. It had been her focus from the moment she'd set foot on station, hadn't it? Did she see him as anything more than what he'd jokingly suggested as being an extra part of the curriculum?

Tama suppressed a sigh. 'Fine. What's the maximum working load for winching?'

'Six hundred pounds.'

'Average cable speed?'

'At six hundred pounds, one hundred feet per minute.'

'What's the emergency guillotine?'

'An electrically fired device the pilot can activate that will cut the cable.'

Tama was asking questions automatically. He didn't have to think hard which made it too easy to have part of his brain still chewing over the cause of that uneasy sensation. Obviously it had something to do with Mikki.

Maybe he was feeling…used. Faced with the focus she was displaying right now, he had to wonder if she had seen a closer relationship with him as a means of speeding up the process of getting what she wanted.

If the thought had occurred to him a month ago, he wouldn't have been bothered. This was a temporary arrangement that most men would think was a dream. A gorgeous, *amazing* woman who was willing to be in his bed as often as he wished with no strings attached. No demands. No expectations that he could and should be offering more than he was prepared to offer.

Why the hell should motivation be a problem? Why did he feel like he was being used?

'What's the thumbwheel?'

'A wheel located on the shrouded upper portion of the hand grip. It controls direction and speed. Moves upwards to lift a load and downwards to lower it.'

Mikki's eyes were shining. She knew she was getting the answers correct. She knew she was well on the way to getting exactly what she wanted.

Like she always had?

The resentment with which Tama had viewed his new recruit surfaced for the first time in weeks. She was a princess, he reminded himself. Spoilt. Yes, she may be capable and courageous and able to do this job as well as him but she hadn't had to fight to get here, had she? There must have been a string of people in her life making things easier for her. Housekeepers and gardeners and probably chauffeurs. He was just the latest, wasn't he?

A kind of employee who was being paid a bonus. She'd move on with her life and he'd be forgotten.

The heavy feeling developed sharp edges.

'I'm good, huh?' Mikki was smiling again. 'Do you think I'll pass the written paper?'

'Yeah. I guess.'

'You don't sound very pleased about it.'

Tama shoved his chair back and stood up, needing movement. He picked up his unfinished sandwich and went to drop it in the bin. 'Maybe I'm not.'

'Why?' Mikki's smile had vanished.

'You're already pushing to do more than you're ready to do. I don't want you to have any more ammunition.'

'Oh…' The tone was thoughtful. 'You're determined to put the brakes on, aren't you, Tama?'

'No. I'm determined that you remain safe and become proficient when you're ready.'

'I've only got a month left. I'm going to be at that interview in London, Tama. With or without my qualification. I would just *prefer* to have it.'

'So you can go off and kill yourself in some war zone? What is with you, Mikki? Why are you so hell bent on doing such a bloody dangerous job?'

'Look who's talking! You spent this morning doing what looked like an exceptionally dangerous job.'

'That's different.'

'Why? Why was it any less dangerous because you were doing it?'

'It wasn't. I have the experience to deal with it.'

'So teach me! That's what I'm here for. If you want me to be safe, then do your job and teach me how to be.'

Tama stared at her. Do his job? She did see him as an employee, didn't she? Just a step up from a gardener or something.

'I was actually worried about you during that winch,'

Mikki continued heatedly. 'I wouldn't have tried to stop you doing it, though. I respect your right to do what you want with your life.'

She was worried about him? The hard knot in Tama's gut changed shape and felt odd. He couldn't identify how it made him feel.

'You're as bad as my father,' Mikki snapped. 'Trying to control me and what I want to do with my life in the name of safety.'

OK. Much easier to stay angry than try and analyse that peculiar sensation, and the mention of Mikki's father made it a no-brainer. The anger grew.

'I'm nothing like your father,' he snapped back. 'I wouldn't have let you do this in the first place. I certainly wouldn't have tried to make it easy for you.'

Mikki's jaw dropped. 'What the hell is that supposed to mean?'

'You know as well as I do.'

'*What?*' The grim, imperious tone was enough to push Tama that bit further. To dredge up and let go of the resentment that had been there right from the start. Buried but not entirely forgotten.

'That your father set this training up. That if the whole helicopter rescue service wasn't dependent on the money he generates for us, there's no way you would have been taken on like this. You would have had to wait for the next intake, like everybody else. You wouldn't have got anywhere near this station until next year at the earliest and you would have been competing with a lot of very fit, very keen guys. No guarantee you would have made the cut.'

Not entirely true. Tama pushed back the memory of

just how competent Mikki had shown herself to be at that pre-requisite challenge. For some obscure reason he didn't have time to figure out he was very, very angry and he was going to win this argument.

Maybe he already had. Mikki was as pale as he'd ever seen her.

'That's not true,' she whispered. 'It *can't* be true.'

'You think I'm lying?' She didn't trust him, did she? Didn't trust his professional judgement and didn't even trust him to tell the truth. 'Why don't you ask him yourself?'

'I will.' Mikki's chin came up and the rest of her body followed. She was pulling her mobile phone from the pocket of her overalls as she turned and walked outside without a backward glance.

Tama could see her outside a few moments later. Pacing back and forth as she held the phone to her ear.

Had she really not known?

Why had he told her?

His anger evaporated and that nasty, uneasy feeling was there again. With teeth now. Gnawing at his gut.

What the hell had he just done?

CHAPTER TEN

MIKKI couldn't get hold of her father.

He had probably turned his mobile phone off because he was on a plane or in the middle of some important meeting that would end up increasing his net worth by another million or so. The kind of money that made it possible to be a major source of funding for a rescue helicopter service.

She didn't need to speak to him, anyway. She didn't *want* to speak to him.

Holding her phone to her ear and pacing about was simply a means of getting a few minutes to herself. To try and sort through the chaotic jumble of her thoughts.

She knew perfectly well Tama was right. It was just the kind of thing her father would do, and he had the power to do it. Mikki kept pacing, her humiliation growing with every extra shred of back-up evidence her mind was only too happy to produce.

Like how miraculous it had been to get that acceptance to try out for a place on the crew.

And how much Tama hadn't wanted her there. She had been so aware of his disdain that first day she'd turned up on his station, and look at the way he'd just walked off when she'd passed that physical challenge. It had been Andy who'd congratulated her and welcomed her on board. The station manager. The middle man between the crew and the board of directors that involved her father.

The way he'd called her 'princess'! Josh must have known, too. Hadn't Tama jumped on him only recently when he'd made a crack about her being given the 'royal treatment'?

The conversation with her father when she'd known there was something odd in the way he'd said Tama's name. He'd lied to her, hadn't he, when he'd said he didn't know her instructor?

Anger edged into the humiliation that came from the horrible notion that Tama and Josh had only agreed to take her on because they'd been told to comply with the request of someone who had major strings they could tweak.

No wonder Tama had glossed over that first job when her performance had been less than impressive. Had he been lying all along, too? Spoon-feeding her so that she could pass and get her coveted qualification because her father had requested the prize on her behalf?

This was all a sham.

Including Tama's attraction to her? He'd said it more than once, hadn't he? That she was 'special'. He hadn't meant *her*, though, had he? She'd been special because of who her father was. Had he seen sleeping with her as part of a game? A bit of fun that didn't really matter because she didn't have to go by the same rules as everybody else?

The anger grew. Mikki was angry enough to march

back inside. Into the messroom where Tama was—astonishingly—cleaning up the bench.

'I'm leaving,' Mikki announced. 'I'll find another helicopter service that'll take me on for training. One that has no connection whatsoever to my father. One where I'll actually get treated professionally. Judged on what I'm capable of doing and not who I am. Or, worse, who my father happens to be.'

Tama didn't interrupt the tirade. He paused in his task, the tea-towel dangling from his hand, his head inclined enough to show he was listening. And he waited until it was clear Mikki had had her say.

'I guess you *didn't* know about it,' he said evenly.

'You thought I did?' Mikki shook her head in disbelief. 'You thought I'd just go ahead and take advantage of a privilege I hadn't earned?' Her outward breath was an incredulous huff. 'Of course! You thought I was a receptionist or something, didn't you? An airhead. You actually believed me when I said I had a manicure booked.'

Tama was twisting the tea-towel in his hands. 'That was a long time ago. I didn't know you then.'

'You don't know me now,' Mikki spat.

That *hurt*, dammit!

She'd spent so much time with this man. Admired him so much. Given him every ounce of her strength and abilities in trying to prove herself and win his approval.

And that was only part of it now. She'd given him everything she had to give in bed as well, and that made her want to cringe in shame.

It counted for nothing. All of it. Tama thought she was simply a spoilt…princess. That she got what she

wanted in life handed to her. That it was all just a
game. He didn't know her and he never would because she was getting out of here. Escaping. Leaving
this station.

Leaving Tama.

Anger, shame, humiliation and something even
darker that felt like...grief jostled each other and Mikki
had the horrible sensation it was all too much and she
was about to burst into tears.

She opened her mouth with the intention of delivering some cutting remark to try and salvage just a scrap
of pride before turning on her heel and walking away.
But no words came out.

And Tama had the nerve to be standing there looking
angry himself.

'I know you better than you think,' he said. 'Yes, I
admit I didn't like the idea of you coming here by cutting through the red tape. And you turned up and you
looked exactly how I expected you to look. Tiny and
pretty and...and fragile. I was all set to give you a challenge I didn't think you'd be able to pass so I wouldn't
have to train you.'

Mikki had opened her mouth again to interrupt. He
had thought she was pretty? Was it a compliment or an
insult? She closed her mouth.

'And you know what?' Tama continued without a
pause. 'You surprised me. Turned out you were determined. Clever. Brave. You blew me away the day of the
HUET training, you know that? I actually started to feel
proud to have you on my crew that day. And since then?'

He had raised his eyebrows. He was saying nice
things about her. Amazing things. He thought she was

clever? Brave? It almost sounded like he really admired her so why was he still looking so angry? He was starting to sound angry as well and Mikki had to throw confusion into the mix of her reaction. What was he going to say now?

Something about that survival training and their time on the mountain?

About their relationship?

Was he going to tell her he would miss her when she was gone?

That he didn't want her to leave?

Mikki's breath caught in her throat and stayed there.

'Since then...no, even before then, I'd decided you weren't really a princess. That you were prepared to work bloody hard and even fight for what you wanted if you had to. And now you're going to walk out? Without the qualification you want so badly?'

The tea-towel was now a scrunched-up ball in his hands. One that was flung sideways into the sink, giving the impression that Tama was disgusted.

'You're right,' he said bitterly. 'I *don't* know you.'

This was the time to say he never would. Too bad. That she didn't care what he thought of her. But that wasn't true, was it? She cared a lot about what Tama thought of her. That was why it hurt so much to think this training had been a set-up. She winced as the tea-towel landed in the sink with a dull thud because she could suddenly see this from Tama's point of view.

She'd been behaving like a princess, hadn't she? Nagging to get what she wanted. Not prepared to trust his judgement on whether or not she was ready. And when he'd said no again, what had she done?

Stamped her foot and thrown a tantrum. She was halfway through throwing her toys—and her qualification—out of the cot.

No wonder he looked disgusted.

Mikki really wanted to cry now. She had never felt so stupid. Small and useless and...still angry, but the anger was being directed inwards now.

She couldn't think of anything to say. A silent plea for something—she had no idea what—formed in the silence that fell.

The plea was answered in a very unexpected way.

Their pagers sounded.

Tama read the message. He went to the phone and spoke briefly.

'We've got a job,' he said to Mikki. 'Are you coming?'

Mikki swallowed. 'For winching?'

Tama eyed her steadily. Oh, God, did he think she was still nagging? Trying to throw her father's weight around?

'Don't know yet,' he said. She couldn't read his expression. His face was set in grim lines and his eyes were so dark they looked black. 'If it is,' he continued calmly, 'it's yours. You can have the job, Mikki. And if you do it as well as you've done every other challenge, I'll sign you off as proficient. And then you can leave if that's what you want.'

And it was Tama who walked out. Heading towards the office to look at the maps and get ready for the new mission.

Mikki dragged in a breath. And then another. This felt like a turning point for something. Her career? Her relationship with Tama? Her *life*?

It didn't feel like there was a choice involved, how-ever. Her feet seemed to move by themselves. Taking her towards the office.

Taking on the job.

Was this it?

The last mission he'd ever go on with Mikki?

From the information they'd received it sounded like it would be a winch job. A teenager had been seen climbing a beachside cliff and he now appeared to be stuck about halfway up. He could be seen hunched on a narrow ledge but wasn't responding to any attempts at communication.

Emergency services were at the top but the area was dangerous. Notorious for being unstable. Too risky for anyone to abseil down because it was too likely to send a rockfall onto the ledge, and it would be impossible to climb up with any gear. Nobody could figure out how the boy had managed to climb up in the first place. Or why.

It didn't matter why.

Tama turned his head from where he sat in the winch operator's seat. Mikki was sitting on the other side and she was staring resolutely from the window on her left. All Tama could see was the back of her helmet.

No. It didn't matter why the boy had chosen to climb a dangerous cliff face. It didn't matter why or how Mikki had won her chance to try out for the team either. She was only here because she had proved worthy of the opportunity and he shouldn't have suggested otherwise.

Why had he? Why had he held onto some immature jealousy that Mikki had grown up with all the advantages money could buy? With the idea that everything had been easy for her and she couldn't imagine what it was like to inhabit his planet? That she would look down on him if she really knew what his upbringing had been like.

That didn't seem to matter anymore either. In so many ways, he and Mikki were the same. He'd said that to her, when? When he'd been hell bent on getting her into his bed? It didn't mean it wasn't true.

They wanted the same things in life. The adrenaline rush of this job. The satisfaction of knowing you'd saved a life. The thrill of sex without a commitment that might have unpleasant long-term consequences, such as interfering with a career you were passionate about.

Except that one day Mikki was going to change her mind about that, wasn't she? When she met the right person.

Why wasn't *he* the right person?

Did he want to be?

No.

Yes.

Dammit! Tama could feel the lines of his scowl etching deeper into his forehead. He felt confused and he hated feeling confused. Maybe what he really wanted was to have the choice.

Maybe he didn't want Mikki walking out of his life as though it meant nothing to her. As though *he* meant nothing to her.

'Target sighted.' But Steve sounded preoccupied. 'I'm getting a call from Control here. I'll patch you guys through.'

'The boy's name is Tim,' Tama heard the voice of someone at the control centre. 'The police are taking his mother to the scene. She's received a text message that makes this look like it's a suicide attempt.'

Tama groaned. This changed everything.

'Copy that,' Mikki said briskly. 'Do you know his age?'

'Fifteen.'

'Any background?'

'Sister died last year. Brain tumour. Single mother. She says he's been very withdrawn since then. In trouble at school.'

'Drugs?' Tama queried succinctly.

'Unknown. Mother doesn't think so.'

Steve was circling above the scene. 'How close should I go?' he asked. 'I don't want to push him into doing anything stupid.'

Mikki was staring intently from her window. 'He's just sitting,' she said. 'He's got his head on his knees. I don't think he's going to jump in a hurry.'

'You still there, Control?' Tama asked. 'Is the boy answering his phone?'

'No. It's going straight to voicemail. Either turned off or dead.'

'And he can't hear anyone from the top?'

'Negative. No response, anyway.'

'The ledge is quite long.' Mikki was still peering downwards. 'If I land well away, it won't be too threatening but I'll be able to talk to him.'

'No.' Tama changed channels so that only Mikki and Steve could hear him. 'The cliff's unstable and, as far as we know, this lad doesn't want to be rescued. This isn't a straightforward job, Mikki. We'll land on top and change places. Alistair can operate the winch and I'll go down.'

'No.' Mikki's head turned. Her face was still as grim as it had been ever since their confrontation in the mess-room but her voice was calm. More determined than

Tama had ever heard it. 'I can do this. I want to do this. You said this was my job, Tama.'

He had. And he'd told her in the past that he kept his word. That she could trust him. This might be his last opportunity to give her anything and he owed her this chance, didn't he? His hesitation was only brief.

'Fine,' he growled. 'But you don't get close enough to touch him.' He wasn't having this kid grab her and then send them both plummeting to their deaths on the rocks below.

Mikki said nothing. She was checking her harness.

'If he moves…' Tama said a minute or two later when the side door was open and locked. 'If he even *looks* like moving, I'm pulling you out. Got it?'

'Roger.' Mikki was looking past him. Waiting for the hook to be brought inboard.

It seemed only a very short time after that to Tama being in control of lowering Mikki. Carefully. Fortunately, it wasn't at all windy, which made it relatively safe to put her down so close to a cliff.

Relatively.

She looked tiny on the end of the cable and the responsibility was weighing heavily on Tama.

This was why he had been trying to slow her training schedule down. He'd known, at some level, how it would feel to be there when Mikki was putting herself in danger. Close enough to watch but not necessarily close enough to protect her.

And he wanted to protect this woman.

When he next met Trevor Elliot he might have to shake the man's hand for succeeding in keeping Mikki safe thus far in her life.

Why *did* she want to do this?

'Minus six...' Mikki's voice sounded as clear as a bell inside his helmet. 'Four...two...'

Tama could see her feet touch the ledge and he tried to help Steve keep the helicopter as still as possible in its hover by sheer willpower.

Mikki tested her footing and the stability of the ledge. She unhooked herself and held the cable out, signalling for Tama to retract it. The boy hadn't moved. He still sat, a miserable hunched figure, about ten metres from Mikki.

She didn't move any closer and Tama let out a breath he hadn't realised he was holding.

He nodded his approval a second later as Mikki crouched down, both to make herself seem less threatening and to give her a more stable position on the ledge.

'Hey, Tim,' he heard her call softly. 'I'm Mikki.'

There was no response.

Steve took the chopper higher on the way to touching down in the clear area at the top of the cliff but Mikki obviously hadn't thought to push her microphone out of the way and Tama could hear her with perfect clarity even though her figure was unrecognisable from this distance. He adjusted his own microphone, so he could speak without Mikki hearing him unless he wanted her to, but he could still hear her.

Her voice would never be unrecognisable. If he never heard it again after today, he would always remember it. So clear. Often eager, almost always resolute. So soft sometimes, it kind of reverberated in his bones.

'Are you hurt?' Mikki was asking now. 'Is it OK if I come a bit closer?'

No! Tama's lips formed the words silently. Don't do that. But he could hear other noises that suggested

Mikki was moving. Squeaks and a soft thud and a tiny catch of breath, as though the footing wasn't as steady as she had expected.

'Let's get down,' he said to Steve. 'I want to get somewhere where I can see what's going on. See if there's a way of at least getting a rope down to her.'

Mikki's voice continued in his helmet as the chopper landed and Tama moved swiftly to liaise with the emergency services already on the scene.

A distraught-looking woman who had to be Tim's mother was being helped from a police car. Fire service personnel, ambulance officers and police were gathered at a point that allowed them to see what was happening, judging by the grim intensity of the group.

'*Please!*' he heard the woman beg. 'Try his phone again. I *have* to talk to him. He's…he's all I have now…'

Mikki's voice continued as a kind of background. Quiet and calm. Trying to win the boy's confidence and trust or at least get him to listen and buy some time.

Had she had any kind of training in counselling or negotiation? Tama hadn't thought to ask. She seemed to be doing all right, though. She was probably as good at this as she was at everything else she was determined to master.

By the time Tama reached the point where he could see down the cliff, Mikki was getting a response.

Everybody was staring at the two figures, now hunched much closer together on the ledge, but only Tama could hear what was going on.

'How do *you* know?' The teenager sounded angry. 'You don't know *anything.*'

'I was fifteen once,' Mikki said. 'And my life wasn't so great either.'

'Your sister didn't die.'

'No. I'm really sorry about that, Tim. It was a horrible thing to happen.'

Her mother had died, Tama thought. She did know how bad things could be.

'Mum hates me. She thinks it was my fault.'

'That's not true, Tim.'

'She wishes it had been me instead, then.'

'What makes you say that?'

'She stopped talking to me. She stopped even looking at me.' The words sounded as if they were being dragged out but he wanted to talk. That was a good sign. Tama silently encouraged the boy. 'It was like...I don't exist anymore. Even when I got into big trouble at school and she *had* to notice me, she didn't care. She didn't even care enough to tell me off.'

The sound of the sobs that came then was heart-breaking. Choked and despairing. Quiet enough for Tama to still hear what Mikki was saying.

'When people are really hurt, Tim, like when they lose someone they love very much, they can get scared. Too scared to let themselves love other people. They can pretend they don't care because that's the only way they think they can protect themselves from getting hurt all over again.'

Tama closed his eyes. Was she talking about herself here? She could almost be talking about *him*. Had he ever let himself love anyone after his mother had gone? Trusted that anyone would want to stay around long enough to make it safe?

'And when *you* love someone and you lose them, it hurts, Tim. It hurt when you lost your sister and now you feel like you've lost your mum, even though she's still around. Yes?'

'Yeah…'

'And when something hurts so much you can't bear it, you want to die because you think it's the only way to make the pain go away.'

Tama heard a sound like a groan, The sound of someone in pain.

'It *is* the only way.'

'*No.*' Mikki's voice had a quiet passion in it. A sincerity that was compelling. 'Feeling like this, Tim— feeling so bad you want to die—it's like being in the worst storm you can imagine. With hail and sleet and thunder and lightning, and every bolt of lightning feels like it's going through your body and you just want to curl up because of the pain.' He could hear Mikki draw in a slow breath. 'What happens after a storm, Tim?'

She waited for the response. When it finally came, it was sullen. 'Dunno.'

'Yes, you do.' Mikki waited again. 'Eventually, what happens?'

Only silence greeted the question.

'Does the thunder and lightning stop?'

'I s'pose.'

'Does the hail and rain stop?'

'Yeah.'

'And then what happens? What happens when the storm ends or gets blown away and the sky is clear? What comes out?'

This time Mikki didn't let the silence continue. 'The sun, Tim. Maybe it's patchy and weak to start with, but it always comes back and one day you know it's going to be blazing. You're going to want to be outside and maybe go to the beach and be warm and feel safe that there's no storm in sight. Maybe you'll never be in a storm quite that bad again.'

Mikki sounded slightly out of breath now. The little catch in her voice as she took in enough air to keep going touched Tama in a very deep place. She really believed what she was saying. She really wanted this lonely, miserable child to believe her.

'That's what life is like, Tim. Being happy is the sunny time. Nobody's happy *all* the time but it's because life's like that that we know how good it is to feel happy. And…and if you die in a storm then you'll never feel the sun again and it's worth hanging on, it really is, because you'll get through this.'

'No, I won't.'

'Yes, you will. You don't have to do it by yourself. If it was a storm you could find shelter. With life you can get shelter, too.'

'How?'

'Through people. People that care. Especially people that love you.'

'Nobody loves me.'

'Why is your mum coming here, then?'

'My mum's coming? Is she here?'

'I expect she's arrived by now. And she's scared, Tim. She doesn't want to lose you.'

'But I threw my phone away. How did she know where I am?'

'People saw you climbing the cliff.'

'Where are they?'

'Up the top. Hey, don't move, Tim! Oh… God!'

Tama saw Mikki reach out and grab Tim's arm. He saw the boy's foot slip and a cascade of small rocks went over the edge of the ledge. He heard the horrified gasp from the onlookers and a similar sound from both Mikki and Tim seemed magnified in his earphones.

'Help!' Tim cried. 'I don't want to fall.'

It was enough. Too much. Tama turned and ran back to the idling helicopter. He grabbed a harness and gave terse instructions to Steve and Alistair.

'Mikki's got a nappy harness she can put on Tim. If he's co-operative, the safest way to do this is going to be if I go down and bring them both up, one at a time. That ledge is crumbling.'

The minute that ticked past seemed much longer. So did the next. And then they were airborne and Tama was talking to Mikki.

'Try to move as little as possible but get the nappy harness onto Tim. Find an anchor you can hang onto. Try one of those shrubby trees or a larger rock. I'm coming down.'

Another minute and he was outside the helicopter. And then he was descending smoothly. Counting off the distance. Keeping his voice calm, even though he saw another boulder come free from the ledge and bounce down the cliff to smash into the rocks at the shoreline.

Mikki was standing, her back to the cliff and her feet planted on an area that looked stable enough. She had her arms around the boy and she had managed to get the harness on him.

'It's OK, Tim,' he heard her saying. 'Tama's the best there is. You're safe. He's going to hook your harness onto his and take you up to the helicopter.'

'*No-o*! I'm scared.'

'I know, honey, but it's safe, I promise. Everything's going to be fine.'

Tama found a smile to reassure Tim as his feet touched the ledge. 'Put your arms around my neck. Hang on, buddy.'

It was hard to turn his head in the panicked grip but Tama had to look back at Mikki. He almost wished he hadn't.

He'd never seen her look this afraid and it went through him like physical pain.

'I'll be right back to get you,' he said gruffly. 'Don't move.'

He couldn't look down again until he was standing on the skids and Alistair was helping pull Tim to safety within the helicopter.

Then he was ready to go down again and rescue Mikki. He looked down past his feet where he could see Mikki still hanging onto the trunk of the small, dead-looking tree.

And then he saw the tree move and her feet slip as the ledge beneath them crumbled.

He heard her soft, stricken cry.

She was hanging. The only thing preventing her from falling to the rocks below was the grip she had on a skinny tree trunk that was clearly as unstable as everything else on this damned cliff.

Tama was about to lose her.

For ever.

'Get me down,' he barked at Alistair. *'Now!'*

CHAPTER ELEVEN

MIKKI was about to die.

There was nothing below her feet.

Just space. A huge space that she knew ended where the waves were crashing onto those unforgiving rocks. She'd heard the rumble and crack of dislodged boulders—a sound that went on and on to let her know just how far she was about to fall.

This wasn't supposed to happen. OK, she'd been happy to flirt with death. She'd pushed hard for the opportunity to do exactly that, but she had never really believed she wouldn't survive. That she would gamble and lose.

She could hear the harsh sound of her own breathing inside her helmet. From outside, now that the rockfall had finally ceased, she could hear a kind of roaring. Faint shouting? Mechanical noises? The roaring of her own thoughts was louder.

Images, like movie trailers. Of the future she had so carefully planned to be full of adventure and new experiences. Enough danger to make her appreciate being alive. Thrills and spills with the cushion of knowing that one day she would have had enough and she'd find a wonderful partner and the safe haven of a family of her own.

Children of her own that she could love with all her heart. Just the way her mother had loved her right to her last moments.

Her breath rushed out in a strange combination of grief and wry mirth. Wasn't it the past that was supposed to flash past in the final moments of your life, not the future?

Her hands were going numb. Her grip so tight the blood supply was probably cut off but she couldn't loosen her hold on that pathetic half-dead tree trunk. Not without just giving up, and she'd never been one to give up. She couldn't hold on much longer, though. When all feeling had gone, she'd lose the ability to control her muscles and that would be that.

Mikki squeezed her eyes shut and could feel a tear escape. Sorry, Dad, she thought. You were right.

Sorry, Tama, she thought next. You were right, too. I wasn't ready for this.

I'm not ready to die.

Panic was edging closer. Fear threatened to obliterate any rational thought.

'Help…' Were the words coming from her lips or still part of the roaring inside her head? 'I need…*help*.'

Her hands were starting to slip. Mikki kicked her feet in a futile attempt to find a foothold. A scream was building inside her head. Gaining strength. She just needed enough breath to release it.

The voice inside her helmet came loud and clear then.

Soft and compelling.

'Be still,' it said.

And somehow it created a barrier to hold back the

scream. Mikki knew that voice. She trusted it. It went with such a solid presence. With arms that could hold her and make her feel safe. It was all Mikki could wish for right then. All she could ever wish for.

The arms were here now, too. Strong and sure. Mikki felt some kind of strap being fastened around her body but when it came time for her to let go of her handhold she couldn't do it.

'Let go, Mikki,' Tama said. 'You're safe now. I've got you.'

Things blurred then. Her awareness of being winched up to the helicopter was hazy. She was strapped into her seat. Tim was there, too, but not for long. It seemed only seconds until they landed on the cliff top and then Tim had his mother's arms around him and they were both crying. Being led away and cared for by other people.

Mikki couldn't cry. She felt totally numb. She barely heard the words of congratulations and relief from Steve and Alistair. Tama deserved the praise, not her. He had saved the day. She had failed spectacularly. Would Tama say anything? Not on the trip back to station, apparently. It was silent.

Their shift was over by the time they got back. Steve was busy with the helicopter. Alistair went home. Tama had gone to do something in the office. Eventually, Mikki sat with a drink that had been hot when someone had made it for her but it was stone cold now. The shock was beginning to recede but it was still hard to think straight.

Tama returned. He stood not far away but Mikki had her forehead resting on the palm of her hand and she didn't want to look up and see her failure reflected back at her. She waited for deserved words of recrimination.

'You OK?'

'Yes.' It hadn't been what she'd expected. The enquiry regarding her welfare was almost enough to make her cry. He sounded like he genuinely cared. 'No,' she added. 'Oh, I don't know.' With a resigned sigh Mikki raised her gaze. 'You saved my life, Tama. Thank you.'

He grunted as he pulled out a chair and sat down. It was a noncommittal sound.

'I rang the hospital. Tim's going to be fine, I think. Both he and his mother have agreed to get help. She's going to have treatment for her depression and they both need counselling to get through this period. The psychologist sounded optimistic.' Tama cleared his throat. 'There was a message Tim's mother wanted passed on to you. She said to say thank you. Very much.'

Mikki gave her head a tiny shake. 'I didn't do much. He just needed someone to talk to.'

'No. He needed someone to talk to who understood.' Tama was silent for a moment. 'I need to apologise,' he said then.

Mikki's chin came up sharply. 'What on earth for?'

'For ever thinking you were a princess. That you'd have no idea what real life was like. You've been through it yourself, haven't you?'

'Through what?'

'The kind of hell that kid was in. Thinking the only way out was to kill himself.'

'I guess.' Mikki closed her eyes as she took a deep breath. 'I never got to the point of thinking about suicide but things were rough for a few years after Mum died.'

'Your father was too scared to love you.'

'And I tried to get him to notice by getting myself into trouble. I was worse than Tim. I got into alcohol and car racing. I discovered the thrill of cheating death. And when I pushed it far enough I got an even better prize. My dad noticed me. He woke up and started living again and…it was all the more exciting doing dangerous things because I knew it made him worried. Made him show that he cared about me. I hope Tim hasn't started a life of chasing danger.'

'I think he got enough of a fright today to cure him of wanting to try it again.'

Mikki's chuckle was wry. 'I think I might have, too.'

'Oh?'

'I hope I never get that close to killing myself again.'

'So do I.' The words were a growl.

'I won't be trying, that's for sure. It was…different this time.'

'How?' Tama was watching her closely.

'I was scared,' Mikki admitted. 'Really scared.'

'You've done scary things before. That underwater escape training was hardly a picnic.'

Mikki nodded. 'That's true. And that was like all the other times I've been that scared. I survived and then I got that amazing realisation that I was safe and it made me feel like…nothing else can.'

Tama was nodding, too. He knew that feeling. Of course he did. That had been the first moment of connection between them, hadn't it? That they'd both felt the same.

'But this time it's different. It hasn't happened. I still feel…scared.'

Tama frowned. He reached out and took hold of her

hand. 'You don't need to be,' he said. 'You're safe now. You're here. With me.'

'I know…but…'

'But what?'

Mikki tried to swallow but her throat felt too tight. 'I can't tell you.'

'Why not?'

She could have said she didn't know. The shock and numbness and confused racing of her brain would have made that true even a few minutes ago but something was becoming very clear to Mikki. Nebulous thoughts were starting to get reined in by talking and things were becoming clearer by the second thanks to the way her hand was enclosed by Tama's. In that strong, sure grip.

'It's just a feeling,' she hedged. 'You wouldn't want to know.'

'Why not?' Tama repeated.

'Girly stuff. I'm not even sure I could put it into words.'

'Try.' Tama's fingers moved over hers. A stroke that was as encouraging as his tone.

Mikki tried to think. If she could put more of it into words, maybe she would understand it better herself. And did it matter if Tama didn't want to hear it? She'd really failed this time and she wasn't sure if she even wanted to try and redeem herself. Maybe this job wasn't what she'd been searching for after all.

'Cheating death,' she said finally. 'It's exciting because of how you feel when you succeed. When you know you're safe.'

'The feeling you didn't get today.'

'But I did. I got it when you came down and got hold of me. When you had your arms around me and I knew

I wasn't going to fall. But as soon as we got up to the chopper and you let me go, the feeling disappeared and I felt scared again.'

She took a shaky breath. 'It was a different kind of safe. I've felt it before with you. When you got me out of that underwater cage and up to the surface of that diving pool. And when we were in that snow mound like two little dots in a place so big we were invisible. It's a feeling I got from you—not from just knowing I wasn't going to die.'

'From when I was holding you?' A chair scraped. 'Like this?'

And Mikki was being drawn up. Held in Tama's arms. Tears were very close. 'Yes.'

'You feel safe now?'

Mikki nodded, her face against his shoulder. She couldn't speak.

Tama's hold tightened. 'But you're shaking. You're still scared.'

'Because it's not real,' Mikki blurted.

'Of course it's real.' She could feel Tama's lips moving against her hair. 'Feel it, Mikki. I'm here and I've got you and it's real, babe.'

Mikki shook her head, her nose rubbing on Tama's chest. 'No. I'm going away and the only way I'll ever feel like this again is by remembering this so it'll never be *real*.'

'You mean real like a real relationship? When you care a lot about what happens to someone?'

Her nose rubbed in the other direction again. Up and down.

'I cared about what was happening to you today,' Tama growled. 'I cared so much I've never been so scared in my life. I thought I was going to lose you. Never be able to hold you again.'

'Don't stop holding me, Tama.'

'I don't intend to.' The words were a murmur. 'Not until you want me to, anyway.'

'Why would I want you to?'

'I mean when you go.'

'Oh...' But why would she want to go anywhere if Tama was here to hold her?

'What is it?' Had Tama sensed her confusion?

'Why do I feel so safe when you're holding me like this? Like you...' She couldn't say it. Couldn't utter a word that had never crossed Tama's lips. One that would instantly conjure up all the kinds of expectations he had said he would never want. She wouldn't see him for dust.

'Like I love you?'

Mikki's heart stopped for a beat. As though she needed to be very, very still so as not to break something precious.

'Is this how it feels?' Tama queried softly. 'Does being in love mean caring so much about someone? Being scared if they're in trouble? Being prepared to risk your own life because you can't bear the thought of being without them?'

'That's weird.' So many impressions were crowding back on Mikki. 'That's what I was wondering when I watched you being winched down to that fishing boat.'

'Did you figure it out?'

'I thought I had. I thought I would get over it because we both knew this wasn't going to last right from the start. That was what made it OK. And that even if I missed you when I went away it would be all right because we could stay in touch with email or something and maybe see each other again one day. But I was wrong.'

Mikki had to pull back to see Tama's face properly. 'I was *so* wrong. It wouldn't be enough just to know you were alive. I need to see that for myself. Every day. To see you and hear you and…and touch you.'

'So is that a "yes"? Is that what it's like to be in love?'

Things were so clear now. 'Yes,' Mikki said quietly. 'Sorry, Tama. I didn't mean to.'

'What?'

'Fall in love with you.'

'It's OK.' But Tama was frowning. He seemed to be collecting his thoughts. 'Listen. I heard you talking to that boy today and I thought you were talking about me. That bit about being too scared to let yourself love someone. Pretending you don't. I'm good at that. So good I believed myself totally. Until today.'

He pulled Mikki close again and dropped his head to rest against hers. 'It's too late not to feel scared of losing you. I'm in too deep. I'm not sure how it happened but it has and, dammit, Mikki—I'm scared now.'

Mikki stretched her arms so they would fit around this big, powerful man whose strength and courage and humour had won her admiration and respect so totally. She tried to hold him so that he wouldn't feel scared. So he would feel safe—like she did when he was holding her.

'Nothing's frightened me since I was a little kid and the worst happened when my mother abandoned me. I've fought ever since and made damn sure I protected myself from ever feeling scared of that kind of thing again. I've never let anyone have the power to really hurt me. But you…' Tama's voice trailed off. There was a tremble in it. 'I never thought I'd ever say this to anyone but you have it, Mikki. You have the power to destroy me.'

'No.' Mikki pulled her arms free so that she could reach up and touch Tama's face. 'I could never do that. I could never hurt you, Tama. I…love you.'

It was one thing to admit to falling in love. Quite another to utter those three, astonishingly powerful little words.

So scary. For a moment, Mikki had the sensation of being in freefall. As though she'd fallen off that cliff she'd been on only a short time ago.

Except she couldn't fall because Tama's arms were still there. Holding her. His head bent further and his lips sought hers and for quite some time there was no need for any further spoken words.

Quite enough was being said.

Asked and promised.

Let go.

There were no ground rules this time. They were both in freefall but they would both be safe if they cared about each other. Held each other.

Tama finally pulled back.

'Just don't ever do that to me again,' he growled. 'Scare me like you did today.'

'It's not like I'm going to get the chance. I failed, didn't I?'

'Hardly. It was a great job. Wasn't your fault the ledge crumbled.'

'You mean I passed? I've qualified? You wouldn't try and stop me doing another job?'

'I can't stop you. Doesn't mean I *want* you to keep
doing it, though. Don't ever think you have to try and
kill yourself to get me to notice you. Or to get me to
tell you that…'

Mikki held her breath.

'That I love you.'

Mikki held Tama's gaze to make absolutely sure she
could believe what she was hearing.

Then she let the words sink in for another long,
blissful moment. To seep into every cell of her body and
make them sing.

Then her lips curved. 'I'm starting to think I might
look for a different job. Or go back to my old one. Keep
my feet on the ground.' Her smile widened. 'My father's
going to really approve of you, Tama James.'

'Not if he hears too much about what happened today.'

'I'll tell him you saved my life. No.' Mikki's smile
faded and she held Tama's gaze. 'I'll tell him you *are*
my life.'

Tama's face was as serious as her own. 'We're the
same, you and me, aren't we? It's more than being in
love. It's being…'

'Soulmates?' Mikki suggested.

'Bit girly,' Tama growled. Then he grinned. 'But it'll
do. Whatever means that we belong together.' He gathered Mikki close again. So close she could feel his heart
beating as strongly as her own. 'Just like this.'

Mikki's echo was a sigh of contentment. 'Just like
this,' she agreed.

Her Very
Special Boss

ANNE
FRASER

Dear Reader,

This is my second novel for Mills & Boon and, believe me, it is just as exciting for me as getting my first one published.

It is such an honour to be part of a reading tradition that is a hundred years old. I can imagine our grandmothers and mothers reading the same romances through the years, and although times and settings have changed, the basics of a good romance are still the same—hunky men and gorgeous women that we know just have to be together.

I love writing romances because you can set them anywhere in the world. My husband, baby daughter and I spent fifteen months in Africa. While my husband—a doctor—looked after the patients, I looked after our daughter and taught part-time at a local school. Evening meals were taken communally, in 'staff house', and it was there I would listen to the doctors and aid workers discussing their days. I think back to the community often and wish we could have done even more. Things have improved a great deal since our time there, but there is still a lot that needs doing. So many children have lost their parents to HIV/AIDS. Therefore I plan to donate some of the earnings of this book to the children of Africa.

I hope you enjoy this story as much as I enjoyed writing it.

Best wishes,

Anne Fraser

Anne Fraser was born in Scotland, but brought up in South Africa. After she left school she returned to the birthplace of her parents, the remote Western Islands of Scotland. She left there to train as a nurse before going on to university to study English Literature. After the birth of her first child, she and her doctor husband travelled the world, working in rural Africa, Australia and Northern Canada. Anne still works in the health sector. To relax, she enjoys spending time with her family, reading, walking and travelling.

To my husband Stewart
and all the doctors and nurses who work
in remote communities for no other reason
than the love of medicine.

CHAPTER ONE

KIRSTY kicked the tyre viciously and squealed in agony as a jolt of pain shot through her ankle. Damn, damn, damn, she cursed as she hopped around on one foot. Could this day—could her life—get any worse?

As if the twelve-hour journey in the cramped rear of the Jumbo hadn't been bad enough, the airline had lost her luggage. And then, instead of being collected, as she had anticipated, she had found that she had to make the five-hour journey to the hospital on her own in this heap of a car. Keys and directions had been left for her, along with a short note explaining that her driver had to be elsewhere and they would expect her before nightfall. It had taken her much longer than she'd anticipated to navigate herself onto the road heading north and she had found herself going in the wrong direction at least once. What sort of place was this she was going to that they couldn't be bothered to look after their new staff? What on earth had she let herself in for?

She was tired—no, scrap that, exhausted—and had planned to catch up on some sleep on the journey to the hospital. Instead, here she was in the middle of nowhere, under an endless African sky, with a flat tyre and no idea of how to go about changing it. Under these circumstances back home, she would have phoned road recovery to come to her aid or, failing that, some friend. But here she couldn't even call for help. She hadn't got around to converting her mobile phone so that it would work in this country.

Impatiently she swallowed the lump in her throat. *No use feeling sorry for yourself, girl,* she told herself. She gritted her teeth and studied the directions on the piece of paper in her hand. It looked as if the hospital was only three or four miles along the road—a walkable distance. The air was hot and turgid and Kirsty was aware that if she weren't careful her pale skin would burn. She should have worn jeans and walking boots, but she had wanted to make a good first impression, so had decided on a white linen blouse, skirt and heels instead. Her shoes with their delicate kitten heels might be the last thing in fashion, but they were no good for a long walk.

One last glance up and down the empty road confirmed what she suspected. She was going to have to complete the rest of the journey on foot. Kirsty had no idea when darkness would fall, but she guessed she'd better get going if she were to make the hospital in daylight.

Alternatively, she could stay in the car. Someone would come looking for her eventually, wouldn't they? But what if they didn't? Kirsty shivered at the thought of spending the night on her own. This country was too strange, too vast for her to feel safe, even within the locked doors of the car.

Grabbing her handbag and the tepid water bottle, she set off. The more time she wasted, the more likely it was that she would find herself walking in the dark.

The red dust beside the road coated her shoes as she walked and her ankle began to ache painfully. It was all

Robbie's fault, she thought bitterly. If it weren't for him she'd never have made the journey to this godforsaken place.

An hour later and, although the sun was beginning to sink in the sky, it was still almost unbearably hot. Kirsty had finished the water and her tongue was beginning to stick to the roof of her mouth. Caked in sweat, she could taste the dust that seemed to cover her body from the tips of her toes to the top of her head. She had discarded her shoes and was walking gingerly on blistered feet. She felt her spirits lift for a moment as she saw the matchbox sized shapes of houses in the distance. Perhaps it was the village where the hospital was based? If not, at least there would be people whom she could ask for help.

Kirsty sat down on a rock and rubbed her feet. She would rest for a few moments, not much longer than five minutes, and then carry on. The chance of her reaching help before darkness fell was small but she also knew that once darkness came, her journey would be much more hazardous. Without streetlights, there would be nothing to guide her steps. An eerie cry in the distance brought her to her feet. Were there wild animals out here? Maybe she should have stayed with the car. Instead, she now risked getting mauled by a lion or some other wild animal.

After a short rest, Kirsty forced herself on. Despite walking for another age, the matchbox houses stayed matchbox size. Just when she thought she could walk no further, she saw the flash of sunlight on an approaching car in the distance. Please, let them stop, she prayed. At least if they wouldn't give her a lift they might have a phone she could use.

She almost cried with relief when the car slowed down before making a U-turn and coming to a stop beside her.

The driver wound down the window and Kirsty found herself looking into a pair of glittering blue eyes.

'Dr Kirsty Boucher?' a deep voice said incredulously, adding before she could reply, 'Good grief, woman, what on earth are you up to?'

Relief that the occupant was someone who knew who she was gave way to annoyance. Did he, whoever he was, think she enjoyed walking in her bare feet in temperatures that surely must be close to 100 degrees? Did he think she was the archetypal mad Englishwoman? She opened her mouth to tell him as much when he turned his face and she noticed the scars that ran from his right ear to his jawbone. Years of medical training meant that she was able to disguise her shock, but perhaps not as well as she thought. Or maybe it was an instinctive response, but the man passed his hand over the scar before leaping out of the car and coming around to stand in front of her.

Kirsty felt dwarfed by his massive frame, despite being over five feet eight in her bare feet. She took an involuntary step backwards.

'I'm Greg. Greg du Toit,' he said, holding out his hand. 'We expected you hours ago. What happened?'

Kirsty's heart sank. This wasn't how she had imagined her first meeting with Dr du Toit, her new boss and the physician superintendent of the hospital. Somehow she had assumed he'd be much older. The man in front of her looked to be no more than thirty.

'Puncture, back a few miles,' was all Kirsty could manage through her dry mouth.

'And there wasn't a spare in the boot? Someone's head is going to roll. I tell them never to allow the cars to go out without checking. But come on, let's get you out of the heat.' For a moment he peered into Kirsty's face. 'And get you a drink of water. For God's sake, don't you know the first rule of Africa? Always carry plenty of water.'

Once again, Kirsty felt herself prickle with annoyance. He had no right to speak to her like she was some school-girl. OK, so she should have been able to change a tyre, but he *should* have ensured that the car she had been left was in better condition. Maybe for the time being she should let him believe that there hadn't been a spare tyre? No, she couldn't do that. If he found out, she would look an even greater idiot than she did already.

She sank gratefully into the cool seat of the four-by-four and she felt his eyes on her as she gulped greedily at the bottle of water he held out to her. When she had finally slaked her thirst she wiped the back of her hand across her mouth.

'There was a spare wheel. I, er…I couldn't remove the bolts,' she lied. Well, it wasn't exactly a lie. They were probably so rusted that she wouldn't have managed anyway. She glanced down at her perfectly manicured hands, which bore no evidence of having been anywhere near a toolbox, and quickly hid them under her thighs. It was only a white lie, she told herself. She just couldn't cope with this man's disdain. Not now. Not today. Her should-have-been wedding day. Swallowing hard, she pushed the thought away. She had promised herself she wouldn't think about it.

Greg glanced at his watch. 'How far back is the car? Are you up to going back for it? I don't want to leave it too long or we might find it stolen or dismantled by the time we get around to recovering it. We're pretty short of cars at the complex.' He smiled and all of a sudden the grim lines of his face relaxed. For the first time Kirsty looked at him properly. He really was quite attractive, if in a rugged sort of way, she admitted to herself. Not even the scar detracted from his looks. In an odd way, it even made him seem more vital somehow. Kirsty was already getting the distinct impression that this was a man who was used to people following his orders. Not that she would ever find another man attractive again—not after Robbie. Men were a thing of the past as far as she was concerned. She closed her eyes against the memories. She must stop thinking of the past and concentrate on the present. What was he suggesting? She stifled the protest that came to her lips. Go back? All she wanted was something to eat, a shower and a bed— and not necessarily in that order.

Still, Kirsty was painfully aware that the impression she had created so far was a million miles away from the one she had meant to make. Instead of the immaculately turned-out, efficient, career doctor she had hoped to present, here she was, bedraggled, dirt smeared and seemingly woefully unable to look after herself. Having to be rescued by her new boss had never been part of the plan.

'Of course we should go back. It shouldn't take long.' She straightened in her seat. 'I suppose they'll keep me some dinner?' She couldn't quite erase the plaintive note from her voice.

Once again she felt his appraisal. This time she was conscious of his gaze taking in her dishevelled appearance and her scratched and bleeding feet. He frowned as he started the car.

'Forgive me,' he said, steering the car back onto the road in the direction from which he'd come. 'You must be exhausted, as well as starving.' Again that brilliant flash of teeth. 'I'll take you to the hospital and come back with one of the others. We usually eat around seven. If we hurry, you'll just have enough time to freshen up before dinner. It'll mean waiting for your luggage, I'm afraid, but I'll bring it over as soon as I can.'

'There's no luggage,' Kirsty told him. 'It's been delayed. Lost somewhere between here and Timbuktu, I imagine. I'll have to find a way of collecting it from the airport tomorrow. Supposing they manage to find it.' She couldn't help sighing at the thought of a repeat journey the next day. But at least she'd have slept by then.

Greg muttered something under his breath that Kirsty suspected she wasn't supposed to hear. 'Bloody airlines. Still, it can't be helped. The driver who was supposed to pick you up, but decided not to come at the last minute, can collect it on his way tomorrow. I did try to contact you to tell you to find yourself a hotel for the night, but I couldn't get through on your mobile. I phoned the airport and they told me you had collected the car and were on your way. These roads aren't safe for a single woman, especially at night. When you didn't arrive by the time we expected you, I thought I'd better come looking. Just as well I did. You don't look as if you were in any shape to finish the journey on foot.'

Once again Kirsty felt chastised, although it was hardly her fault. Instead of apologising—after all, the car was the hospital's responsibility—the man was making it clear she was causing a lot of extra work.

'I'm sorry,' she said again, willing her voice to remain steady. 'I really didn't plan to cause all this bother.'

'No problem,' he said brusquely, but somehow Kirsty didn't believe him. She was beginning to think she had made a dreadful mistake in coming here. She wondered bleakly if she would be able to work with this man. He was far too autocratic for her liking and already seemed to have taken against her. But there was nothing she could do about it right now. She was far too tired to think logically so she closed her eyes and within minutes was fast asleep.

She was jolted from her dreams by the sound of an explosion. She opened her eyes to see a minibus swerve erratically across the road in front of them, bits of rubber flying from a rear tyre. Disorientated, Kirsty sat bolt upright in her seat and, as Greg veered to avoid the out-of-control vehicle in front of them, she spread her hands to brace herself for impact. For several breath-taking moments the minibus continued to career from one side of the road to the other, churning up clouds of dust in its wake before finally spinning off the road. Its front wheels hit a shallow ditch and Kirsty held her breath as, with the sound of crunching metal, the vehicle slowly tipped over on its side.

As Greg carefully brought his vehicle to a halt at the side of the road, Kirsty was immobilised with horror. She was barely conscious of him leaning across her to open the cubbyhole and scrabble for something inside, except, incongruously, the clean lemony smell of his skin.

'Double-glove before you do anything,' he said tossing an unopened pack of latex gloves onto her lap before reaching into the back for his medical bag. 'Let's go,' he ordered, and, without waiting for a response, was out of the car. Hastily, Kirsty pulled on the gloves and followed.

It all felt surreal to her. The music emanating from the vehicle's unbroken stereo system was a blast of happy sounds, a sharp, eerie contrast to the moaning and crying voices and the still-spinning wheels of the tilted minibus. Bodies spilled out and lay around, arms and legs twisted at unnatural angles. Still others were slowly extracting themselves from their seats and stumbling, zombie-like, away from the disaster.

Despite the warmth of the African sun on her bare arms, she shivered. *For God's sake,* she thought, *I've been in the country less than four hours and a doctor for not much longer. This can't possibly be happening.*

'Dr Boucher—Kirsty.' She became aware of a hand on her arm and looked up into calm blue eyes. 'I have to phone for help. In the meantime you have to start triaging the casualties.' He turned from her and opened the boot of his car. He shoved a pile of lines and bags into her unwilling arms. 'Take this. Once you've finished triaging, put in lines where you need to.' She looked at him, still in shock. He shook her arm impatiently. 'Look, you can do this. I need you to help me.' He held her eyes for a few moments, and then with a final shake of her arm he was gone.

Out of the corner of her eye, Kirsty became aware of a small figure stumbling away from the wreck. A child, no older than two, toddled purposefully up the side of the ditch towards the road. It was the impetus she needed to shake her loose from the paralysis that had gripped her in the first dreadful minutes since the crash. 'Stop! Come back!' she called out. Tossing the equipment Greg had given her onto the passenger seat, she lunged for the child, grabbing the small bundle seconds before he reached the road. The frightened and bewildered child squirmed in her arms. She looked around at the passengers and, finding a woman who seemed uninjured, thrust her small charge into the woman's arms.

'Hold onto him. Don't let him go. Not even for a second.' She wasn't sure if the woman understood her words, but she must have understood her meaning as she engulfed the child in her embrace.

'Move away from the bus,' Kirsty instructed her. Still unclear whether the woman understood, she indicated a stretch of ground away from the bus and the road. 'Bus could explode,' she added miming an explosion with her arms. Thankfully the woman seemed to grasp enough of the exchange and moved away with her charge.

Kirsty retrieved the equipment Greg had given her and scrambled down the slope to the bus, oblivious to the small stones that scraped her bare legs and feet. The vehicle had come to rest at the bottom of the ditch, its front badly crumpled. The wheels on the driver's side had mounted a small hillock and the bus tilted precariously over to the left. The driver had been thrown through the windscreen and hung there like a casually tossed rag doll. Kirsty reached up and felt for a carotid pulse. As she suspected, the driver was dead.

Moving around the front of the bus, she attempted to open the passenger door. Unfortunately the angle of the bus prevented her from opening it more than a few inches. Through the narrow gap, she could see that there were two more people in the front seat—an elderly man, who was conscious and moaning with pain, and a young woman, who was crying but seemed uninjured. She recalled her training. *It's the quiet ones you have to worry about.* With these words ringing in her head, she decided that both casualties could wait until she had assessed the rest. 'You are going to be fine,' she said softly. 'I'll be back as soon as I can. In the meantime, try not to move.' With a final re-assuring smile she left them and went to check up on the remainder of the passengers. Despite her initial impression, most of them seemed relatively unhurt, apart from possible fractures, lacerations and shock. They too could wait. 'I'll be back in a minute,' she promised the frightened and shocked figures. 'Those that can, move away from the bus. The rest of you, keep as still as you can.'

Leaving them she found Greg bent over a young man in his early twenties, doing chest compressions. He had been joined by a middle-aged woman who, apart from a few cuts and bruises, seemed to have escaped from the minibus unscathed.

'This is Sister Matabele,' Dr du Toit said tersely, barely glancing at Kirsty 'She was on her way to work in a taxi when the accident happened. She'll help me here. You carry on treating the rest of the casualties. The paramedics should be here shortly.'

Before Kirsty had a chance to move, a voice called urgently. 'Help! Over here!'

She hurried over to where a man was cradling a woman on the ground a short distance from the wreckage. She bent over the woman who was lying pale and unconscious. 'My wife—she needs help. She was awake until just now. Now she is asleep. She is bleeding very badly from her leg, I think.'

Kirsty checked that the woman's breathing was unrestricted before examining her. Her pulse was rapid and weak. The heart was still beating, but only just. Swallowing her fear, she removed the T-shirt the woman's husband had laid over the wound. Gently lifting the fabric, she revealed a hole the side of a child's fist at the top of her leg. Bright red femoral blood pulsed onto the ground.

Once again Kirsty felt the rising paralysis of her fear. *Keep calm,* she told herself. *You've dealt with worse than this before.* But that had been in the controlled environment of a large inner-city A and E department with the latest

equipment and a team of experienced doctors and nurses.
Nothing could have prepared her for this. She looked over
for Dr du Toit, but he was still bent over his patient. For
the time being she was on her own. These two people were
depending on her. She needed to stop the bleeding, and
soon. She placed her hand over the wound and pressed
down hard. Her hand wasn't enough to stem the gushing
flow of blood. She needed something bigger. A quick
glance around told her there was only one option. Taking
a deep breath to calm her shaking hands and to steady her
voice, she slipped off her linen blouse, placing it onto the
hole in the woman's leg. 'Hold this. Press down hard,' she
instructed the frightened man, taking his hand in hers to
demonstrate exactly what she wanted him to do. Kirsty
knew if the woman were to stand a chance, she would have
to replace the blood she had lost with fluid as quickly as
possible. Kirsty used one of the lines she had been given
and, ripping off the protective cover from the needle with
her teeth, slipped the needle into a vein in the arm. *Bingo!*
she thought with some satisfaction as she hit the vein first
time. 'What's your wife's name?' she asked the distraught
man.

'Maria. Is she going to be all right?' Kirsty heard the fear
in his voice. She smiled and kept her voice low and calm. 'I'm
sure she will be,' she said, although she wasn't sure at all.
'Talk to her. Let you know that you're here. Reassure her.'

As she worked on her patient, she felt a shadow fall on
her shoulders. She glanced up to find Greg looking down
at her. 'Are you OK?' he asked from what seemed to be a
great distance. 'Do you need any help? My patient is breathing by himself now. Thank God Sister Matabele was here
to help. She'll stay with him until the ambulances arrive.'

'This is Maria. She has a ruptured femoral artery. I've applied pressure and got a drip going. Her pulse and blood pressure are up, but we need to get her to hospital stat.'

Greg examined the woman briefly but expertly. 'She's doing fine for the time being. Good work,' he said warmly. 'I'll carry on assessing the rest. I'll let you know if I need you. But first…'

Kirsty felt him wrap something around her shoulders. 'Apart from the obvious distractions of a half-naked woman, you'll get sunburnt unless you cover up.' He smiled down at her and despite the situation, Kirsty could have sworn she saw a wicked twinkle in his eyes. Suddenly very aware that she was dressed only in her bra and skirt, the colour rose in her cheeks. Quickly she slipped her arms into the shirt. She needed to roll up the sleeves several times and it came well below the hem of her skirt. Her day was going from bad to worse. Now she was dressed like some kind of hobo. Never, in a month of Sundays, would she normally be found less than perfectly groomed. She shook her head impatiently. What was wrong with her? Thinking about clothes at a time like this!

'Someone! Please. Over here!' Another cry for help, but before Kirsty could react, Greg was already moving. Within seconds he was crouched beside the bus. A moment later he called out, 'I need assistance over here.'

There was little more Kirsty could do for Maria for the time being. In calm, measured tones she instructed her helper to keep pressure on the wound and, grabbing one of the uninjured passengers, told him to keep the bag of fluid raised. Once she was satisfied that her patient was in capable hands, she hurried over to Greg.

He was kneeling by the side of the bus, his mouth set

in a grim line. The upper body of a young woman in her late teens or early twenties was visible from under the bus.

'This is Lydia,' Greg told Kirsty tersely. 'Her right leg is pinned underneath the bus.'

'I don't know how I missed her,' Kirsty said, upset.

'Hey, it's not your fault. You couldn't have known she was here. We need to give her some morphine and get some fluids into her while we work out how we can get her out.

'We're going to give you something for the pain,' Greg told the frightened young woman, taking a syringe of morphine from Kirsty. 'We'll have you out just as soon as we can.' While Greg administered the pain relief Kirsty set up a drip.

Large brown eyes darted from Greg to Kirsty. 'My son. I need to find my son. Please.' Lydia squirmed, trying to pull her leg from under the broken fender.

'Is your son a toddler of about two? Wearing a blue jumper?' Kirsty asked.

'Yes, yes. Did you see him? Is he all right?'

'He's perfectly fine. Someone's looking after him. We'll bring him over to you once we've got you sorted.'

Lydia's head sank back on the ground. 'Thank you,' she whispered gratefully, before closing her eyes.

Kirsty looked at Greg. 'How are we going to remove her safely?'

'The pressure from the bus on her leg is probably helping to stem the bleeding.' Greg said softly, his voice thoughtful. 'We'll wait until the ambulance gets here, then we'll have help to lift the bus. We'll need to be ready to control the bleeding.'

To Kirsty's relief, the wailing of sirens signalled the arrival of the ambulances. There were two, each with a paramedic. 'Tell the paramedics to deal with the injured, but get the drivers over here,' Greg told Kirsty.

As the paramedics set about seeing to the other patients, the two burly ambulance drivers came over to the wrecked minibus.

'OK, guys. Once I'm finished here, I need you to lift the bus. Kirsty, you keep the leg stabilised while I pull her out. Watch out for any sudden haemorrhage. It's quite possible the weight of the bus is preventing us from seeing any big bleeders, but once we lift it, that's when we'll know the true extent of her injuries. Get ready to apply pressure.'

Greg knelt and said something to the woman in a language Kirsty didn't understand. But whatever it was, it seemed to reassure her because she nodded and even managed a small smile.

At Greg's count of three the two ambulance drivers lifted the minibus, their muscles bunching with the effort. The vehicle was lifted a couple of inches, but it was just enough for Greg to gently pull Lydia out. Once she was clear, the men let the bus drop with gusty sighs of relief.

Although Lydia's leg was a mess, clearly broken several times with her tibia showing white through her ebony skin, the anticipated spurting that would indicate a torn artery failed to materialise. Kirsty breathed a sigh of relief and bent to cover the wounded leg with padding before stabilising it with one of the inflatable splints the ambulancemen had brought over.

'The rest of the patients are loaded and ready to go, apart from this one,' one ambulanceman informed the two doctors. 'The rest are walking wounded and one of the passers-by will bring them in by car.'

Greg looked at Kirsty and grinned, dimples appearing

at either side of his mouth. His smile sent a shiver down her spine 'Good work. Not bad at all for a city girl.'

Kirsty felt inordinately pleased at his praise but before she could think of a reply he went on, 'I'll need to go in the ambulance with the two critical patients. Would you mind driving my car?'

'Wouldn't you prefer me to go in the ambulance?' Kirsty asked.

'I think you've had enough of a baptism by fire for the time being, don't you? The keys are in my car. Just follow the ambulance,' he said, continuing to supervise the loading of his patients. 'The hospital is only a few miles up the road. I'll see you there.'

Kirsty decided the easiest thing to do was to do as she was told. She hurried over to his Jeep and leapt in. She spent a couple of minutes familiarising herself with the vehicle. She had to move the seat at least a foot forward before she could reach the pedals.

Driving in convoy, they arrived at the hospital as evening descended. Kirsty was oblivious to the setting sun casting its halo of orange rays behind low, distant mountains. Instead, her only thoughts were for the accident victims and the doctor who'd worked so unstintingly to help them. What had caused the scarring on his face? It looked like burns. She had noticed that his right hand was also scarred, although the movement didn't seem impaired. Despite his rather cool manner, there was something about him that inspired confidence. Kirsty was sure he'd be a patient, if demanding teacher. She knew that if the rest of her new colleagues were half as skilled and dedicated as he was, she was going to find being part of the team an experience she wouldn't want to miss. For the first time she was really able to believe that coming to Africa might be so much more than simply running away from her past.

When the ambulance doors opened, a squad of staff surged around the injured. There wasn't time for introductions as Greg barked orders to them, instructing which patients needed to go immediately to Theatre and which required X-rays and tests before a proper diagnosis of the extent of their injuries could be determined.

'Jamie, take this one will you? Kirsty, give the boy to Sister Shange here. Elspeth, what's the status of the other casualties?'

'Would you like me to assist in Theatre?' Kirsty asked.

Greg stared at her, as if for a moment he couldn't remember who she was.

'I think you've done enough for the time being. We'll cope from here on. If you give me a minute, I'll find someone who can show you to your quarters.'

'But…' Kirsty started to protest.

Greg lifted a hand to stem the flow of words. 'I don't have time to argue. You don't know the layout of the department. Right now, we've enough staff to help. You'll only get in the way. Please,' he added firmly, 'leave it to us.' Then he smiled as if to soften his words.

Kirsty glared at him, her eyes flashing. He was treating her like some incompetent medical student.

Greg must have sensed her frustration. He raised an eyebrow at her. 'You did very well back there. Now go get some rest. You'll be in a better position to help tomorrow.' He turned his back to her, but not before something in those cool blue eyes told Kirsty it'd be useless to argue further. Reluctantly she looked at his retreating back.

* * *

Later that night as Greg wrote up his notes, he thought about Kirsty. The image of her standing before him in his bloodstained shirt and the short skirt which did nothing to hide her long slim legs kept intruding on his thoughts. She was undeniably attractive with her thick auburn hair escaping from her ponytail and her elfin face with those flashing green eyes. Although on the surface she appeared sophisticated, there was something vulnerable about her— and it wasn't just her age. He cursed under his breath. She had only been qualified for a couple of years. Despite the way she had performed at the accident scene, she was still far too inexperienced to work in such a remote and challenging setting. He had tried to refuse to accept her as a member of his new team, but had been overruled by the hospital manager. 'You can't keep working night and day, Greg,' he had said. 'This hospital should have twelve doctors, not the four we have. We need help, at least your colleagues do, and it's not as if we're overrun with applications to come and work here. You might be able to work all the hours God sends, but your colleagues need a break. If they don't get some time off, we could lose them.'

There was no denying his argument, but Greg knew to his cost that an inexperienced doctor could be worse than no doctor at all. With her delicate features and slim build, Kirsty looked as if she had just come out of medical school, although he knew that she was twenty-five. The last thing he needed was to babysit some inexperienced doctor who thought spending a few months in a rural hospital in Africa would be fun or, worse, a good way of practising newly acquired medical skills. He'd had enough of those types in the past and they had proved more of a hindrance than a help. Most of them had only stayed a short while. Long enough to realise that the incredibly long hours and hard work was too much.

He shook his head in frustration. He had been tempted to take Kirsty up on her offer of help earlier. Perhaps working through the night in the primitive and gruelling conditions would have been enough to see her immediate return to the UK. But the temptation had been fleeting. It wouldn't be in the best interests of the patients to have an exhausted and inexperienced doctor working on them. Still, he had to admit she had done well at the crash scene. Apart from that initial hesitation she had worked calmly and efficiently. He knew that more than one patient had reason to be glad she had been there. It didn't help that something in those luminescent green eyes had sparked feelings that he thought had gone for ever. No, it was best all round if she could be made to see that Africa wasn't for her.

CHAPTER TWO

THE sun streaming into her room woke Kirsty. Anxious that she'd overslept, she glanced at her watch and couldn't believe it wasn't quite six yet. She stretched, breathing in the unfamiliar but heady scents that drifted in from her open window. Last night, one of the kitchen staff had escorted her to her accommodation after serving her some mashed pumpkin and roast beef. The rest of the staff had all been busy with the aftermath of the accident, so it had been a solitary supper for Kirsty.

Although she had been a little disappointed not to meet and work alongside her new colleagues, part of her had been relieved to get the opportunity of a much-needed early night. She had barely managed to stay awake long enough to shower the blood, sweat and dust away, before collapsing into bed. She had expected to fall asleep the moment her head had hit the pillow, but instead had found herself replaying the events of the day and her introduction to the strangeness of this wild, untamed patch of Africa and its people, including the enigmatic Dr Greg du Toit. Although she couldn't say her new boss had been unwelcoming, she'd sensed he wasn't altogether happy to have her there. She had tossed and turned, wondering if she had made the right decision to come to work in this hospital deep in rural Africa. Would she cope? Everything seemed much more basic than she had imagined. But she'd had to get away. Put as much distance between herself and her memories as possible. She wanted—needed—to start afresh make a new life for herself. When at last she had fallen asleep, it had been to dream of Robbie. She had woken up to find tears drying on her cheeks.

But Kirsty was determined that today would be the beginning of her new life. Curious about her new home, she jumped out of bed. There was a set of scrubs on the rickety chair in the corner of the room. They hadn't been there the night before. Greg must have asked someone to bring them over. She was surprised that he had remembered, with so much going on.

The accommodation certainly wasn't lavish but, then, Kirsty hadn't expected it to be. Nevertheless she appreciated the gleaming polished earthen floors smelling faintly of lavender, cool and smooth under her bare feet. And although the furniture was sparse, she knew that with a few touches she could make her new home more appealing.

The house was at least half a century old, with a hodge-podge of additions over time to what must have been the original structure—a circular room from which a tiny scullery, her bedroom and a spartan bathroom led off at various angles, each serving to create interesting nooks and crannies.

The circular room—or rondavel as it was traditionally known—was divided down the middle by a freestanding granite unit that separated the living-room area from the kitchen. On closer inspection Kirsty realised it must have been an autopsy slab from bygone times. However, its antiquated, well-scrubbed appearance amused rather than repulsed her.

While the kettle boiled, she searched fruitlessly for something to eat. In hindsight, she remembered being told that staff meals were served daily in the dining room. If she preferred to prepare meals for herself, she'd have to do her own grocery shopping. Hell, there wasn't even tea or milk! Dispirited, she flicked the kettle off. Breakfast in the staff dining room it had to be!

She took a quick shower, pleased to find that while the furniture and fittings might be sparse, there was a plentiful supply of steaming hot water. However, she remembered that Africa often suffered severe water shortages and limited her shower to the minimum amount of time needed to soap her body and rinse the last of the dust from her long auburn hair.

She wasn't expected on duty until the following day but she was eager to see how the victims of yesterday's accident were faring so she dressed quickly in the scrubs, which were a surprisingly good fit. She wondered if Greg had selected them himself—if he had, he had an accurate idea of her size.

Looking around for a socket for her hairdryer, she was dismayed to find that although there were a few, none fitted her UK plug. Mildly put out, she towel dried it instead, before plaiting it into a thick braid. She would simply have to learn to adapt as best she could to her new environment. After all, she thought with some longing, she was unlikely to find all the conveniences of her home city several hours' drive into the African bush. Nevertheless, she thought with exasperation, there were some things she couldn't possibly be expected to do without, and a hairdryer was one of them!

Following the footpath that led from her cottage, she entered the rear of the hospital where most of the wards were situated on different sides of a long passageway. She stepped into the first room on her right through double swing doors and was greeted warmly by a smiling Sister Ngoba, the night sister whom she'd met the previous evening and who was now busy writing up reports before handing over to the day staff. As Kirsty's eyes roamed the length of the ward, she was surprised to see a familiar head bent over the bed of a female patient whose leg was in traction. When he looked up she could see the stubble darkening his jaw and the fatigue shadowing his eyes.

'Kirsty?' he said, sounding surprised. 'You don't need to be on duty until tomorrow. Everyone needs a day to settle in.'

'I know. I wanted to check up on how our patients from the accident yesterday were doing. And I'm longing to get started. I don't need a day off. Anyway, you're on duty,' she challenged.

He smiled tiredly. 'But I'm *meant* to be on duty.'

'You haven't been up all night, have you?'

'Almost, but not quite,' he said, wryly thinking that the hour's sleep he'd managed to get hadn't been nearly enough. 'Thank you for your help yesterday, by the way, and a belated welcome to the team. You'll meet everyone later.'

'I look forward to that.' She paused to smile hello at the patient Greg had been examining. It was the young woman whose tibia and fibula had been badly crushed by the overturned minibus. Lydia, her eyes cloudy with painkillers, managed a weak smile in return, before closing her eyes.

'How's our patient?' Kirsty asked quietly.

'I think we've managed to save her leg. Once I'm sure

she's stable, I'll arrange to send her to one of the hospitals in the city. They have better equipment than we do, as well as access to physio. For cases like this we patch them up, stabilise them and then send them on.' He smiled down at the girl and said something to her that Kirsty couldn't understand.

'You speak the language?' Kirsty asked impressed.

'One or two of them—there are around fifteen different languages or dialects in this country, but I know the ones that are spoken in this neck of the woods. I find it's pretty useful for communicating with my patients.' He stretched, working the kinks out of his muscles. 'But obviously you'll need a nurse or an assistant to help you translate when there are patients who don't speak English.' Kirsty made a mental note to try and master as much of the language as she could. She had learned a few words before coming out, mainly greetings, but intended to learn more.

'I'm just telling Lydia that the morphine that we've given her is what's making her sleepy. She'll probably be out for the count for the rest of the day,' Greg explained, and sure enough Lydia had closed her eyes and seemed to have already succumbed to the sedating effects of the drug. Kirsty and Greg moved away from the bed.

'I also hoped for a tour of the rest of the hospital. I'm really keen to see it all.'

Greg wrapped his stethoscope around his neck. 'I could show you later,' he replied.

'Please, don't worry. I'm sure you've got enough to do. One of the nursing sisters can—or, if everyone's busy, I can see myself around. I won't get in anyone's way—I promise. But first I need a cup of coffee! I haven't had any yet and I'm a bit of a caffeine junkie.'

Greg hit his forehead with the heel of his hand. 'Damn, I'm sorry about that. I meant to organise some provisions for you yesterday but with everything going so crazy here, it completely slipped my mind.' His sheepish grin was contrite. 'I'm almost finished the ward rounds so if you can hold on, I'll show you the dining room. Then unfortunately I'm due in Outpatients so I'll have to leave you to your own devices.'

'I'll come with you to Outpatients, if that's OK. I'd really like to get stuck in as soon as possible. A coffee and toast will do me until lunch,' she said.

Greg looked at her appraisingly. Kirsty couldn't help notice how the corners of his eyes crinkled when he smiled. But even when relaxed there was a presence about the man, an animal-like energy that seemed to fill the room.

'We could do with the help. Jamie and Sarah are in Theatre this morning and Jenny is anaesthetising for them, so quick rounds, followed by coffee and Outpatients it is.' He went on, 'This, as I'm sure you've gathered, is the female surgical ward.' He moved to the next bed. 'You recognise this young lady?'

It was the woman who had had the femoral bleed, Maria. A quick look at her chart told Kirsty that she was stable.

'I take it if she's not in Intensive Care, she's going to be all right?'

'We had her in surgery most of the night, but it looks hopeful. Once we're sure she can tolerate the journey, we'll send her by ambulance to one of the teaching hospitals in the city. They'll be able to take it from there.'

'And Lydia's little boy? Where is he?' asked Kirsty, suddenly remembering.

'He's in the paediatric ward for the time being. There

was nowhere else to put him. He's been driving the staff crazy with his loud wailing. He won't be consoled. We'd let him see his mother if she looked a little less frightening. Can't you hear him?'

And Kirsty did, faintly. She found herself moving in the direction of his cries.

'Any relatives we can contact?'

'No one's come forward to claim him but it's early still. When the mother surfaces properly, we'll get more information.'

'I think he should see her,' she said firmly.

'Would that be wise?'

'He's, what...about two years old? Old enough for some understanding. I think he needs to *feel* his mother's still alive, even though she's "sleeping".'

'It might make things worse. Surely it's better to wait until she's alert enough to reassure him herself?' he suggested.

'How could anything be worse for him than what it is now? He's not crying just because he's miserable and wants to make a loud noise. He's crying for his mother, and he can't understand why she's not coming. In his mind she's abandoned him.'

'If you're sure...'

'I'm not sure. It depends on his ability to comprehend. But he seemed so well cared-for I'm willing to take a gamble... Besides, I do know a thing or two about children.' Kirsty felt the familiar crushing pain as she said the words. She ignored Greg's searching glance and turned towards the cries before he could say anything.

They entered the children's ward together. The toddler was not the only one crying but he was certainly the loudest. Kirsty's greeting of the staff on duty was cursory as she focused her attention on the unhappy child. Picking him up, she depended on the natural inherent curiosity of toddlers for him to be distracted long enough for her to talk to him. She was confident that, like most very young children, he understood a lot more than most adults would give him credit for. Recalling the desperate concern of the mother at the accident scene, this child knew love.

'Shh,' she said, soothing the distressed infant, dangling her stethoscope in front of him. It took a while but he quietened eventually as, momentarily distracted, he explored his new toy. Kirsty knew that it wouldn't be long before his cries resumed.

She caught sight of one of his fingers, which had a sticky plaster on it, a superficial pre-crash wound she'd noticed yesterday.

'Ow,' she said, lifting his hand and kissing the well-wrapped injury. The little boy seemed hypnotised by her attention. 'What's "Mother sleeping"?' she asked the staff while the boy gazed, astonished, at his finger, as if seeing it for the first time in a new light. 'Tell him his mummy has a big "ow" and is sleeping.' The nurse spoke to the child and he listened, taking in what was being said to him.

Armed with a few new words of the language, Kirsty followed Greg back to the surgical ward.

'Mummy's sleeping—*bomma robetsego*,' she tried in his language as the toddler stared down at his mother. His bottom lip quivered and Kirsty knew tears were not far behind. In an age-long gesture, he leaned out of Kirsty's arms, his arms stretched pleadingly towards his unconscious mother.

'Mummy's sleeping. Shh,' Kirsty repeated softly, allowing him to touch the still figure. 'Let her sleep.'

The little boy crumpled in her arms. This time, though, his tears were quieter as she took him away and returned him to the children's ward.

'Well, I'll be damned!' Greg said, walking alongside her.

'It doesn't always work,' Kirsty admitted, 'but I thought it worth a try. He's exhausted so hopefully he'll sleep now, and when he wakes up someone should take him back to see his mother. With a bit of luck she'll wake soon and comfort him herself.'

'And if she doesn't?'

'Then he'll know why,' she replied simply. 'If not now, then later when it matters. Children are more able to cope with a parent who can't help or comfort them. It's those who think their parents have abandoned them who suffer most.'

Greg flinched and he looked off into the distance, before striding out of the ward, leaving Kirsty to scurry along in his wake. It seemed she had touched a nerve. She was dismayed and not a little curious. What on earth had she said that had affected him like that?

In the male surgical ward, Dr Jenny Carter was taking a blood sample from a patient. She looked up as she heard the ward doors swing open.

Kirsty found her instantly likeable. Plump, with a thick bush of greying hair tied back at the nape of her neck with what looked like a shoelace, she had a gregarious, warm manner.

'Ah, our new recruit! Come to check we're taking good care of your patients from last night?' But there wasn't an ounce of malice in the question. 'Here's Mr Mhlongo. Says we can call him Eddy! And he must be doing fine because he's already been teasing the nurses. Perhaps we should plaster the other arm, what do you think?' A nursing sister cheerfully translated the doctor's words to Eddy.

'*Dumela*,' Kirsty greeted the chuckling man, covered in plaster on one side of his chest all the way down to his fingers with his neck stabilised in a brace. He might not have realised it yet but he owed his life to the seat belt that had prevented him from meeting a similar fate to the driver when the front of the minibus had slammed into the ground. She felt his pulse and although she'd been concerned he might have sustained a serious concussion, his bright eyes told her otherwise. A broken shoulder and a severe case of whiplash seemed to be the worst of his problems. Not so the patient in the bed closest to the nurses' station or the one in Intensive Care, but the two other patients in the ward she'd attended to yesterday were doing fine.

Kirsty was surprised at the number of patients in the hospital cared for by a very small complement of staff. In fact, some wards were so crowded that some patients were sleeping on mattresses on the floor or, as the case in the children's ward, doubled up in cots.

'What about the risk of cross-infection?' she asked Greg.

'We are as careful as we can be. Most of those sharing are siblings with the same condition.'

'Surely not those with HIV or AIDS?'

'Actually, contrary to popular belief, it is these patients who need to be protected from infection and not the other way around. After all, it is their immune systems that are compromised, rendering them vulnerable to every infection and germ around,' Greg told Kirsty. He turned to the nursing sister who was accompanying them. 'Isn't that right, Sister?'

The nursing sister shrugged her shoulders. 'Too many

with the disease. We try to take special care but…' The shake of her head told much without words. It had been a fact of life for so long that it was difficult, if not impossible, not to become desensitised.

'Come on, let's get you fed and then, if you're still up for it, you can come and help me in Outpatients. Although it's Sunday, we'll have a full clinic. Days of the week have no meaning out here. Most of them will have walked for days just to get here and I don't like to keep them waiting any longer than necessary. I've eaten…' he glanced at his watch '…but I've time for a quick cup of coffee, so I'll show you where the staff dining room is then leave you to it. The other staff will probably be there, except for the Campbells who tend to eat breakfast in their own house.'

When they entered the dining room she was pleased to find Jenny there if no one else.

'Jenny will show you to Outpatients when you're ready. Take your time,' Greg said, and after a quick gulp of coffee left the two women to it.

'Does he ever slow down?' Kirsty asked, looking at Greg's retreating back.

'Not really,' Jenny acknowledged. 'The man is a human dynamo. I can't remember the last time he took a day off. The rest of us are more human: he insists we take a couple of days at least every third week.' She eyed Kirsty's thin frame thoughtfully. 'Don't worry, no one will expect you to work these hours, dear.'

'I'll do my share,' Kirsty said. 'I'm stronger than I look.' She stirred the lumpy porridge thoughtfully. 'Maybe Greg works too hard,' she said, choosing her words carefully. 'Sometimes he seems a little…well, abrupt. Or is it just me? Have I done something wrong?'

'Oh, don't mind Greg. His bark is worse than his bite. He's a real softy really. As you'll find out.'

'Softy' was the last word Kirsty would have used to describe Greg. 'What happened to him?' she asked, curious to know more about this man she was to work with over the coming months.

'You mean his face? The scars? I hardly notice them any more.' Jenny hesitated for a moment before seeming to make up her mind. 'Oh, well, you'll find out sooner rather than later anyway. It's impossible to keep secrets in a community of this size. He got them trying to rescue his wife and child from their burning house. They were on their own, just before Christmas—five years last Christmas, in fact. He had been called to the hospital—some emergency I expect. He arrived home to find his house in flames and the fire brigade battling to get it under control. His wife and daughter were still inside. Greg tried to get to them even though the firemen had already failed. They couldn't hold him back. He went in and brought them out. But it was too late. They had both died from smoke inhalation. Apparently the fire started from the Christmas-tree lights. He was devastated. They were his whole world. I don't think he has ever come to terms with the loss—I'm not sure that one does.'

Kirsty was stricken. Memories of her own tragedy came flooding back. Although fifteen years had passed, there wasn't a day when she didn't think of her mother or Pamela.

Jenny shook her head sorrowfully, unaware of Kirsty's reaction. 'I think Greg blames himself, God knows why. There wasn't anything anybody could have done. The poor man was in hospital himself for weeks. Once he was discharged he left Cape Town. I expect he couldn't bear to stay anywhere near the place where they had been so happy. He came here and has been here ever since. He works so hard. It's as if he is trying to exorcise his demons through sheer hard work. He never talks about it or them, and if I were you, I wouldn't ever raise the topic. I tried once and got my head bitten off.'

'How awful.' Kirsty blinked away the tears that threatened to surface. No wonder he was brusque. Now she knew, she would have to be more sympathetic.

'He still wears his wedding ring,' she said.

'You noticed, then?' Jenny cast a mischievous look at Kirsty. 'I wouldn't get any ideas in that direction. There has been many a young doctor and nurse who has tried to offer Greg comfort, but while he doesn't seem adverse to the odd casual fling, I doubt somehow that he'll ever let anyone really get under the barrier of ice he seems to have wrapped around his heart.'

Kirsty felt her cheeks flame at the implication. 'I can assure you,' she said stiffly, 'a relationship with anyone is the last thing on my mind.'

Subconsciously she fingered her now bare ring finger. 'I've had enough of men to last me a lifetime.' She ignored Jenny's curious look. 'I'm here to work and to learn. Nothing more.' She drained her coffee. 'Sorry.' Kirsty grimaced, suddenly aghast at the turn the conversation had taken. The kindly doctor in front of her must think her rude. 'I'm not usually so prickly, it's just…new place, new people, new challenges. It'll take me a day or two to settle in, I guess.'

By the time Jenny left Kirsty outside the outpatient clinic, with a hasty apology that she had another Theatre list due to start, there were several patients sitting outside, waiting their turn to be seen. Most of the women still wore traditional dress and despite the intense heat had their children strapped onto their backs with thick blankets. For the most part the children seemed quiet—subdued even. One little boy squatted in the dust, lazily poking at the ground with a stick. When he looked up Kirsty could see that one of his eyes was sticky with what looked like a chronic infection. She tilted his chin—he needed something for his eyes, the sooner the better. She glanced around and spotted a nurse moving between the patients, taking histories and writing notes. Kirsty guessed she was probably assessing who needed to be seen first. Just before Kirsty could grab her attention she noticed a young woman clutching a bundle to her breast. There was something in the woman's posture—an air of despair—that made Kirsty catch her breath. She moved closer, and gently lowered the blanket to reveal a small, painfully thin child who was making no effort to take the proffered breast of the young mother. The child's face was so thin it seemed almost skeletal, the skin clinging to the fragile bones of the skull. Flies settled and buzzed around the tiny mouth and closed eyes. For a heart-stopping moment Kirsty thought the child was already dead. She felt for a pulse and was rewarded with a faint flutter beneath her fingertips. The child was still alive, but surely not for long. With one swift movement she lifted the infant up, its tiny frame feeling no heavier than a feather, and rushed into the department. This child couldn't wait. It needed fluids in the form of a drip straight away or he or she would die.

Ignoring the wails of the young mother, she searched frantically for Greg. She found him crouching in front of an old woman, examining a suppurating sore on her foot.

Greg took one look at Kirsty's anguished expression and stood up.

'What is it?' he asked, bending forward to look at her small bundle. 'Not another case of marasmus—starvation,' he said despairingly. 'OK, bring her into the treatment room and let's see what we can do. If there is anything we can do.'

Within moments the small child, a girl, was lying on the couch, her mother sitting close by, her eyes flitting from Kirsty to Greg. One of the nurses had joined them and was talking to the mother in rapid Sotho.

'The child stopped taking the breast two days ago. She's been sick for over a week. A traditional healer gave her mother some herbs to give her, but when they didn't help and she stopped taking the breast, the mother decided to bring her to us. It's taken two days for her to get here.'

While the nurse repeated the history, Greg and Kirsty had been searching for a vein in which to insert a drip. Kirsty knew that they had to get the small child rehydrated as soon as possible.

'I can't find any in her arms. They all seem to have collapsed,' Kirsty told Greg, fear catching her voice. They had no time. The child could die if they didn't treat her right away.

Greg looked up at her. 'Slow down. We'll find one. Look here just above the foot. We'll need to do a cut down. It's not ideal, but it's all we have. Have you done one before?'

'I have, but I'd rather watch you first, if that's OK,' Kirsty said. This child was so small, so desperately ill. What if she was too slow?

'You'll have to do it, I'm afraid. You may have noticed my right hand only has restricted movement. It's fine except for the most delicate stuff.' Kirsty could only guess what it cost Greg to admit his limitations. At the same time she admired him for it. She had once seen a doctor attempt to perform procedures above his capabilities and the results had almost been disastrous.

Greg noticed Kirsty's hesitation. 'You'll be fine. I'll talk you through it.'

Somehow his belief in her gave her confidence and with very little assistance from Greg she performed the procedure perfectly and without any wasted time.

'Excellent job.' Greg's praise was fulsome and genuine and Kirsty felt elated. She thought that she might grow to like her job here.

'OK, let's get her started on the usual regime.' He directed a few rapid words towards the mother.

'She's three years old,' he translated for Kirsty.

Once again Kirsty was horrified. Three! It wasn't possible. The child looked no older than nine months, a year at the most. She was so tiny.

'Obviously we can't use her age to work out how much we need to give her. By my guess she weighs just over eight kilograms. Could you pop her on the scales?' he asked the nurse.

The nurse scooped the child up and laid her gently on the scales.

'Just right—eight kilos,' she told Greg.

'Any thoughts on the dosage we should be administering?' Greg asked Kirsty.

Kirsty thought frantically. She had completed six months in paediatrics as part of her houseman jobs. But the children there had been so much bigger, stronger than this child in front of her. She had never seen anyone in such an advanced stage of starvation before. How could she have?

But she remembered a child, physically handicapped, who had been brought in following a severe episode of diarrhoea. The child's condition had been similar to if not quite as drastic as that of this child in front of her.

She was about to hazard a guess, but Greg hadn't waited for her response. He adjusted the drip and straightened up. She could sense the fatigue and something else—could it be anger?—behind his professional exterior.

'We've done everything we can for the time being. It's in the lap of the gods now.' He tossed his gloves into the bin. 'The main problem is caused by formula. The government spends substantial sums of money promoting breast-feeding, but the problem is with the women who are HIV positive. The danger of them transmitting the disease to their infants through breast milk is just too large, so they are encouraged to give their babies formula. Unfortunately formula is too expensive for most of them, so they start diluting it to make it go further. Then the children simply don't get enough calories or nutrition. And as if that isn't bad enough, a large number of the outlying villages still don't have access to clean water. So the women mix the powder with water from the river. And what you see before you is the result.'

'Can't we do anything about it?' Kirsty asked. 'Surely it's just a matter of education?'

Greg smiled, but there was no humour in his eyes. 'Education and clean water. That's what is needed. In the meantime...' He let the words hang in the air for a moment. 'In the meantime we do the best we can. Come on, Kirsty, as you're about to see, there is plenty more for us to do.'

'But doing the best we can isn't *enough*. Is it? Not if children are still dying?' Surely he wasn't going to tell her there was nothing they could do to prevent this? He didn't strike Kirsty as a man who let anything stop him from doing what was right.

'We'll talk about it later,' Greg said quietly but firmly. 'Right now we have work to do. You take the consulting room next door. I'm just across the hall. If you need me, give me a shout, but try the nurses first. I think you'll find that there is precious little they can't help you with.' And without waiting for a reply, he turned on his heel and left the room.

CHAPTER THREE

THE rest of the morning passed quickly. Kirsty saw many children with the swollen bellies and stick-like limbs of kwashiorkor, a condition the nurses told her was caused by poor nutrition and lack of vitamins. The nursing staff were fantastic. They worked unstintingly throughout the day, pausing to answer Kirsty's questions with unfailing good humour and patience. Kirsty felt humbled to be part of their team and full of admiration for their level of expertise. The patients too were remarkably stoic and, despite long waits in the overcrowded department, were universally grateful for everything Kirsty did, however small. Occasionally, to her surprise, she could hear laughter filtering through the walls of the consulting room.

Eventually the clinic quietened down, until all that was left was dressings and vaccinations that the nursing staff on the back shift would finish off.

As Kirsty leaned back in her chair, a wave of exhaustion washed over her. But it felt good. She closed her eyes.

'Lunch?' Greg popped his head around the door and as if in answer Kirsty's stomach growled. Now that he mentioned it, she was starving. The cup of coffee and the watery porridge she had eaten at breakfast-time had made her appreciate why the others ate at home. As soon as she had the opportunity she was going to stock up on provisions, but in the meantime…

'Lead me to it,' she said, jumping out of her chair. *I hope he doesn't think I've spent the morning snoozing,* she thought.

'Come on, then. I gather you did pretty well this morning. The nurse told me you worked throughout without a break. Well done.'

Kirsty felt herself glow with pleasure. Maybe he wasn't going to be so difficult to work for after all.

'I am going out to one of the villages tomorrow to do a clinic, if you'd like to come with me,' Greg said as they made their way to the staff dining room. Kirsty almost had to run to keep up with his long strides. 'You've seen the bad, now I'd like you to see the good.'

'I'd love to,' Kirsty said, 'but I'd like to check up on the child we saw this morning before lunch, if that's OK. I don't mind missing lunch if we're pushed for time.'

Greg's eyes swept over her figure. He shook his head. 'You look as if you could do with a good feeding up yourself, so missing lunch isn't a good idea. You've been working hard and a sick or weakened doctor is no good to anyone. Of course we can take the time to pop into Paediatrics before we eat, but if you are going to survive out here, you'll need to become less emotionally involved. I find too much emotion can cloud a doctor's judgement.'

So much for thinking he was going to be easy to work for! It hadn't taken long for his habitual curtness to resurface. And who was he to tell her when she had to eat? And as for telling her not to become too involved, she had heard those words before. She thought it would be different out here. She thought, if anything, doctors came here to work because they wanted to be involved. But clearly not Dr Greg du Toit. The man had no feelings. He was simply a working machine.

'I think I'm old enough to look after myself,' Kirsty said frostily. 'I don't mind you commenting on my work, but what I eat and what I feel is up to me, don't you think?'

Her words stopped Greg in his tracks. He turned to look at Kirsty with glittering blue eyes. Suddenly he smiled.

'OK, OK.' He put his hands up in mock surrender. 'You win. However, no missing meals—is that understood?'

'Yeah, yeah, and no late nights or alcohol or strange men in my room after midnight. Gotcha.'

Greg's smile grew broader. 'God, I do sound like a Victorian father, don't I? Kathleen was always telling me to lighten up.' His smile disappeared and Kirsty could see the pain in his eyes. For a moment she was tempted to reach out to offer him comfort. She touched his arm gently, feeling the muscles tense beneath her fingertips.

'Was Kathleen your wife?' she asked softly.

He drew back from her touch as if she'd caused him physical pain.

'Ah, I see people have been talking,' he said, his lips set in a grim line.

'Jenny told me what happened. I'm so sorry, Greg. I don't know how anyone can bear such a loss.'

'Well, let's hope you never have to find out,' he said, rubbing his hand across his scars. 'Some things are just better not thought about.'

That's where you are wrong, thought Kirsty, feeling the familiar flicker of pain.

'You must miss them,' Kirsty ventured. Inexplicably she felt the need to get closer to this man.

'As you told me just a few minutes ago, everyone has a

right to their privacy. I've agreed to respect yours and I'd be grateful if you would respect mine.' Despite his words, his tone was mild. But Kirsty could see by the set of his jaw that he was holding himself in check.

Nevertheless, Kirsty felt as if she'd been slapped.

'I'm sorry,' she said stiffly. 'I didn't mean to pry.'

Greg rubbed his scar. 'No, forgive me,' he said. 'I didn't mean to have a go at you. I've probably been here too long and have forgotten the social niceties. Let's just forget it.'

He paused next to a path that led away from the hospital towards the perimeter of the compound. 'If you follow that path for a few minutes, you'll come to a large concrete reservoir. We use it for swimming. Jamie makes it his business to keep it clean. We often congregate there after work or at weekends.' He carried on walking. 'There are four doctors here, as you know—you make the fifth. We take turns at being on call, and we all operate but Sarah is nominally in charge of obstetrics, Jamie paediatrics, Jenny anaesthetises and has responsibility for the medical wards. The surgical wards are mine. There's a rota for outpatients as that involves a bit of everything.'

'What will I be doing?' Kirsty asked

'You'll be learning.' He looked at her intently. 'At this point you have no idea how quickly you'll be learning. A couple of weeks and you'll be expected to manage on your own, although, of course, we will always be available for advice. I'm afraid, Dr Boucher, we can't carry people here. It's a case of see one, do one, teach one.'

There was no mistaking his meaning. If she didn't live up to his expectations, she'd be on the next plane home.

For a moment she felt a flutter of anxiety. She was a good doctor, she knew that—but it was all so different here.

He stopped outside the staff house. 'Come on, let's get you fed.' He grinned as he caught her warning look, his smile making him look younger and carefree, and for a moment Kirsty could see a different side to her boss. 'And introduce you to the rest of the team, of course.'

There were five or six people seated at the table. Jenny smiled a greeting and Greg introduced a striking-looking couple as Sarah and Jamie, the doctors Campbell. There were two men who were introduced to Kirsty as outreach workers. 'Thandi and Johan spend their time sinking wells in the outlying villages. We'll be going to one of them tomorrow. Clean water is one of the things that really makes a difference to the health of the villagers.'

There was also Sibongele, a young man with chocolate skin and deep brown eyes. Sibongele stood and, grabbing a couple of roast potatoes, headed towards the door.

'Pleased to meet you, Dr Boucher,' he said in faultless English, 'but if you'll excuse me, I'm due in Theatre.'

Catching Kirsty's look of confusion, Sarah explained. 'Sibongele is our foster-son. He helps out as a Theatre orderly when he's not at school. He plans to study medicine when he finishes high school. All his spare time, apart from the odd game of football, is spent hanging about the hospital.'

'I thought he looked a bit young—even to be a medical student.' Kirsty admitted.

Sarah laughed. 'Believe me, Sibongele is twice as good as some of the medical students we've had.'

Kirsty was drawn to Sarah, with her open smile and sparkling eyes. Her husband Jamie stood and pulled out a chair for Kirsty. 'Welcome, Kirsty. You've no idea how badly we need an extra pair of hands.'

'I think she's probably got the picture, Jamie,' Greg said, passing Kirsty a bowl of sweet potatoes. 'She's seen for herself how busy we are. She worked like a Trojan this morning.'

Kirsty felt herself flush at his praise. She knew that he was being kind. All the clinical staff were so much more experienced than her. She was terrified she'd end up being more of a hindrance than a help.

'Don't worry, Kirsty, if you find it all a bit overwhelming,' Sarah said. 'I did at first. It's all so different to being in a properly equipped and orderly A and E department. But when you get used to it, there is nothing like it. You really feel that here you can make a difference.'

Before Kirsty had a chance to reply, all eyes turned towards the door. A gleeful toddler rushed into the room, followed by a clucking woman. 'Hey, Calum, you're too fast for Koko now. Leave Mummy to finish eating.'

'It's all right, Martha,' Sarah said, scooping the chuckling toddler into her arms. 'I've finished and I need a cuddle with this young man,' she added, tickling the delighted boy. 'Kirsty, this is our son, Calum.'

'Your son?' Kirsty echoed 'You brought your son here? Aren't you worried about bringing him up here? So far away from civilisation. And exposed to so much disease.' The words had slipped out before she could prevent them. For a moment there was a deathly silence. Sarah's smile froze and Jamie narrowed his eyes.

'Mmm. Civilisation—whatever that is. But I can't say I feel Calum is deprived. We've been here about six months and, as you can see, he's thriving,' Sarah said. 'He has plenty of attention and there are lots of other children he can play with. And as for disease—obviously he has been vaccinated. Naturally, we don't let him near any of the contagious patients,' she finished softly.

The smile returned as she turned to her husband. 'I did worry about bringing him out here at first—of course, any mother would—but I knew Jamie would never expose his child to danger.'

The look that passed between Sarah and Jamie was affectionate. It was obvious they were very much in love. 'We would never risk anything happening to our child. We almost lost him once, so would never do anything that would put him at risk, believe me.'

'I'm sorry…I didn't mean to imply… You must think me so rude. Of course you would never put your son in harm's way. I'm such an idiot. Sometimes I open my mouth without engaging my brain. You're obviously not the kind of parents that would put their child in danger.' As soon as the words were out of her mouth Kirsty could have bitten her tongue. She glanced over at Greg just in time to see him flinch. How could she have been so insensitive? She should just shut up instead of making matters worse! 'Oh, dear…' she began.

The sound of a chair being scraped back stopped Kirsty in mid-flow. Greg tossed his napkin onto the table, his face pale and his mouth set in a grim line.

'I've had enough,' he said quietly. 'I'm going back to my house. Jamie, perhaps you could take Kirsty around the wards with you this afternoon?' His gaze swung to her, his eyes cool. 'Or, since this is meant to be a day off for you, maybe you'd prefer to go to the shops with Sarah? I'm afraid that's as close to civilisation as we can offer you. You might even find one or two clothes shops.'

'I didn't mean…' Kirsty felt herself go pink. No matter what, she seemed to say the wrong thing in front of Greg. She felt a stab of disappointment as his cool eyes flicked over her. Was that what he really thought of her? A shallow city girl obsessed with shopping? She stifled the words of protest that sprang to her lips. She'd already said too much. She took a deep breath. 'Of course I'll need to go shopping at some time, but only to stock up on food. I could give you a list, Sarah, if that's OK with you? Then I could stay and do rounds with Jamie.'

'Whatever,' Greg said. 'See the rest of you at dinner.' He left the room, leaving an embarrassed silence in his wake.

'Don't worry, Kirsty,' Sarah said, noticing her distress. 'Try not to take it personally. You hit a sore spot. But he's really a lamb under that tough exterior.' Sarah ignored her husband's snort of disbelief. 'It's just that we've been let down badly by doctors in the past. They come out here, looking for God knows what, and then within a couple of weeks they find it's too remote and too basic so they just leave. Then we have wasted our time training people who don't stay. But I'm sure you're going to be different. What brings you here anyway? You were a last-minute substitution for someone else, weren't you?'

Kirsty thought rapidly. She couldn't possibly tell them the truth now. If they knew why she'd come here, they'd believe their worse suspicions confirmed. And suddenly Kirsty couldn't bear them to think less of her. Perhaps when she had accepted the job at short notice it had been for the wrong reasons. In that she was no better than the doctors Sarah had talked about. And, yes, she had been horrified—was still horrified—at how basic and isolated the hospital was. She was a city girl used to first-class medical amenities after all. There was nothing wrong with liking clubs and theatres and shopping, was there? You could still like all that and be a good doctor, couldn't you? But now she had made the commitment to the hospital, she intended to stay and play her part. She had no intention, no matter how tough and no matter how disagreeable her boss was, of leaving. All she really worried about at this stage was whether she could cope. Not just with the work, but the lifestyle, the bugs. She shivered, remembering the large insect that had scuttled across her foot that morning.

'Er, I had just finished a stint at A and E and I had taken six months off to travel across Australia with a friend. But that fell through at the last minute.' It wasn't exactly a lie, Kirsty thought, mentally crossing her fingers. 'Then a work colleague mentioned this place and that you were desperate for doctors. So it seemed perfect,' she finished triumphantly.

'Well, we are glad to have you,' Sarah said. 'I only work part time so I can spend time with Calum. I usually end up doing the shopping trips. And, of course, I'm happy to take your list. When you do have some time off, we can go together, if you like. I for one miss the occasional trips to civilisation, and another female for company.' She winked at Kirsty.

Jamie stood up. 'If you two have finished, we'd better get on. Ready, Kirsty?'

Kirsty unwound her stethoscope from around her neck and lifted her hair off her collar to ease the tension in her neck. Her skin felt clammy and she longed for a breeze to cool her overheated body. The last few hours on the wards had been so busy she hadn't had time to notice how inadequate the air-conditioning was in the hospital building but now she was aware her clothes were sticking to her. Waving a tired goodbye to the nursing staff, she remembered the pool that Greg had mentioned. A swim would be ideal right now. Incredible that even with the sun so low in the sky, it should be so hot and humid still.

Finding the path again, she turned down it, enjoying the shade cast by a magnificent jacaranda tree and a fence listing under the weight of bougainvillea. The circular reservoir was virtually hidden by the lush growth of honeysuckle and other shrubs surrounding its high walls. Wondering if the water would be clean enough to swim in, she climbed the ladder at the side until she was standing on top of the broad wall. The water was clear, blue and extremely inviting. The thought of it on her skin was too tempting for Kirsty to resist. Glancing around to check there was no one about, she stripped off her scrubs and stood in her underwear. She hesitated only a moment before taking a deep breath and lowering herself gingerly into the water. She gasped as found herself submerged in the icy water. Despite the initial shock, it felt wonderful after the searing heat.

She swam a few lengths before turning on her back and letting herself float. She gazed up at the cloudless sky and let her mind wander. It had been an eventful day. She hadn't really thought about what she would face when she had got here. She had been too desperate to put as much distance as possible between her and Robbie. Kirsty knew she would have gone to the moon if it had been the only place left to get away to. But now she was glad that she had ended up here. Already she felt drawn into this world and cared about the people who depended so desperately on this team of highly skilled and dedicated doctors and nurses.

A shadow fell across her face. Opening her eyes, she squinted into the sun to find Greg's tall figure standing looking down at her. He was dressed only in a pair of Bermuda shorts and was holding a towel in his hand. His chest was bronzed and muscular and Kirsty was disconcertedly aware of the dark hair on his lean abdomen. Her eyes travelled back upwards, her breath catching in her throat as she saw the scars that marred his chest and shoulder. She forced her eyes away and found his eyes, which seemed to glitter in the dying light.

'I'm sorry,' he said,' I didn't realise that anyone was using the pool. I'll leave you in peace to enjoy your swim.' Something in his expression made her suddenly conscious that she was only wearing her underwear and, glancing down, she was horrified to realise that it had become transparent. Quickly she began to tread water, trying to hide herself beneath the swirling water.

'Don't go,' she said. 'There's room enough here for both of us. Besides, I was planning to get out soon.' She turned away and started swimming, hoping to hide her confusion in action.

She felt a splash as Greg dived into the water. She rested for a while and watched his swift, sure strokes as he swam to and fro. Clearly he was an experienced swimmer. She wasn't a bad swimmer herself, but she was slightly out of breath after a couple of minutes. He surfaced beside her, shaking the water from his thick hair. She could make out the faint crinkles around his eyes. Excruciatingly aware of his nearly naked body next to hers, separated only by a couple of inches of water, she felt a tingle of desire low in her abdomen. What was wrong with her? She was still in love with Robbie, wasn't she? She couldn't possibly be lusting after another man. Maybe it was her dented ego, wanting to check out whether she was still desirable. Perhaps an affair, no strings attached, was just what she needed. But if it was, her libido had chosen the wrong man. She couldn't imagine Greg being interested in any woman, least of all *her*. Catching Greg looking at her speculatively, she prayed the man couldn't read her mind.

'I think I'll get out,' she said, needing to get away from the confused thoughts his proximity was generating.

'OK,' Greg said, before plunging back into the water.

She turned to get out, only to discover that the water level was too low for her to grab the side of the reservoir and pull herself out. She looked around for a ladder and realised there wasn't one on the inside.

She made a couple of attempts to heave herself over the side before conceding failure. She just didn't have the upper body strength necessary to do it.

How mortifying, she thought as she realised she was going to have to ask for assistance. It was either that or spend the night in the pool. Little as she liked having to ask for Greg's help, it was marginally more appealing than passing the night in a watery bed. She turned around to find him watching her, a grin playing on his lips as he trod water.

'Can't manage?' he said. 'I thought you city girls were all into the gym.'

'This city girl has been too busy with work—*and other things*,' she added under her breath, 'to go to the gym. So if you wouldn't mind helping me?'

Greg narrowed his eyes at her as if the thought of leaving her had also entered his mind, then with a fluid bunching of muscles he hauled himself out of the pool and came to stand in front of her.

'Take my hands,' he ordered.

Kirsty felt her hands grasped in his and as if she weighed nothing at all he pulled her out of the pool. The speed of her removal made her stumble against him and they both stepped back as Greg put his arms around her to steady her. She felt the cool heat of his skin against hers and the strength of his arms as he held her. Once more desire hit her like a tidal wave. Through the thin fabric of her underwear she could feel his answering response.

His hands moved over her shoulders, sweeping down to the small of her back. For a second she thought he was going to pull her closer but then he put her away from him.

'I told you, you don't eat enough. God, you hardly weigh more than a child.'

She felt his eyes rake her body, taking in her frame. His eyes paused on her breasts before slowly dropping downwards. She thought she heard him groan, before he cursed and bent to pick up his towel.

'Here, take this.'

Once again she was aware of her scanty attire. Heavens, she was practically naked in front of this man! She took the towel from him and wrapped it around her body. The sun was sinking in the sky, shooting ribbons of purple and pink, silhouetting the stark outlines of the acacia trees. The sound of rising starlings filled the air. Kirsty was bewitched. Africa was beginning to weave its magic.

'We'd better go,' Greg said brusquely. He turned his back and whipped off his wet shorts. Kirsty could just make out the lean contours of his naked buttocks before he pulled on his scrubs.

'Don't worry, I won't look if you want to do the same.'

'It's OK. I'll just get dressed over my wet clothes. I

don't have far to go. My underwear will probably dry out in a minute.' She was aware that she was babbling but she felt confused by what had just happened. And what had that been? Nothing. He had helped her out of the pool—that was all. He had responded to her half-naked body like any other red-blooded male would have. But she suspected there was more to it than that. She was attracted to this man, despite being still in love with Robbie. It was crazy—she wasn't sure she even liked Greg du Toit. There was something too masculine, almost old-fashioned about him. And she was a thoroughly modern woman. She liked her men to be firmly part of the twenty-first century.

'By the way, your suitcases have arrived. What on earth have you brought? There seems to be at least four of them. Are you planning to stay here indefinitely?' Greg's voice broke into her thoughts.

Once more Kirsty felt defensive. 'It's probably my medical books. I thought they'd come in handy.' She winced inside at another white lie. OK, obviously there wasn't going to be an opportunity to wear all six of her party dresses, and perhaps she didn't need to bring quite as many pairs of shoes—but, bush or no bush, a girl still had to come prepared for any eventuality, didn't she?

'You must show me what you've brought,' Greg said with a sideways glance. 'We're always looking to update our skills with modern thinking—with all that literature, you're bound to be able to teach us a thing or two.'

Kirsty was aghast. But then, glancing up at him, she noticed a wicked twinkle in his eyes. Could he be teasing her?

Thankfully, before she could dig an even deeper hole for herself, he turned on his heel and, whistling, left her standing in the gathering dusk.

CHAPTER FOUR

DINNER that evening was a relaxed affair. As it was Kirsty's first proper evening everyone had turned up for the meal at staff house to welcome her. The dining room was bubbling with medical chat as everyone filled each other in with the day's events. Kirsty was relieved to note that all the staff sought opinions from each other. It seemed that sharing and discussing cases was the norm. Nobody seemed to hesitate to ask for advice.

'It's impossible for us all to know everything, and even what we do know counts for little out here where we have basic facilities.' Greg had turned to Kirsty after a particularly heated, though friendly debate with Sarah about a case. 'We often have to make different decisions out here than we would in a fully equipped hospital. Here we have to be aware of our limitations and the environment our patients are living in. For example, there is little point in asking someone to attend as an outpatient if they have to walk ten miles each way every day. Similarly we have to make decisions about performing surgery here versus waiting until the patient can be transferred to a major hospital, bearing in mind the trip takes several hours. Sometimes it's better not to give a C-section to a woman in labour—even when it seems on the face of it that it's clinically indicated.'

'But surely we have to do everything to ensure the survival of children or those who haven't been born? Isn't it fortunate that the patients end up here where we can section them and where we have at least basic facilities to support the neonates?'

'Well, yes and no,' said Greg, appearing to choose his words with care. He was leaning forward, elbows propped on his knees, his blue eyes holding Kirsty's with an almost magnetic pull. 'In the hospital, the child will have a reasonable chance of survival, but after that? You know that many neonates require intensive nursing for many months. We can't offer that here. They will have access to that kind of care if they can make it to the city. Not many do.'

Kirsty still couldn't quite believe what she was hearing.

'You can't possibly be suggesting we do nothing in these circumstances. It's our job, for God's sake. I for one could never stand back when I could help. And you can't ask me to.'

'No one is suggesting you do nothing. What I am suggesting is that we put the mother's life first—think of the implications surgery might have on her. What if she has one C-section, but then in subsequent pregnancies doesn't make it to the hospital in time, and her uterus ruptures and she dies? What of her unborn child then? More importantly, what of the children she has already? This country has been decimated by AIDS. There are already too many orphans even for the extended families to cope with.'

Kirsty sank back in her chair. Although instinctively she hated and rejected everything Greg was saying, she tried to see it from his point of view. But she couldn't. She hadn't become a doctor to stand back when she could help. But she remembered her father's words with a shiver—*You become too emotionally attached, Kirsty*—and he hadn't been the only person to say these words to her. She looked around at her colleagues. Why wasn't anyone arguing with him? Was this what happened when you worked in places like this? You became immune? You stopped thinking with your heart?

'So we just stand back,' Kirsty said, 'and do nothing.'

'We do what we can, Kirsty, but...' Greg stood, implying that as far as he was concerned the conversation was at a close. 'Whatever we do, we do it because it is best for our patients. Not because it's best for us. Now you are here, remember always to ask yourself the question, "Am I treating this patient because it will make the patient better or because it will make me feel better?"'

Kirsty opened her mouth to argue with him. Even if everyone else seemed to accept everything he said as gospel truth, she saw no reason why she should. *Except he has more experience than you*, the rational voice in her head argued, *years more experience. But*, the other more persistent voice argued back, *he's emotionally distant. Whatever happened to him in the past has removed his ability to care. And that can't be right either.* Before Kirsty could find the words to argue with him, Greg put his empty wineglass down and headed towards the door.

'If you'll excuse me. I had an early start this morning and I have another one tomorrow. Remember you're coming to the one of the clinics with me tomorrow, Kirsty. We leave at 6 a.m. sharp.' And then, with a goodbye to the others in the room, he was gone.

Kirsty turned to Sarah, who was gathering up Calum's belongings.

'Do you agree with him? You can't possibly believe that we should ever stand back and not use our medical skills whenever we can. That we act like we are gods, deciding who we should help and when.'

'I don't think that's what he meant at all, Kirsty,' Sarah said quietly, rising to her feet and passing her sleeping child to Jamie. 'Once you get to know Greg you'll know he always acts in the best interests of his patients. No matter how difficult that can be.

'What he's trying to say is that every day we face diffi-cult choices here. Choices we never thought we'd have to make. Sometimes we have to make decisions that go against everything we have learned up until now. That's why we discuss cases with each other, ask each other for an opinion, a point of view. Nobody, least of all Greg, is asking you to make those kinds of decisions alone. Not until you've gained enough experience and confidence, and that will take time. A week or two, at any rate.' She smiled and Kirsty hoped that it meant she was joking.

'Don't tease her, SJ,' Jamie admonished gently, winking at Kirsty. 'We'll be here to help and advise you for a lot longer than a couple of weeks. Greg and I have both spent a long time working in these conditions and we still run situations past each other—there is no shame in that. Where doctors do get themselves into difficulty is when they don't seek advice, but I'm sure you aren't that kind of doctor.' Jamie cocked an eyebrow in her direction.

For a second Kirsty felt flustered. What was he implying? But then, just as quickly, the moment passed. There was no malice in either Sarah or her husband. It was

simply that she was feeling overly sensitive. All of a sudden
a wave of fatigue engulfed her. Although it wasn't quite ten
in the evening, she was exhausted. Normally at this time
she'd be getting ready to go to some club with Robbie or
some of her friends. Here, however, all she wanted to do
was crawl into bed and drag the covers over her head.

'I guess it's another thing I have to adapt to in Africa,'
Kirsty replied, with a self-conscious smile. 'And I certainly hope I never become the kind of doctor that feels
above asking a colleague for advice or an opinion.'

Sarah nodded. 'There's a lot to take in when you come
here, but I can tell you're going to fit in just fine.'

Kirsty stifled a yawn as she said goodnight to everyone.
It had been an interesting evening, she mused as she made
her way back to her rooms. She had been worried that
Greg would still have been annoyed with her, but to her
relief it seemed as if he had totally forgotten her earlier faux
pas. Oh, well, she decided, tomorrow was another day and
she had no doubt that it was going to be as challenging as
today had been. As long as she didn't say the wrong thing
again in front of Greg, Kirsty ruminated, although a tiny
voice wondered why the thought of upsetting Greg should
bother her so much.

The Jeep rattled its way over the dusty and bumpy dirt
roads. They had left the tarred road almost an hour before
and this road showed no sign of ever coming to an end.
Kirsty almost felt travel-sick from being bounced around
like a sack of potatoes. But there was no way she was
going to complain.

Greg had knocked on her door at five-thirty that
morning, just as she had emerged from the shower.

Wordlessly he had held out a flask of coffee and bowl of fruit salad.

As she had stood at the door, her hair wrapped in a towel turban and her thin dressing-gown clinging to her still damp body, she'd noticed Greg's appreciative look as he'd taken in her curves.

Seconds later she'd thought she must have imagined it. Greg's eyebrows had drawn together as he'd frowned at her.

'I thought at the very least you'd be dressed by now,' he said shortly. 'When you didn't appear for breakfast I thought I'd better check you were up.'

'I am not in the habit of sleeping in. For heaven's sake, Dr du Toit, I thought we'd agreed that you were going to stop treating me as if I were a child. And,' she added quickly, seeing him open his mouth to interrupt, 'I'm afraid that checking that I'm up and ready for work counts. As does making sure I'm fed.'

He had the grace to look slightly sheepish. He gave a lopsided smile and Kirsty was dismayed to feel her heart somersault.

'I know we agreed, but then I realised I hadn't told you the village was a good couple of hours' drive away, and it might be a few hours after that before we get something to eat.'

Kirsty smiled to let him know he was forgiven. It had been longer than she cared to admit, even to herself, since anyone had considered her needs.

'I'll just throw some clothes on if you want to come in. I haven't sorted my hairdryer so I'll just plait my hair. All in all it'll take me five minutes.' She was about to turn and head for her bedroom when she remembered the coffee. She took it from his unresisting grip.

'The kettle's just boiled for my coffee. We can keep this for the journey.'

Now all she longed for was a cold drink of water. Her mouth felt as if a herd of elephants had set up home. The dust from the dirt road had penetrated everywhere.

She and Greg were alone in the Jeep. The nurse who was to accompany them had left earlier with Thandi and Johan, who had been responsible for drilling the wells. Greg had explained that they all stayed a few miles away from the hospital compound and it was easier for them to travel together.

'I don't know why I bothered showering,' Kirsty muttered, 'and as for washing my hair, well…'

Greg's glance at her was fleeting.

'You'll get used to it.'

'I'm sure I will.' She looked around at the sunburnt ochre hills that gave the dust its reddish hue. 'It is beautiful. Stark, but beautiful. You can imagine it being like this since the beginning of time. Oh, look!' In her excitement she tugged at Greg's arm. 'Over there!'

In the distance a herd of buck, as graceful as ballerinas, danced across the veld. Every so often they would soar into the sky as if for the sheer joy of it.

Greg grinned. 'Impala.' He looked at her intently, as if struck by something.

'I think I must have been here too long. I've become so accustomed to the beauty of Africa I have stopped seeing it. You'll have to visit one of the game reserves when you have time off,' he said.

'Do I get time off?' Kirsty said, feigning disbelief. And just as Greg's brows drew together she winked at him. Suddenly he laughed, sounding surprised.

'Touché,' he said.

A short time later the Jeep drew into the village. A group of children came running towards them, yodelling and laughing. Women with baskets of firewood balanced precariously on their heads walked between small huts made of mud. Kirsty couldn't imagine how the women managed to balance the heavy loads on their heads as if they weighed nothing. They could teach the catwalk models of New York a thing or two, she thought.

Over to one side Kirsty saw a makeshift tent where a number of women and children squatted patiently. Kirsty could make out the tall figure of Sister Matabele as she weighed babies and small children. While she took in the scene around her, she helped Greg to unload the Jeep.

'This is one of the more fortunate villages,' Greg informed Kirsty as they carried supplies of vaccinations and medical equipment over to the tent. 'Operation Health finished putting in a well here a couple of weeks ago. For the first time ever the villagers have access to fresh water all year round. Not just for drinking and cooking, but for bathing and washing clothes. At this time of year the streams have all but dried up and the water is sluggish and contaminated, and in the past, for lack of any other options, they were forced to bathe and wash clothes in what little water there was, then use the same water to drink. Now, however, they have enough clean water for all their needs, including irrigation. Now they can grow crops.' He pointed to a group of women bent low in the distance. 'See there? That will be their first real crop of mealies and vegetables. Starvation and gastroenteritis will soon be a thing of the past.' Kirsty could see how pleased he was. 'Clean water and education, that's what really makes the difference.'

'Where are all the men?' Kirsty asked. Apart from one

or two elderly men sitting by the doors of the huts, it was mainly women and children in the village.

'They leave for the cities. It's where the work is, and the money. Some send money back, but often that eventually dries up and the women are left to do what they can.' As they had been talking they had been setting out their supplies on a table. Greg snapped on a pair of gloves.

'OK, Kirsty, we'll start at the beginning of the queue. Nurse Matabele has already triaged the patients. When I first arrived at the hospital a child died while the mother was waiting her turn.'

'How awful,' Kirsty said, aghast. 'How on earth could that have happened? Why didn't she insist on being seen earlier?'

'The child had already been ill for a week. Then the mother walked with the child for four days to get to the hospital. I guess she thought everything would be all right if she just waited her turn. The women aren't used to making a fuss. So now we make sure all the patients are triaged when we do these outlying clinics. Maybe this way we can save one or two who might otherwise have died.'

For a moment Greg looked into the distance. Maybe he wasn't so good at keeping his emotions tightly under control after all. But there was no more time for talk. Kirsty and Greg divided the patients between them. Soon it became obvious that the easier patients had been allocated to Kirsty: the children and elderly who needed vaccinations or vitamins. But quickly Kirsty became immersed in the steady stream of patients, who, just like those they saw in the hospital clinic, waited patiently, grateful for the smallest effort. Kirsty found it very humbling. More than once, confronted with the desperate poverty and deprivation, she had cringed, recalling her lifestyle back in the UK. She had taken so much for granted. How often had she spent more on a pair of shoes than most here had to spend on food for months?

During an examination of an elderly woman Kirsty became aware of a nurse by her side.

'Dr Greg asks if you can go over to him,' the nurse said. 'I'll see to these patients in the meantime.'

Kirsty found Greg examining a boy of about three or four.

She drew in a sharp intake of breath when she saw the young boy's arms. They were covered in burns, at least second-degree, Kirsty thought, and the right arm had swollen grotesquely from just above the elbow to the fingertips. Greg was asking the boy, who stood with wet eyes, to try and flex his fingers. The child was finding it impossible.

'Dr Boucher,' Greg greeted her, barely glancing up. 'I would be interested to hear what you think of the case.' He said something to the nurse aide who scurried off.

'This little chap—Mathew is his English name—pulled a paraffin heater over onto himself a couple of days ago.' He went on, 'His mother took him to the local healer who prescribed some herbs which haven't improved matters. What do you think?' While he was talking he pulled a packet of sweets from his pocket and proffered them to his patient, who took them with a shy smile of thanks.

Kirsty felt her stomach clench as she examined the boy. There were some burns to the chest, but they were mainly superficial. He had also been splashed with the burning paraffin on the lower part of his face. It was his arms that had been most badly affected. To make matters worse, the burns had blistered and were badly infected. Kirsty knew that the burns on their own were significant, but add infection to the equation and the boy's chances of a full recovery were severely diminished.

'Second-, possibly third-degree burns to the arms and face. First-degree burns to the chest. The arms are infected and clearly Mathew has restricted movement in his right hand.' Kirsty made notes as she called out her assessment.

Kirsty looked at Greg when she had finished and was surprised to see his jaw clenching, his mouth set in a grim line. As he looked down at his own hand, flexing it and failing to achieve full inflection, Kirsty knew he was reminded of his own injuries.

'Why didn't she bring him to us at the hospital when it first happened?' Kirsty asked. 'He needs to be started on IV antibiotics and hospitalised straight away to get that infection cleared up. As for his hand…' she shook her head, averting her eyes from the mother '…it's possible that he may have lost full use permanently.'

'And how was his mother going to get him to hospital? It's thirty miles away at a guess and she would have had to carry him every step of the way. At least the healer lives in her village. She knew we were coming today and decided to wait. We can't blame her for doing what she thought was best. However, you're right—he does need to be in hospital, but first we have to sort out that hand.'

The nurse aide returned, carrying a procedure pack which she opened while Greg spoke in quiet, urgent tones to the mother. It was only when Greg picked up a scalpel that Kirsty realised with horrified fascination what he was about to do.

'You can't operate here,' she said.

'I can and I will. If you don't want to watch, go back to your patients, otherwise hold the boy's arm firmly for me.'

'But without anaesthetic, without analgesia? He's only little, Greg,' Kirsty pleaded.

Greg looked at her steadily. 'You need to trust me on this, Kirsty. But if you want, you can leave now. If you stay, I need to know I can rely on you. Can I?'

For a moment Kirsty held his eyes. Did she trust him? As a doctor, unquestionably. It was only his apparent lack of compassion that bothered her. Was he immune to the suffering and pain he was about to inflict on this child who gazed up at him with unwavering trust? Had his own experiences blunted him to the point where the outcome was all that mattered?

As if he could read Kirsty's mind, Greg said gently, 'It won't hurt him, I promise you. The burns are so deep the nerves have been damaged. If I thought that it would hurt him, or if there was any other way, believe me, I would take it. But if there is any chance at all of saving function in the hand, I have to do this here and now.'

Kirsty nodded, knowing it mattered little to Greg what she thought.

Smoothly, without the slightest hesitation, Greg drew the scalpel across the charred skin along the length of the boy's forearm. Immediately the flesh parted, revealing the pink muscle underneath, and the hand began to lose its dusky hue.

Mathew flinched, but more out of surprise, Kirsty realised, than pain.

Greg straightened. 'That will do for the time being. When we get him to hospital, we can tidy things up.'

Once more Kirsty could detect bleakness in his eyes. She wondered if she'd misread him. Could it be that he wasn't as detached from his patients as he'd have her

believe? Or was it just this little boy with his horrible burns
in particular? Did he remind him of his own child?

'I'll go back with him if you like,' Kirsty volunteered,
as she sought a vein in an undamaged limb for a drip. The
nurse began bandaging the boy's burns. Once she had
finished dressing his burns and they had started him on IV
antibiotics, it would just be a matter of keeping him comfortable and pain-free until they got him to the hospital.

'No,' Greg said abruptly, without looking up from his
notes. 'Sister Matabele will go with him. She has more experience.' He looked up just in time to notice Kirsty wince.
'It's for the best, Kirsty,' he said not unkindly. 'You need
to be here so you can learn. With me to keep an eye on you.
The child needs to be in the safest pair of hands. It means
that you'll have to do what Sister Matabele would have
done, as well as helping me.'

How patronising, Kirsty fumed, but knew better than to
argue. It wasn't as if Greg was asking her. It was clear that
as far as the job went he was in charge and would brook
no arguments. Everyone would do as he said or heaven
help them.

Kirsty worked tirelessly throughout the rest of the afternoon. Despite the new well, there were still children and
adults suffering the long-term effects of malnutrition.
There were also sores which had turned septic and a large
number of patients requiring antibiotics.

Greg worked alongside her, checking her diagnoses
without implying that he had any reservations about her
medical skills. Often he would catch her eye and nod encouragement. Kirsty could feel her confidence growing
under his supervision. Although there were some occasions
when she had to ask for his help, he was always patient.

Whatever else she thought of him, Kirsty realised she had found a fine teacher in Dr du Toit.

It was mid-afternoon by the time the last patient had been seen and Kirsty's stomach was beginning to growl with hunger.

'Food?' she suggested to Greg and laughed at his look of surprise. 'Whatever you might think,' she said, 'I do like to eat.'

'Is it that time already?' Greg asked. He sniffed the air appreciatively. 'Mmm, I think lunch is ready.'

They had no sooner finished clearing up when one of the women called them over to a circle of logs, arranged as seats, around a fire. In the centre a buxom woman with a wide smile stirred a large black pot suspended over the burning coals. Kirsty and Greg and the rest of the team were urged to sit by the woman and were handed battered tin plates.

Greg and Kirsty shared one of the logs. Given Greg's large frame, it was a tight fit and she was uncomfortably conscious of his muscular thigh against hers. For some reason her heart was beating faster than usual. Just the heat and hunger she reassured herself.

'Are we going to eat their food?' Kirsty whispered, perturbed.

'Why?' Greg asked. 'Not to your cosmopolitan taste?' The frown was back. 'You'll eat it whether you like it or not.'

'Good God, Dr du Toit,' Kirsty said exasperated, 'of course it's not the food. I love trying new tastes. It's just…' his eyes followed hers as she looked around the village '…they don't seem to have enough for themselves, let alone us. Couldn't we have brought something with us?'

She smiled her thanks as one of the women ladled a

thick stew and some white stuff that looked like a mix between porridge and rice onto her tin plate.

Greg turned to face her and his face relaxed into a smile. Once again Kirsty was aware of her pulse going out of kilter.

'We did bring food. And it was gratefully received. But it's important to the villagers that they share what little they have with us. They are a proud people and it's the only way they can thanks us. You have to trust me on this.'

'I have to trust you on a load of things,' Kirsty said. But she too smiled to show there were no hard feelings. 'But what exactly is it I'm about to eat?' she whispered

'Oxtail stew and mealie pap, a type of porridge made from maize meal,' Greg answered. 'Mealies are the staple food in this part of Africa, eaten at every meal. It grows fairly easily, given a water supply. And it's nutritious and cheap. Try some with a bit of the stew.'

Kirsty did as he'd suggested and was pleasantly surprised. The porridge didn't taste of very much on its own, but with the stew it was tasty enough. Besides, she was ravenous. She would have eaten almost anything.

Greg ate with the same concentration and efficiency he seemed to do everything. She decided that now was not the time for small talk and instead let her gaze travel around the village. Most of the work had stopped for lunch and the villagers sat around in groups, chatting and casting openly curious looks in Kirsty's direction. A group of children ran through the village, squealing happily as they used sticks to propel old tyres and race each other. Kirsty wondered absent-mindedly where the tyres had come from. Apart from the clinic's and the Operation Health's cars, there were no other vehicles in sight.

She handed her empty plate back to one of the women,

indicating with sign language that, no, she wouldn't take any more, she was full up, it was quite delicious and thank you so much. Greg was deep in conversation with Johan and Thandi from Operation Health so Kirsty thought she might take the opportunity to explore.

Just as she stood, she was startled by a high-pitched cry as one of the women who had been peeling vegetables dropped her knife and clutched her hand.

Before anyone else could react, Kirsty was at the stricken woman's side. The woman was on her feet, moaning with pain. 'Let me see,' Kirsty said, putting out her hand. 'Please,' she said as the woman hesitated.

'Stop right there.' Greg's voice halted her in her tracks. Her hand froze mid-air. She turned to see him striding towards her while pulling on latex gloves. 'Don't touch her, Dr Boucher,' he said as he reached them. Kirsty let her hands drop to her sides. What had she been thinking? She watched as Greg quickly examined the woman's hand. 'It will need suturing,' he said to Kirsty. 'Which you can do, once you have double-gloved.'

'Of course,' she said, feeling the colour rush to her cheeks. 'I'm sorry. It was an instinctive reaction.'

'You never ever touch anyone, particularly someone who is bleeding, unless you are double-gloved,' Greg ground out between clenched teeth. 'The risk of infection is too great. Surely you were taught that?'

'Yes, of course, but…' Although Kirsty knew there was little she could say in her defence, at least he should understand it had been a normal reaction to another human being in distress.

'No buts. It's not only your own life you put at risk but

your patients'. Remember that. Now, let's get this hand
sutured.' Before she could reply he had walked off.

Kirsty felt her eyes smart, followed quickly by a wave
of anger. That kind of attitude had gone out with the ark,
surely. But she knew she had almost made a mistake and
was deeply embarrassed. Just when she thought she was
making a good impression—a medical impression that
was, of course. She didn't care what other sort of impression she had been making—or did she? Why else would
she feel as if she had taken a blow to the solar plexus? Did
it really matter what Greg thought of her—apart from her
medical skills? Unfortunately a little voice was saying that
it did. It was beginning to matter a whole lot more than
Kirsty would have thought possible.

Later, the vehicles were packed and ready for the return
journey. The sun was beginning to drop in the sky and
if they wanted to make it back to the hospital compound
before dark, Greg knew they should get going. He looked
around for Kirsty, realising the last he had seen of her
had been when she had gone off to suture the woman
with the knife wound, but that had been a long time ago.
He felt a little guilty about earlier. He had been a bit
brusque after what had been a genuine attempt to help.
But, damn it, he wanted her to do well. There was something about that look in those green eyes, a look of
defiance mixed with vulnerability, that seemed to be
getting under his skin. Why she seemed to have this
effect on him, he had no idea. He had worked with count-
less doctors before and had never been drawn to any of
them the way he was drawn to Kirsty. It had been one of
his unwritten rules—never get involved with his junior

colleagues. He wasn't above having affairs, but never with his medical subordinates.

Suddenly the full realisation of what he'd been thinking hit him. He had been thinking of Kirsty as a woman he'd like to have in his bed. She was someone who was beginning to make him think that some rules could be broken. He almost groaned aloud. Kirsty Boucher was becoming a complication he could do without. Maybe he should try and convince her to go home. After all, he'd be doing her a favour. She obviously wasn't cut out for the harsh reality of Africa. She'd be much better off back in the UK in a city hospital, close to friends and family. And he, if not the hospital, would be better off without her, too. But for now he needed to find her and take her home.

CHAPTER FIVE

GREG eventually found Kirsty where he least expected to find her, in the fields, working alongside the women who were back at work, planting the next season's crops. The stillness was punctuated by the sound of the women singing, their beautiful ululating voices carrying through the air. Every now and again one of them would break off and bend towards Kirsty with a laugh and correct her movements. Kirsty had rolled up her khaki chinos to protect the bottoms from the damp soil. But her once crisply white blouse was now more of a pinkish brown and she had undone a couple of extra buttons against the heat.

Greg was dismayed to find himself stir as she bent, copying the women's actions and offering him a tantalising glimpse of her breasts. He called out to get her attention. She looked up at the sound of his voice, pushing a strand of auburn hair away with the heel of her hand. The gesture left a grubby smear across her cheek. Greg had to fight hard to resist the temptation to rub the mark away with a finger. Her face was glistening with her efforts, her cheeks flushed, and she was ruefully examining a broken nail, but Greg thought she looked more beautiful than ever.

'I hope you don't mind, but I thought, since we had

finished work and you still had unfinished business, I would lend a hand here.' She indicated her companions with a sweep of her hand. 'They have all been so patient with me and have been trying to teach me the odd word here and there.'

'It's time to go if we want to get back before dark.'

'I'd like to stay a little longer. We're almost finished. We've only got a couple more rows.' She looked so determined Greg didn't have the heart to refuse her, even if it meant they were late leaving.

'OK, then,' he said, pulling off his shirt to expose tanned skin and well-developed muscles. 'I'll help. That way, we'll be finished quicker.' Ignoring the giggles of the women, he took a hoe from one of them and set about furrowing rows with a will.

Thirty back-breaking minutes later they had finished. Kirsty looked down at her hands in horror. It would take a week of Shona's sought-after manicures to get her blistered hands back into shape. And what had been one lamented broken nail had turned into four. She looked up from her doleful scrutiny of her hands to find Greg's eyes on her, his expression inscrutable except for—surely it couldn't be—a flash of approval in his eyes.

'Let's get going,' he said gruffly. 'We've wasted enough time as it is.'

'I need a moment to wash,' Kirsty said. 'I couldn't bear the journey home caked in this dust. And I'm pretty sweaty, too. I don't think I'll make a very pleasant passenger.'

The expression in Greg's eyes changed. This time Kirsty could have sworn she saw a glint of amusement.

'Fancy a quick shower before we leave?'

This was a sudden change of heart, coming from Greg.

Kirsty frowned, dismissing her suspicions. She did need to wash and cool down.

'OK, then. Come with me. I'll show you how we shower African style.'

He led her over to one of the few trees that provided shelter to the villagers from the worst of the sun. Kirsty could see that some sort of rope and bucket contraption had been rigged in one of the trees but, nonplussed, she looked around for even the suggestion of a shower.

'Wait here.' Greg led her by the arm to a spot beneath the tree.

Kirsty did as she was told, glad even for the limited relief from the heat the shade of the tree offered.

Then, without warning, she was soaked in icy cold water that was falling from above her. Spluttering and gasping, she could see Greg grinning broadly. Suddenly she was furious. She stormed up to Greg, grabbing an abandoned blanket from a rock as she passed.

'Highly amusing, I'm sure,' she said through gritted teeth. 'I wanted a shower but not fully dressed or in full view of everyone. Have you not had enough fun at my expense?'

'I'm sorry. I shouldn't have sprung it on you, but it is how we all shower in the bush. Usually with fewer clothes on, it has to be said.'

'Not funny.' Kirsty glared, aware that she was the object of much amusement as all the villagers looked her way. A group of children pointed, covering giggles behind small hands. As quickly as it had come, the anger left her. She did feel wonderfully cool. And her clothes were already beginning to dry. 'I'll get you back one day,' she admonished, smiling to show she bore no malice. 'I am a patient woman with a long memory.'

* * *

The sun was setting as they left the village, bathing the roads and hills in a wash of red. The villagers turned out to wave them off, singing and dancing. As she waved back, Kirsty felt a lump in her throat. Africa wasn't turning out the way she had expected. Although in her haste to leave Glasgow she hadn't, if she were honest, given much thought at all to what she had been coming to. It had been a bit of a shock when she had arrived, but she hadn't been prepared for the country and its people getting under her skin.

She turned to the man sitting beside her. In the gathering darkness his scars were almost invisible. Indeed, Kirsty thought she could no longer imagine him without them. To her they had become an essential part of the man. Part of who he was.

But did they remind him of his wife and child every time he looked in the mirror? How could they not?

The dusk gave Kirsty the courage to ask, 'What was she like—your wife?'

For a moment she thought he was going to tell her to mind her own business again, but instead he looked thoughtful. He started to speak, slowly at first, as if the words were painful.

'We met at university. She was studying English and drama and I was a medical student. We both belonged to the fencing club, but she was much better than I could ever be.' He smiled, remembering. 'She was beautiful, but more than that she had an aura about her that drew people to her. She wanted to be an actress, and had already been offered a part in a play in her last year of university, but she fell pregnant and that was that. There was no other way for her except to have our child and support us while I finished my medical degree. She said she could always return to acting when I started earning. But—that wasn't to be. The opportunities never came around again.' He closed his eyes for a brief moment as if to shut away the memories.

He continued, his voice husky with regret. 'I owed her so much. She never complained, never resented the hand life dealt her, even when she was so often alone with our child in those early years while I was completing my training. The hours were horrendous back then. You guys have no idea how much easier you have it today.'

'I know,' Kirsty said. 'But the shorter hours have their own disadvantages. It is much more difficult to get the experience. Most of us feel we're qualified almost before time. We've done about a third of the time our predecessors did, and we don't always feel ready.'

'Is that what brought you out here? I know someone pulled a few strings. I have to be honest, I didn't believe you had the experience for this job. I was against employing you for that reason. And…' he looked sideways at her '…despite your performance so far, I still think I was right.'

Kirsty looked down at her hands. She was gripping them tightly together. She hadn't fully appreciated until now how much she wanted to stay. And not just because of Robbie.

'You have every right to think that,' she said slowly. 'I don't really have enough experience for this job but, as you said last night, none of our training in Western city hospitals can really prepare any of us for working in Third World rural communities. Believe me, I didn't come here to practise my medical skills, although I am desperate to learn as much as I can, but only so I can be of some use. No, I came here because…' As soon as the last words were out of her mouth Kirsty would have done anything to take them back. If Greg knew the true reason she had come, his worst fears about her would be confirmed.

'One of the reasons I came here was because of my father. You've probably heard of him? Professor Keith Boucher?'

Greg shook his head slightly. 'Doesn't ring a bell.'

'Well, you must be one of the few people in the Western medical world who doesn't know who he is.'

'Wait a minute,' Greg said as the penny dropped. 'Professor Keith Boucher.' Of course he knew who he was. He had simply never connected the charismatic world re-knowned professor with the under-confident Kirsty.

'No. I'm afraid I never made the connection. It didn't cross my mind.'

'I can see why it wouldn't,' Kirsty said with a slight twist of her mouth. 'We are nothing like each other.' She paused. 'I hardly saw my father as I was growing up. He was always speaking at one international conference or another or building up his private practice. I wasn't always an only child. My mother and younger sister were killed in a car accident when I was ten. From then on I saw even less of him. It was as if he couldn't bear to be in the same room as me. Sometimes I wondered if he wished it had been me who had died instead of them.' Her voice trembled slightly before she managed to get it under control.

Greg reached across and squeezed Kirsty's hand.

'I'm so sorry, Kirsty.'

'I always felt guilty,' she went on, 'for not dying. Can you believe that?' She glanced across at Greg, who nodded almost imperceptibly. The memories were flooding back. The anguish of losing her mother and sister—then the rejection by her father. The feelings of being alone and unwanted.

'It was as if he no longer had a reason to come home.

So I tried to make him proud of me. I guess I wanted to make him notice me, so I worked hard, got top grades...'

'And became a doctor,' Greg finished for her. 'Not the best of reasons perhaps?'

'I became a doctor *despite* my father, not *because* of my father. Don't you see the last thing I wanted to do was end up in the same field as him? One in which I could only ever be compared unfavourably. Where people would always have unrealistic expectations of me. But in the end medicine was what I wanted to do. I needed to become a doctor. There was no other career that felt right.'

And, Kirsty thought bitterly, it was probably the reason Robbie had wanted to marry her. The reflected glory of being Professor Boucher's son-in-law. If he had really loved her he would have shared her longing to have children. After her lonely childhood, she knew, when the time was right, that she wanted to have at least a couple of kids. Why bother with marriage otherwise? But Robbie, it seemed, had had entirely different plans.

'And your mother? What was she like?' Greg prompted.

'She was also a doctor—I come from a family of high achievers. I didn't see all that much of her either before she died. But at least I knew she loved me,' she said.

Greg looked at her expectantly, waiting for her to go on. But Kirsty decided she had revealed as much of her private life as she was prepared to. Too much, in fact.

'So what about your parents?' she asked, determined to steer the conversation away from herself. She was also genuinely curious about her companion.

'Both alive and well. They live in Cape Town. I don't see them as often as I'd like, but we keep in touch.'

Kirsty fell silent as they drew up outside their living

quarters. She could hardly believe the journey was over. The last couple of hours had flown. Suddenly now they were back she felt shy again, mortified at how easily he had steered the conversation back round to her and embarrassed that she had revealed so much of herself. Had it been because she really needed his good opinion? In the same way she still sought her father's? Or was it because she needed to let him know that she knew what it was like to lose the people you loved most in the world?

Greg leant over to open the door for her and she could feel the heat from his body. For a moment she had the ridiculous notion she could turn towards him and rest in his arms. She'd feel protected there. But in the next instant her head cleared. She didn't need protection. She was more than able to look after herself, despite what everyone seemed to think. And being here, coping—and she *was* coping—was proving it. And as for her and Greg, the idea was laughable. The man was still in love with his wife. That much a blind man, or woman, could see.

'Home,' Greg said. 'I'll see you at dinner?'

Kirsty shook her head. 'I don't think so. I'm still pretty full after that late lunch and, besides, Sarah was going to town and said she'd pick up some supplies for me. I'm sure I'll find something to snack on if I get hungry later,' she said pointedly, before Greg could open his mouth. She was tired, not particularly hungry and for some reason she felt the need to have some time on her own to get her thoughts in order. Talking about her father and thinking about her mother and sister had dredged up feelings that had left her emotionally drained.

'Suit yourself,' Greg said. 'I'll see you tomorrow.' He lingered for a moment, as if about to say something else, but then with a final puzzled look he disappeared into his own house.

Sarah had indeed been shopping and she or someone else had thoughtfully stocked Kirsty's fridge and cupboards with bread, butter, eggs and cheese, as well as fruit, fresh salad, vegetables and pasta. Everything she needed. The house felt cool now that the sun had set and Kirsty shivered a little. She showered and changed into her pyjamas. She thought she'd go to bed with her book. It had been an early start and she knew she could expect a busy day the following day.

No sooner had she found the scene in the detective novel she had started on the flight when the phone rang with an unremitting jangle. Kirsty couldn't ever remember seeing a phone that looked quite as antiquated outside a museum. It was made of black Bakelite and instead of buttons had a handle on the side. If you wanted to make a telephone call you had to rotate the arm several times until someone at the hospital switchboard picked up. You would then be connected. Kirsty hadn't as yet attempted to make a call— after all, who would she ring? She had heard the others complain bitterly about aborted calls and most used their mobiles. She, on the other hand, still needed to get hers modified.

As she picked up the phone she wondered who could be ringing. Perhaps it was Sarah, checking she had got her supplies. With a flicker of dismay Kirsty remembered she had intended to pop over to Sarah's house to thank her. She had simply forgotten in her tiredness.

But it wasn't Sarah's voice she heard. It was Robbie's. Her heart leapt, then fell as she recognised his voice. She wasn't ready to speak to him.

'How did you find me?' she said. 'I made my friends promise not to tell you. Whoever did so had no right.'

'It wasn't any of them Kirsty. It was your father.'

'Dad.' She should have known. He had been unsympathetic when Kirsty had told him that there wasn't to be a wedding. Although she hadn't told him the reason, if he knew anything about her, he'd have known that she wouldn't have broken off her engagement lightly. A father who cared would have supported her decision unquestionably. But he hadn't said much, just made it obvious he disapproved. Yet for the first time she could remember he was getting involved in her life. Once that would have made her happy. Now it made her angry.

'He had no right to tell you either. It's none of his business. If I wanted to speak to you, I would have called.'

'Look here, Kirsty. We need to talk. You never gave me the chance to explain. You just refused to let me near you and then ran off. Come home. We can talk about it. Sort it out. Please, darling, I need you.'

'Need my father more likely,' Kirsty ground out. 'Do you think I haven't realised that he's the reason why you wanted to marry me? Getting a share in his private practice must have seemed like an excellent reason to get married,' she said bitterly.

'My wanting to marry you has nothing to do with your father,' Robbie protested. 'I love you. And you love me. Come home,' he said again, 'so we can sort this all out.'

'You've a funny way of showing someone you love them,' Kirsty said. 'And as for my loving you—well, maybe I thought I was in love with you, but I was mistaken. Maybe I thought I wanted the life you were offering to me, but I'm not so sure now. I just know there is no going back for us. I'm sorry, Robbie. Really I am. But you can't say you didn't bring all this on yourself. I'm pretty certain Dad will honour his promise to involve you in his private practice. He's not the kind of man to allow a small matter like loyalty get in the way of a good business arrangement. So I wouldn't worry on that score.'

The line started to crackle with static electricity, drowning out Robbie's protests. She could just make out the words 'mistake' and 'need to see you' before the line went dead. Kirsty was relieved. There wasn't any point in continuing the conversation. When she had found Robbie in bed with another woman she had thought her heart would break. Until that moment she had believed that she had found someone who loved her unconditionally. How wrong she had been. Robbie's betrayal had made her feel fury, hurt and humiliation in equal degrees. Running away had seemed the only answer. She couldn't have endured seeing him every day at the hospital, knowing that she was the cause of the whispers and sly glances. So she had run away. And it dawned on her she had barely thought about Robbie since she'd arrived! Admittedly there had been too much going on, but perhaps she hadn't been as in love with him as she had thought?

Maybe he had done them both a favour. It was a novel idea, but one that made sense. Perhaps Robbie's actions had prevented her from making the worst mistake of her life.

Kirsty could have only been asleep for a couple of hours when something ran across her face. She jumped out of bed, swatting at her arms and legs in a frenzy lest the wretched beast—whatever it was—was still attached to her. Cursing out loud—she *hated* creepy-crawlies—she did a one-legged dance across the room until she reached the light switch. Even in the full glare of the bare light bulb there was no evidence of her visitor. Heart still pounding, Kirsty made a thorough search of the room, through her bedclothes, under the bed and in the cupboards, but whatever it was had gone. Or so she thought until she looked upwards.

There, on the ceiling, a few feet above her pillow, almost looking at her, was the most enormous and certainly the hairiest spider she had ever seen. She felt ill at the thought that this was what had woken her up. There was no way she could stay in this house with the spider. Had she really thought barely hours ago that she could fall in love with this country? She must have been under the influence of some hallucinatory drug. She just didn't do countries that sheltered spiders that big.

Looking at her watch, she confirmed the time. It was almost midnight. What was she to do?

Seeking a weapon, her eyes alighted on the floor brush. It wasn't much, but perhaps she could use it to chase the spider out of her house. She didn't particularly care where it went as long as it wasn't within two hundred feet of her. Carefully manipulating the brush, she nudged the spider with the handle. At first it refused to budge and then without warning it dropped to the floor before scuttling over her foot. Kirsty screamed, thrashing frantically at her feet. Before she could recover, Greg appeared in her room, bare-chested, tugging at the zip of his jeans.

'What the hell's going on?'

'A spider—huge.' She gestured, with the broom clenched defensively in front of her. 'I think it's hiding under the bed.'

Her eyes slid briefly to Greg as he let out an incredulous snort of laughter.

'A *spider?* God, Kirsty, I thought you were being murdered.'

'It's enormous,' she said, backing out of the bedroom, still holding the broom. 'I've never seen anything like it.'

Greg's lips twitched. 'All that noise because of a spider?'

'Believe me,' Kirsty said indignantly, 'this was no ordinary spider. It's clearly mutated or something. It's at least the size of a rat.' She shivered with revulsion.

His eyes crinkled and the small smile broadened into a grin. Flustered, she dropped her eyes and then became riveted by the sight of his naked torso, muscles taut, the skin golden except for the path of dark hair disappearing below the waistband of his jeans.

'Trust me, big spiders are usually perfectly harmless. It's the small ones you have to watch out for. These are the ones that can be, well, venomous.'

'I don't believe you. And, anyway, I don't care. Either that spider goes or I do. There is no way I'm spending the night with that monster if there's any likelihood it's still under this roof.'

There was no disguising Greg's amusement now. 'You'll have to get used to it, Kirsty. Africa is chock-full of insects. Many of them perfectly harmless.' But when she failed to budge he relented. 'OK, let's see if we can evict your guest so we can all get some sleep.'

Despite an extensive hunt, Kirsty's eight-legged visitor remained elusive. While they searched Kirsty burned with mortification. More evidence, she thought grimly, that she was unsuited to working in Africa. As if he'd needed any more. But it wasn't fair. She couldn't help her phobia. She searched frantically for a solution. No matter how silly and pathetic he thought her, there was absolutely no chance she was spending the night in her house. Perhaps she could intrude on Sarah and Jamie? As a woman, Sarah was bound to sympathise.

'I'm sorry,' Greg said at last. 'We aren't getting anywhere with this. You probably frightened it half to death and it made its escape while the going was good. I'm sure it's more scared of you than you are of it.'

'I don't care what you say. I am not spending the night here.' Kirsty folded her arms across her chest and anyone who knew her well could have told from the mutinous set of her mouth that there was no way she was going to change her mind.

Greg stepped closer, his eyes narrowing. 'Are you suggesting that you sleep at my place?' he asked, a dangerous glint in his eyes.

Kirsty fought the temptation to take a step back. She refused to let this man ridicule or intimidate her. He must already think that she was some pathetic female who liked nothing better than to lean on a strong man's shoulder. Unfortunately, she shuddered, it was easy to see how he might have gained that impression.

'Don't be ridiculous,' Kirsty replied indignantly. 'I said I had a phobia about spiders, not that I was off my head. It'll take more than a spider—no matter how huge—to get me into bed with you,' she said, her temper rising. The moment the words were out she wished she could have bitten them back. The man was still her boss after all, although thinking of him as anything other than a sexual predator was proving difficult.

Greg raised an eyebrow. 'Who said anything about

getting into bed with me? I meant stay at *my place,* that was all. Although now that you suggest it, maybe that's not such a bad idea.' His eyes raked over her body.

Once again Kirsty felt the hot tide of embarrassment suffuse her body. She had forgotten that she was wearing very little, and self-consciously brought her arms up to cover her body. Quickly she scooped her lightweight dressing-gown from the bottom of the bed.

Idiot, idiot, idiot, she berated herself mentally. Was there any way at all she could give Greg a worse impression of her?

'I was suggesting no such thing,' she said hotly, shrugging into the gown, after giving it a thorough shake. Luckily, before she could say anything more she noticed the wide grin on Greg's face. It was amazing how humour transformed his face. She hadn't thought of him as having a sense of humour. Up until now he had seemed, well, a little taciturn.

'OK, OK. You've had your fun at my expense—yet again,' she said, attempting a grin of her own. Maybe she could convince him she had been kidding, too?

However, *nothing* was going to make her sleep in this room. She would keep vigil in one of the chairs in the sitting room. Naturally there wasn't anything as civilised as a sofa in her accommodation. She could always curl her feet underneath her. In the morning she'd get someone, anyone, to give the house a clean sweep from top to bottom.

Greg must have seen her uncertainty. He assumed the slightly exasperated expression that she seemed to inspire.

'You have my bed,' he said. 'Alone,' he added pointedly, as Kirsty started to object. 'I'll sleep here. In yours. At least, that way we'll both get some rest some time tonight. I don't think there are any monster spiders in my house—

but I'm afraid that's a chance you'll have to take. Unless, of course, you'd rather I kept you company, although I can't guarantee you'd actually be protected from danger.' Once more the amused look was back, but this time there was something else, something that Kirsty couldn't quite read.

'That's very kind of you,' she said stiffly. 'If you're sure you don't mind having my bed for the night?' She lifted her chin. 'I am well aware that you find this perfectly ridiculous and completely incomprehensible. I can only assure you, that it won't happen again. Now, if I can just collect my toothbrush, and I'm sure there are one or two things you'll need from your place, I'll say goodnight and let you get some sleep.'

'I don't need anything. I was in bed when I heard you scream,' Greg replied. 'I'm pretty bushed. All I want right now is a bed and a few hours' sleep.'

'Goodnight, then, Dr du Toit,' Kirsty said politely as she left the room, knowing all the while it was far too late to try to remind them both of their professional relationship.

Hours later Greg was still wide awake. He had thought he'd fall sleep the minute his head hit the pillow, but he hadn't allowed for the fact that the faint scent of Kirsty's perfume and the memory of her half-naked body was doing things to his libido that he truly resented. It had been a while since he had taken a woman to his bed—he was no saint, but on principle he never had affairs with colleagues—and there was something about Kirsty, a vulnerability that made her untouchable as far as he was concerned. The women he had slept with had all known the score, that he would never marry or have children again. He would never risk the pain of loss again. Anyway, no one could replace Kathleen. He would always love her.

Or did he? His thoughts turned to Kathleen, as they did so often. Lately he had been able to think of her without the gut-wrenching anguish he'd once experienced. The guilt was still there—God knew, it would stay with him the rest of his life. Not just guilt that he had been unable to save them but guilt that he hadn't spent more time with them when he'd had the opportunity. Guilt that she had abandoned her dreams for him and their child. 'I have everything I want right here,' she used to say. 'There will be plenty of time later for acting. I can always play the mother-in-law if I get too old.' She would laugh, looking up at him with her soft brown eyes. And his child, his beloved Rachel—he had missed so much of her growing up. He had always thought there would be time. If only he had known how little time there was going to be.

Cursing, Greg abandoned sleep and Kirsty's bed and strode to the window. There were no streetlights here, but the light from the moon and the sprinkle of stars lit the sky.

He breathed in the cool scent of frangipani that drifted through the open window. He loved this place, and he had found some measure of peace living and working here. Although the lack of proper facilities was frustrating, he knew that his medical skills were making a difference in a way they wouldn't anywhere else. Until Kirsty had stumbled into his life he had thought he was reasonably content. Not happy—he didn't expect to be happy ever again—but content. Now he was aware that there was something missing in his life, something that niggled at him like an itch that needed to be scratched. Maybe that was it? Greg wondered. He should break his rules, bed Kirsty, and then perhaps the irritating itch would be gone. But somewhere deep in his soul he knew it wasn't quite that simple.

CHAPTER SIX

KIRSTY left Greg's house just as the sun was beginning to rise. She had thought she wouldn't be able to sleep in the disconcertingly masculine surroundings, but she had quickly fallen into a deep, dreamless sleep. She had felt safe in Greg's bed. She smothered a laugh. She was pretty certain nothing would dare enter without an invitation!

Her curiosity had got the better of her that morning, so she had taken a few moments to explore Greg's home. There had been little to see. It was the exact reverse of hers, with no personal items to show who lived there except for a single framed photograph. She had picked it up to examine it more closely and had recognised Greg, a smile on his scar-free face. He had an arm around a woman with a little girl on her lap. The woman could only be his wife. Her long black hair framed a delicate face. She was beautiful with an impish expression, as if she held a naughty secret. The child was instantly recognisable as Greg's. The forget-me-not blue eyes could only be his. The little girl was looking up at her parents with an expression of such utter happiness and trust it made Kirsty's heart ache. How could he bear it? she wondered.

She made the bed and returned to her own house to get

ready for work. She needed to shower and dress before hitting the wards. She showered quickly and, wrapping her hair in a towel, with another one tied round her body, she slipped into her bedroom, tiptoeing so as not to disturb the man who occupied her bed. Greg was still asleep, his long limbs tangled up in the sheet as if he had been fighting demons in his dreams. He clutched a pillow in one arm as if to block out the unwelcome glare of the sun.

Kirsty looked down at him for a moment. In sleep he looked less severe, almost vulnerable, despite the small crease between his eyebrows that made it seem as if he was frowning, even in his dreams. Averting her eyes from his naked limbs, she opened her wardrobe and cringed as the doors creaked. She spun around to find Greg staring at her, his blue eyes alert and unreadable.

'I'm sorry,' she said, 'I didn't mean to wake you. I'll be out of here in a minute and you can get back to sleep.' She gathered up her clothes and made to squeeze past the bed, when without warning Greg's arm shot out and grabbed her arm.

'It's still early,' he said lazily, tugging her towards him. He slid a hand further up her arm and Kirsty shivered at his touch. Powerless to resist, she allowed herself to be drawn downward until he brushed her lips with his. A spasm of lust shot through Kirsty that made her toes curl.

'Do you always have to be half-dressed around me? I'm only human, you know,' he said, his voice low.

Kirsty pulled away from his grip. Surely the man didn't think she was deliberately parading herself in front of him? He must have an even dimmer view of her than she had imagined.

'I had to get my clothes and my watch. You were in my

bedroom so I had to come in. I didn't want to wake you up, otherwise I suppose I could have yelled from outside the door and then waited until you had left my room before I went for my shower.'

'Hey, remember it wasn't me who wanted to swap beds for the night,' Greg said. 'I was perfectly fine where I was until the wail of a banshee brought me running. I don't think I can be blamed for your predicament.'

'What predicament? There is no predicament. Now, would you behave like a gentleman and let me get dressed?'

'Sure,' he drawled. 'It's time I was on the wards anyway.' Greg sat up in bed and made to pull the sheets away. Kirsty backed away, realising that, as Greg obviously slept in the nude, unless she acted pretty darn quickly, she was about to be confronted with his naked body.

'I'll leave you to it,' she said, beating a hasty retreat to the bathroom.

By the time she emerged dressed, Greg had left. Kirsty sat on one of the rickety chairs in her sitting room, sipping her coffee. What just happened there? she wondered. The image of Greg's long naked limbs kept tumbling around her head, along with the memory of his hands on her arm, the touch of his lips. She felt a frisson of heat deep in her belly. For a head-spinning moment she had wanted nothing more than to abandon all caution, accept his invitation and join him in bed. Thank God she had come to her senses in time, but she still felt shaken by the power of her reaction to his touch, to the need she had seen in his eyes. She hadn't responded to a man like this since... Well, now she thought about it—never. Not even to Robbie, she realised with some amazement. *He* had never made her feel as if she wanted nothing more than to be in his bed. Oh, she had enjoyed his love-making, so much so she had imagined herself in love with him, thought she had wanted to spend the rest of her life with him. Now she realised that what she had told Robbie last night on the phone was true. She knew with absolute certainty there would never be a future for them.

She tried to conjure up the image of the man with whom she had planned to spend the rest of her life. She could bring his face into focus, but the features she'd once thought handsome now seemed insipid and weak compared to Greg's. Although Robbie had been good company, always charming and thoughtful, keen to wine and dine her at every available opportunity. Keen to lay material things at her feet. That's what she still wanted, wasn't it? A comfortable, easy life? Why, then, did she find herself comparing Robbie and Greg?

Kirsty stood up and started to tidy away the detritus of her breakfast. It must be the backlash of feeling rejected by Robbie combined with finding herself in a new situation that was making her feel this way. That was all, she told herself firmly. She simply needed to get her hormones under control. Work. That was what she needed. Plenty of honest-to-goodness hard work that left her too exhausted to think of anything else. And, she thought wryly, there was no shortage of that here.

Kirsty eased her aching back and pushed a strand of damp hair from her forehead. A swim would be lovely right now, she thought, but there were still over twenty patients in the clinic waiting to see her.

The days had settled into a routine. Work, then a couple of hours study followed by an early night. She had seen a variety of illnesses, injuries and diseases in the hospital and her confidence was continuing to grow. She had spent time with all the medical staff on the wards, with the exception of Greg, who since the spider episode seemed to be avoiding her. She didn't know whether she was sorry or relieved about that. Mainly relieved, she thought on reflection. For some reason, which she refused to examine too deeply, she felt awkward and tongue-tied in his presence and her heart had an annoying habit of beating a little faster whenever she caught a glimpse of him.

She knew that she had been allocated to the clinic because the nursing staff were very experienced. If she was honest, there wasn't much they couldn't do, and essentially Kirsty was simply another pair of hands. They remained fantastically patient with her and she was learning so much. She hadn't dreamed how much the work would absorb her. There was so much she needed to know, and she found herself furiously reading up on tropical diseases every night after work. She was determined to learn so she could be a real help to her patients and the staff.

Everybody was going out of their way to make her feel supported and every day her admiration grew for all her colleagues who gave so much of themselves to their work. Her life back in the UK seemed shallow by comparison. The thought that she had almost married Robbie dismayed her now. If she had, she would never have known what else life had to offer.

Earlier that day there had been another nasty road accident, with multiple casualties, and all the other doctors were in Theatre, dealing with the aftermath. Once again Kirsty's offer of help was politely but firmly rejected.

'We get one of these most weeks,' Greg said. 'If we stopped the clinic and pulled all the medical staff in every time, the queue at Outpatients would become unmanageable. And as I am sure you are aware, they need to be treated just as urgently as our accident victims.'

'I'd like to assist some time,' Kirsty protested. 'With the way staffing is here, there are bound to be times, especially at night, when you'll need me in Theatre.' So far Kirsty had not been allowed to be on call at night. The others continued to cover it between them.

Greg rubbed a tired hand over his face. He works too hard, Kirsty thought. They all do.

'I know this isn't a teaching hospital, Greg, but you're going to have to let me do my share of nights on call sooner or later. And the more I've assisted, the better prepared I'll be.'

Greg eyed her thoughtfully. 'You're right. It's simply that I wanted to give you enough time to ease yourself in gently before putting you on nights. As you know, Kirsty, we don't have the luxury of staffing that would let us give you the next morning off to catch up on sleep. You would still have to do a full day's work in Outpatients the next day, regardless of how much sleep you'd had. And as I've told you before, an inexperienced doctor is one thing, but an inexperienced and exhausted doctor is another matter all together.'

Kirsty felt inordinately disappointed and not a little indignant at his words. Clearly, as yet, she had not convinced him that she could cope.

'There you go again,' she said crossly. 'Treating me like a child. What about if I do on-call with one of you? I can shadow you, be another pair of hands. That way you'll see I'm tougher than I look. You're on tomorrow night—I could do it with you. I'm not scheduled to work on Saturday or

Sunday, so I'll have plenty of time to recover.' She was determined to get her way.

'Actually, I was going to speak to you about that. Sarah and Jamie are covering the weekend and have insisted that Jenny and I take some time off from the hospital. You see…' he smiled tiredly '…you're not the only one who gets ordered about.' He looked rueful and Kirsty could tell from his expression that there must have been quite a battle. Having spent some time with Sarah, she knew that her colleague could be a force to be reckoned with. Nevertheless, she guessed Jamie had backed up his wife if they had managed to persuade Greg to take time off. She smiled to herself at the thought of Greg getting as good as he gave for once. It was a distinctly pleasant image—let him feel what it was like to be bullied.

'Anyway,' Greg went on, 'Jenny is determined that she and I visit one of the nearby national parks and has suggested you come along too. She says it might be some time before you get the opportunity again, especially once you take your share of being on call.' He raised an eyebrow at her little smile of satisfaction. 'But perhaps you'd rather go to the city for the weekend. Do some shopping? Go to a restaurant, take in a movie? A couple of the nursing staff are going to see family and would, I'm sure, be delighted to give you a lift.'

'I hadn't planned to do anything this weekend,' Kirsty said, 'except possibly more studying. And as for going to the city to shop, spending money on clothes seems impossible under the circumstances.' In fact, Kirsty had given away quite a few of her possessions to some of the patients. There had been more than one young woman who had left with one of Kirsty's favourite brightly coloured scarves or even a T-shirt or skirt. She loved seeing the delight on their faces, even though in the greater scheme of things it was such a small gesture on her part. The women often exclaimed over her hair. The nursing staff explained that most of them had never seen a redhead before. Kirsty was growing accustomed to their curiosity and the fact that the patients liked touching her hair.

'But I'd love to see more of the country,' she went on. 'I've never been to a game reserve before. If you're sure Sarah and Jamie won't need the extra help and you wouldn't mind me coming along. I wouldn't like to intrude.'

'That's settled, then,' Greg said. 'We'll leave on Saturday after the clinic and rounds. It's only about an hour's drive away, so we'll be there in plenty of time to do some evening game viewing. I'm warning you, though,' he cautioned, 'this isn't one of the luxury camps you might have read about. This one's pretty basic. Tents rather than cabins.' Before Kirsty could protest that he was once again talking to her as if she were some kind of spoilt rich kid, he went on, 'I must go. I can hear the ambulances in the distance.' And with that he turned on his heel and left.

Two hours later when Kirsty thought she had seen the last patient of the day, Bounty, one of the nurses, came to her looking perplexed. 'There's another patient for you. He's just turned up. He has come far. Usually at this time I'd send him to our emergency department, but none of the doctors are available. They're all still in Theatre.'

'That's all right, Bounty,' Kirsty said. 'I'm quite happy to see him.'

'I'll bring him in, then,' she said. 'I don't know what can be wrong with him. And if I don't know…' She didn't need to finish her sentence. Kirsty knew what she meant. If the highly experienced nurses didn't know what was wrong, it was unlikely Kirsty would know either. Regardless, Kirsty thought defiantly, she would make her own assessment. If, after that, she couldn't make a diagnosis, then she would call in the troops.

Moments later Bounty ushered in a gaunt-looking man of about forty. His breathing was laboured and Kirsty could see from the dusky hue to his lips that he was struggling to take in enough oxygen. Briefly Bounty filled Kirsty in on the history.

'According to the patient, the breathlessness came on quite suddenly. There's no history of heart or lung problems.' Her brow crinkled. 'His blood pressure is only 70 over 30.'

Kirsty felt a surge of adrenaline. She had to do something—and quickly. He was in imminent danger of collapse, so there was no time to wait for help. She examined him quickly but thoroughly. 'Right, A,B,C,' she told herself. 'Airway, breathing, circulation.' His airway was clear, with nothing obvious causing the breathing difficulties, but there was something odd about his pulse. Every time he gasped for breath, his pulse almost seemed to disappear. Suddenly Kirsty knew exactly what was the matter with her patient.

'It's cardiac tamponade. It's quite rare, so you won't see it very often. But I saw it when I was on a surgical rotation. It fits the pattern. I'm going to have to insert a needle to drain the fluid around his heart.' Kirsty was pleased that this time she was going to be able to teach the nurses something. For once she was going to be of real help.

Quickly Kirsty made her preparations. She asked Bounty to explain to the patient what she was going to do.

Taking a breath to steady herself—she needed to be very precise—she directed the needle upwards from his stomach towards his heart with one single movement. Just as the needle pierced the skin, Greg threw open the door to the treatment room.

'What the hell are you doing?' Although his voice was calm and level, Kirsty could see from the expression in his narrowed blue eyes that he was alarmed. Alarmed and angry. 'I thought I told you to call me if there was anything—'

'We tried to call you. You were tied up in Theatre. Besides, I knew what I needed to do and there was no time to waste.' As she talked, she drew back on the plunger and straw-coloured fluid filled the syringe. Almost immediately the patient's breathing improved and his lips lost their bluish tinge. She emptied the first syringe and filled another before withdrawing it from the chest. As Greg watched in silence, Kirsty turned to the nurse. 'The fluid has been building up around his heart, stopping it from pumping properly. That's why he's been so breathless and his blood pressure low. Now we need to find out what caused it in the first place. Could you send this to the lab for cytology and culture, please?'

'I see I underestimated you,' Greg said finally. 'That was an inspired diagnosis. How did you know?'

'I do know a bit of medicine,' Kirsty responded tartly, before relaxing and grinning broadly. She couldn't quite manage to disguise how pleased she felt with herself. 'Actually, I saw a case like this fairly recently. Pretty impressive, huh?' She blushed, realising that her words could be misconstrued. 'I mean the procedure and the outcome, not me.'

'I think the doctor was pretty impressive, too,' Greg said quietly. 'Never refuse to take credit for a job well done. Maybe there is more of your father in you than you realise, girl.'

Girl? What did he mean, *girl?* He was at it again. Patronising her. Making her feel too young as well as too inexperienced. And what was that remark about her father supposed to mean? Hadn't she made it clear that the last thing she wanted was to be compared with him? Hadn't Greg understood what she had been saying on the drive back from the village?

'Anyway…' she went on, biting down on her anger. She wouldn't let him see that he had infuriated her. Not until she got what she wanted, at any rate. 'Does that mean you'll let me do my share of on-call now?'

Greg laughed. 'OK, you win. You can do tomorrow night with me. On condition that you call me if there's anything at all you're unsure of. And, yes, if there is a case that needs to go to Theatre, you can assist.'

'How very gracious of you.' This time Kirsty couldn't keep the sarcasm from her voice.

'I am trying to protect you as well as the patients, Dr Boucher. This isn't personal, no matter what you think. I'm sure that in a short time you'll be managing fine on your own—most of the time.' Kirsty knew there was little point in arguing. She would just have to continue to prove herself. In time she would make him revise his opinion of her. She couldn't wait to see the mighty Dr du Toit eat his words.

CHAPTER SEVEN

THE next day the whole team managed to gather in the staffroom for lunch. Kirsty was beginning to realise what a rare event this was. The sheer numbers of patients meant that there was always someone in Theatre or on the wards, but today everyone had made it for lunch at the same time and there was almost a party atmosphere.

'I gather you've been enticed away by Jenny and Greg for an overnight stay at Pelindaba Game Park,' Sarah said. 'Lucky you. Jamie and I took Calum there once, but he kept squealing with excitement every time we got close to the animals and frightened them away.' She laughed. 'We didn't make ourselves too popular with the rest of the group. I think we'll have to wait until he's a bit older before we go again.'

'Or perhaps leave him with Sibongele,' Jamie said pointedly. 'It would be nice to get away, just the two of us.'

'He's a bit young yet, Jamie. Not that I don't trust Sibo, but it would be unfair to burden him when he has so much on his plate already,' Sarah protested, and from the looks on their faces Kirsty suspected that this was a discussion that they'd had before. It seemed as if Sarah couldn't bear to be parted from her child, even for a short time.

'I could look after him some time if you'd like,' Kirsty offered.

Sarah looked at her speculatively. 'No offence, Kirsty, but you don't strike me as the kind of woman who has had much experience looking after young children.'

'Well, that's where you'd be wrong,' Greg interjected quietly. Kirsty hadn't even been aware that he'd been listening. 'I've seen her in action with a child, a very frightened and bewildered boy, and she worked miracles with him. I think if you ever left Calum in Kirsty's hands, they would be safe hands indeed.'

Everyone looked at Greg, surprised at his support of Kirsty.

But no one could have been more surprised than Kirsty herself.

'Do you come from a large family, then?' Sarah asked.

Kirsty felt uncomfortably aware that everyone had stopped talking and were now regarding her with interest.

'I'm an only child,' Kirsty said. At least, she was now. 'But I worked at a children's hospice during the university holidays and my last rotation before coming here was in paediatrics. The children seemed to take to me—perhaps it was because I didn't talk down to them.' Kirsty couldn't help slide a pointed glance in Greg's direction. But he seemed oblivious to her hidden meaning.

'Oh, well, perhaps we will take you up on your offer soon. Once Calum has got used to you,' Sarah conceded, earning Kirsty a warm smile from Jamie.

'And we'd all chip in, wouldn't we, Greg?' Jenny added. 'You know I would have offered, Sarah, but as much as I love Calum I'm simply not the maternal type. Never wanted children, and it's probably just as well I never had them. The kids here are more than enough for me.'

'What about you, Kirsty? Do you want children?' Jenny asked

'Yes. Not for a while, but eventually.' Kirsty desperately wanted to steer the conversation away from herself. As much as she liked and trusted her colleagues, she wasn't prepared yet to go into her private life. What she had told Greg had been an aberration, but she felt certain he wouldn't have repeated her confidences.

As if sensing her discomfort, Greg changed the subject.

'I think Kirsty will enjoy the game reserve,' he said. 'I have warned her that it's pretty basic.'

'And pretty close to the wildlife,' Jamie added. 'At night it feels as if you are right in the thick of things. When we were there Sarah was certain a lion was about to have us for supper. She almost made me pack up and leave there and then.'

'I wouldn't have minded so much being eaten as long as you were too, sweetheart, but the thought of Calum being some wild animal's aperitif was a bit much.' Sarah slid a mischievous look Jamie's way.

'It's perfectly safe,' Jenny interjected. 'There is no way the animals can get to you. They're on the other side of an electric fence. It only sounds as if they are close by. It's wonderful,' she continued. 'You really feel part of the bush.'

'Oh, I don't think Kirsty would be frightened of a lion,' Greg said. 'I have a suspicion her fears lie in another direction.' Kirsty shot him a withering look, daring him to go on. But it seemed as if Greg had no intention of sharing her secret. 'I suspect it's the lack of creature comforts that will scare Kirsty off,' he went on, just as she was beginning to feel benevolent towards him.

'I don't know where you get this idea I'm unable to tolerate a bit of discomfort,' Kirsty countered. 'I was in the Guides. And we went camping once.' She didn't add that it had been the camping that had finished the Guides for her, and that after only a couple of weeks. What anyone ever saw in camping was beyond her. Give her a comfy bed, a plasma TV and top-quality toiletries. Add in a spa—now, that was bliss. Or it had been once. Lately she wasn't at all sure if the new Kirsty would find the experience quite as enjoyable as she would once have done. But, still, a tent!

'Does it have to be a tent?' Kirsty said. 'Isn't there anything available that is slightly more upmarket? Even a simple cabin would do me—as long as there was a bed.'

'Don't worry, Kirsty.' Jenny laughed. 'These are tents but not as you know them. They have camp beds and small fridges. There is even a separate bedroom for the two of us. Greg will make do in the main area. They are just like mini-homes. Trust me, you'll find them perfectly adequate.'

'Oh, are we in one tent, then?' Kirsty asked. For some reason the thought of having Greg sleeping under the same roof dismayed her. But, she reassured herself, Jenny would be there.

'They are very spacious. You'll see,' Jenny said, standing. 'Come on, guys, we'd better get moving. Theatre starts in ten. I gather you're to assist Greg with the list this afternoon, Kirsty?'

It was the first Kirsty had heard of it, but at Greg's nod she realised that she must have finally passed some sort of test. 'You'll need as much experience of operating as possible if you are to start doing your own on-call in a couple of weeks,' he said. 'And from what I've seen so far, you're a pretty fast learner.' Kirsty felt her heart lift. It seemed that at last she was being given the chance to prove herself. Surgery was where she had hoped to specialise and although she loved Outpatients, operating was where her heart was.

The afternoon passed quickly. Kirsty found Theatre every bit as interesting as she had hoped.

Her first patient was a woman at full term of pregnancy. She had four children already, the last two delivered by Caesarean section.

'I thought you didn't believe in doing Caesars on the women out here,' Kirsty said as she and Greg scrubbed up.

'I only don't believe in inappropriate Caesars. However, because the patient has had two previously there is a very real danger of her rupturing her uterus if we attempt to let her deliver normally. Happily she has attended the hospital regularly, so we have been able to monitor her closely. She has also decided to have her tubes tied while we are at it. She's content with the size of her family and doesn't want to risk another pregnancy. If you do the section, I'll do the sterilisation and you can assist. Are you OK with that?'

Kirsty nodded. Immediately before her paediatric rotation she had spent six months in surgery. Her consultant had been a patient teacher, happy to let her assist in as many cases as she was able to. Still, this would be the first time she would actually be the primary surgeon.

'Wouldn't you prefer to do it? And I can assist?' Kirsty said, the responsibility suddenly hitting causing her new-found confidence to desert her again.

'You'll be fine doing the op,' Greg said. 'I'll be right beside you, watching you every step of the way. Don't worry, by the time you leave here you'll be able to do them in your sleep. The more practice you get now, the better.

There is a good chance that you may find yourself in a position where you are the only person available to do one in an emergency, so it's best you get as much experience in a controlled situation—where one of us is around to help you out if need be. But, if you'd rather not, that's OK, too.' Greg lifted an eyebrow in question. Kirsty knew that a gauntlet had been thrown down. She had been asking him repeatedly to give her more responsibility. Now she needed to show him that she was ready. And she knew what to do. Silently, she pulled on her face mask and held out her hand for a scalpel.

Greg said very little as she operated on the woman, just watched carefully, ready to step in if Kirsty showed any signs of faltering. But she didn't need his help, although his presence gave her confidence. She took her time and was pleased with the result. Once the baby had been delivered, a healthy boy who had disrupted the quiet of the theatre with his gusty cries, she had swapped sides with Greg and assisted as he had quickly and efficiently tied the woman's tubes. His right hand had shown no indication of being unable to manipulate the scalpel.

As if reading her thoughts, Greg said, 'I used to be a neurosurgeon, but the damage to my hand put paid to intricate brain surgery. Most days my hand is fine, but some days it stiffens up. On good days, which, thank God, are most days, I can still operate, but I leave the very fine or delicate stuff to Jamie. And obviously brain surgery is out of the question. Not that we'd do that here anyway, except if we had no choice in an emergency. We really don't have the facilities.'

'He was one of the best neurosurgeons in the country, and well on his way to gaining an international reputation,'

Jenny said from her position at the top of the table, where she was monitoring the patient's vital signs. 'Still, their loss is our gain.'

Greg looked at Jenny. Above his mask his eyes glittered. 'Jenny exaggerates,' he said. 'However, the teaching hospital where I learned offered some of the best experience in the world in the field. I was very fortunate to have the opportunity to train there.'

Despite the even tone, Kirsty knew it must have been a blow for Greg. Not only had the fire cost him his family, but it seemed it had cost him his career, too.

'You miss it?' Kirsty asked.

Blue eyes turned in her direction. They seemed to drill right through her.

'My life is here now,' he said. He stood aside. 'Would you like to close?'

Kirsty finished stitching the wound in the woman's abdomen before standing back to admire her handiwork.

'You have very neat hands,' Greg said approvingly. 'It seems, Jenny, that we have a surgeon in the making here.'

Kirsty felt a warm glow at his praise. Whatever else she thought of him, he was generous when it came to praise. However, she suspected he'd be equally unstinting with his criticism if he thought it would make her a better doctor. She hoped that she wouldn't find out.

After they finished the list, Kirsty slipped away to check on her first patient. She found the mother in the maternity ward fully conscious and her baby suckling contentedly. Kirsty peered into the blanket, catching a glimpse of long eyelashes that lay against chubby cheeks the colour of dark chocolate. She felt a twinge of longing. She wondered if she would ever know the joy of motherhood. To have children, be a part of a large, happy family. To love and be loved in return. Unconditionally. For herself. She had once thought that was to be part of her future, now she wondered if it was ever meant to be.

Greg had insisted that she take a couple of hours off before making herself available to share the on-call.

'We might be quiet,' he said, 'although, being a Friday night, we do tend to get our share of road accidents and one or two stabbings. As it's your first night, Jenny is going to be second on call. That way we won't have to disturb either Sarah or Jamie if things get busy. They need as much rest as possible before the weekend. And you should get some rest, too, while you can. You're off until nine. After that I'll call you if I need you.'

'What about you?' Kirsty asked. 'When will you get some rest? You've been up since the crack of dawn,'

'I'll have a run then a swim. That's usually enough to recharge my batteries. I find I don't need much sleep.' He stretched and his top rode up, offering Kirsty a tantalising glimpse of his bronzed abdomen. Her stomach flipped. She had a brief memory of him in her bed, his arms circling her waist and his hands on her bare arms, his breath on her face. She couldn't stop herself imagining running her hands over his abdomen, up to his chest, pulling him close.

She shut her eyes in case he read her thoughts. What *was* she thinking? What was it about this man that made her think this way? She had never experienced pure animal attraction before. Had thought it was impossible. How could you lust after someone when you didn't really like them? But, she realised, she was beginning to like Greg du Toit. She was beginning to like him very much indeed.

'OK, I'm off. Enjoy your swim, run—whatever. I'm

away for a shower and a nap. Actually, I might pop over and see Sarah and Calum for a bit first. He is so adorable. And I should let him get to know me in case Sarah and Jamie take me up on my offer of babysitting. I know Jamie would love to have a couple of days with Sarah.' God, now she was babbling. Greg was looking at her as if she were slightly deranged. Kirsty decided that removing herself from his company until she got her wayward thoughts back under control—if she could get them back under control—was by far the most sensible course of action. 'So I'm off,' she repeated, pointing in the vague direction of her house. As Greg's look of confusion deepened, she turned and walked away.

'And don't forget to have something to eat,' Greg shouted after her retreating back. 'I don't want you collapsing with hunger on me through the night because you haven't consumed enough calories.'

Kirsty felt her spine stiffen. There he went again. He really was the most patronising, old-fashioned, sexist man she had ever met. She couldn't imagine him talking to one of the male doctors like that. Maybe she didn't like him so much after all.

Kirsty sat drinking a cup of coffee in Sarah's house. She had showered and tried to nap, but she hadn't been able to relax enough to sleep. So in the end she had decided to do what she had told Greg she might do—go and see Sarah. Perhaps the company of another woman would bring her back to reality.

Calum had been a ball of energy as he'd torn around the house, dragging Kirsty after him. He'd seemed determined to point out every last toy and item of furniture in the house. Sarah had watched fondly with her feet up.

'Thank God you came!' she exclaimed. 'This seems to be a new game. I've been around the house five times this afternoon, trying to explain why a chair is called a chair. Actually, he's learning a few words from Sophie, who looks after him when I'm at work. I'll probably end up learning more of the language from him than from the tapes and books I bought. Never seem to find a spare moment to look at the wretched things.'

'Can I borrow them for a bit, then?' Kirsty asked eagerly. 'I really want to learn, too.'

'Be my guest.' Sarah waved tiredly at the pile of books that lay in a haphazard heap on the coffee-table. 'If you take them, at least I won't have to feel guilty every time I look at them.

'How are things going anyway?' Sarah asked. 'Finding your feet? I hear you've done some great work—with out-patients and in Theatre.'

'Thanks,' Kirsty said with a smile. 'Everyone's been fantastic. Making me feel part of the team. There to offer advice and help when I need it. Particularly Greg.' Kirsty laughed ruefully. 'Although he's been mostly very positive, I'm not so sure he's convinced I'm up to it yet.'

'Greg's a hard taskmaster,' Sarah said slowly, 'but when it comes to making sure the patients receive the best possible care, he doesn't allow personal feelings to get in the way.'

'That's just it,' Kirsty said. 'I'm not sure that he *approves* of me. I still wonder if he'd be happier if I wasn't here—if I gave up, packed my bags and went home, tail between my legs.'

Sarah looked at Kirsty keenly. 'Do you think so? I hadn't got that impression at all. I get the feeling that our Greg is getting used to having you around.'

Before Kirsty had time to consider Sarah's words there was a loud crash from the kitchen, followed by wails of outrage. They both jumped to their feet and ran into the kitchen to find Calum sitting on the floor, surrounded by pots and pans. Despite his cries, he was clearly uninjured. Sarah picked him up and calmed him down with soothing words.

'Fell on me,' Calum whimpered.

'Pulled them on top of yourself more like, young man,' Sarah said, 'but you're all right now.' She glanced at Kirsty with a rueful smile. 'Being the mother of a toddler, you need eyes in the back of your head.' She kissed Calum until his tears were replaced with squeals of laughter.

'Does this little monster put you off having children?' Sarah asked Kirsty over the top of Calum's head.

'No, I want children,' Kirsty said quietly. 'But first I have to find the right man.'

'No one serious in your life, then?' Sarah asked, setting Calum back down. 'I'll need to get you ready for bed in a moment.'

'There was…' Kirsty hesitated. 'Once. But, no, no one at the moment.'

Sarah looked at her quizzically, inviting her to go on.

'A month ago I was engaged. I should be on my honeymoon right now,' she admitted, straining to keep the bitterness from her voice.

'Do you want to tell me about it?' Sarah asked softly.

'There's nothing much to tell. Robbie and I went out for years. I met him when he started working with my father. We seemed to have a lot in common. We both enjoyed the same things—the theatre, restaurants, clubbing. Last year we got engaged. At the time it seemed the right thing to do, the inevitable next step. I thought I had my life mapped out. A career I love, a life with the man I loved, children in the future…' She tailed off.

'What went wrong?' Sarah prompted.

'I found him in bed with someone a couple of weeks before the wedding. My wedding day was supposed to be the day I arrived here.'

'Sounds like you're better off without him. But you must have been deeply hurt,' Sarah said sympathetically.

'I was—at first. Now I'm just angry and, I have to admit, relieved. It wasn't just the fact he had been sleeping with someone else—what really made me furious was that I had agreed that we wouldn't have children. He didn't want them. Told me that we didn't need them in our lives. Of course, I hoped that eventually I would be able to change his mind, but I *was* prepared to give up my dreams for him. For a man who couldn't even be faithful to me. How stupid was that?'

'You can't blame yourself, Kirsty. Just be glad you found out that he was a snake before you got married.'

'I wonder now if I ever really loved him,' Kirsty said slowly. 'It's only been a few weeks, but I don't miss him at all. Now all I can think about is how close I came to making the worst mistake of my life. I suspect that all along he was only using me; that he thought marriage to me would cement his position in my father's private practice. It's worth an awful lot of money.'

'Is that the real reason you came out here, then? Running away from a broken love affair?' Sarah held up her hands as Kirsty started to protest. 'Don't worry, I don't blame you. Whatever your reasons for coming out here, it's clear to us that you are prepared to work hard and to learn. At the end of the day, that's what matters.'

'I'm not sure Greg would share your view,' Kirsty said. 'I suspect if he knew why I came here, he'd believe his initial assumptions about me were right. And although it may have been the reason I came initially, it's not why I'm staying. So, please, Sarah, don't tell him.'

Sarah looked at Kirsty, a small frown creasing her brow. 'His good opinion matters to you, doesn't it?' she said. 'Be careful that you don't allow it to matter too much.'

'What do you mean?' Kirsty replied defensively. 'Of course I want Greg to think well of me professionally. That's all.' But she could see from Sarah's expression that she wasn't convinced. 'Believe me, Sarah,' she went on, 'I have no aspirations in any other direction.' She laughed shakily, knowing as she said the words that they weren't quite true. Greg's good opinion did matter. It mattered much more than Kirsty wanted to admit. Even to herself. She stood up. Suddenly she needed to be on her own.

'I should leave you to it,' she said. 'I'm on call tonight, so I need to try and get some rest.'

'And I'll need to get this young man ready for bed,' Sarah yawned. 'I'm pretty well ready for bed myself. Enjoy your weekend if I don't see you. Try and force Greg to relax. That man could do with some rest and recuperation.'

Make Greg relax? Kirsty thought. She couldn't imagine anything more difficult. The man was a like a coiled spring and she couldn't imagine him being any other way.

The night on call went smoothly. Kirsty spent the first part of the evening accompanying Greg on his rounds.

'We'll start in Paeds,' Greg said. 'There are a couple of patients there I want to see.'

As they entered the ward Kirsty was struck afresh at the

drabness of it. The paediatric wards back home had been stuffed with toys, televisions and mobiles. There were always plenty of nursing staff and even play leaders to keep the children occupied. But here it was a different story. The ward was empty except for the rows of cots, some with two children in each. With only two nurses on duty, most of the children lay quietly, looking up at a bare ceiling. With the exception of three or four children whose mothers comforted them or lay sleeping on the floor next to their cots, there was no one free to offer the children the cuddles and attention they needed. Kirsty thought her heart would break as she looked down at the innocent faces that gazed up at her not expecting comfort. There was one child in particular who had kicked off his blanket, his cries of distress unheeded. To her surprise, Greg scooped the wailing infant up into his arms as he passed the cot and carried the child across to the nurses' station. As he talked to the nurses he rocked the child absent-mindedly until his sobs turned to whimpers and then his eyes closed in sleep. Still carrying the sleeping child, Greg accompanied the nursing staff to another cot where a toddler lay semi-conscious, oblivious to the tubes that snaked out from its tiny limbs.

'This child has pneumonia,' Greg told Kirsty. 'As you can see, she's on IV antibiotics and oxygen. However, she's not responding as well as we hoped. Any suggestions?'

'HIV?'

'No. We've tested her and she's negative.'

'TB? Malnutrition? Has she had a skin test? Have the rest of the family been checked? Could also be unrecognised heart disease.'

'Good thinking. I'll leave you to sort that out.'

The next child they went to check was the child from the village, Mathew.

'He's doing well,' Greg said. 'His burns on his arms are getting better, but we won't be sure for some time how much function he'll have retained in his hand. The burns to his face are also healing. Unfortunately, given the infection, there is likely to be scarring. Again we won't know the full extent until the scars have healed completely. But you'll be pleased to hear he has some movement back in his hand.'

'I heard. Sister Matabele told me movement came back when he was in the ambulance.'

Greg looked at her quizzically.

'What? You didn't think I wouldn't go and find out as soon as I could? Anyway what next?' Kirsty asked. 'Plastic surgery?'

Greg smiled ruefully. 'I wish. There is no way this child's parents will be able to afford remedial surgery for their child. They can barely afford food, never mind anything else. No, I'm afraid the best they can hope for is their son returned in one piece with full use of his limbs.'

Once again Kirsty felt outraged and then ashamed. Before coming here she hadn't really given much thought to the privileged life she had been living. As a child she had wanted for nothing, apart from her father's attention perhaps, and as an adult she had never thought twice about how she had spent her money. But if these children didn't have material possessions, at least some of them had their parents' love.

'Where are the parents of the other children?' she demanded. 'I know the nursing staff are too short-handed to play with the children, but what about the families? Surely it can't be good for them not to be with their children at a time like this?'

Greg looked around the ward. 'Most of these children don't have parents. The HIV/AIDS virus has wiped out a large proportion of the adult population in this region. Almost all of the children here are here because they are suffering the consequences of the infection. We didn't get the drugs in time to help the parents but hopefully, with the increase in funding available for retroviral drugs for children, most of these children will lead long, healthy lives.'

'What? In an orphanage? Without parents? Not good enough.'

'No, it's not.' He looked around. 'You're right to be angry. I guess we've become slightly inured to it. We do what we can, but it's not nearly enough. Sarah and Jamie buy toys for the children, but the children take them with them when they leave. Most of them have never had a shop-bought toy. We all wish we had money to do more. We need more staff, better facilities, more drugs.' He stooped down to replace the sleeping infant in his arms back in his cot, covering him with a blanket. 'I go along to local meetings to try and raise more money, and we have been successful to a degree. We have a lot more equipment and drugs than there were when we first arrived, but we could always do with more. In the meantime, until we can get more, we prioritise.'

'Still not enough,' Kirsty repeated.

'I know. In the meantime, as I said before, we do what we can. We try and keep an emotional distance. We can't get too involved with our patients. We need to remain objective so we can treat them as best we can.'

'Emotional distance. Huh,' Kirsty retorted. 'And how much emotional distance did you feel towards that child you just held in your arms?'

Greg frowned and Kirsty could see she had scored a point. Greg was always going on about not getting involved with the patients, but she could see, and not just from the way he had held the child, that the fate of the children touched him deeply. Perhaps the macho Dr du Toit wasn't as good at keeping his emotional distance as he thought. And as for Sarah and Jamie, they were fostering one of the children!

'That doesn't count. I had a free pair of arms. And now, Dr Boucher, shall we move on?'

A couple of hours later they finished their rounds. There were a few patients who would require monitoring through the night, but apart from that, and some minor injuries requiring suturing, the hospital was quiet. Greg suggested they go back to staff quarters once they had finished seeing to the patients.

They found Jenny there, reading a paper. She looked up as they entered.

'Hi, you two. I was hoping you'd be back here before I went to bed.'

'Why? What's up?' Greg asked settling himself down on one of the sofas, indicating to Kirsty with a sweep of his hand that she should do the same.

'I'm afraid I'm going to have to call off tomorrow,' Jenny said, regret evident in her voice. 'I've had a call from a close friend who is having some sort of personal crisis, and I think I need to go and see her tomorrow instead of going on our trip.'

'No problem,' said Greg. 'We'll reschedule for another time.'

Kirsty was dismayed at how disappointed she felt. She

hadn't appreciated how much she had been looking forward to going away. And she had to admit it wasn't just disappointment at missing out on seeing more of the country.

'Oh, you two must still go,' Jenny said. 'Heavens knows when the opportunity will come your way again.'

'If you're not going—' Kirsty began.

Jenny cut her short. 'It was difficult enough to get Greg to agree to go in the first place,' she said to Kirsty, 'so don't back out now because I can't go, or he'll never take time off.'

'I don't need time off,' Greg protested. 'And, anyway, I've been to this particular camp at least twice so I don't need to go again.'

'Ah, but Kirsty hasn't been. I'm sure she's been looking forward to it. Think of your staff,' Jenny admonished. 'They need to get a break even if you don't.'

'Don't worry about me,' Kirsty interrupted hastily. 'I'm sure there'll be plenty of other opportunities for us all to go.' The realisation of what Jenny was suggesting was beginning to sink in. The thought of spending the best part of a weekend alone with Greg was disconcerting, to say the least. As far as Kirsty was concerned, there was safety in numbers.

'You see, Kirsty doesn't want to go either,' Greg said— with an undue amount of satisfaction, she thought. It appeared as if he were no more keen to spend time alone with her than she was with him.

'You listen to me, young man,' Jenny said, drawing herself up to her full five feet two inches. 'Everyone needs a break—even supermen like yourself. You'll go as planned and take this young lady with you. Otherwise I'll be forced to ring my friend and tell her I can't make it after all. And that will make me feel bad. And you don't want that, do you?' Jenny wiggled an eyebrow at Greg. Despite her slight smile, Kirsty could tell she meant every word. And clearly Greg did, too. He laughed before holding his hands up in mock surrender.

'See what I have to put up with. Just because Jenny has known me since I was a kid, she thinks she can boss me around.'

'Well, someone needs to,' Jenny retorted. 'For your own good. Now, can I assume that's settled? You and Kirsty will go as planned?'

'OK, OK. You win—if you can persuade Kirsty, that is. You may well find that there are a thousand things she'd rather do than spend time with her boss.'

While Kirsty was searching for an excuse that would let Greg off the hook, she felt the full force of Jenny's severe look turned on her.

'No, no, I would love to go,' she found herself saying. 'I mean, if Greg doesn't mind.'

She was rewarded by a warm smile from Jenny. 'That's settled, then. I don't want to hear any more about it. If I come back and find the trip was cancelled…' she wagged a finger at them both '…there will be hell to pay. Do I make myself clear?'

'Yes, ma'am,' Greg and Kirsty said simultaneously. They shared a smile. It seemed as if there was no backing out for either of them. Kirsty was amused to see Greg find himself outmanoeuvred by his older colleague. Before this evening, she would never have guessed that anyone would have been able to make him do anything he didn't want to do.

After Jenny left, Greg yawned and turned to Kirsty. 'Why don't you go home? It's pretty quiet. I'll call you if anything comes in.'

'I'm happy to stay.'

'There's no need. I'm going back to my house. They'll call me there if they need me. Do you want to hang about here on your own?'

'I might as well go home, too, then,' Kirsty said reluctantly. 'But you promise to call me?'

'I promise,' Greg said. 'But don't be surprised if there's no need. I know you'll find this hard to believe, we do sometimes get a quiet night. And the nurses are used to coping with most things.' He stood up. 'Come on. I'll walk you back.'

Once she was back in her own place, Kirsty found herself too restless to sleep. The image of the children in the ward kept coming back to haunt her. She couldn't accept that there was nothing to be done about the ward or that there was nothing to be done about Mathew's face. Slowly an idea was beginning to form in the back of her mind. No, she tried to dismiss the thought. She couldn't ask. He had never helped her before, so why would he agree to do so now? But the idea wouldn't go away. It was, she thought, at least worth a try. Making up her mind, she crossed over to her rickety dressing-table, pulled out some writing paper from one of the drawers and sat down and wrote a letter.

CHAPTER EIGHT

She hadn't been called by anyone through the night, and when Kirsty arrived on the wards shortly after sunrise, Greg had already finished rounds.

'I promise, there was no reason to call you,' Greg said before Kirsty could berate him. 'And because we were quiet, I though I'd make an early start on rounds so we can leave in plenty of time to get to the camp before sundown.'

'I'm not sure I believe you, but it's too late now. I'll just make a start in Outpatients, shall I?' Even though it was still early on a Saturday morning, Kirsty knew that there would already be a queue of patients waiting to see her.

'I'll come and help as soon as I'm done here,' Greg said.

'I can manage fine on my own,' Kirsty said stiffly.

'Don't be so prickly, woman. I'm sure you'll manage fine. But two pairs of hands are better than one. And the sooner we finish, the sooner we can leave. Now I'm committed to going, I'm quite looking forward to it.'

And, sure enough, once Greg arrived to help, the clinic was finished in record time. Kirsty had to admit to herself they made a good team. It was almost as if instinctively each knew what the other was thinking. As far as the patients were concerned, that was.

Once they had finished the clinic and had had lunch, they set off. Kirsty had dressed in a pair of beige shorts and a white T-shirt. She had brushed her hair into a high ponytail to keep her neck cool. Uncertain of what to pack, she had eventually decided on a pair of jeans, a dress, a couple of T-shirts, a skirt, a couple of sweaters and limited herself to three pairs of shoes. Heels, walking boots and sandals. With a swimming costume and a sarong, as well as a couple of novels thrown in for good measure, she considered herself prepared for any eventuality.

Greg, however, had raised an eyebrow when she lugged her case out to his car.

'Good grief, woman, we're only going for a night, unless you're planning to make an early escape back to the UK?'

'I'm not going back. Not until my time is up or you fire me. Accept it,' she responded tartly. 'And, unlike you, I have no idea what one wears on safari, so I've come prepared.'

Greg laughed. 'Lucky there's plenty of space in the boot, then. Come on, let's go.'

As they drove, Greg and Kirsty chatted easily about patients. Kirsty repeated tales of her life as a medical student and as a junior doctor that made Greg laugh.

'I can't believe some of the things we thought.' She smiled. 'We were all so naïve.'

In turn, Greg shared with her some of the difficult cases he'd had to deal with when he'd first arrived. It was clear to Kirsty that, despite the hardships, he found the work immensely rewarding.

'It was just Jenny and I to begin with,' he told Kirsty. 'Until Jamie arrived, we split the workload down the middle.'

'That must have been tough,' Kirsty volunteered. 'Weren't you overwhelmed at all?'

'It was challenging. There's no doubt about that. But Jenny was—still is—a great support. And there was no time for thinking… It wasn't altogether what I did for the hospital. It's what the hospital and the patients did for me. In some ways I think they might have saved my life. Instead of the other way round,' Greg said slowly. 'Hey,' he went on before Kirsty had a chance to respond, 'there's something here I want to show you.' He pulled over to the side of the road. On the left where the veld fell away from the road, Kirsty could see a river.

'Come on,' Greg said, slinging a rucksack over his shoulder, 'it's just down here.'

Kirsty followed Greg for a few hundred yards along the bank. The dry grass of the bush tickled her bare legs.

'There's no snakes here?' she questioned nervously.

'They'll hide when they feel the vibrations from your footsteps. They are only likely to bite if you surprise them. There's not much danger of that.'

When they came to a cluster of sun-bleached boulders, Greg gestured to Kirsty to sit down. He pulled a bottle of water from a rucksack and passed it to her. As she swallowed she listened to the silence, unbroken except for the swish of the long grass as it moved in the breeze. Greg stayed quiet, although his eyes seemed to be searching the river for something. Suddenly an animal poked its head out of the water with a cry not unlike that of a bull. Its mouth was open, revealing rows of large teeth. Kirsty scampered to her feet, but Greg pulled her back down.

'Don't move,' he ordered.

'What is it?' Kirsty whispered, fascinated.

'A hippo. There's a whole herd that lives in this part of the river.'

'Aren't they supposed to cause more injuries than any other wild animal?' Kirsty asked, not altogether certain she was happy to be in such close proximity to them.

'We're perfectly safe as long as we stay still and keep our distance,' he whispered. 'And, anyway,' he said, reaching into his knapsack and placing a hunting rifle on the ground beside him, 'I have this in case of emergencies.'

Kirsty recoiled. She didn't know which frightened her more—the hippo or the gun.

'Is that legal?' she yelped, sliding away from Greg and the weapon.

'Of course. And don't worry. I was brought up on a farm so I know how to use it. Although I have no intention of doing so unless I have to.'

'Well, if you think for one minute that thing is coming anywhere near our tent, you have another think coming.'

'Don't worry. I'll unload it when we get back to the car. The bullets stay locked in the car, the gun stays with me.'

They sat in silence and watched as another two hippos appeared. Kirsty was captivated by their size and quiet presence. If the animals were aware of their audience, they gave no indication of it. After a while they sank below the surface of the water.

'Time to go,' Greg said, unloading the rifle before pulling Kirsty up by the hand.

He held onto her, guiding her around him so that she would be in front as they made their way back to the car. As she squeezed between him and the boulders she stumbled slightly. Greg caught her around the waist, drawing her away from the river. For a moment he held her against him and Kirsty could feel the steady beat of his heart. She looked up to find his eyes locked on hers.

'Careful,' he said huskily, tracing her cheekbone with a long finger. 'You don't want to get hurt.'

The underlying message was clear. Kirsty returned his gaze.

'I'm a grown woman, Greg,' she said. 'You don't have to worry about me. There's no danger of me getting hurt.' But even as she said the words she wondered if they were true. Something told her she was in very real danger indeed.

They arrived at the camp when the sun was still high in the sky, although the heat was beginning to leak from the day. Kirsty was delighted to find that Greg had understated the facilities in the camp. There were tents, but they were perched in the treetops. Theirs had a small balcony with an uninterrupted view of a waterhole. One side had been sectioned off to form a bedroom with a couple of single beds pushed together. In the main part of the tent, there were a couple of chairs, a table and another single bed. Kirsty raised an eyebrow at Greg.

'I guess you won't mind if I have the bedroom?' she said.

'No problem.'

In one corner open to the sky, hidden from view of the other tents, was a shower. Thankfully Kirsty noted it also had a screen to offer privacy from other occupants of the tent. Dumping her bags, she went out onto the balcony. From there she could see that in the centre of the camp was a thatch-roofed structure where they could have a barbeque or sit around a fire with their fellow guests. To one side, just within the perimeter fence, was a small, inviting pool with sun loungers. Kirsty knew where she'd be heading just as soon as she could.

'Isn't this awfully expensive?' she asked Greg as she looked around, the thought tempering her delight somewhat.

'It's not as nearly as expensive as you think and, because the camp is quiet, they've given us an upgrade free. All the profits go back into the upkeep of the reserve and to the villagers, so don't worry, anything we spend here finds its way into the right pockets.'

'In that case, I'm not going to waste a precious minute. I'm off to the pool before the sun goes down. Coming?' Ignoring Greg's astonished look, Kirsty began to remove her T-shirt.

'I was hoping there would be a place for a dip,' she said, 'so I put my costume on underneath my clothes.' And with another brief movement she removed her shorts. Pausing only to grab a towel, she left Greg standing.

Greg stared after Kirsty as she left. He had been taken aback when she had stood in front of him dressed only in the tiniest floral bikini, which emphasised the curve of her breasts, her narrow waist and her abdomen with just the smallest hint of roundness. Her auburn hair contrasted with the alabaster whiteness of her shoulders and, as she turned to leave, he had to admit she had one of the cutest back-sides he had seen in a long time.

Despite everything he had been telling himself since Kirsty's arrival, Greg knew with a twist in his guts that he was in trouble. There was no longer any doubt, he was seriously attracted to Kirsty Boucher, and he could think of only one way to get her out of his mind. But an insistent voice needled at his thoughts. It wasn't just a physical attraction. Despite Kirsty's professional inexperience, contrasting with her curious mix of sophistication and vulnerability, Greg was beginning to recognise and admire the determination that underpinned everything she did. It couldn't have been easy for her since she arrived. And, God knew, he hadn't tried to make it easier for her, but she had never complained. Quite the opposite, in fact. She was always asking to do more. He looked down at his hand, twisting the gold band he never removed. He couldn't remember laughing as much in a long time as he had on the journey here. Around Kirsty, he felt happier, more relaxed than he had, well, since Kathleen had died.

The thought made him frown. Not that anyone could ever replace Kathleen. There was no question of that. What he felt for Kirsty was pure animal attraction. That was all. Not for the first time, he regretted agreeing to come here alone with her. It would have been far better, for both their sakes, if there was someone else around. Still, it was too late now. He'd just have to exercise some willpower and he was good at that, wasn't he? Satisfied that he had it all under control, he changed into his swimming shorts and, whistling, went to join Kirsty at the pool.

Greg found Kirsty sitting by the pool. She had grabbed one of the sun loungers, and although the sun had lost most of its heat she was slathering herself in sunscreen. She was attempting to put some on her back but despite her contortions, was failing miserably.

'That's the problem with fair skin,' she muttered to Greg, as he tossed his towel onto the lounger beside her. 'If I don't make sure every inch is covered, I burn so easily.'

'Here, let me,' Greg offered, holding his hand out for the bottle of lotion.

'It's OK, I can manage,' Kirsty said.

'Don't be silly,' Greg responded, taking the bottle from her. 'Turn round and I'll do your back.'

Knowing it would be useless to argue, Kirsty gave in and lay face down on the sun bed. His first touch sent tiny sparks tingling down her spine as his strong hands kneaded her skin. Kirsty buried her face in her towel, lest a low moan of pleasure escaped unbidden from her lips. She couldn't stop herself from imagining his hands roaming all over her body.

'There, that should do.' Greg's voice interrupted her thoughts as he snapped the cap shut on the bottle, bringing her back to earth.

It occurred to her that she should offer to return the favour, but one look at his smooth, tanned skin told her it wasn't necessary. In fact, she thought as she studied him from beneath her lashes, he really had the sexiest physique she had ever seen. She resisted the urge to reach over and run her fingers along his back.

'I think I'll go for a swim,' Kirsty announced. *I could do with cooling off in more ways than one,* she thought.

She felt his eyes on her as she walked to the edge of the pool before diving in. The cool water made her gasp. Within moments, however, her skin had adjusted to the temperature and as she trod water she savoured the coolness of the water on her overheated skin.

'Are you coming in?' she shouted over to Greg.

He shook his head. 'In a while. I'm going to catch up on some reading first.'

He did want to catch up on some reading, Greg thought, but it wasn't just that. He knew he didn't trust himself to be in the water with Kirsty. He opened his book, but found he had no interest in getting back into the complicated plot. Instead, his eyes were drawn back to Kirsty as her slim arms sliced through the water. She certainly was beguiling, he had to admit. But it was nothing more than sexual attraction, he reminded himself as she emerged, dripping, from the pool. Her skimpy bikini clung to her body, emphasising the curve of her breasts, her narrow waist and her long shapely legs. How could he have ever thought she was too thin? She was just right. Greg felt heat low in his abdomen as she padded back to her sun lounger and snatched up her towel.

'I needed that.' She laughed, rubbing her hair. 'But I think I'll go up for a shower.' She looked pointedly at his book, her lips twitching mischievously. 'Leave you to catch up with your reading.'

Greg frowned, wondering what she was finding so amusing, when to his embarrassment he realised he was holding his book upside down.

Kirsty stood under the pounding needles of water, enjoying the novel experience of showering under the sky. When she had finished she dressed in a skirt and T-shirt and unpacked the rest of her clothes.

By the time Greg appeared she was ready.

'I've organised a game viewing. We leave at five in the morning, if that's OK.'

'Sounds good to me.'

'Dinner's at seven. I'm going to take a shower.'

Kirsty stood on the balcony, enchanted to see that a herd of buck and a couple of zebras had come to the water-hole. The sky was a blaze of red as the sun sank in the sky. A faint breeze cooled her skin.

I'm happy, Kirsty thought, surprised. Could it only have been a couple of weeks since she had thought her heart shattered? She wrapped her arms around herself. She couldn't have loved Robbie. Not the way a woman should love the man she planned to spend the rest of her life with. Not if her heart was healing so quickly. She had almost made a terrible mistake. If she had married Robbie, it wouldn't have lasted.

Kirsty was disturbed from her reverie by a distant rumble of thunder. Suddenly she was aware that a bank of dark clouds was rolling in with the night. The air began to fizz with electricity and she shivered as the wind rippled through her skirt.

She felt rather than saw Greg join her on the balcony. He had just stepped out of the shower, a towel wrapped low on his hips and his hair still beaded with waterdrops.

'It looks like a storm's coming,' he said. 'Heaven knows, we can do with the rain.'

Kirsty's gaze was drawn to his broad shoulders, the muscles rippling beneath the skin. Unable to help herself, her eyes took in his narrow waist with the thick trail of dark hairs that led downwards. Feeling a stirring of desire, she turned away abruptly and concentrated on the view.

'Look,' she said, pointing to the waterhole. A herd of elephants was making its slow majestic way to join the zebra and buck, who were already drinking at the water's edge. Unconsciously she held out her hand to Greg. They stood watching the animals for a moment as darkness descended. Kirsty sighed contentedly.

'It's such a magical country.'

Kirsty felt Greg put his arm around her shoulders. Without thinking, she leaned into his body. Suddenly with a muffled curse Greg turned her towards him. He studied her intently, his blue eyes mirroring the stormy sky, before bringing his mouth down on hers.

Kirsty swayed, drowning with desire. She clung to him, returning his kisses with a need that left her breathless. As his kiss deepened he dropped his hands to her hips and pulled her closer. Unable to help herself, her body melted into his as she responded to his touch. She let her hands explore his back, her fingers, as light as feathers, gently tracing the ridges of scars on his body. Suddenly the world was lit up as the sky flashed and another roll of thunder, louder than the one before, rent the air. Greg picked Kirsty up by the waist and she wrapped her legs around his hips. He moaned and his kisses grew ever more insistent as he carried her over to the bed. The room had darkened and Kirsty could barely make out his features as he laid her on top of the sheets. He stood for a moment, his eyes lingering on her body. She reached for him and he lay down beside her. His fingers skimmed over her breasts, tugging at her T-shirt. With trembling hands she assisted him to remove it.

With a swift movement he turned on his back and lifted her onto his hips, where she could feel the strength of his desire. He reached behind her, undoing her bra with one hand, allowing her breasts to spring free before capturing them in a gentle grip. As he explored her body, Kirsty arched her back, soft moans of pleasure escaping from her lips. Her skirt had ridden up and she could feel his hands sweeping over her thighs ever upwards until he found what he was seeking. Wave upon wave of sensation rocked her body until at last he entered her and then she was lost somewhere she had never been.

Afterwards, as they lay in each other's arms, Kirsty

knew she had found a place where she felt cherished. Raising herself on one elbow, she traced the scars on Greg's face, following them down across his chest. He circled her wrist with a hand, bringing her fingers to his lips, his other hand gently stroking her shoulder before continuing on to the dip of her waist.

'I didn't know it could be like this,' Kirsty whispered. 'It was never like this with Robbie...' She froze as she realised she had spoken her thoughts out loud.

'Robbie?' Greg asked. His hands stopped their restless exploration of her body.

Kirsty sighed. She didn't want to talk about Robbie right now, but she had no choice. 'My ex-fiancé. We were going to get married. The day I arrived here, in fact. But obviously we didn't—get married, or are ever going to get married.' Grief, she was babbling again. But she needed him to know that it was over between her and Robbie. She looked at Greg, trying to gauge his reaction. But in the dim light his eyes were cool, expressionless.

'I didn't know. I'm sorry,' he said, his voice flat. He hesitated for a moment. 'Tell me about him,' he said quietly.

'There's not much to tell. We met, fell in love—or so I thought. We were going to get married, and then I came home from work early one day. I wanted to surprise him. I surprised him all right.' She couldn't keep the taint of bitterness from her voice. 'In bed with another woman. You know the old cliché. Never thought it would happen to me.'

'Bastard,' Greg said succinctly.

Kirsty laughed. 'I'm beginning to realise it was for the best. He and I disagreed on too many things. We wanted different things from life.'

'Such as?' Greg prodded gently.

'For a start, I wanted children. Oh, not right away, but some time in the future. He didn't.'

'That's a pretty big difference, Kirsty.'

'I thought if I loved him enough, it wouldn't matter. Or that perhaps I could change his mind in time. If he loved *me* enough.'

'A dangerous assumption to make. And now? How do you feel about him? Do you still love him?'

'I'm beginning to realise that I never did truly love him.'

Kirsty laid her head on Greg's chest and continued her exploration of the scars that covered his chest and shoulder with a finger.

'Were you in a lot of pain?' she asked, knowing it wasn't just the physical scars she was referring to.

'The physical pain was nothing compared to…' Greg let the words tail off. Abruptly he flung off the sheet that entangled their limbs and leapt out of bed. Picking up his discarded jeans, he slipped them on and stood by the window, looking out, his back towards Kirsty. There was something in the set of his shoulders that chilled her. She fumbled for the light switch. She needed to see his expression. But as she flicked the switch, nothing happened.

'The power's gone off,' Greg said. 'It happens often during storms. There should be a lantern here.' A few minutes later he found what he was looking for and lit the lamp, which cast shadows across the room. The storm was passing, the thunder now little more than a low rumble in the distance, and the lightning had stopped. When Greg eventually turned back to Kirsty his eyes were dark, his mouth set in a grim line.

'This was a mistake. I'm sorry, Kirsty. I should never have allowed it to happen.'

Kirsty could hardly believe what she was hearing. One minute he was holding her, making love to her, now he was looking at her almost as if he couldn't bear the sight of her.

'What do you mean, *allowed* it to happen? As far as I am aware, we both wanted it equally. And I don't—can't—regret it.'

'It's not fair on you. You were about to be married, Kirsty! Hell, no one gets over a love affair that quickly. If I had known…' He rubbed his scarred cheek in the gesture Kirsty was coming to know. 'It's too soon—for both of us. I can't be a replacement for Robbie. Ever.' His tone softened. 'You want more than I can offer. You deserve more than I can give.'

'And who gives you the right to decide what I need or want? Why don't we just let things develop between us? See where it takes us?' Kirsty drew her knees to her chest and pulled the sheet tighter around her. Suddenly she felt very vulnerable.

'That's precisely it, Kirsty. There is nowhere for this relationship to go. I can give you nothing. I can never, will never, fall in love or marry again. I will never have more children.'

Kirsty shivered as the blood turned to ice in her veins. 'For God's sake, Greg. It's your wife who is dead, not you.'

As soon as the words were out Kirsty could have bitten her tongue.

'Don't bring Kathleen into this.' Greg almost spat the words. 'It has nothing to do with her. I'm content the way I am. I like my life the way it is.'

Kirsty recoiled.

'And how is that, Greg?' she asked quietly. 'Empty, except for your work. You've mocked me for being afraid. But my fears are nothing compared to yours. I'm prepared to risk being hurt again. To take a chance. But you? You are afraid to live. And there's no fear worse than that.'

'I'll take my chances,' Greg said grimly. 'Don't you see? I could never give another woman everything she needs. I'm not like your ex-fiancé. I wouldn't offer a woman half of me. It wouldn't be fair.' He looked at her bleakly, his eyes glittering as if they held raindrops. 'There is no future for us. Not ever,'

'We don't need to think of the future,' Kirsty said, desperate to convince the man in front of her. 'We could take one day at a time. Simply enjoy being together. See what happens from there.'

'And then what? You give up your career to stay with me here because, make no mistake, Kirsty, I will never leave Africa. And if you stayed I would have ruined another woman's life. And for what? For nothing.' He shook his head. 'I made that mistake once before, Kirsty, putting *my* needs, *my* career in front of those of the woman I loved, and what happened? I let her down in every way possible.'

There was no disguising the anguish in his eyes. Kirsty almost backed away from the naked pain she saw there. But instead she lowered her feet to the floor and, wrapping the sheet tighter, took a step towards Greg.

'I won't pretend that this…' she indicated the bed with a sweep of her hand '…meant nothing to me. I can't and you know that. Perhaps if I'd been able to pretend it didn't matter, you wouldn't be pushing me away.'

Greg strode across the room, closing the gap between them. Gently he tilted Kirsty's chin and looked deep into her eyes.

'Please, Kirsty. Let this go. It's for the best. You must

believe me. I won't be responsible for ruining your life. I have ruined two lives already. The two people I loved most in the world. The two people I would have given my life for.' His voice was ragged with grief. He passed a hand across his forehead. 'I shouldn't have let this happen. You have every right to be angry with me. I had no right.'

Suddenly Kirsty was furious. She moved away from him.

'OK, you win. If you aren't ready to face life, with its risks and uncertainties, then you're not the man I thought you were.'

'That's just it. I am not that man—and I never will be.'

Kirsty was dismayed and embarrassed in equal measure. She had made a terrible mistake. She had read much more into a simple case of lust than there had been. She should accept it for what it was. After all, it was the twenty-first century. Men and woman slept together for all sorts of reasons that had nothing to do with feelings. But she wasn't that type of woman. Never had been. Her heart and pride was still bruised after Robbie and it seemed both were to get another beating. At least sex with Greg had made her realise that what she had shared with Robbie was nothing compared to the short time she had spent in this man's arms. However, there was no point in prolonging this humiliating conversation.

'Well, it was fun while it lasted,' she said, trying to keep her voice light. 'If you don't mind, I'll wash then we can go to dinner. I don't know about you but I'm ravenous.' It was a lie, of course, but the last thing she wanted was for Greg to know how much he had hurt her. At the very least she needed to get out of the situation with a tiny bit of dignity still intact. She made her way towards the bathroom, hobbling slightly in the sheet that threatened to trip her up. *Please, God, don't let me fall* she thought. *Even I can take only so much embarrassment.*

Behind her, Greg said quietly, 'I am sorry, Kirsty.'

'We made a mistake, that's all. Let's just pretend it never happened. We still have to work together and we are both grown-ups.' Kirsty winced as she closed the bathroom door behind her. What on earth had she gone and done?

A short time later Kirsty left their tent and wandered off to find the bar. Greg had already gone. The recent scene kept replaying in her mind. Despite everything he had said, she knew he had wanted her as much as she had wanted him. There had been no pretence in his response to her. Or had she completely misread the situation in the first place? Had she been the one who had unthinkingly pressed herself into his arms and raised her mouth to his? She felt her cheeks colour with mortification. Did he think she had seduced him? In which case, no wonder he wanted to put as much distance between himself and his hormonally rampant colleague as possible. She almost groaned with horror. But, she told herself, her reaction had been the normal response of a red-blooded female to a man she found sexy. And while she found him attractive, he was right—there was no way she needed another relationship with another man so soon after her disastrous engagement and certainly not with someone as emotionally repressed as Greg.

Finding herself at the bar, she accepted the drink that the barman thrust in her hand almost without thinking and gulped the cool beer down. The bar was simple, with one side completely open to the night air. Myriad candles and lanterns lit the space, flickering in the breeze. Outside a fire had been lit and several people sat around it, chatting and drinking. There were about a dozen other guests staying at the camp and most of them came up and introduced themselves to Kirsty before going on to describe what animals they had spotted that day. Kirsty caught a glimpse of Greg across the room. He was deep in conversation with a tall man with dark skin, and an elegant woman, who was dressed in a brightly patterned robe with a matching scarf. Kirsty felt her heart thud as she caught his eye. He looked devastatingly gorgeous in his crisp, white, short-sleeved shirt and light-coloured trousers. Unwilling to hold his gaze, lest he read the shiver of desire that raced down her spine, she looked away. She was obviously still suffering the effects of a libido that was temporarily out of control. That was all, she told herself firmly.

The next moment Greg and his two companions were at her elbow and Greg introduced them. 'This is Nelson and his wife, Grace. They own this place. Nelson and Grace, Kirsty Boucher, a colleague and a, er, friend.'

'Any friend of Greg's is welcome here,' Nelson said, shaking Kirsty's hand. He turned to Greg. 'Why didn't you let us know you were coming?'

'I'd heard you were both out of the country. Besides, I didn't want special treatment. I knew if I let you know you'd have the staff pull out all the stops. You know when I come here I like to pay my way—and you always try and stop me.'

'Greg saved my wife's life,' Nelson told Kirsty. 'Back in the city. She had a brain aneurysm and luckily Greg spotted it. He operated and removed the clot.' He thumped Greg on the shoulder. 'Of course we'd do anything for him.'

'Nelson exaggerates,' Greg told Kirsty, looking embarrassed. 'I did no more than any doctor would have done. That was all.'

As the men continued to catch up, Grace pulled Kirsty to one side. She was one of the most beautiful women Kirsty had ever seen, with enormous brown eyes the colour of peat, fine chiselled cheekbones and a graceful neck adorned with beads.

'So are you only "friends"?' Grace quizzed Kirsty.

Kirsty nodded, unable to describe, even to herself, the nature of her relationship with Greg.

'Are you sure? Earlier—before you came in—it was as if he had been waiting for you, and then when you walked in, he only had eyes for you.'

Kirsty winced, her smile sad. 'You couldn't be more wrong.'

Grace didn't pry. 'Pity. I hoped for him there was more between you. He's such a wonderful person. He did save my life, you know,' she said quietly. 'And more. I was at university at the time. I could easily have been left brain damaged. Instead, I finished my degree with honours. He was a fine neurosurgeon. One of the best.'

'What did you study?' Kirsty asked, grateful for the change of topic.

'Geography. Nelson and I met while we were studying. He was doing environmental law. Once we had finished we got married and came up here to start this place. It quickly became evident that there was a real shortage of medical facilities. When we heard what had happened to Greg, we persuaded him to take the position at the hospital.'

'You knew Greg before his accident?'

A cloud crossed Grace's face. 'We knew the whole family. It was awful what happened. Neither of us thought that Greg would ever recover. But coming out here to work seemed to give him a reason to carry on.'

'What was she like? His wife?' Kirsty couldn't help but ask.

'Kathleen?' Grace looked at Kirsty searchingly for a moment before seeming to read something in Kirsty's eyes that reassured her. 'She wasn't beautiful. Not in the way you are.' She ignored Kirsty's shake of the head. 'But she drew people to her wherever she went. Whenever she was in a room it seemed to light up. She made people laugh. She was a wonderful mother and a good friend. We loved her. We loved them all. Greg was different when his family were still alive.'

'In what way?'

'Just different. Happier. More carefree.' She looked intently at Kirsty. 'But it's almost been five years and we think its time for Greg to move on. Find happiness once more. Perhaps fall in love. Get married again.'

'I'm pretty sure that's not what Greg wants.' Kirsty looked away from Grace's searching eyes. 'I don't think anyone will ever replace Kathleen.'

'No,' Grace sighed. 'I don't expect so. Not as long as Greg blames himself for the deaths of his family. Unless he accepts it wasn't his fault, that he was powerless to save them, I guess he'll always be alone. But tell me about yourself. What brings you to Africa?' As the two women chatted, Kirsty's thoughts kept straying back to Greg and what Grace had said. How could she have ever thought there could be something more between her and Greg than sexual desire? Not when it was clear to everyone that there would only ever be one woman for him.

Greg couldn't help himself. Despite his best intentions, his eyes kept straying back to Kirsty as she chatted with the other guests. Her auburn hair seemed to reflect the glow of the candles, making her face look paler than ever. He cursed under his breath. He had behaved despicably. He had made love to a woman who was on the rebound, who had recently broken up with her fiancé, for God's sake. If he had known he would never have given in to the raging lust that she inspired. Why did she have to be so beautiful? But he knew it wasn't simply her beauty. Kirsty made him feel alive for the first time in years. An unfamiliar sensation twisted his guts as he noticed that Kirsty was surrounded by a group of men who seemed to be hanging onto her every word. Surely he couldn't be jealous?

He'd had sex with other women since Kathleen had died, but those encounters had been different. He hadn't felt anything for them, or they for him. Both parties had been happy to take what they'd needed and leave it at that. None of them had got under his skin the way Kirsty had. The thought shook him to his core. Was that what made him feel so bad? The fact that he had made love to Kirsty, not just had sex with her? That for the first time he had betrayed the memory of his wife?

He wandered off outside. He needed to be alone without the distraction of Kirsty hovering in the periphery of his vision. He looked up at the sky. Another storm was moving in and it was unlikely the power would be on any time soon. His thoughts turned inexorably back to Kirsty. What, in God's name, was he going to do about her? No doubt she believed him the worst kind of man and he deserved it. It didn't stop him wanting to make love to her again. He knew that as long as she was around it would be difficult to resist her—although after the way he had behaved he doubted that she would want anything to do with him.

He shook his head despairingly. When he had thought his desire for her had been an itch he'd just needed to scratch, how wrong he'd been. Now he wanted her even more. Maybe they could have an affair, as Kirsty had suggested? See where it went?

But straight away Greg knew he couldn't. He hadn't been lying when he'd told Kirsty he'd never marry again or have more children. He felt the familiar stab of agony as he thought about his daughter. No, he would never allow himself to love again. Not when loving brought so much pain.

CHAPTER NINE

KIRSTY was woken up by a soft tapping. She was sitting up in bed when Greg came in. He looked rumpled, as if he hadn't slept much, and shadow darkened his jaw line. She wasn't surprised. He had insisted on sleeping in the car, and there couldn't have been much room for him to stretch his legs. Served him right, she thought viciously. As if she would have got up during the night and crawled into bed with him. When he'd suggested that he sleep elsewhere, it had been on the tip of Kirsty's tongue to tell him not to. Of course he shouldn't when there was a perfectly good bed in a separate room. But she hadn't. If he wanted to put as much distance between them as possible, that was fine by her.

'Its time for the drive, Kirsty,' he said, passing her a scalding cup of coffee. 'Take this. We'll get breakfast afterwards.' She accepted the coffee gratefully. At least he'd remembered that she couldn't function without a hit of caffeine.

It was still dark and cool as the open-topped Jeep rumbled down the track, stopping in front of their tent. Greg directed her into the seat at the rear of the Jeep behind the driver and guide, and climbed in beside her.

As his leg brushed against hers, Kirsty tucked the blanket Grace had thoughtfully supplied under her thighs. It wouldn't only serve to keep out the chill, it would provide a barrier between them because his proximity was stealing her breath.

She caught sight of the rifle resting against the front seat.

'It's not dangerous,' Greg had reassured her, noticing her eye the rifle anxiously. 'It's a precaution, that's all.'

But Kirsty's attention had shifted. 'What's that?' she asked, as the headlights caught the glitter of eyes in the shrubs.

'Wild dogs,' the driver replied, shifting into a lower gear as the Jeep started to climb a slope. Taken by surprise, Kirsty couldn't stop herself from sliding into Greg. His arm came around her shoulders.

'Steady on, Mike,' he admonished. 'This isn't a rally.'

Kirsty tried to lift herself away from him but the angle was too acute. She was forced, ignominiously, to grip his thigh, the muscles bunching under her hand, and yank herself upright by grabbing her doorhandle. It came away in her hand. She fell against him again. She could feel his heart beating beneath her cheek. All she wanted to do was close her eyes and melt further into him. Resisting the impulse, she struggled once more to sit upright.

Greg looked at her in amusement, a wry smile tweaking the corners of his mouth. 'Give it up, Kirsty,' he whispered in her ear. 'We're almost there.'

And they were. The Jeep levelled out before coming to a slow stop beneath some wide-spreading acacia trees. Below them a dark pool of water glinted beneath fading stars as the sun's rays stretched tentative fingers to a lightening sky. Impala, warthogs and giraffe sipped at the water, only a few casting anxious glances for predators. Kirsty was enthralled—more so when a rhino with a calf made their ponderous way to the waterhole.

Mike's radio crackled. 'Over and out,' he ended, before turning the key in the ignition. 'Lion spoor further on. Let's see if we can track them.'

After trailing the spoor for almost an hour, Kirsty was thrilled when they came across a pride stretched out under a tree. Unthinkingly she reached out to Greg, grabbing his arm to get his attention. He looked down at her, grinning at her excitement.

'It's wonderful, isn't it, the first time you see them in their natural habitat?'

They watched for some time as the cubs played with their father who would reach out a large paw and swat them away from time to time. Eventually a lioness rose and padded away. The Jeep followed, keeping its distance downwind. After some time the lioness crouched in some deep grass and was hidden from their view. 'Over there,' Greg whispered to Kirsty, pointing at a herd of wildebeest in the distance. He handed Kirsty the binoculars and through their lenses Kirsty could see several young grazing close to the adults. Suddenly something seemed to startle them and they took off, heading in different directions. Kirsty swung her binoculars to find that the lioness had left her concealed position and was moving towards the herd at speed. She followed her with the binoculars and was horrified to find that a young wildebeest had become separated from the rest and the lioness was in full pursuit. She lowered the binoculars, unable to look any more. 'Oh, no,' she whispered. 'Somebody, do something. Fire in the air. Warn her off.'

Greg, too, had seen what was happening. He placed his

hand over Kirsty's. 'We can't intervene. It's not fair on any of the animals.'

Within moments it was all over. The lioness had caught her prey. The other animals stopped running and soon went back to grazing some distance from the large cat. Kirsty was still aghast. 'It's too cruel,' she said. 'That poor animal.'

'It's life, Kirsty. She has to feed her cubs if they are to survive. Death is a necessary part of the circle. We all know that.'

Kirsty looked at him. He was staring into the distance, his jaw clenched. 'Isn't it better,' he went on, 'knowing these animals have lived well before they died? Rather that than not live at all?' Kirsty wondered if he realised what he was saying. It was just a pity that Greg couldn't apply the same principles to his own life.

They took leave of the camp and Nelson and Grace a short while later, after sharing breakfast with them. While they ate, the couple shared their plans of setting up a small clinic for the local population, most of whom worked on the reserve. Greg and Kirsty joined in enthusiastically and Greg promised to return soon to help them with their plans. 'Come, too, Kirsty,' Grace pleaded. 'I feel we could be friends.' She looked from Greg to Kirsty before nodding complacently. As she kissed Kirsty goodbye, she whispered, 'Don't give up on him.' Kirsty didn't know what to say. Grace had simply got the wrong idea.

'Wait up for me, Kirsty, will you? I'm just about finished here,' Greg called out as she passed the surgical ward on her way back to her house. He was scribbling notes on the chart of a patient. For a moment hope flared. It died when he continued, 'There's a case I'd like to discuss with you if you, have a moment?'

Progress of another sort anyway. At least he was starting to take her medical skills seriously. 'Sure, Greg. I'll be outside.'

It had been a long day. While she waited for him she leant against the warm brick of the hospital wall, closed her eyes against the bright morning sun and breathed in the honeysuckle-scented fresh air. Although she tried to stop it, her mind kept flitting to Greg. The past couple of weeks, since the trip to the game reserve, had been both painful and difficult.

The journey back to the hospital from the game park had passed in silence. Kirsty had felt the tension between them almost like a physical force. But there had been little left to be said. Greg had made his position clear. As far as Kirsty was concerned, she had badly misjudged a man for the second time. She couldn't fight the ghosts of his wife and child. She knew that with chilling certainty.

And nothing in his behaviour since had led her to believe otherwise. When they had to work together, he was polite but distant. If he looked wan and haunted, it could only be because he was working too hard.

His footsteps brought her to the present. She pushed herself upright and greeted him with a tentative smile that matched his own.

They walked towards their accommodation immersed in conversation about the patient Greg had wanted to discuss. Since the trip to the reserve, the only conversations they'd had had been about medical cases.

Kirsty didn't notice the car parked outside their accommodation until they were almost there.

Greg looked at her. 'Expecting a visitor?' he asked.

'I don't know anyone here,' she said. 'Much more likely to be for you.' But then, to her astonishment, she recognised the tall, silver-headed man and his younger companion coming towards her.

'Dad! You could have let me know you were coming. And Robbie!' she added, glaring at him. 'What on earth are you doing here?'

'I'm presenting a paper at a conference in Cape Town,' her father said, bending down and kissing her cheek. 'So I thought a detour to see the situation here for myself would be a good idea. When he heard my plans, Robbie decided to come with me. We've come to take you home.'

'Take me home?' Kirsty echoed disbelievingly. *Over my dead body,* she thought grimly. She'd had just about as much as she could stand from men deciding her future.

'Kirsty, darling.' Robbie tried to reach out and hug her, but Kirsty stepped away from his arms. 'I told you on the phone I was coming.'

Kirsty was aware of Greg standing beside her, his expression grim. The easy camaraderie that had arisen between them while they'd discussed treatment options had disappeared as if it had never been.

'Dad, Robbie, this is my boss. Dr Greg du Toit. Dr du Toit meet my father and Robbie Knight.'

Greg shook their proffered hands. 'Pleased to meet you both. Professor Boucher, if you'd give me a moment, I'll show you around. I'm sure Kirsty and Robbie have plenty to talk about.'

He turned towards her, lowering his eyelids too late to hide the brooding darkness she could only read as disapproval in his eyes. 'Kirsty, please invite your guests for dinner. I'll let Cook know to expect two more.'

At that moment Kirsty would have done anything to prevent Greg from leaving. Whatever else had passed between them, she could have done with his presence now. The last thing she wanted right now was to be left alone with Robbie. However, there was nothing for it but to let Greg leave.

'Come inside,' Kirsty said, as Robbie took the pile of case notes she had been planning to review that evening from her unprotesting grip. 'I'll show you around after we have a drink. And then I'm sure you'll want to get on your way before night falls.'

'On the contrary,' Kirsty's father said, 'I've got a couple of days free and Robbie here is planning to stay as long as it takes to persuade you to put this nonsense behind you and come home. And the sooner the better—the clinic can't survive too long with both of us away.'

'May I remind you that I never asked either of you to come? When I wrote to you about the desperate situation here, Dad, it wasn't because I wanted to be rescued. I simply thought you might be able to help—from the UK,' Kirsty said frostily. 'So, while you are welcome to stay the night, I'm too busy to act as hostess. Neither do I have any plans to "come home", as you put it.'

'I'll go and join Dr du Toit for that tour, shall I?' Keith Boucher said. 'Leave you two to talk.' And with that he beat a hasty retreat towards Greg. He'd always been good at avoiding emotional scenes, Kirsty thought ruefully. But what had brought him out here? Surely Robbie hadn't brought him along to help persuade her to return to him?

As Kirsty boiled the kettle she felt her temper rise. Her

father and Robbie had no right to dictate how she lived. She whirled to find Robbie standing behind her, a contrite expression on his face.

'Think about what you are doing, Kirsty. How can you bear it out here? It's all so primitive. Not your sort of place at all. Surely you can see that? Why can't you forgive me and come on home? I know it was a stupid thing I did. I'll never do it again, I promise you. It was just a final sowing of wild oats. It didn't mean anything. Let's just pick up where we left off.' He stepped towards her, a pleading smile on his face. Once that smile would have melted her, but that had been before… She left the thought unfinished. Better not go there.

'I'm not leaving here. At least for a while. And I'm certainly not coming back to you. Ever.'

'I know you're still angry with me and you have every right, but if I ever meant anything to you, you need to give us a chance,' Robbie persisted.

Kirsty whirled on him. 'No, I don't. You stopped meaning anything to me the moment you were unfaithful. For goodness' sake, Robbie. We were about to get married.'

All of a sudden the anger left her, replaced with sadness. Robbie would never know true love, she was certain. He would always be too wrapped up in his own needs. He wasn't a bad man, Kirsty knew now. Just a weak and selfish one.

'Let's leave it at that, Robbie. I'm happy here. Of course I was hurt and humiliated when I found you and Karen together. I couldn't bear telling everyone the wedding was off, particularly the reason why. I couldn't face their sympathy and I couldn't face you. But everything is different now. I don't love you any more. I'm not sure I ever did. You have to believe me when I say it's over.'

'I don't believe you. Unless…' Robbie's eyes narrowed suspiciously. 'Unless you've found someone else. That man Greg, your boss. What's he to you? They said when we arrived that the two of you were on some trip. I thought when they said it was with your boss, they meant someone a lot older.'

'It's got nothing to do with Greg.' Although as Kirsty said the words she wondered if they were true. 'Greg's not interested in me.' She couldn't quite keep the note of regret from her voice.

Robbie stepped closer, searching her eyes. Kirsty's gaze fell under his scrutiny.

'I'm right, aren't I? You do have feelings for him. That didn't take long.'

'Whether I do or whether I don't is no longer any concern of yours,' Kirsty reminded him, putting down her cup of coffee. 'Now, as far as I am concerned, this conversation is over. Shall we join my father and Greg on the wards?'

But his words had unsettled her. As they walked in silence towards the hospital, she thought of Greg, the strong planes of his face, the way he was with his patients, the way life seemed more exciting whenever he was around. She knew that in the short time she had been here she had changed. He had made her see that there was more to life than sports cars, new shoes and going out. She couldn't help but think what life would be like with Greg. It would always be an adventure. He'd never be satisfied with settling down in suburbia. He'd always be looking for new challenges and expecting the woman by his side to rise to those challenges, too. And then, with heart-stopping conviction, Kirsty knew that more than anything she wanted to be that woman.

The realisation made her head spin. She had never felt like this before. She glanced at Robbie. He had never made her go weak at the knees, never made her ache with need, the way Greg did. Robbie had never made her heart thud when she caught his eye across a room. But Greg did. With Greg she wanted nothing more than to be with him. Nothing else mattered. She would live in a tent in the desert if that's what it took to be with him. What she had felt for Robbie had been a pale imitation of what she felt for Greg. The truth hit her like a sledgehammer. She loved Greg. Completely, hopelessly and for ever.

But with equal certainty she knew that he would never love her. He was still in love with his Kathleen and *she* could never hope to compete with the memory of his dead wife.

Robbie was looking at her curiously. 'Are you all right? You look as if you've seen a ghost.' Kirsty almost laughed at the aptness of his description. Kathleen's ghost would always be there, between her and Greg. It was pointless to think there was any hope that Greg would ever allow himself to love her. All she would ever have was the memory of that brief interlude at the reserve. She shivered, wrapping her arms around her body.

'I'm OK.' She paused outside the paediatric ward. 'I think we'll find them in here.'

Sure enough, that was where they found them. The two doctors were bent over Mathew, deep in conversation. The little boy was sitting up in his cot, playing happily, his watchful mother by his side. Kirsty could barely look at Greg, scared he'd see her feelings written all over her face. She could have done with more time to collect herself.

'Professor Boucher—Keith—has shown a keen interest

in Mathew,' Greg told them. 'In fact, he thinks he may be able to help.'

'I won't be certain until I make some calls, but I believe I might be able to persuade some of my colleagues at the hospital in Cape Town to let us use their facility to operate on this lad's face.' Kirsty was surprised. Although she had pleaded for his help in her letter, she hadn't really believed he would do anything. She had never known her father to do anything that didn't enhance his reputation or finances.

'That would be wonderful, Dad,' Kirsty said. 'If you could swing it?'

'If I can't then we'll operate here,' he said firmly. 'I have to say, Kirsty, this hospital of yours is exactly how you described it. Even the patients and staff. Greg introduced me to Jenny earlier on. She's a pretty tough cookie. Gave me quite a lecture about how the privileged should be doing more for the less fortunate.' Kirsty had rarely known anyone take her father to task and rarer still was the fact he had agreed to do something.

'I've got another patient I'd like you to see, Dad. You, too, Robbie,' Kirsty said, knowing that it was unlikely she'd get another opportunity to get her father's help.

Kirsty led the way to the medical ward. She opened the door to a side room. In it was a woman lying in a bed with a small child in her arms. Over the top of her sleeping child's head the woman looked at them in mute supplication, her brown eyes wide with fear. Kirsty knew that her father and Robbie wouldn't need to look at the woman's notes to know that she was dying.

'Thabisa here has end-stage AIDS. We have done all that we can, but sadly there is nothing left for us to do.' Kirsty reached over, tucking the blankets around the dying patient. It was so little. She took a deep breath, before going on. 'Her child has probably inherited the HIV virus but with the right treatment and drugs could go on to lead a productive life. Sadly, our supplies of the drug are limited. We need more, much more, if we are to ensure that every infected child has access. Furthermore, even if we do get the drugs we require, there are thousands of children in this country who have been left orphans. We need more homes for them, clothes, food and schools. The government is doing what it can, but there is so much need.' Kirsty struggled to keep her voice calm. She knew that any emotion on her part would weaken her argument in her father's eyes. She leaned over and touched the child's cheek with a finger, saying a few words of the African language she had been studying. She put her arms around the dying woman, gently lifting her into a position where she could manage a few sips of water. The woman smiled weakly, grateful for the small attention. Greg unwound his stethoscope and listened to the woman's chest. Wordlessly he shook his head at Kirsty.

Kirsty's father looked shocked. Robbie, on the other hand, appeared dismayed. Neither said anything until they had left the room.

'This is why you can't stay here,' Robbie said. 'Can't you see it's not your problem? Leave it to the government agencies who know what they're doing.'

'I can't accept that we can't do something. I won't accept it. What about your contacts, Robbie? Dad? Can't you persuade them to help?'

'Aren't you getting too involved, Kirsty?' her father asked. 'I think Robbie is right. Leave it to people who know what they're doing.'

'I don't think either of you know Kirsty as well as you think if you believe she'll give up on this,' Greg interjected quietly. 'And she's right. As doctors all we can do is stem the flow of the disease. It's a drop in the ocean. We can't just patch the children up and send them out to God knows what. It's easy to say there is nothing that can be done. But it doesn't absolve us from our responsibilities to our fellow human beings to try.'

Kirsty was surprised but pleased at Greg's intervention.

'I don't know what I can do, Kirsty. OK—operating on the child with the burns is one thing, and I can write you a cheque,' Keith offered.

'Any help you can give would be appreciated, of course, but I was thinking more of fundraising. You're always speaking at these large conferences, Dad.'

'So you mentioned in your letter, Kirsty. But I've never chosen to get involved in causes.'

'But there's no reason *you* couldn't, Kirsty,' Robbie interrupted. 'What about all these well-connected friends of yours? That's another reason for you to come home. You could do more back there than you ever could here. After all, it isn't as if you have much experience to offer out here.'

Kirsty felt as if she'd been slapped. She'd always known that Robbie didn't take her career seriously. He had often hinted that she could give up work once they were married. Not to stay at home with children—that he had made clear—but to network with other wives, lay on dinner parties and in general help his career.

'I wouldn't say that,' Greg said quietly, his mouth set in a grim line. 'Kirsty has been an enormous help out here. Her patients and colleagues all think very highly of her medical skills and knowledge. She learns fast and has shown that she's more than prepared to roll her sleeves up and get stuck in.'

All eyes turned to Greg, as if they couldn't quite believe what they were hearing, Kirsty not least. It was the second time in the last half-an-hour that Greg had defended her and her clinical ability. Didn't he realise by now that she was perfectly able to stand up for herself?

'Let me think about it, Kirsty,' her father said. 'I'm not promising anything, but I will give it some thought. Now, if someone could point me in the direction of a shower and dinner? I don't suppose there's a decent restaurant in the vicinity?'

Kirsty and Greg shared a smile. 'No, I'm afraid not. But as I said earlier, you're both welcome to have dinner with us in the staff dining room. I've already alerted Cook that there'll be another two to feed. In the meantime, will you excuse me? I have some more patients I want to check on.'

By the time Kirsty and her two visitors made it to the staff house, the rest of the team was already waiting, drinks in hand. She introduced everyone as they took their seats, aware of the curiosity her visitors—particularly Robbie— were causing. Freshly showered, shaved and dressed casually but elegantly in trousers and sports jacket, he looked every inch the charming, successful surgeon he was.

They had almost finished dessert when one of the nurses came running into the room.

'Come quickly! There has been a bad accident. Two minibuses and many casualties.'

Jenny stood up. 'It's my shift.'

Sarah, Jamie and Greg stood, too. 'We'll help. Sibongele, could you take Calum home and stay with him, please?'

'I'll come, too,' Kirsty said, getting up from the table.

'Its OK, Kirsty, you stay with your guests. We'll cope,' Greg said, barely glancing in her direction.

'I'm coming, whether you like it or not.' Kirsty had had enough of the men in her life talking about her and making decisions about her. And hadn't Greg just told her father that she was a useful member of the team?

Greg paused and looked as if he was about to protest. But something in her expression must have told him that she had made up her mind.

'OK, but stick with me,' he said

'Perhaps I can be of some assistance?' her father said, a spark in his eye. Kirsty couldn't remember seeing him look so animated.

'I suspect I'll only get in the way,' Robbie said. 'So I'll just head off back to your place, Kirsty, although if you need me, give me a shout.' He yawned and Kirsty wondered that she'd never realised how selfish he was until today.

'The door's open. Make yourself at home,' she tossed over her shoulder as she left the room.

The scene in the emergency room was chaotic. There were several patients with life-threatening injuries and many more with minor injuries requiring attention.

As they worked, more staff arrived from the nearby village to lend a hand. The crash had happened close to the village and a couple of nurses had rushed to the scene to help.

Another ambulance pulled up. 'These are the last of the casualties. One we had to cut out of the vehicle and the others are walking wounded. They can wait. But...' The nurse hesitated. 'One of the minibuses exploded. The veld is on fire. Many are trying to put it out but the grass is so dry. The wind is blowing it towards the village.'

'Make sure that the villagers are being evacuated. Has the fire service been called?' Greg demanded.

'Yes, but it will take them at least an hour to get here. I don't think it's going to be soon enough. The village will have burnt down by then unless the wind changes direction,' Jamie replied. 'Apparently Kirsty's friend—Robbie—has gone to help.'

Greg cursed under his breath. 'Idiot. He knows nothing about veld fires. They take hold so quickly and shifts in the wind can cause the fire to move behind you. Unless you know exactly what you are doing and have the right equipment, it's foolhardy to try and tackle them.' He must have noticed the alarm in Kirsty's eyes because he added hastily, 'I'm sure he'll be all right. The villagers will look after him.'

'I should go and find him,' Kirsty said. 'You don't know Robbie. He won't be told by anyone.'

'There's no way you're going anywhere near that fire,' Greg said firmly. 'They'll have enough to do keeping that boyfriend of yours safe without you adding to the problem.'

'I don't remember asking you for permission,' Kirsty ground out, trying to keep the fury and fear from her voice. 'I can't stop you ordering me about here, but you have no jurisdiction on me outside this hospital.' She pealed off her surgical gloves. 'Everything here is under control. The others can manage fine without me. So I'm going,' she held up a warning hand. 'And nothing you can say will stop me. I can drive myself. I don't need your help.'

'You can't go on your own, woman. See sense. The last thing we need here is to add you and Robbie to the list of casualties. Let the fire brigade handle it. You stay here and I'll go and make sure he's out of danger.'

'I'm coming, too,' Kirsty's father said quietly. 'He's my

responsibility as much as anyone else's. But Greg's right,
Kirsty. It's no place for a woman.'

'Stop it. Both of you.' This time Kirsty made no attempt
to keep the anger from her voice. 'No more, do you hear?
No more telling me what to do. I'm going and that's final.
Whatever you choose to do is up to you.'

'Atta-girl,' Jenny cheered from across the room. 'You
tell 'em. Too many men here think they're Rambo or some
other kind of hero. Need a woman to keep them real.'

But Kirsty was out the door. Greg and her father looked
at one another before shrugging and following her.

'We'll go in my car,' Greg said as he caught up with
Kirsty. 'Or were you planning to walk?'

They piled into his vehicle in silence, Kirsty worrying
about Robbie. Whatever had happened between her and
Robbie, she'd had feelings for him once. She didn't want
anything to happen to him.

As soon as they left the hospital grounds they could see
the flames lighting up the sky over the village. The fire was
bigger than anything Kirsty had ever seen or expected.
She shivered.

'I hope the villagers are all right and that no one's
been hurt. But their homes! They could lose what little
they have.'

'The fire might still pass by the village,' Greg said,
although Kirsty could tell from the tone of his voice that
he didn't hold out much hope.

They reached the fire in less than five minutes, passing
groups of people with their possessions balanced on their
heads, hands hanging onto fearful children.

'They'll be planning to take refuge in the hospital overnight, or at least find space for the kids there,' Greg said.

'It's a warm night. At least if the adults do have to find shelter outside, they'll be OK.'

As they suspected, the flames had reached the perimeter of the village. A line of villagers stood flinging buckets of water on the fire, while others beat at the flames with coats or blankets—anything they could find. Kirsty could see immediately it was hopeless.

Greg pulled to a stop a safe distance away and they spilled out of the car. Kirsty slung her medical bag over her shoulder and ran after Greg, determined to keep up with him as he ran down the main street. A fire engine had mercifully arrived, its flashing lights adding to the sense of chaos and urgency as the wind steered the fire ever closer to the fragile village homes. But, Kirsty thought, surveying the mayhem around her, one fire engine was unlikely to be enough.

She glanced over her shoulder to make sure her father was following, relieved to see that he was at least keeping a safe distance from the inferno that was raging around them. Sparks of burning debris floated in the swirling air, and the intensity of the smoke and heat caught in the back of her throat.

The hairs on the back of Kirsty's neck stood on end as ear-piercing screams split the air. She caught up with Greg as he stopped short, frantically scanning the mud huts to locate where the heart-wrenching sounds were coming from. Through the dense smoke, an older woman staggered towards them, her face streaked with soot and tears.

Her words were incomprehensible to both of them, but her frantic pulling of Greg's arm and her pointing backwards towards a cluster of huts spoke of her urgency and desperation.

'I think she's trying to tell us someone's trapped back there,' Kirsty shouted to Greg, running forward. 'Come on!'

For a split second Greg stood immobilised by the wall of flames around them, the terror and confusion bringing that fateful night his family had died sharply into focus. He thought he could hear the cries of Kathleen and Rachel over the crackling flames. He remembered the heat of the fire, the flames licking his skin, the taste of smoke in his mouth, choking lungs. He hadn't been aware of it then, he had been too focused on reaching his family, but afterwards, night after night, the scene replayed in his mind. Could he have done more? Why had he left them alone? Every time he thought of that night he willed the outcome to be different. In his dreams he saved them, only to wake up, his heart crushed with the realisation of their loss. He had thought he couldn't bear it. Only immersing himself in work had saved him from going mad.

Gritting his teeth, he forced his mind back to the present. It was that night all over again. Could he bring himself to face the flames once more? He knew there was no choice. He was damned if anyone was ever going to die while he stood back and did nothing. Spurred on by a renewed sense of urgency and an anger that surpassed any fear, he ran after Kirsty as she darted into the labyrinth of pathways that snaked between the dwellings.

He grabbed Kirsty by the arm, spinning her towards him.

'Go back!' he shouted over the noise of the burning houses.

'No, I *won't*.' She shook herself free of his grip. The determination he saw there made his blood run cold. He knew that unless he picked her up and carried her back, she wouldn't go. For a split second he considered it, then another scream cut through the air. There was no time.

'Stay right beside me.' He had to lean close and shout in her ear to make himself heard above the sounds of the crackling flames. 'For God's sake, stay near me,' he beseeched her, not caring if she saw the fear in his eyes. He couldn't—wouldn't—lose her, too.

She saw the fear in his eyes and nodded mutely. Greg ran a finger over her lips before cupping her chin in his hands and pulling her against him. For the briefest moment she felt his lips touch hers and then he was off, running towards the huts.

Kirsty could feel her breath coming in gasps as she struggled to keep up with him, the thick, cloying smoke filling her lungs and stinging her eyes. Every now and again Greg would glance back to check she was following.

They emerged from the narrow path that skirted the village into a clearing. Most of the houses seemed to have been built around a circular space in the middle of the village. It was difficult to see through the smoke that hung over everything, but it looked to Kirsty as if most of the villagers had managed to flee in time. Greg was running from house to house, trying to locate the source of the screams.

Robbie emerged from the chaos and grabbed her arm, almost wrenching it out of its socket. She spun around, frowning in shock and bewilderment but relieved that he was safe. But where was Greg?

'Kirsty! No, don't!'

She struggled to free herself from his strong grip. 'I've got to, Robbie!' she yelled wrenching herself from his grasp. 'I can't just do nothing. I've got to help.'

'It's madness Kirsty. You'll get yourself killed.'

This was getting them nowhere, she thought in exasperation. Her eyes pleaded with him. 'Robbie, I know these people, I've got to help them.' She laid a hand gently but firmly on his. 'If you want to help me, please go help the others with the casualties.' And with that she turned on her heel and disappeared into the smoke.

Robbie stood transfixed, gazing after her until he could no longer see her. He dropped his arms to his sides, knowing it was futile to run after her.

'I should never have let you go...' he murmured to himself, as he turned back to help the others.

Kirsty's heart was beating so loudly in her ears she thought it was going to burst out of her chest. Her eyes darted around as she scanned the area frantically, trying to find Greg. *Where was he?* She suddenly felt completely alone and vulnerable in the cauldron of yellow and red flames. And then she saw him. He staggered from a hut, carrying a small child of about two and a bundle of rags in his arms. On closer inspection, Kirsty discovered, the rags were, in fact, a swaddled baby.

Greg thrust them both into her arms. 'Get them out of here now!' he ordered.

'What about you? Aren't you coming?'

'There's a young girl still inside. I'm going back for her. I couldn't carry all of them. Now go! There's not much time!'

'Greg!' She shouted but her words were whipped away by the roar of burning bush. Knowing that she had to get the children out of danger, she hitched the toddler onto her back where he clung to her neck, almost forcing the last remaining breath from her throat. She ran back as fast as she could, oblivious now to her aching lungs, intent on getting the children to safety. The toddler held on, coughing and crying, his mouth open in a perpetual wail of despair and fear. The baby lay worryingly inert and silent in her arms.

After what seemed an eternity but was probably only a few minutes, the smoke thinned and Kirsty burst through the haze.

Jamie and Sarah surged forward, gently taking the children from her and immediately laying them on the ground to examine them. For a moment Kirsty sank, exhausted, to her knees. Jamie looked over at Kirsty as he slipped an oxygen mask over the toddler's face. Sarah did the same with the baby.

'You could do with some oxygen, too, Kirsty,' Jamie said. 'Wait there and I'll get someone to see to you once I've seen to this little fellow.'

Kirsty shook her head. 'I'm fine. See to the children.'

'I'll be back as soon as I can, but in the meantime sit still,' Jamie said.

As he turned away, she staggered to her feet. Robbie darted forward, catching her before she fell. She struggled in his arms.

'Greg's still back there. I've got to help him.'

'Don't be a fool, Kirsty! You've done all you can,' Robbie said hoarsely.

She pushed against his chest but was too weak to make any impact. Tears of exasperation and fear pricked her eyes. 'I can't leave him…'

Robbie studied her face for a moment, before realisation dawned on him. He had lost her for ever, he knew that now. Her heart belonged elsewhere. Sighing inwardly, he berated himself for being such a blind fool as to lose the one woman he had truly loved. Now it was too late. But at least now he could do something to repair the hurt and damage he had caused her.

'Your father's helping with the other casualties. I'll go look for Greg. You stay here and get seen to, OK?'

Kirsty looked up at him. She had almost no strength left to argue.

'I'm coming, too,' she said, getting to her feet.

Robbie ran a finger gently down her cheek. 'Leave this to me. Greg will be fine, don't worry.' Pulling off his shirt and soaking it in a bucket of water, Robbie held it over his mouth and ran back into the swirling nightmare of flames.

Taking a deep gulp of air, Kirsty followed Robbie back towards the burning houses where she had last seen Greg. Every breath brought a sharp pain in her chest. The smoke was thicker now and she could barely see. All of a sudden she tripped and went flying. She hit the ground with a thud and an excruciating pain jolted up her leg. Instantly she knew she had broken her ankle and Robbie was nowhere to be seen. The smoke muffled everything except the sounds of the fire around her. To her right the flames leapt closer with every second. Panicking, she looked around frantically for an escape route, but even had she found one she knew she'd be unable to escape the fire. With a sickening feeling in the pit of her stomach, Kirsty knew she had run out of time.

She tried to get to her feet, but when she put weight on her broken ankle she fell back to the ground. She bit back the screams of pain and horror that rose to her lips. Don't panic, she told herself. Whatever you do, don't panic. Spotting the branch of the tree which had probably caused her to lose her footing, she crawled towards it, biting down on her lip against the pain the movement caused in her foot. Inch by inch she moved towards the branch, convinced it was hopeless but refusing to give up. When she reached it, she used it to lever herself off the ground.

If I can just take a few steps, she thought, if I can just stay alive for a few more minutes, he'll find me. She didn't know where the certainty came from, but she knew deep in her soul that Greg wouldn't rest until he found her. All she had to do was help him find her.

'Greg,' she yelled as hard as her aching lungs would allow, 'I'm here, help me.' She manoeuvred the branch under her armpit and, using it as a crutch, took one painful step at a time. In front of her the flames had died a little having consumed all the dry grass there was to be had, and were now greedily making their way towards a small clump of trees to feed its hunger. But as faltering step followed faltering step, she knew she was too slow. Just as she was ready to give up and accept her fate, she heard Greg's voice calling her name. He sounded close.

'Over here. I'm over here,' she gasped. Tears from the smoke and fear ran down her cheeks.

'Hold on, Kirsty. I'm coming. For God's sake, hold on.'

Kirsty turned in the direction of his voice, almost blinded by tears and smoke. She hardly recognised Greg when he burst through the flames. Covered in ash, only his eyes were visible.

'Kirsty, thank God,' he cried as he crushed her in his arms. 'Are you all right?' He held her as she collapsed in his arms, relief robbing her of the last of her strength. She looked around frantically. 'Where's Robbie? Is he safe? You've got to find him.'

'He's fine. He's with the others.'

'My leg,' she whispered hoarsely. 'I think I've broken my ankle. I'm so sorry, Greg, for making you come after me.'

'Shh now,' Greg said, picking her up as if she weighed nothing at all. 'Did you think I'd let anything happen to one of my doctors?'

And that was all she was, Kirsty thought as her eyes closed. Just one of his doctors. Another responsibility. As she lost consciousness, she was unaware of Greg's lips on her hair.

'Don't leave me,' he murmured. 'Don't you dare leave me, too.'

CHAPTER TEN

KIRSTY woke up to find herself in one of the hospital beds. Images from the night before flashed in her head. She remembered Greg picking her up in his arms. After that she must have floated in and out of consciousness as she had been placed on a stretcher and put in an ambulance. She could recall being given oxygen, her ankle being X-rayed and someone's gentle hands wrapping her ankle in a cool, soothing cast. Her father's face had drifted in and out as had the faces of Jamie, Sarah and Jenny. But she couldn't recall Greg's presence. Or Robbie's. Were they all right?

She tried to sit up, fighting the fear that gripped her and weight of the bedclothes pinning her down. She had to find out.

As she struggled someone pressed her gently back into the pillows. Her eyes flickered open and her heart soared. It was Greg. Despite the bandage on his right hand and singed eyebrows, he was here, in one piece. Thank God. Regardless of how he felt about her, she knew she'd be happy as long as he was in the world. Unbidden and deeply resented tears washed her eyes.

'Greg…' was all she could manage through her aching throat.

His voice was husky. 'Hey, hey, take it easy. You're safe now. You won't be walking without crutches for a while, but otherwise you'll be out of here by tonight.'

'Robbie—what about Robbie!' she asked grasping Greg's wrists. 'Is he OK?'

Greg flinched before smiling down at her. 'He's fine, too. Jamie's giving him a final once-over, then you'll be able to see him.'

He disengaged Kirsty's hands from his wrists.

'I'll tell him you were asking for him when I see him. Your father's just outside. He wants to see you, but I've limited him to five minutes only. You need to rest some more before I'm prepared to give you the all-clear.' He paused, and it looked as if he was about to touch her, but instead he rammed his fists deep in his pockets. Despite the events of the night before, it seemed as if he intended to keep his distance.

Greg left the room as her father entered.

'How are you, Kirsty?' her father asked softly, looking down at her. For the first time in as long as she could remember his eyes were tender. She had rarely seen him looking so subdued. He seemed uncomfortable.

'I'm perfectly fine. I don't know why everyone is making such a fuss.'

'Perhaps because they are fond of you? You seemed to have made quite an impact in the short time you've been here.' He shuffled his feet. 'I'm very proud of you, Kirsty. I hope you know that. I know I haven't been around very much for you since your mother died, and I wanted to say how sorry I am. She would have been so proud of you, too.'

He cleared his throat. 'You remind me so much of her.'

The rare display of emotion touched Kirsty deeply. She

reached out for his hand. 'I do? I miss her, too, Dad. And I've missed you as well.' Kirsty felt the familiar ache, thinking of her lost childhood. She swallowed the lump in her throat. She had to try and reach her father one last time. 'I always wondered if you were sorry it wasn't me that died in the accident. Sometimes it seemed as if you could almost not bear the sight of me.'

Keith looked horrified and then ashamed. 'I am so sorry. I know I was weak and selfish, but every time I looked at you, I saw your mother. You were always so much like her—and not just in looks.' He leaned over Kirsty and tucked a strand of hair behind her ear. 'When she and your sister died, I thought my life was over. The only way I could deal with missing them was to throw myself into my work. The only time I didn't think of them was when I was working. All I wanted was to come home too exhausted even to dream of them. And there you'd be, refusing to go to sleep until I had tucked you in. Wanting to tell me all about your day. Everything you'd done. Making demands when I'd exhausted myself with the effort of forgetting.'

'I was desperate to make you notice me. I wanted to make you proud of me, but you never seemed to care. You never once came to prize-giving, even in my final year when I won all those prizes. Why, Dad? I was so alone. I missed them, too. I needed you more than ever.'

'I don't expect you to ever forgive me, Kirsty. As you got older you stopped telling me things. I know it was my fault that a chasm had opened up between us, but by the time I realised how far apart we were, it was too late. You had your own life, university and your career. I didn't know how to get close to you again. But I was always so proud of you. That fierce determination to succeed. Your ability to stand on your own two feet. You did all that by yourself, Kirsty—you are so much stronger than you think.'

Kirsty smiled. 'I know that now, Dad. Being out here has taught me that at least. Life no longer holds any fears for me—not even being alone. I suspect now that was the reason I thought myself in love with Robbie. I wanted so much to belong somewhere.'

'And now?' her father asked gently. 'You know you'll always have a home with me. We can start to get to know each other properly. Spend time together. I know I have no right to be part of your life, but if you'd let me—I'd be grateful.' He looked at her and Kirsty could see that he meant every word.

'I'd like that, Dad.'

Her father squeezed her hand. His look of relief told Kirsty how much it had cost him to open up and expose the wounds that lay beneath the austere surface.

'By the way, that Jenny woman is something else,' he said admiringly. 'She gave me a real rollicking about my apparent selfishness and my parental obligations. Anyway, it seems as if I have agreed to set up an exchange programme with one of the teaching hospitals in Cape Town for some of the patients here to be treated free of charge. I'll give them some of my time on a regular basis in return. What do you think? It means I'll be coming out to Africa on a regular basis. We'll see much more of each other and more of the patients will be getting the specialist care they need. Perhaps it will go some way towards making things up to you?'

'You shouldn't do it just because of me, Dad,' Kirsty said.

'You're not the only one who has learnt something out here, my girl. What matters...' His voice wavered. 'Is I have my daughter back. And medicine has given me so much, it's about time I gave something in return. After all, it's why we all trained, isn't it? To make a difference.'

'Then I think it's a great idea. Thank you.'

Father and daughter smiled at each other. Kirsty felt her heart shift. Something good had come out of her time in Africa. It would take time for her and her father to learn to know each other properly—but it was a start.

'Have you seen Robbie?' she asked, changing the subject.

'Yes, I have. I rather think he's enjoying being the centre of attention. He's told me it's really over between you and why. I gather he is planning to leave tomorrow morning,' Keith replied, pulling up a seat. 'Will you be very sorry to see him go?'

'No, Dad. Really. Robbie and I have had a narrow escape in more ways than one. I was never the right woman for him nor him the man for me.'

'Is it Greg? He's got something to do with this, hasn't he?' Keith asked. 'I can see why you'd find him attractive in a rough sort of way. And he's one hell of a doctor. You look at him the way your mother used to look at me. My God,' he said, realisation dawning. 'You're in love him, aren't you?'

'Yes, but it's no use. He doesn't want me.'

Keith looked at her disbelievingly. 'Doesn't want you? Are you sure about that? You should have seen him when he realised you'd gone back into the fire. I suspect he would have happily knocked Robbie to the ground for not stopping you, had there been time. No, I think you're mistaken there.'

'There's other complications, Dad. Trust me. There's no future for us,' Kirsty said, closing her eyes wearily. 'I think

I'll just rest for a while, if that's OK.' And before she knew it she had drifted off into a deep sleep.

When she next woke up, Greg was back. He had showered and changed and, apart from the bandage, he looked as he always did. Kirsty felt her heart squeeze. She knew she'd have to leave Africa. She didn't think she could bear to be around Greg—loving him but never being able to have him. But the thought of leaving him and the people who had begun to mean so much was almost too much to bear.

'I have someone to see you,' he said softly, and stood aside.

Robbie too had showered and changed, but he looked uncharacteristically disheveled, as if the night's events had taken their toll. 'I had to make sure for myself you were all right. For God's sake, Kirsty, what on earth got into you? You could have been killed.'

'But I wasn't. Although I'm sorry I put anyone else in danger.' She glanced over at Greg who was standing with his arms folded. He looked grim.

'I'll leave you two alone,' he said abruptly. 'I'm sure there are things you want to say to each other.'

'Please, don't go,' Kirsty said quickly, but he was already pushing the door open. 'There's nothing Robbie and I have to say to one another that you can't hear.'

Greg shook his head, his eyes expressionless as he looked at her. 'I'd rather not,' he replied, and left.

His departure sent a chill through Kirsty. Did he think she and Robbie were going to have a lovers' reunion? she wondered in despair. If she had the energy, she'd get out of bed and run after to him to explain. But what was the point? He had made it all too clear that there was no future for them.

Suddenly aware that Robbie was saying something to her, she dragged her attention back to him as he leant over the bed and kissed her on her cheek. 'Do you forgive me?' he asked.

Kirsty's eyes met his. *How could I have thought I was once in love with Robbie?* she asked herself, noting his hangdog expression which in the past used to make her go weak at the knees. Now, she realised, it just made her pity him all the more.

Kirsty managed a small smile. 'I do, Robbie. It's all in the past now.'

He leaned over, clasping her hand. 'Is there any chance we could…?'

'No.' Kirsty shook her head and gently disengaged her hand. 'If we had been right for each other, you would never have cheated on me. And if I had loved you enough, we would have found some way to have made it work.'

Robbie stood up, his expression regretful. 'I was stupid and I guess I'll have to live with the consequences.'

'I suspect it won't be long before you've forgotten all about me.'

'And you'll be wrong.' He hesitated. 'I'll see you soon? Back in the UK?'

'Yes.'

'Goodbye, then, Kirsty,' he said quietly, kissing her gently on the forehead. 'You'll always be in my heart, no matter what you think.'

'Goodbye, Robbie. Look after yourself.' Despite what had happened, she hoped he'd find happiness one day.

Robbie took a deep steadying breath as he walked down the corridor. He could hardly believe that he had lost Kirsty for good. Deep down he had been sure he could win her back. How wrong he'd been. What a fool he'd been. But there was something he had to do before he left tomorrow.

He eventually found Greg outside in the hospital gardens. For a second he doubted the wisdom of what he was about to do. What if he was wrong? No. Robbie straightened his shoulders. Being out in Africa, even for this short time, had made him a better man. It was time he started acting like one.

Greg looked round as Robbie approached. He nodded at him. 'Did you and Kirsty sort everything out then?' he asked tersely.

'Yes, we did.'

The muscles in Greg's jaw tensed. He stared out over the horizon. 'So she'll be joining you back in the UK, then?'

Robbie paused. He hoped he was doing the right thing. 'You know, Greg,' he said softly, 'some people go through their whole life never finding that special someone. Someone mentioned you lost your wife and child some years ago. I can't even begin to imagine how hard that must have been for you, but you were damn lucky to have had a love so special the first time round.'

Greg glowered at him. He didn't have to listen to this. 'It's none of your damn business. I know how blessed I was—I don't need you of all people to remind me. I trust *you* appreciate what you've got.' Greg turned on his heel. 'I hope you'll both be very happy.'

Robbie grabbed his arm, ignoring the dangerous narrowing of Greg's eyes. 'I lost my chance of happiness. I threw it away. Kirsty and I are over for good. The way is clear for you.'

Greg's heart slammed in his chest. For a moment happiness flooded his body, only for it to be dispelled a second later. What was the use? he thought, raking his hand through his hair. 'I can't…' His eyes were anguished.

'Can't…or won't?' Robbie demanded, suddenly frustrated. 'I know how you feel about Kirsty, and it's taken every ounce of my nerve to come out here to talk to you. Do you think this is easy, trying to persuade another man to make the woman I love happy?' Robbie shook Greg's arm gently, his tone softening. 'Would your late wife really want you to punish yourself for the rest of your life?'

Greg raised his eyes. The question had never occurred to him. 'No, she wouldn't,' he answered after a while.

Of course she wouldn't. He could imagine what she'd say if she knew how hard he'd being trying to hide from life. She of all people would have wanted him to move on. Find happiness wherever, however he could. But was it too late? He knew he had hurt Kirsty badly. Could she ever forgive him? There was only one way to find out.

'Well, then?' Robbie half smiled. 'Don't you think it's time you stopped punishing yourself?' He clapped Greg lightly on the shoulder, leaving him alone with his thoughts.

Greg stole into Kirsty's room, careful not to wake her. He quietly pulled up a chair alongside her bed and sat down, resting his forearms on his thighs. In the dim overhead light he noticed how her long lashes cast shadows on her cheeks, her long hair framing her delicate features. He thought she had never looked more beautiful.

Almost as if she had sensed his presence, Kirsty slowly opened her eyes. She smiled sleepily when she saw him.

'Hi, you,' she murmured.

'Hi, you, back.' His voice was soft. 'How are you feeling?'

Kirsty turned over on her side to face him, her hand resting

under her cheek. 'Much better, thank you,' she replied
politely. She paused. She would have to tell him sooner
rather than later. 'Greg…I'm going to go back to the UK.'

Greg frowned, startled. 'To be with Robbie?'

'No. Not in the way you mean. I guess we'll always
have contact. Especially as he works for my father. But as
I said before, Robbie and I are over. What love there
was….' She left the words unfinished. 'But I *am* going to
leave. I'm not much use here, not with this cast on. So I
may as well go back.' Although she tried, she couldn't
keep the sadness from her voice.

'Are you certain it's over between you and Robbie? Out
there in the fire, when you thought he was in danger… And
then when you woke up, he was the first person you asked
for. Are you sure there's no hope of getting back together?
He stills love you.'

'But I don't love him.'

'Perhaps given time?' Greg persisted.

Kirsty finally lost her temper. 'Greg du Toit, you have
no right to interrogate me about my love life. I can see why
it might make you feel better to believe that Robbie and I
still have feelings for one another. It lets you off the hook.'
Seeing he was about to protest, she held up an admonishing finger. 'You have made it perfectly clear that you and
I have no future. I accept that. Now, once and for all, butt
out of my life. Besides…' she glowered at him '…aren't
you needed elsewhere?'

'I'm exactly where I need to be,' Greg said, his eyes
sparkling. 'With one of the most difficult women I have
ever met or ever want to meet. And I have no intention of
leaving her again.'

Kirsty's heart thudded.

Greg slid onto the bed beside her and pulled her close. She smelt the same lemony aftershave, and felt the muscular hardness of him.

'I've been such a fool,' he groaned. 'When I almost lost you, I knew I couldn't live without you. But then you seemed frantic about Robbie. And I thought it was too late.'

'And Kathleen? What about her?'

Greg pulled her closer. 'I loved Kathleen and part of me will always love her. I thought I didn't deserve happiness again. It was my fault that she and Rachel died. What kind of man doesn't protect his family?' Kirsty made to interrupt him, but he held a finger to her lips. 'Let me tell you, while I can. The grief and the guilt almost destroyed me. I felt I didn't deserve happiness. And then you came into my life. You, with your odd mixture of vulnerability and sophistication. I tried so hard not to fall in love with you, but it was no use. I tried to tell myself that it was just lust. And then we made love and I knew I could never get you out of my mind. It was the worst kind of hell, Kirsty— believe me. Wanting you, but feeling as if it was so wrong, as if it were the worst sort of betrayal to fall in love again.'

'Well, thank you very much. I can assure you I didn't plan any of this either,' Kirsty muttered under her breath. She couldn't make out what he was trying to tell her. Something about not wanting to fall in love with her. Something about not succeeding. She felt a small surge of happiness, followed sharply by a needle of exasperation. How did he feel about her? And what—if anything—was he going to do about it?

'And then there was the thought of you sacrificing your career to be with me,' Greg went on. 'It was Kathleen and I all over again. I couldn't let it happen.'

'It isn't entirely up to you, Greg,' Kirsty said crossly. 'Do you think for one moment I wanted to fall in love so soon after being engaged? And with a man who really still belongs in the Dark Ages? Do you think for one moment I planned to fall in love with someone who lives in deepest Africa, as far away from civilisation as you can get?' Kirsty took a deep breath, ready to continue to list all the reasons she had never intended to fall in love with him, but he stopped her words with a finger on her lips again.

'What did you just say?' he asked, his eyes glittering.

'I said it wasn't in my plans to fall in love with a man and have to start a new life, particularly a man as impossible as you...'

But once again Kirsty was stopped in full flight—this time as Greg brought his lips down on hers. 'Let's stop at the bit where you said you loved me,' he said, once he had kissed her soundly. 'The rest can wait until we both have our strength back.' He released her. 'I shouldn't overtire you. You need to rest.'

'For God's sake, Greg. There you go again. Don't you know by now I'm stronger than I look? We're going to finish this conversation right here. I want to know what happens now.' Greg gathered her in his arms again, and rested his chin on top of her head.

'Last night—the fire. At first I was terrified. The smoke, the flames. It brought it all back to me. I felt paralysed with fear. But you didn't hesitate. You were so brave—but reckless, too.' He couldn't resist admonishing her. He would much rather she had stayed safely away from the fire, but then she wouldn't be the woman he adored.

'And then when no one knew where you were, only that

you had gone back in, I thought I was about to lose the woman I loved all over again.'

Kirsty turned towards Greg so she could look him in the eyes. She felt her throat close at the naked pain she saw there. Reaching up, she kissed his eyes as if her touch could take away his anguish.

'But you saved me. You rescued that woman and her children. Robbie, too.'

'I think it's the other way round. You and the fire saved *me*. In some way it felt as if I had been released from my burden of guilt. In some small way I had paid back the debt I owed my wife and child. I'll never forget them, Kirsty. They will always be part of me, but if you are prepared to take the risk, prepared to spend your life with a stubborn fool…'

Happiness soared through Kirsty's veins. Whatever it took, she knew she wanted nothing more than to spend the rest of her life with this man. But she needed to hear the words.

'What exactly are you saying, Greg?' she asked, a small smile playing on her lips.

'I love you and want to marry you. Isn't it bloody obvious?' he said tersely. 'But if it's too much or not enough, I'll understand.'

'You mean I'll have to stay with you here? In this country? Without access to my beloved shops? Hmm, let me see,' she teased. But from the look in Greg's eyes she knew he needed an answer.

'Of course, Dr du Toit. You know I always like to do as you ask.' She had just enough time to see his eyes glow before he brought his lips down on hers and she knew at last she was exactly where she belonged—for good.

The Surgeon's Marriage Proposal

MOLLY
EVANS

Molly Evans has worked as a nurse from the age of nineteen. She's worked in small rural hospitals, the Indian Health Service, and large research facilities all over the United States. After spending eight years as a Travelling Nurse, she settled down to write in her favourite place, Albuquerque, New Mexico. Within days she met her husband, and has been there ever since. With twenty-two years of nursing experience, she's got a lot of material to use in her writing. She lives in the high desert, with her family, three chameleons, two dogs and a passion for quilting in whatever spare time she has. Visit Molly at www.mollyevans.com.

To those who helped me get here: my family,
my friends, the Kick-Ass Sisterhood
critique partners, Gabriella Anderson,
Barbara Simmons and Sheley Wimmer,
the Land of Enchantment Romance Authors,
and my husband, who will always
be the hero in my life.

CHAPTER ONE

THE front doors of the Kodiak Island Medical Clinic crashed open and rebounded off the walls. Dr. Jack Montgomery jumped from his chair as an air ambulance crew rushed a patient through. An unfamiliar woman rode the gurney and performed CPR on the fly.

Jack rushed to hold the doors of the trauma room open. "Dammit, Kyle," he barked. "Why didn't you radio? We're not ready for this."

"Couldn't," Kyle said. "Radio's out."

"Ready...to...change," panted the nurse who was performing CPR.

Amos, one of the Alaskan clinic nurses, positioned himself to take over. "Right behind you."

"Ready... Change."

Amos and the air ambulance nurse swapped places without missing a compression.

She jumped down from the gurney, stumbled backward and fell right into Jack. He caught her under the arms and helped her regain her balance, but not before he'd inhaled her fragrance. Musk or sandalwood or something else earthy wafted over him in those few seconds and lingered in his senses.

"What's your name?" he asked as he released her and stepped a pace away.

"Thanks. Just a little wobbly from all the exertion."

"Who are you?" Jack asked again, and looked at the blonde with bright blue eyes and a pink flush to her cheeks.

"Maggie." She sucked in a few deep breaths, recovering from the labor of administering CPR.

"OK, Maggie. What happened to this guy?" Jack asked, starting to examine the man.

"Blunt force trauma to face, chest and abdomen," she said, and pulled her clipboard from beneath the gurney. "A crab pot hit him," she said as a frown of confusion wrinkled her brows.

"He's lucky to still be alive." With his stethoscope, Jack listened to both of the man's lungs. "He's got a pneumo for sure on the left."

"It might be a hemo-pneumothorax with that kind of trauma. He's probably bleeding into the lung, as well as having a collapsed one," Maggie said.

"Probably," Jack acknowledged. "Hold CPR, Amos. Let's check for a rhythm," Jack said.

"V-fib," Maggie said after one look at the monitor. She dashed to the code cart and dragged it to the patient's side.

"Kyle, keep bagging. Amos, resume CPR," Jack instructed. "Maggie, get the defibrillator ready."

"Yes, Doctor." With hands that visibly trembled, she charged the machine. Waiting for it to fully charge took seconds that felt like days, and Maggie's insides tied up in knots.

"Defibrilate, two hundred joules," Jack said.

Maggie tapped a foot as she waited for the beep. "Charged," she said, and pressed the defib paddles to the patient. "Clear!"

Maggie discharged the paddles and the patient spasmed in response.

"Again," Jack said, a muscle twitching in his jaw.

"Charging." Tense seconds passed as the machine re-charged and sweat poured down Maggie's back.

First day, first code, first everything. *Welcome to your new job.*

Jack glared at the persistent squiggles on the monitor and started to curse. "Again, dammit," he said, and ran a hand through his hair.

No one breathed as the defibrillator whined. The tension in the air choked Maggie, and she had to draw a deep breath as she hit the button for the third time.

Everyone stared at the monitor. "Asystole," Jack said, his shoulders slumping in defeat as he blew out a long breath. "Damn."

"Give it just a second," Maggie said, and clasped Jack's sleeve, needing a connection to someone, even a stranger, to help get her through this moment. After a few seconds more the monitor blipped and beeped. "Sinus rhythm," she cried, and clapped her hands once. "We did it. Should I start a lidocaine drip?"

"Yes. No. Wait a minute." Jack shook his head and frowned, and had to look away from those blue eyes shining with triumph. He picked up the patient's dog tag. "He's got an allergy to 'caine'-type drugs."

"Bretyllium drip it is," Maggie said, and exchanged the drugs with a happy grin.

"First a bolus, then a drip."

Maggie programmed the IV pump and connected it to the IV site in the patient's arm. "All set, Doctor."

"Jack, please. We're pretty informal around here."

"OK," she said, and dropped her gaze from his, unaccustomed to such familiarity. Maybe it was a sign that things were going to be different for her here.

Jack studied the monitor. "I'm not sure I like his rhythm just yet."

"There's still the collapsed lung," Maggie said, and taped the IV tubes together. "If someone could tell me where the chest tube trays are kept, I'll get one ready," Maggie said.

"Over there." Jack pointed to a supply cabinet and scrubbed at the sink.

"What do you want to use instead of Xylocaine?" Maggie's hands trembled as she searched through the drugs in the code cart. There had to be something else they could use. Did she dare make a suggestion to a doctor who didn't know her or her skills? For a second Maggie bit her lip as she stared at him.

"Something you want to say, Maggie?" Jack asked, and punched his arms into the yellow disposable gown she held out.

"A few milligrams of morphine for pain control and two milligrams of Versed for the sedation and amnesic effects would work."

Jack nodded. "All right. Have you used them before?"

Finally! Something she knew about and could offer without feeling like she was in over her head. "Yes. I'm certified in advanced sedation. Just have to give the Versed slow IV push so the patient doesn't lose his respiratory drive. Same with the morphine."

Jack's glance lingered for a few seconds on her face and a light blush colored it, but she held his gaze.

"That would be bad, wouldn't it?" Jack asked, his eyes crinkling up at the corners.

"Very," Maggie said with a quick smile at his teasing, and then moved to the patient. Maybe this wasn't going to be so bad after all. At least he seemed to have a sense of humor.

"Go ahead, prep him." After giving the sedation Maggie swabbed three quick applications of Betadine solution to the skin. "Ready here," she said, and pulled a blue surgical mask over her face.

"Scalpel."

Maggie slapped a metal scalpel into Jack's palm.

His hand closed around the handle, but he winced behind his protective goggles. "Ouch. Maybe a little lighter next time."

Maggie cringed, a sick feeling twisting tight in her chest. "Sorry. Sorry. God, I'm sorry! First-day jitters."

"It's OK. Just relax. You're doing fine," he said, trying to instill a sense of calmness in her. She was obviously an experienced nurse, but her nerves were overwhelming her.

Maggie took a stack of gauze from her tray and dabbed Jack's forehead before a bead of sweat dripped into his eyes.

"Thanks," he said. "Looks like you've done this before."

"Had a lot of trauma where I came from." When Maggie hooked the collection container to suction, dark red blood drained into it, and a feeling of satisfaction flowed through her. She loved being right, especially when it meant saving a patient.

"Good assessment, Maggie. Clamps and a curved needle, and I'll sew him up."

Jack's simple words of encouragement and approval sent warm heat through her chest as she handed him the instruments. So many times in her last job she'd wished for approval and not gotten it, but here on her first day she'd earned it, mistakes and all. This was going to be a great job.

After Jack had placed a few tight stitches, Maggie stepped closer, her fragrance again washing over him, lingering in his mind and going places he'd thought were locked up tight.

Maggie handed him the appropriate dressing materials in the correct order without him having to say a word. He liked that. Neat, tidy, orderly and mostly calm. Great qualities in a nurse. They would come in handy in this clinic where anything and everything happened twenty-four hours a day. Jack finished applying the tape and patted the dressing. "That ought to do it."

The phone in the room interrupted conversation, and Kyle picked it up. "Plane's here."

After the patient was loaded into the ambulance, Maggie and Jack stood by the clinic doors as it pulled away. He looked down at her until she met his gaze. "You weren't here three weeks ago."

"No. The locum hired me. Today's my first day." She gave a hesitant smile, hoping that he'd approve of the locum's decision. After having come all this way to embark on her first real-life adventure, she'd hate to

have to turn around and go back. Then Maggie remembered her resolution. *She'd never go back.*

Jack held out his hand, and she clasped it for a brief
moment, but that's all it took for him to feel something
tingle in his palm. "I'm Jack Montgomery, the medical
director here. Pleased to meet you, Maggie…"

"Wellington."

"Glad to have you on board, Maggie. Welcome to
Alaska." He released her hand and opened the door to the
clinic, but stopped. "See you later." He turned back into
the clinic before he could get lost in those baby blue eyes.

She watched his gait and the rhythm with which he
walked and knew instantly that he was a runner.

A sigh of pure female appreciation almost poured
from her, but she squelched it. Here and now was not
the place or the time to be attracted to anyone, especially the medical director. This was the adventure of a
lifetime, and she wasn't going to mess it up.

On her first break in the staff lounge, Maggie reached
for the pot of coffee.

"Don't touch that," Jack said from behind her.

Maggie whirled around, her heart fluttering wildly.
She placed a hand to her chest with a sigh of relief. "Oh,
you startled me."

"Sorry, but I was passing by and wanted to stop you
before you poisoned yourself. The coffee is really bad
here." Jack entered the small lounge and made it seem
smaller.

"Thanks." She returned the Styrofoam cup to the stack.

"I was going to the diner. Care to join me? Coffee's
a little better there, but not like in Seattle."

"Caffeine addict?" Maggie asked with a smile, relating to the cravings that hit her every morning.

"Certifiable."

Maggie shoved her hands into her scrub pants pockets as they walked to the ER, hoping that Jack didn't want to take her someplace private to fire her. That would be just her luck, if there'd been a mistake after she'd uprooted her entire life to come here.

At the nurses' station they approached the charge nurse. "Catherine, I'm going to the café, and I'd like to borrow Maggie if you're not too busy here."

"It's pretty slow now, and I'm sure she can use the break, too. I'll page you if anything big comes in."

"So what brings you to Alaska, Maggie?" Jack asked minutes later as they settled into a booth at the café.

"Adventure, I suppose." She smiled up at him, hoping to read something in his face, but his expression remained guarded, watching her as if trying to see inside her brain.

"You're from Boston, right? Aren't there enough adventures in Massachusetts?"

Maggie avoided his glance and fiddled with the handle of her mug. "None that I wanted," she said. "I wanted someplace far from home." Very far.

"You can't get any farther away without leaving the country. What made you leave Boston?"

"I needed a change of pace, change of scenery, change of everything," Maggie said, knowing that was true but leaving out a few details didn't hurt.

"Your résumé said you worked the ER at Massachusetts General Hospital. I'll bet that had plenty of excitement."

"Not the kind I'm looking for," Maggie said, and shook her head, not wanting to think about her time there. "I don't want that any more." She looked up, and her cheeks warmed beneath his probing gaze. Hazel eyes were usually dull, but his were brilliantly colored.

"Where are you staying?"

"There's an inn just down the street, Brownies, that I'm staying in until I can find an apartment or something."

"There are plenty of efficiency apartments around, but they're overpriced during the summer." Jack sipped his coffee but continued to observe her, wondering if she could truly handle it here or if she'd take off when the weather turned cold, like others who had come before her. "Let me ask around and see if there is anyone who might have a place for rent."

"No, you don't have to do that," Maggie asserted. "Really, you shouldn't. I'll find something." She sat up straight and looked at him, concerned he'd go to too much effort on her account and think her nothing but trouble from the start.

"I don't mind," Jack said. He paused and stared into his coffee-cup. "Don't take this the wrong way, but are you planning on staying a while?"

"I don't know. Why?" It would just be her luck if the locum had hired her and Jack didn't approve. "Has there been a mistake in hiring me?" She may as well ask straight out and know right now whether she had a future in Alaska or not.

"No. No mistake. My concern is that I've seen people come to Alaska for a great adventure and leave after a few months. They decide that Alaska is too far, too cold, too something for them, and they return to the lower forty-eight, leaving us with another staffing shortage."

"You're making too many assumptions. I have no intention of leaving," Maggie said, and cocked her jaw to the side, determined to prove him wrong. "I just got here."

"I understand, but as medical director I have to prepare for every outcome, and new staff bolting is one of them," Jack said, his expression grim. "You'll be on probation for sixty days, or until you prove that you can hang in there and aren't going to go back home when things get tough. At the end of your probation we'll reevaluate."

"I'm not going anywhere, Dr. Montgomery." Maggie leaned back against the red vinyl upholstery of the booth and stared at him.

"Good. But in the meantime we still need to find you some decent housing."

They ordered and ate a simple meal in awkward silence.

"So what about you?" Maggie asked and indicated his left hand. "Wife and kids?"

He looked down and touched his thumb to the simple gold ring he wore. His vows had meant something to him. "No. My wife died before we had children."

"Oh. I'm sorry." Maggie looked away.

Jack stood. He'd heard the words often enough over the years and didn't need to hear them now. "Let's go back to the clinic."

"How long have you been in Alaska?" she asked, hoping she wasn't going to anger him with her questions.

"Six years."

"Did you need to make any adjustments when you came?" She already knew the answer, but had to ask. Something made her curious about Jack, and she wanted to know more.

"Sure, but—"

"So it *is* possible for someone to come from another place to Alaska, and be able to do well here, then?" Maggie slanted a glance at him and waited. She held her breath.

"Yes, of course, you're right—"

"Oh, I love to hear those words. Twice in one day, too." Being right wasn't something that her family credited her with, so she savored the feeling now.

"But, Maggie, I'd planned to come here for years." Jack stopped and stared down at her, his eyes dark and serious.

"How do you know I didn't?" she asked, hoping her pulse would settle down. Confrontations always unnerved her, and she avoided them, but her life depended on this one, and she faced it head-on.

"From what you said, it sounded like an impulse."

"Well, it wasn't. Maybe I didn't plan as long as you did, but this was definitely an intention. I need to be here as much as you do." Probably more, she thought.

"Probation. Sixty days. I'm not changing my mind."

Maggie smiled up at him, and he returned it with obvious reluctance. "OK, but you're going to be eating your words, Jack, and it won't take sixty days."

CHAPTER TWO

JACK left Maggie in the company of Catherine after they returned to the ER. Though it was a small clinic, the flow of patients seemed constant due to the high traffic of village residents, fishermen, and tourists with the occasional fishhook stuck where it wasn't supposed to be.

Two hours later Maggie insisted that Catherine take a break. "Why don't you sit for a while and let me handle the next few who come in?"

"Oh, no, I couldn't," Catherine protested.

Maggie led Catherine to the nurses' station and sat her in a chair. "When are you due?"

"When am I...? How did you know?" Surprise widened Catherine's eyes.

"You've been very discreet, but you've placed your hand over your abdomen several times. Unless you have day-long indigestion, I'd say you're pregnant." Maggie smiled, pleased her observations had been correct and hoping that Catherine wasn't overdoing it.

"You're right. It feels good to tell someone," she whispered.

"No one else knows?" Surprised, Maggie hoped for

an explanation. Having a baby should be something you shouted from the rooftops. Why wasn't Catherine?

"No. I'm only about two months along, and so many things can go wrong in the first trimester." Catherine looked away, but not before Maggie had caught the shine of tears in her eyes.

"Have you had trouble before?" Maggie didn't like to see her new friend suffer, but some women seemed to be plagued with fertility issues. Mother Nature could be a cruel mistress.

Catherine nodded and blew her nose. "Yes. That's why I don't want to say anything. Not until I'm sure this one's a keeper." She patted her abdomen in a protective gesture.

Maggie gave her a quick hug. "I hope so, too. Just take a rest now, will you?"

Catherine dabbed her eyes. "That's what my husband Charlie says, too."

"Well, he's right." Two things Maggie never thought she'd ever have—a husband and a baby—and Catherine had them both. Since her flight to Alaska, her life had already changed for the better. Maybe some day she'd fulfill that dream, too.

"Who's right?" Jack asked as he entered the room, unaware of the intimate conversation between Maggie and Catherine.

Maggie closed her eyes, her heart palpitating in chagrin. How much had he heard? Not much, she hoped. This was Catherine's secret, and Maggie wasn't going to betray it. Her mouth went dry. "Uh, the medical director is always right." She smiled and turned, wide-eyed, to Catherine, hoping she'd go along with it. "Isn't that what you told me?"

"Uh, yeah," Catherine agreed with a choked snort.

He looked back and forth between them, amused doubt shining in his eyes. "I'll believe that when I see it," he said. "Catherine, mind if I borrow Maggie again?"

The women exchanged a glance, and Maggie experienced a measure of relief as the tension in the room evaporated. "Sure, go ahead."

She touched Catherine on the arm, whispering, "I'll be back in a bit. Don't overdo it." Then she turned to Jack. "What are we doing?"

"I know a lady with a room for rent."

"You didn't have to go to the trouble, but I'm grateful."

"I'll take you over and introduce you."

They strolled with silence between them, his loping gait slowed to match hers. Seagulls screeched overhead, looking for any tidbit of food to scavenge, and the breeze whispered softly over her face.

They turned down a narrow street that looked like an oil painting come to life. Every possible color of the rainbow jumped out. Bold reds, the brightest yellows and impossible blues burst from pots and window planters. Even a pair of old boots hanging from a hook boasted an array of playful pansies. "This is lovely," she said, taking in the charm of the street. "It almost doesn't look real."

They walked to a small pink and yellow house at the end of the short row, and Jack knocked on the door. Rubber tires and more old boots had found new life as pansy planters here, too.

"Coming!" The door was yanked open by a gray-haired woman with a pair of striking green eyes. "Hey, there, Doc."

"Ella McGee, meet Maggie Wellington, our newest nurse."

Maggie shook the older woman's hand, smiling into a face filled with the wrinkles of life.

"Nice to meet you," Ella said. "I hear you're looking for a place to stay."

"Yes. Jack said you might have something available." So far so good. Maggie liked the look of the place, warm, inviting, and Ella was friendly enough.

"Come in and have a look," Ella said, and stepped back from the door.

Before Maggie entered the little house, she turned to smile up at Jack. "Thank you. I'm going to like living here." A puzzling warmth flowed through her at Jack's thoughtful gesture. Maybe he didn't think she was going to bolt after all.

Maggie observed Jack during the shift change several hours later. She had been so grateful to him for finding her somewhere to live, and she was certain she had felt something between them as they had walked through the house. But perhaps she was only imagining it. She could only imagine how painful his wife's death must have been. Would he ever consider another relationship? Maggie blew out a sigh and shook her head, trying to clear it. Was his pain any of her concern?

No. She had to prove herself, that's all she had to do, and she had sixty days to do it. Proving herself had been a life-long endeavor, so she was good at it, even when she didn't want to be.

Just then Jack looked up and captured her gaze. Though he was still speaking to a nurse, his piercing gaze remained locked to hers. A vibration charged through her, and her breathing caught as her heart trembled unevenly.

Someone called his name, and his attention turned away from Maggie. The interaction had lasted only seconds, but something intangible and seductive had passed between them. That simple look, that momentary connection, shook her more than she cared to admit. With her head down she took a few deep breaths, clearing her mind and focusing again on the job she had come here to do. Nothing in her plans left room for any sort of liaison, especially with her boss. No lust, no love, no nothing but the job. That was the only thing she could count on.

No, no, no, Maggie. You can't think of that man as anything but your boss.

"Are you OK?"

Maggie turned to face Jack standing beside her, his eyes cool but concerned. The tension that had started to ease rushed back with full force. "I didn't see you come over." Damn. Of all the people in the clinic, it had to be Jack standing there.

"You were hanging on to the desk like there was an earthquake." Jack's sharp gaze moved over her, assessingly.

"An earthquake?" she asked. "Don't tell me I moved to an earthquake zone." Great.

"Out here we're on a fault line bigger than the one in California. Did you feel a tremor just now?"

"I felt something, but I don't know what." Maggie

swallowed and tried to keep her face expressionless. As she stared at him, her mouth went dry.

Jack held her gaze. "Me, too."

Maggie woke in the middle of her first night at Ella's to an emergency call to come in to the clinic. Things that went bump in the night were usually traffic accidents. Bad ones.

Catherine was waiting by the door of the first patient room. "Maggie, go with Jack. I'll take the second patient and get him settled."

Maggie slipped a face shield onto Jack and one on herself. No time for anything else except gloves as the patients came through the doors.

Jack ignored the fluctuation in his heart rate as Maggie's fragrance washed over him, singing through his senses. He was probably just excited about the trauma, that was why his heart beat erratically and why his mouth suddenly went dry.

"Grab a flashlight," he said, and they checked the patient's pupils.

"The left one is sluggish," she said. "Did he hit his head?"

"Yes. I'm worried about a serious brain bleed." Jack looked behind him. "Amos, set up transport to Anchorage."

Sharp footsteps rushed through the ER and arrived at the door of the trauma room. "Where is he? Is he here?" a female voice, bordering on hysteria, cried.

"Oh, dear." Maggie rushed to the doorway to intercept the heavily pregnant woman who had just burst in.

Her eyes were wide with shock, and she panted while keeping a hand on her rounded abdomen. "Where is he?" she asked again, and tears flooded her face as she spied a man on a gurney. "That can't be him. Where is he?"

"You're looking for…?"

"Gerald. Gerald Turvick." She sniffed, but the tears still ran.

Maggie curved an arm around the woman's shoulders and took one of her hands. "Are you his wife?"

"Yes," the woman said. "Anita. Now where is he?"

"We're treating Gerald right now. Can you sit outside for just a few minutes while we make him stable?"

"Yes, but where *is* he? I have to know."

The shrill tone of her words scraped Maggie's nerves raw, but she didn't react. The woman was frightened and needed calming comfort right now. "That's him." Maggie gave what she hoped was an encouraging smile, but knew that it couldn't be.

"But look at that man. He can't possibly be my husband."

"Sometimes swelling in the face makes people look different for a while, but it's him." Maggie led Anita to a chair outside the trauma room. "Stay right here for a little while, and I'll come get you as soon as you can see him."

"Was that his wife?" Jack asked when Maggie returned. A muscle in his jaw twitched.

"Yes. You're going to have to talk to her soon. There's no one with her, and she's easily eight months pregnant."

"Great. Just what she needs right now." Jack shook

his head, hating to be the bearer of bad news, but it came with the job. "We'd better talk to her before the transport comes so she can make arrangements. Or something." He felt so helpless when it came to delivering bad news. Every time, he returned emotionally to his wife's illness and the sick feeling in his gut when they had been told the news. The telling never got easier.

They sat beside Anita. "Mrs. Turvick?" Jack asked, and cleared his throat. He reached out for one of her hands. It was ice cold, and he placed his other hand on top of it, hoping to impart a little bit of warmth into her.

"Yes," she whispered as her chin trembled, and her eyes searched Jack's for the truth. "Is he dead?"

"No, but he is seriously injured and is going to need to go to Anchorage for possible brain surgery." It had to be said but, God, he wished there was another way to say it.

"Oh, no," she cried, and covered her face with her hands.

"He's young and physically strong, so those are excellent points in his favor," Jack said, hoping his words would offer her some comfort. But when he'd been told of his wife's illness nothing had helped. Jack's gut twisted into knots as he listened to Anita's sobs. Nothing tortured him more than listening to a woman cry, and as he watched her he froze. Unable to speak, he looked at Maggie.

Sympathy filled her eyes and the sad smile she gave him said she understood his pain.

Something was happening to Jack. She didn't quite know what it was, but there was a plea for help in his eyes. How could she not move to help? That's what she did. She helped people. No matter who they were.

Maggie put an arm around Anita's shoulders and hugged her close.

"That damned man. I told him to sleep more, but when he gets off the boat he wants to sleep in his own bed." She dabbed her eyes. "This was his last trip out before the baby came. Can I see him now?"

Maggie helped Anita to stand and placed a hand on Jack's shoulder. Palpable tension oozed out of him, and he met her gaze. The contact hummed between them as Jack squeezed her hand, then rose. Maybe he needed a friend.

"Dr. Montgomery? Why don't I take Anita in, and you can finish the transport arrangements?" Maggie suggested, then spoke again to Anita. "I'll tell you everything that he's hooked up to so it doesn't frighten you."

"OK, I'm ready," she said, and clutched Maggie's hands as they entered the trauma room, with Jack following behind, feeling useless in the face of the woman's tears and Maggie's obvious control of the situation.

Anita cried softly as Maggie explained everything. As the transport crew arrived Anita leant over his head and kissed his forehead.

Gerald stirred, and his hand moved. Anita grabbed it and held on. "He's squeezing my hand," she cried, and brought his knuckles to her mouth for a kiss.

"He hears you, he really does. He just can't reply with all the tubes in him," Maggie said with tears in her eyes, overjoyed at his response, and she looked at Jack who watched from the doorway. He nodded, his expression grim, and Maggie's heart wrenched. His pain was so overwhelming she could feel it across the room.

"Thank you," Anita said as they left the room. "I

don't know how I'm going to get through this, but if Gerald can be strong, then I can be strong, too."

"Do you have any family or friends who can help you for a while so you're not alone?" Maggie hoped so. Being alone through such a tough time was unthinkable in Anita's condition. If she had no one, Maggie would find a way to help Anita herself.

"Yes, my sister. I don't think I'll be able to go to Anchorage because I'm too close to the due date. I'm sure she'll want to go for me," Anita said, her eyes bright with new hope.

"Why don't you go home now?" Maggie suggested.

"I will and thank you again." Anita hugged Maggie to her.

Maggie watched as Anita left and sensed Jack beside her. "I hope he makes it," she said, and heaved a sigh as they re-entered the clinic after the patient had been transported.

"Think you're up to a lifetime of this?" Jack asked as they entered the staff lounge.

Maggie let out a quick laugh, letting the tension of the last few hours drop away from her. "A lifetime? Let me get through the first week, OK?"

"Fair enough." Jack's lips made an effort to smile, but the gesture didn't reach his eyes.

He dropped into the couch with a sigh and rubbed his face in his hands.

Maggie watched him a few moments. She wanted to go to him, offer him a shoulder in friendship, but was that overstepping the boundaries between boss and employee? She offered comfort all the time to strangers. What was stopping her from reaching out to Jack?

Maggie sat down and blew out a long breath. "That was tough, wasn't it?" she asked, and hoped that he'd respond, not shut her out.

"I think he's going to make it."

"I meant telling the wife about her husband." As soon as she'd said it, Maggie bit her lip, hoping Jack didn't take her head off for probing into his pain.

Jack sat up. After a moment he spoke. "Yes." He turned and looked at her. "Yes, it was hard."

"Want to talk about it?" Maggie cringed a little, waiting for Jack to respond.

"No." He shook his head and looked away. "Thank you," he added in a hoarse whisper.

Maggie's heart was breaking for Jack and the pain he'd suffered, still suffered, and couldn't seem to share. "Well, if you ever need to talk, I'm here, Jack." At least she had offered and now it was up to him whether he'd reach out or not.

Jack nodded, patted Maggie once on the knee and left the lounge.

The day passed with unusual slowness compared to the busy pre-dawn. By noon Maggie was yawning at the triage desk when Jack approached. "I've asked another nurse to come in for a few hours so you can go home."

"Did I do something wrong?" Panicked, she jumped up from behind the desk, not wanting to disappoint him. So many times she'd been a disappointment to her family—she didn't want to be one here, not when probation loomed over her head and the potential loss of her job. "Whatever I did, I'm sorry," Maggie panted as she stared at Jack.

"Whoa, Maggie, slow down. You haven't done

anything wrong." He moved toward her and placed his hands on her shoulders.

"Don't treat me differently because I'm on probation."

"I'm not. Calm down. I'd do this for any of the staff. Catherine's gone home, why shouldn't you?"

Maggie stared at Jack as her heart palpitated in her chest. Slowly she unclenched her hands, which she hadn't realized were knotted in front of her. After a deep sigh the sweat trickling down her back stopped. The fist in her gut evaporated, too. Why had she reacted so strongly? Old fears haunted her and surfaced when she wasn't holding them back. "God, Jack. I'm sorry." She sent an apologetic glance his way and was relieved to see a calm expression on his face.

Jack smiled lopsidedly. "You're just tired. Why don't you go home and get some sleep? It's been a rough shift."

"I'm OK. A few more cups of coffee and I'll be good for the rest of the shift." Another yawn caught her off guard, and she clamped a hand over her mouth.

"You know, if you suppress a yawn it leaks out your ears," Jack said, not taking his eyes off of her.

Maggie snorted a laugh and dropped her hand. "It does not." She thought a second and then narrowed her eyes at Jack. "Does it?"

Jack gave a quick laugh. "If you're even considering it, you're too tired. Go home, have a nap. If you're up for it later, I'll give you a tour of the island." Keeping his eyes on the chart, he didn't look up as he made the offer.

"I'd like that."

Jack sensed the pleasure in her voice and watched her leave. Why had he made such an offer? But how could he retract it now without feeling like an idiot? He sighed and headed to his office, irritated with his impulsive gesture. Rubbing a hand over his face, he groaned. After locking the door to his office, Jack went home, too.

That evening, while the sun still blazed high overhead, looking much like a pleasant afternoon, Maggie explored the village of Kodiak. After meandering down a side street crowded with quaint gift shops carrying Alaskan-made foods and gifts, she started back toward Ella's. Maggie didn't consider it her home yet, because it wasn't.

That was another thing she'd need to think about—calling someplace home, putting down roots and establishing herself in a community. She'd volunteered at several charities in Boston. Maybe she could find some place in Kodiak to volunteer, too.

As she wandered in and out of stores, Maggie made several purchases and tucked the bags under her arm. Kodiak was a lovely village, and she was happy she'd come here. Perhaps one day she'd call this place home.

When she got back to the cottage, after putting her purchases away, she looked at the answering-machine and stifled a blip of disappointment that Jack hadn't called. Then the phone rang and her heart pulsed with anticipation as she picked it up.

"Hello? McGee residence."

"Hi, Maggie. It's Jack."

When he spoke her name, she paused. The quiet of

the line and the empty house lent an unexpected intimacy. She shivered. *Focus, Maggie. Focus.*

"Hello, Jack. H-how are you?"

"I slept for a few hours, so I'm ready for another round. You?"

"Oh." Disappointment chased away the initial excitement his call had inspired. "Is there another emergency I need to come in for?"

"No, everything's quiet at the clinic. I meant the island tour. You still interested?"

Pleasure pulsed in a throbbing wave. *So much for focus.* She switched the phone from one ear to the other, but her suddenly moist hand slipped on the receiver. It bounced off the counter and clattered to the floor. Horrified, she scooped up the phone and clutched it to her ear. "I'm so sorry, Jack! I dropped the phone." She cringed, even though he couldn't see her. Chalk up another mistake to her growing list of them.

"If you didn't want to go, all you had to do was say no," Jack said. "You didn't have to deafen me in the process."

Maggie heard the smile in his voice, and gave a relieved laugh. "I'd love to go."

"See you in ten, then."

After a quick change into a fresh shirt, she grabbed a light jacket and waited on the porch for Jack. In minutes the squeak of brakes alerted her to his arrival. Maggie stuffed her jacket in the back seat and reached to buckle her seat belt, but it resisted the efforts of her suddenly trembling fingers.

"It sticks sometimes," Jack said, and placed his hand over hers.

Startled, Maggie looked up as he leaned toward her. His mouth neared hers. Anticipation flooded her as her lips parted. Then Jack pulled back with a can of oil in one hand, which he had grabbed from under the seat.

"Just needs a little coaxing," he said.

The quick spurt of pressurized oil made Maggie jump and the belt snapped into place. "Oh," she said, trying to forget the way she had just thought about kissing Jack. "It scared me."

He gave a wicked grin. "Wait till you see me drive."

CHAPTER THREE

"So, WHERE are we going?" Maggie asked, eager to see more of the island and have the wind blow away any intimate thoughts of Jack. Getting cozy with the boss wasn't in her plans. Not now, not ever, despite the budding attraction she had for him. He wasn't available. She couldn't believe that he was still emotionally attached to his deceased wife. How did a woman compete with that anyway?

"There's a lot to see. Want to just drive around for a while?"

"Sure."

Jack drove out of town where the road paralleled the inlet. Maggie watched as a pod of killer whales made their way through the water. "Oh, how magnificent!" Maggie cried. "I've never seen a group of whales like that. Can we stop?" Without thinking, she clutched Jack's sleeve.

"We can stop at the viewing station up ahead." Maggie's excitement blossomed in her cheeks and left a sparkle in her eyes. Jack was captured by the spell, powerless to resist her charm.

"Thank you, Jack," she said. "I've only seen them in captivity, never like this."

Before Jack had pulled off to the side of the road Maggie had unbuckled her seat belt and almost dove from the Jeep. A large orca breeched, shooting out of the water and landing on its back, splashing water higher than any building on the island.

She stood breathless, awed by the power of the whale and the roar of the splash. Tears came to her eyes at the overwhelming sight. Never in her life had she seen such a beautiful thing. Never had she been allowed the freedom to explore. As she stood beside Jack and watched the group of killer whales feed just yards from shore, she realized her past was behind her—she just had to keep it that way. Breathless, she turned to Jack. "This is just remarkable. Do you see this every day?" she asked, emotion choking her voice.

"No, not every day, but frequently. They summer here." Jack watched her. The excitement in her eyes pleased him, as if he had brought her there for just this moment, as if knowing the whale was going to perform just for her. He'd almost forgotten how powerful the animals were, but now, watching them through Maggie's eyes, the wonder was almost new again.

The breeze pulled a lock of hair from her ponytail and teased her cheek with it. Just as Jack reached out to tuck the lock away, Maggie's hand moved to do the same. Their hands collided, and Jack pulled back as if stung.

"I'm sorry. I shouldn't have…" Jack's voice trailed off. What was the matter with him?

"Shouldn't have what?" she asked.

"Tried to, um…push your hair back. I used to do that… I didn't…" He felt like a schoolboy with the embarrassment of first attraction. Was that what this was? Attraction? Wanting to touch Maggie? "It was inappropriate of me. I'm sorry." Jack shoved his hands into his pockets and faced the water. It was safer than facing Maggie.

"It's OK, Jack. I understand. Old habits." She turned back to watch the whales, seemingly undisturbed by it.

Jack nodded and cleared his throat. "Let's get going," he said.

"Can I ask you a personal question?" Maggie asked as they drove along.

"Do we know each other well enough for personal questions?" Jack asked, a frown darkening his expression.

"We're going to." She really wanted to know. This wasn't just polite conversation. Jack interested her, despite her efforts not to be attracted to him.

"OK, what do you want to know?"

"What happened to your wife?" The question was seemingly rude, but there was no simple way to ask, and she hoped she didn't alienate their developing friendship by being too personal too quickly.

"She had ovarian cancer. She was twenty-eight."

Maggie gasped and in an instant wished she hadn't asked the question. "She was so young. I'm sorry."

"Yes, she was."

Maggie clenched her hands in her lap, unsure of what to do with them. She wanted to reach out to him, but she didn't. A muscle twitched in Jack's jaw, and he stared ahead at the road, his expression closed off, and Maggie sighed. To try to console him, even with a light squeeze on his shoulder, was too personal, so she opted for a lighter mood and a different subject. "OK, tour guide, give me some history on this tour, will ya?"

Jack slid her a sideways smile, and she knew she had pleased him with the change of topic. As he talked, his shoulders relaxed, and he rested his wrist casually over the steering-wheel.

"There's a great little dive that I'd like to take you to, if you don't mind." He looked at her and his eyes were calm, the turmoil of emotions now gone.

Maggie gave a quick laugh, relieving any lingering tension between them. "In my experience, *great* and *dive* aren't usually used in the same sentence. I take it you've eaten here before and survived."

Jack grinned. "Many times."

After they were seated, Maggie looked at the menu and they shared drinks. "I'm not sure what to have. It all sounds good."

"This is your first trip to Alaska. You've got to have salmon." After the waiter had taken their order Jack spoke. "So, Maggie, tell me your story."

Maggie looked into his eyes, but didn't suffer any anguish at what could have been an uncomfortable question. Gone was the interrogation of the medical director. This was something different. Reading people's eyes came as second nature to her, both in her job and in her family. Something deeper motivated Jack, and he was really interested in the answer.

"My story?" Before answering, she looked away from the intensity of his gaze and ran one finger around the rim of the glass.

"Yeah. Everyone's got a story," he said, and sipped his wine.

He'd offered her a gesture of friendship, and she took it. She had to trust sometime. "If I had stayed where I was, I would have died."

"Were you sick?"

"Yes. Sick of the life I was living, having my life micromanaged by my father. I had been searching the journals and online ads for jobs, but nothing sounded right until I found this job. I handed in my notice, hopped a plane, and here I am."

"Just like that?"

"Just like that." Maggie saluted him with her wineglass and took a long drink. "When something is right, you know it. And when it's wrong, you know that, too."

"How so?" Jack focused his entire attention on her.

Maggie trembled a little under the intensity of his gaze, but went on. "Because my entire life has been dictated by my father. I've always been a project to him, never a person who might have needs or wants of her own. And I did." She shook her head, correcting herself. "I do. The time had come for me to make a break from a life that was killing me. Simple as that." She huffed out a quick breath and took a gulp of her drink as fiery heat overtook her cheeks. She hated it when it her emotions betrayed her.

"I'm sorry if I made you uncomfortable. That wasn't my intention."

"Well, now you know the deep dark truth about Maggie Wellington," she said, and looked away.

"Maggie?"

"Yes?" Here it came. The let-down. Hating to do it,

she looked up anyway, and met Jack's gaze. There was nothing but a friendly light shining in it.

"It's not that deep or dark."

"I won't disappoint you, Jack. I promise."

Her face brightened, and Jack was glad to see it. He knew she had worried about his expectations, but trying to put her at ease had only seemed to make her anxiety worse.

"There are many things I don't know about frontier medicine, but every day I'm learning more, and I won't let you down." Eagerness tore through her. "Why don't you tell me about some of the unusual cases that come in? I'd love to hear about them," she said, as the waiter arrived with their meal of blackened salmon on a bed of angel-hair pasta for both of them.

"If you don't mind while we eat." Jack hesitated.

She waved away his concern. "Please. I'm a nurse. We talk about bowel surgery while eating sausage."

Jack described some of the cases that had come through the clinic doors. Things Maggie never would have experienced anywhere else.

"And then a native family came in with a massive case of food poisoning from eating fermented beaver tail," Jack said, and speared a chunk of salmon.

Maggie quit eating and placed a hand to her throat. "OK, stop. Now you're going to make me sick," she said, and sipped her wine.

"Sorry." He laughed. "But I warned you."

"I know. Try another story that's less descriptive, will you?" She shivered as Jack moved on to another, less nauseating story.

Sated, they returned to Kodiak in a companionable

silence. As they drove along, Maggie watched for more whales, hoping to see more of those wondrous creatures. A strange movement at the edge of the receding water caught her eye. "What's that? Another group of whales?" She pointed to the area past the viewing point they had stopped at earlier.

"The tide's gone out," Jack said, and swung the vehicle into the parking area, his curiosity also aroused. "Let's take a closer look."

They hurried to the viewing platform and hung over the side, trying to get a better look. "It's a whale in the mud!"

"Sometimes they beach themselves when they lose direction or follow a school of fish in too far." Jack didn't want to think how Maggie would react to this after seeing them in the wild for the first time.

"That's terrible. Can we help it?" The danger the whale was in overwhelmed the wonder of the previous sighting.

Jack led her to a gate, the concern in her voice urging him on. "I think we can get through over here. I'll help you over the rocks." Maggie followed, clutching his arm. "Don't go too far in. People digging for clams or walking out on the tide flats have gotten stuck."

"Really?" Maggie backed away from the mud, her eyes wide.

"Yes, and when the tide came back in again, they drowned."

The magic in Maggie's eyes was fading quickly to horror. "You're serious?"

"Very. That's why it's good to explore with someone who knows the area."

"What can we do to help the whale? I don't want to just stand here and watch it die."

Maggie's gaze bored into his, and he was helpless against the plea. Jack looked at the huge animal as it thrashed, trying to right itself. It was still half-covered by water, but it would be completely exposed when the tide receded.

"I don't know anyone at Fish and Game, but Ella will." Jack pulled out his cell phone. Not only was it important that they get help for the beached whale, but also for some reason he wanted to help the animal for Maggie. She was the first woman he'd been attracted to since his wife's death. That meant something, didn't it? She cared about people and animals, that was obvious. Though he couldn't physically or emotionally reach out to her, he could do this. That was the most he could give her.

Dialing the number Ella gave him, Jack clenched his jaw, irritated that his thoughts had strayed to any sort of romantic liaison with Maggie. He took a few steps away from her, needing a little space to clear his head. Aside from his commitment to his vows, he was Maggie's boss. How irresponsible could he be, allowing himself to be attracted to her?

"Thanks," Jack said, and ended the call. "Fish and Game will be here soon. They'll know what to do."

Maggie clutched Jack's arm briefly then released it. The whale no longer thrashed about but lay still in the water, having exhausted its energy. Maggie pointed to a place farther out in the inlet where spouts of water flew high in the air. "Look. More whales."

"They're probably family to this one. From what I

know about orcas, they travel in family pods. This could be a young whale that got separated from his family, and they're out there, waiting for him to come back."

Jack went to fetch a bucket from the Jeep and returned to Maggie. "Don't get near its head. It may try to bite you out of fear, and those teeth could take off your leg."

"OK." She stepped back. "Look at the tide. I can't believe how fast it moves."

Jack could hear the fear in her voice, and he cringed inwardly. "Don't worry. F and G will be here soon. But, Maggie," he warned her, hating to dampen that beautiful light in her eyes but unable to lie about the risks, "sometimes Mother Nature can be harsh. The whale may not live, not even with all the help we can give it."

Solemnly she nodded, her mouth turned down. "I know, but we have to try, don't we?"

There was no doubt in Maggie, and her courage urged him on. "We do."

Together they approached the orca, now almost completely exposed by the receding tide. Maggie stroked its dorsal fin, affection and concern for the animal obvious. "You're going to be OK, baby," Maggie said, and stroked it once more. They filled the container with seawater and poured it over the whale, bathing the animal's skin. Though late in the evening, the sun was still high in the sky, and the whale would dry out quickly.

Three hours later, exhaustion overcame Maggie. F and G officials finally arrived, but they couldn't do anything more than what Jack and Maggie had done. Mother Nature would take its course.

"This is so frustrating," Maggie said, her hands clenched into fists at her side. "We should be doing more. Isn't there something else we can do?"

Jack looked across the whale at her. Tears filled her luminescent blue eyes, and he wanted to go to her, offer her comfort, but he couldn't. Could he? What stopped him? The ring of gold burning on his left hand?

Maggie turned away and wiped her eyes. Without thinking, he walked around the whale and pulled her into his arms. "It'll be OK, Maggie," Jack whispered. "It's OK." Too many emotions churned inside him to be held back. Jack had been dead inside for a long time. But now, standing in the mud, holding Maggie as the glorious midnight sun set, he was coming alive.

For a minute or two she clung to him, then she pushed back. "I'm sorry. I must really be tired." Maggie wiped her face on her sleeve. She had to be strong in front of Jack, show him she could take it here, not fall to pieces in an emergency, even if it was an animal emergency.

"You're not blubbering, and I'm not sorry. Not sorry at all," Jack said. He wanted to keep her in his arms, but he let her move away. It was safer that way.

"I guess we'd better get back to town, but I hate to leave in the middle of this," Maggie said. She dropped her hands to her sides and lowered her gaze to her boots.

Jack ran his hand down the tangle of her hair blown wild by the wind. He squeezed both of her arms and then tipped her face up. He gave her a gentle smile and was rewarded with a curve of her lips, but sadness still swirled in her eyes.

Looking at her, something shifted inside him. For a

second he pondered his wedding band, then his gaze returned to her.

She didn't even know yet how long she'd be staying in Kodiak. How could he be starting to have feelings for her? He'd only known Maggie Wellington a few days and certainly not well enough to embrace her or imagine kissing her. She came from money and was used to grander surroundings than a small village like Kodiak. When the novelty of living here wore off, she'd move on to bigger and better things than this island and he could offer. A man without emotion was nothing inside. And that's all he was.

Maybe that was just an excuse on his part. Shoving his clenched fists into his pockets, he walked out onto the mud flat and stared at the sea. After Arlene had died he'd thought about walking onto the flats and letting the tide take him. But something, some sense of responsibility to his community and his profession, had held him back.

The whale exhaled and redirected Jack's attention from his maudlin thoughts. He strangled his emotions, pushing them back where they belonged.

"Is there anything else we can do?" he asked one of the rescuers.

"No, but thanks for the help. We'll be at this until the morning tide turns," he said.

Jack looked at Maggie in her muddy and bedraggled state. "What do you think? Is this enough adventure for one day?" Jack asked.

Maggie gave a tired nod. "What a night," she said as they returned to the parking lot.

"This wasn't quite the drive around the island I

expected." Jack smiled at her, liking the look of her sleepy face. She would look like that after spending a passionate night in her lover's arms. Jack clenched his jaw and wished he could squash his thoughts as easily.

"I guess we'd better get back," Maggie said, and covered a yawn with the back of her hand. "I'm beat."

The silent drive lulled Maggie nearly to sleep. At four a.m., Jack pulled up at Ella's door with a squeak of brakes and made a mental note to get them checked.

Maggie faced Jack, her eyes barely open. "Thanks for the tour."

"You're welcome. Next time maybe it won't be quite such an adventure."

"I'm glad we helped the whale, though." She moved to an upright position and kept her gaze locked with his. "I hope it lives."

Without understanding why, Jack took her hand. A scar on the middle finger could have marred the perfect skin, but most people wouldn't have noticed it. Jack's thumb traced the tiny raised line. "What happened here?"

Maggie looked at the spot. "Oh, I got carried away with a large vegetable knife, trying to chop like the chefs on television. Cut it to the bone." She smirked at her own stupidity. "Hurt like the blue blazes, too."

Jack raised her hand and kissed the scar then, without thinking, pulled her close and kissed her lips. Exploring their dewy softness pulled a thread of desire taut in his belly, and almost unraveled the control he kept wound tight. As she opened her soft mouth beneath his, his tongue tasted the lingering freshness of the sea, and Jack savored the feel of her against him. Lord help him, but he wanted her. He really wanted to take her home and make love to her, but it would be a dreadful mistake. Until Maggie showed up, he'd almost forgotten what desire felt like. Emotions and physical needs only complicated life, and Maggie unleashed both of those in him. He pulled back with an apology.

"I'm sorry." Jack placed one small kiss on her forehead as he breathed in her fragrance and tried to still the beating of his heart, desire still pumping through his veins.

"Don't worry. We're both tired." Maggie's arms held on to him, and her breathing was as uneven as his.

"But I shouldn't have…"

"It was a kiss, Jack. That's all." She touched his cheek with her palm.

"OK. See you tomorrow." Jack nodded and released her.

Maggie slid from the seat and entered the house.

He was unable to offer Maggie a relationship. So why bother to think about having one with the most interesting woman to wander into his life in a long time? They could have an affair, a lovely, passionate, glorious affair, but in the end they'd both get hurt. That pain could be avoided simply by not becoming involved in the first place and keeping his emotional distance.

After the short drive home, Jack entered his quiet house. After being with Maggie, his home suddenly looked drab and pale. Too tired to think, he stripped and fell onto the bed. Dreams came in swirling mists that clouded his mind, leaving behind the memory of soft curves and passionate kisses.

CHAPTER FOUR

MAGGIE struggled into a light jacket and bolted from the house with a bagel clamped in her mouth. Coffee would just have to wait until she got to the clinic.

The clock showed one minute before seven a.m. as she signed in for her shift. Angry voices from one of the patient rooms forced Maggie to abandon her breakfast on the desk, and she hurried to investigate the disturbance.

Jack stood beside a gurney with an angry fisherman on it who struggled to get up, flailing his legs and arms in all directions. The fisherman looked like a plaid turtle that had landed on his back. "I don't need no goddamn stitches," he yelled. He took a swipe at Jack, but the man was too drunk to aim well, and Jack moved too quickly.

"Hey, sailor, what's going on?" Maggie asked the patient. She strolled into the exam room, ignoring Jack for the moment.

"He's poking needles in my face," the man cried to Maggie. "Help me. I don't like needles," he said, sounding like a youngster who had just been told to eat his broccoli.

"Well, why don't you look at me instead of at that nasty needle? Don't worry, the doctor is a real expert stitcher." Maggie sat on the edge of the gurney and took the man's hand in hers.

"Lookin' at you's a whole lot better than looking at him," he said, darting a quick glare in Jack's direction.

"Concentrate on my eyes and listen to the sound of my voice, and everything will be fine," she said in a soothing tone. She continued in a soft monotone, reciting a silly rhyme she'd learned as a girl.

Jack flashed a grin at her and went to work, stitching the gaping laceration over the man's left eye. The man never moved, except to allow his eyes to drift downward, and his breathing eased into snoring grunts. Just as Jack finished and snipped the thread, the man's hand went limp in Maggie's.

"Nice work," Jack said, his brows raised in amazement. "You hypnotized him."

Maggie stood and adjusted a sheet over the slumbering drunk. "Me and Jack Daniels." Maggie sighed in relief. "Relaxation techniques can work wonders."

"I see they do. Your approach was great. I was halfway to calling for some muscle to hold him down, and you did the job in ten seconds with no effort at all." Jack slapped a hand on the desk, enormously pleased with the outcome of the situation.

"I disagree. It was an effort," Maggie said.

"How? It didn't look like it."

Maggie enjoyed putting the confusion in Jack's eyes. "I had to say something nice about you. You don't know how hard that was." Maggie grinned and jumped back as Jack tossed a wadded-up towel at her.

"Smart ass," he said and chuckled. "We'll let him sleep some of this off."

"OK. I'll get report from the other shift and see you later." But she cast a glance over her shoulder and hesitated. Her gaze met his and held for a long moment. Another nurse called to Maggie, and she hurried to the report room. "Coming!"

Jack watched as she left the treatment room. She had really amazed him with that trick. Holding down a drunk was no easy task, but Maggie had accomplished it with the touch of her finger. He wondered how many other men she had wrapped around those fingers. The dull blast of water into the metal sink sounded hollow and jolted him from his mental musings. *What an idiot I am to think of Maggie in that way.* He saw the silent questions in her eyes before she left the room. Even though she had said the kiss was nothing, she wanted to know what was between them. He wondered himself. He'd spent half of the previous day berating himself for giving in to his attraction to her. And he'd spent the other half thinking about how good she'd felt in his arms. If he closed his eyes and thought about it, he could almost taste her lips again, smell the sea in her hair and feel the future in her arms.

The squawk of the radio drowned out his daydream, and he sighed, picked up the microphone and spoke to the air ambulance.

"Kodiak base. November romeo eight zero eight zero. Go ahead."

"Jack? This is Kyle. We've got a bad one coming in."

"What is it?"

"Bear mauling," Kyle said.

Jack blew out a breath. "What's your ETA?"

"Thirty minutes."

"We'll be ready." Jack signed off.

He gathered the staff to prepare them for the case coming in, but Maggie wasn't there. Irritation made a tight knot in his jaw. This had better not be the time she went AWOL on him. He dismissed the staff and entered the clinic's waiting area. "Excuse me, everyone," he called, and all of the patients looked at Jack. "We're really in for a bad case that's going to require all of our attention for a while. If any of you can wait for a few hours, please, go home and come back after lunch. I apologize for the inconvenience." There were a few stifled coughs and covered sneezes, but no one complained. They all knew that in a small community such things happened. Everyone rose to leave. "Thanks. We'll get to you as soon as we can," he said, and turned to go.

"What you got coming?" one crusty old salt asked. He rose on bowed legs that didn't look as if they would hold his weight and held on to the chair with gnarled hands, disfigured by rheumatoid arthritis.

"Bear mauling," Jack answered and took the man's arm to assist him to the door. "Tom, are you having trouble that can't wait?" Jack asked as he noticed Tom's unusually slow gait.

"No." He pulled a zipper bag filled with prescription bottles and shook it once. "Just need to get me some refills."

"Do you want to leave the bag? I can have one of the nurses call in the refills."

"No. I'll just head to the diner for a bit and come back later. You don't need a crippled old man distracting you right now." Tom patted Jack on the sleeve and shuffled his way out of the clinic. Reaching down to grasp the handle of a beaten old red wagon filled with discarded cans and bottles Tom had collected along the way, he made his way across the street to the diner.

Jack's attention returned to the situation at hand. *Where the hell was Maggie?* Jack returned to the trauma room and jerked back the curtain to find Maggie, dressed in protective gear. A face shield lay on the counter, and the entire room was set up for a critical trauma.

"What's going on, Maggie? Who did all this?" Stupefied, he entered the room.

"I did." She slid an intubation tray onto the counter.

"You weren't there when I made the announcement to the staff."

"I heard your conversation on the radio. I didn't realize you were having a press conference about it," she said, and held out a gown for him to put on. Jack placed his arms in the sleeves, and Maggie tied the gown at the back.

"But...how...?"

"As soon as you signed off the radio I came in here to get the room ready. At least as ready as I could. If there's something I haven't thought of, tell me, and I'll get it ready." After ripping open the sterile gloves, she held each one out for him to shove his hands into. "Hell, Jack. Did you think I'd run away or something?" she asked.

The flush creeping up Jack's neck answered for him. With her lips pressed tightly together, she placed the face shield over his ears. Unable to avoid his gaze, she looked at him and could see the apology in his eyes, but it wasn't enough to soothe the hurt. As he opened his mouth to speak, the patient and flight crew burst through the doors.

"He's not looking good, Jack." Kyle, one of the flight crew, reported. "I've got him as high as I can go on oxygen. You're going to have to intubate him so we can control his airway better."

Jack listened to the man's lungs. "He's really tight." He turned to Maggie. She was already opening the intubation tray. She just knew, seemed to read his thoughts as she sprang into action, anticipating his every need.

Maggie held up a syringe. "Ready with succsinylcholine when you are," she said.

"Dammit, Maggie. You're such a good nurse you're taking all the fun out of having to tell you what to do next," Jack said. "Go ahead."

Maggie injected the medicine that would temporarily paralyze the patient's vocal cords into the IV line, making the procedure easier. "If you have any trouble, I'm pretty good at intubation," she offered.

"I hope we won't need it, but thanks. Glad to know it."

"Ready with ten milligrams of Valium as well," Maggie said.

"Valium, OK," Jack said as he inserted the tube through the now paralyzed vocal cords and into the patient's lung. "Respiratory, bag him."

"I'm on it," the respiratory therapist said. "There's a ventilator set up and waiting."

"Good," Jack said. "Maggie, assess his lungs to make sure I've got good placement of the tube."

Maggie took the stethoscope from around Jack's

neck and listened to both lung fields. "Good ventilation. Good tube placement."

"Let's get this show on the road," Jack said. Once everything could be done to stabilize the man, Jack started to relax. "We're going to need to transfer him to the trauma center in Anchorage." He looked at Maggie. "You're next on the list to take a transport. You up for it?"

"Yep. Just need to change into my flight suit and I'll be ready to go," she said. Despite his absent-minded compliment that she was a skillful nurse, remembering his immediate thoughts to the contrary still stung. She had her pride and her nursing skills were at the top of the list. No one would ever again question her skills. Not even Jack.

"That's fine." Jack nodded. "Unless we can get someone else to take the flight."

Maggie stopped him. "Oh, no, I want to go. But I don't want to leave you short-handed here."

"Everyone in the waiting room earlier had minor complaints. I think we can handle it."

"Give me a minute, and I'll be right back," she said to the crew. On her way out of the restroom, Jack stopped her. "I'm sorry."

"I don't have time to chat now, Jack," she said, and walked past him. "Everyone's waiting for me." Re-entering the trauma room, Maggie prepared the patient for the trip, hooking him to the smaller transport machines that fit into the airplane. She worked silently but listened to the conversations of the other staff around her, ignoring Jack's presence at the door.

"We should stay overnight," Kyle suggested. "By

the time we get him there and settled, it will be time to eat. We could catch a dinner theater. What do you think, Maggie? Want to see a little of Anchorage while we're there?"

Maggie finished attaching all of the electrodes to the patient's chest and flipped on the small transport monitor. "Sure. Why not?" she said. "I could use a good time about now."

"Great," Kyle said. "Unless we get called for another transport right away, we'll be back in the morning."

Jack watched as they closed the ambulance doors and drove away. Jealousy wasn't an emotion Jack had experienced very often in his life. But now, watching Maggie plan an overnight trip with another man, even under the most professional of circumstances, and watching her drive away with him stirred that feeling. He had no right to be angry or jealous or anything where Maggie was concerned.

And he didn't like it one bit. He wasn't even sure he liked Maggie. And if he did, he couldn't, no, *wouldn't* do anything about it. Looking down at the wedding band on his finger, he clenched a fist and shoved it in his pocket.

Knowing Maggie hadn't had time to call Ella, he called her, knowing she'd worry if Maggie didn't come home after work.

"Ella? This is Jack."

"Hi, there. Problem at the clinic?"

"No. I just wanted to let you know that Maggie won't be home tonight."

"My, my, my, Jack. When a pretty girl lands in your lap, you do move fast," Ella said. Her coarse laughter scratched down the line.

A muscle in Jack's jaw twitched at the implication. "Ella McGee, shame on you. Get your mind out of the gutter."

"Why? I like it there."

"Maggie's gone on a transport to Anchorage and won't be back until morning. That's why."

"Well, too bad for you," Ella said with a sigh. "I'd rather hear that she was having an evening at home alone with you."

"I don't think so."

"Excuse me, Jack, but you're an idiot if you think Arlene would have wanted you to waste your life."

"Mind your own business."

"You've never told me to do that before—why should I start now?"

"You've never been such a busybody before."

"I'm not the one with my head in the sand," she said.

"Ella! What's wrong with you?"

"What's the matter with you? You've mourned Arlene long enough. It's time for you to get on with your life."

"I am getting on with my life. The clinic—"

"I mean your personal life, and you know it."

"You don't understand—"

"Jack, I do understand. I do. I know what it's like to lose someone and feel like you want to die with them." She took a deep breath and let out a long sigh. "It's time to let her go now. Life is meant to be lived, not watched like some parade passing you by."

Jack paused. "I'll think about it," he said, but doubted he would. Long ago he'd resolved to live alone. It was simpler that way.

"Think about that when you're all alone in bed and wondering why you're cold inside and out." Ella cleared her throat. "Thanks for letting me know about Maggie. I'll talk to you later."

The line went dead. Ella never did waste words. He was sitting there, staring at the phone, when a quick knock at the door roused him. "Come in if you have to," he said.

Amos popped his head through the door. "It's pretty quiet out here, so I'm going to head home unless you need me for anything."

"Can't think of anything," Jack said.

Amos grinned. "Good. My daughter is having her fifth birthday party tonight, and I don't want to be late." Amos started to leave, but hesitated. "If you don't have other plans, you're welcome to come by. Free cake and ice cream."

Jack tried to come up with a reason not to go, but couldn't think of one. Not on a low-gluten diet, or lactose intolerant. "Maybe."

"It's quitting time, Jack. Go home." Amos rapped the door once on his way out and left Jack staring at the door.

Why not? He had to start living sometime. Amos and his family were safe. Suddenly filled with warmth and contentment at attending the little party, Jack locked his office and left the clinic.

Maggie wiped the tears from her face. Laughing, she grabbed a napkin from the table and buried her face into it with a squeal.

Kyle patted her on the back. "You OK, kiddo? What do you think of the Fly By Night Club?"

"I've laughed so much tonight my face hurts," Maggie said, and tried to control the lingering giggles. "Please, tell me it's over. I can't take any more of this," she said.

"Show's over, but the sun's still up and the night is young," Kyle said. "Chilkoot Charlie's, here we come."

"Chilkoot Charlie's? What's that?" Maggie asked as they left the dark interior of the low building for the bright light of early evening. Maggie blinked and reached for her sunglasses. "I'll never get used to this light thing," she said.

"You will. Summer's the easy part. Just wait until winter. Then it gets tough."

"I can hardly wait."

Kyle, Maggie and two other crew members spent the night visiting Chilkoot Charlie's nightclub until the four a.m. closing. From there the small group adjourned to an all-night diner and gorged on giant omelets, gallons of coffee and Alaska chocolate silk pie. On the return flight to Kodiak the medical crew napped, sleeping off the indulgences of the night.

Once home, Maggie let herself into the house and guzzled coffee before dragging herself to the shower. Her thoughts drifted back over the short time she'd been on the island and how the people here had made her feel welcome. An image of Jack lingered as well as the memory of his kiss. Why had he kissed her? Probably all the pent up emotions over the whale. Just needed an outlet. Men didn't react to her with passion. Not really. After her one fiasco in college she'd never been tempted to jump into bed with anyone else. That experience had been a disaster. She'd mistaken his lust for love and had vowed never to do that again. She would never give herself to someone who could make her feel empty and alone. She had closed herself off to the thought of a physical relationship. Until now.

She'd enjoyed the feel, the smell and the taste of Jack. But she was terrified it meant nothing to him. Could she be sure of that? That lone tendril of desire he'd inspired in her wasn't going away like she'd hoped it would.

Over the hiss of the shower she heard the phone ring, but she ignored it, content to let the water soothe her aching body. She hadn't been out all night since college, four years ago. Her body wasn't used to it, and the shower offered some relief. Sleep would be best, but she didn't want to waste an entire day sleeping when she could be out hiking or discovering treasures around the island.

After the shower, Maggie dressed in casual clothes fit to hike, bike or adventure around the island, and returned to the coffee-pot for another infusion of life support.

The flash of the answering-machine light drew her attention, and she pushed the button to listen to the message. Seconds later she clutched the counter, her knees weak at the sound of her father's voice on the machine. She dragged in deep breaths and dropped into one of the kitchen chairs with her head between her knees.

"You'd better not faint," Ella grumbled from beside her.

Maggie turned her head and got a look at Ella's knobbly knees. "Why not?"

"'Cos I'm not picking you up." She sipped at her cup. "Bad back."

Cautiously, Maggie sat up and pressed a trembling hand to her forehead, noticing her skin felt clammy to the touch. "I need to lie down."

"What's got you all knotted up? Oh, there's a message," Ella said and hit the play button on the answering-machine.

Listening to the message the second time wasn't any better than the first. Her father's voice insisted that she return home. Maggie dropped her head between her knees again and groaned. "I can't, I won't."

"Your family got a problem with you living in Alaska?" Ella asked.

"It's not just Alaska." Maggie swallowed. Pain throbbing in her head from an excess of blood forced her to sit upright again. "They just didn't have any idea where I was until now, dammit." Tears clouded her vision, but she blinked them away, determined not to give in to fear, or guilt, or any of those things her father made her feel. She wasn't a little girl any longer. This was her life, and she wasn't going to let him run it or ruin it. Not when she'd finally found a place where she fit in.

"Is there a good reason you don't want your family to know where you are?" Ella asked, and sat beside Maggie, watching her.

"My father has run my life up until a few months ago when I escaped from the asylum that's the family home." She gulped down more coffee. "I just packed up and drove away. Alaska was as far away as I could get and still be in the same country." Maggie met Ella's watchful gaze. "I love my father. I just don't like what he does to me or what he thinks I need to be."

"Don't worry, girl. You're a grown woman now, and you can make your own choices."

Maggie snorted out a derisive laugh, hoping Ella was right but afraid she wasn't. "You don't know my father. He has a way of making the simplest thing seem stupid, and he twists everything until he's right. He's very stubborn."

"You've got new friends here, and I've got a shotgun that packs quite a wallop." Ella laughed, immediately lightening the mood.

Maggie smiled. "That's exactly what he needs," she said, and gripped Ella's hand. "Thank you." Kodiak was going to be her new home. No one, not even her father, was going to take it away from her.

"Why don't you crash on the couch for a while and rest? You look like you could use it." Ella watched as Maggie wandered into the living room.

Maggie dropped onto the couch with a yawn. "I'm sure you're right." Exhaustion had crept up on her. Nothing short of an earthquake could have kept Maggie from falling asleep. The couch was lumpy, but she found a position that suited her and closed her eyes. A nap was all she needed.

Ella pulled a colorful quilt over Maggie. "Whether you know it or not, this is where you belong, honey. I'm gonna help you realize that, or my name ain't Ella McGee."

CHAPTER FIVE

JACK'S pager went off. It was Ella's number and a thrill of anticipation jolted through him at the thought of talking to Maggie again. He hadn't heard from her since she'd returned from the transport, so why would she page him now? An irritable band of guilt hung around his neck when he thought of how they had parted. It had only been yesterday, but already it felt like weeks had passed, and he didn't like it.

"This is Dr.—Jack," he said. "I was paged."

"This is Ella, your fairy godmother."

"What's up, Ella? Cat got a furball again? Dog need its nails cut?" Disappointment escaped in his tone, though he tried to hide it.

"No. It's Maggie."

"She got a furball?"

"No, you twit." Ella hesitated. "Something's wrong with her," she whispered.

Jack jerked upright to attention. "What's wrong with her?"

"I can't wake her up."

Jack relaxed. "She's probably just hung over."

"She's not. Earlier she was dizzy, cold and clammy and almost fainted in the kitchen."

Frowning, Jack tried to imagine what could be wrong as nightmarish thoughts assaulted his brain. Anaphylaxis? Hypoglycemia? A cerebral aneurysm? "Call 911."

"No. She's breathing OK, and I checked her pulse. Can you come over here and look at her before we call in the cavalry?"

"I'll be right there." Jack slammed the phone into its cradle.

Minutes later he burst through Ella's kitchen door, black bag in hand. "Where is she?"

Ella pointed to the living room and backed out of Jack's way.

Jack knelt on the floor and dug a penlight out of his bag. With one hand he pried open one of Maggie's eyes and flashed the light across her pupil, looking for a reaction. It constricted instantly, and he sighed in relief.

"Ow," she said, and scrunched her eyes closed. "What are you doing?" She opened her eyes and glared at him. "Jack? What are you doing here?"

"Ella called me." With expert and gentle hands Jack palpated Maggie's neck, checking for suspicious lumps.

"Why?" She pushed his hands away.

"She said she couldn't wake you."

"Really? I don't think she tried." Maggie started to sit up, and Jack moved back onto his heels as she adjusted her position.

"Are you OK?"

"Yeah. Sure," she said, but her tone was flat.

"Did something happen? Did something go wrong on the flight?" Jack was starting to get worried.

"Nothing went wrong. It was fine."

"Was your date with Kyle OK?"

"My date with…" Maggie stared at Jack and then frowned. "We didn't go on a date. We went on a transport." She stood and swayed, her color ebbing.

Jack eased her back down to the couch before she fell over.

"You don't almost faint for no reason. What's going on, Maggie? Why did Ella call me? She doesn't worry over nothing."

Tears flooded Maggie's eyes, and she covered her face with her hands. "I can't tell you."

"Why not? Did someone hurt you?" he asked, and pulled her close against him. It didn't even cross his mind to be upset that he'd been called away from the clinic for no reason.

"You'll be mad at me if I tell you and send me away," she said, and hiccuped into his shoulder as the tears poured out of her eyes. "I didn't lie to you on purpose. I didn't."

"Tell me," he whispered, her crying lacerating his heart.

"I tried to run away as far as I could. I'm sorry. I can't go back. Don't make me, Jack."

Trepidation settled in Jack's gut like a glob of worms. "What's happened? Who's after you?" He gripped her shoulders and made her face him. He searched her face and cringed at the anguish written there.

"My father," she whispered, as her chin trembled again.

Confused, but relieved it wasn't an ex-husband

hunting her down, Jack relaxed his hold and waited for her to go on.

She pushed a hand through her hair, pulling it back from her face, and met his gaze. "I shouldn't even be telling you this."

"Why not?"

"Because once you asked me if I was running away from something, and I am."

"You can tell me anything. We're friends, aren't we?"

"Are we? Or are we co-workers? Or something else?"

He thought about her question for a moment before he could find an answer that seemed reasonable. "I want to be, if you'll let me. Sometimes I want to be more, but...I can't."

"Can't?" she asked, her gaze searching his for the answer.

"Let's solve one dilemma at a time, shall we?" He smiled and squeezed her hand, offering her some comfort. "Go on with your story."

Unable to hold Jack's gaze, Maggie stared at the floor as she talked. "My father is a controlling, angry man, never happy with anyone or anything. Nothing is ever good enough, especially me. I've always been a disappointment."

"You are not a disappointment," Jack said, his face grim.

Grabbing a tissue from a box on the table, Maggie wiped her face and then proceeded to shred the thing in her hands. She picked up a cushion from the couch and hugged it to her. "According to my father, I'm supposed to return to school immediately, pursue my Ph.D., graduate early and with honors, secure a position teaching at the university level, marry someone worthy of my social status, procreate, and hire adequate caregivers to raise my progeny while I pursue my career."

Jack flopped back against the couch. If it wasn't so serious, it would almost be funny. "What about your wishes?"

"They're irrelevant." She shrugged. "That's why I took off. I've wasted enough of my life following my father's plan and it was time that I made my own path." A deep breath in and a long slow sigh out failed to calm her frayed nerves. "I know I'm still on probation but, please, don't send me away for not telling you the whole story. I'll make it up to you, Jack."

"How did he think he was going to force you into doing what he wants?"

"Oh, he threatened to cut off my finances and all that kind of stuff. I can make my own living, so that really didn't impress me." Maggie stood and paced the room. "I was so careful when I left. I paid off my credit cards. I used cash on the trip up here, and I even took precautions against my nursing license, because it would be simple to trace me through it." She threw the cushion against the wall, wishing it was her father's head.

"So what's wrong with staying here?" Jack asked.

"You don't know my father." She resumed pacing. "He can bully, threaten and browbeat anyone into doing anything, including his children."

"You have siblings?"

"Yes. One brother, James. I call him Jamie just to irritate him." She hugged her arms around her waist.

"How's he dealing with your father?"

"Like a champ. His desires fall in line with my father's wishes, so he never had the challenges I face."

"So, what are you going to do?" Though Jack asked, he wasn't sure he wanted an answer.

"I don't know." Maggie stopped in front of the large picture window that faced the inlet. She watched the ships coming and going, people busy on the docks, and wished she could climb aboard and sail away, never to return. She didn't want to leave, but keeping a step ahead of her father was the only way to hang on to her freedom. Being emotional about it would only hamper her, and give him a chance to turn her away from her wishes.

"What if you just stayed here? What would happen?"

Maggie stared at Jack a full minute, contemplating the possibilities. "I don't know. He'd probably send the company jet for me, expecting me to just get on board and return to Boston."

"You're an excellent nurse, you have a job that you've just started and seem to like. You're an adult woman making your own living, and you've given me a commitment. Why don't you make your stand against your father now? You've got friends you can count on."

Jack approached her from behind and stopped just inches away from her. Tremors still shook her shoulders now and then, the emotion stored inside her muscles twitching in need of release. "Facing your demons is a large part of life and growing up. Why don't you stop running?"

She turned to face him, her blue eyes intense as she held his gaze. "Face *my* demon?"

He nodded.

"Why don't you take your own advice, Doctor?" Maggie asked, and placed her hands on his shoulders. Her gaze dropped to his mouth, and he couldn't move. He knew what she wanted, what she was asking, but he didn't know if he could do it. Without thinking about it, his hands moved to her waist and settled on the inward curve.

The movement stirred her fragrance, and it swirled around him, sinking into his mind. Sandalwood and musk. It was a clean but heady fragrance which stimulated his emotions and his hormones. There must be some sort of pheromone in that combination, because every time he got near her he wanted to touch her and kiss her and forget everything except pouring himself into her. Living in the moment was something he hadn't done in a long time. Something he hadn't even considered until Maggie. But Maggie made him want to change. "Things will turn out OK."

"I don't know. This is new territory for me."

Unable to stop himself, Jack stepped closer to her.

Surprised, Maggie stiffened, but she didn't move away. "What are you doing?"

"I want to kiss you again."

The teasing before a kiss held an intoxicating eroticism, and Jack drew those few seconds out into eternity. Drawing her closer by sheer will, he parted his lips in anticipation of tasting hers, but the scent of her, the texture of her skin and the aura around her held him captive. His head tilted as he watched her eyes close, anticipating his touch, wanting it. Desire for Maggie ripped through him like nothing he'd ever felt before, and he captured her mouth with his.

The first tentative strokes of his tongue against hers broke through any semblance of control he might have at one time possessed. A moan, deep in her throat, told him more than words could have that she wanted this, wanted him. The desperation in her kiss was more than just seeking sanctuary from an emotional upset. She wanted him and his body responded, growing hard from that knowledge and the taste of her.

Unable to control his desire and fearful of what could happen if he didn't, Jack tore his mouth from hers and buried his face in her hair. Trembling from the onslaught of powerful emotions pouring through him, he held Maggie close, needing to hold on to her for support.

"Jack," she whispered. "What are you doing? When you kiss me like that I can't think straight."

"I know. I don't know. Me neither," he said, finally admitting the truth to her, to himself. Pulling back, he searched her eyes and found desire for him unmasked in those incredibly blue eyes.

"What do you think we should do about it?" she asked. There was no guile in her eyes, but they bewitched him just the same.

"We can't really avoid each other, considering we work together," he said. As he'd wanted to do the other evening, he curved his hand around her ear, pushing the hair back from her face.

"Do you want to avoid me?" she asked in a whisper that revealed her vulnerability and tugged at his protective instinct.

He pulled back from her, not sure if he did or didn't. "Not right now I don't. But we have to maintain our professional relationship no matter what else happens between us."

"Agreed." Maggie's eyes curled up at the corners. "Does that mean I can pinch your butt when no one is looking?"

Jack laughed and stepped away from her. The laugh rumbled in his chest and burst from him. He couldn't help it. It felt so good and right to laugh again. Joy threaded its way into every molecule and nerve ending in his body, and he craved the pure happiness it brought him. "No, you cannot pinch my butt."

Jack smiled to himself. Maggie inspired him. *Life was meant to be lived.* But then Ella's poignant words returned to him at that moment. And he knew she was right.

"Maggie, I don't know what you can see in me. I'm not a whole man." The thought sobered his mirth. "You deserve to have someone who can give you everything you want, and I can't." He stroked her cheek as regret stole into his heart, replacing the happiness that had momentarily resided there.

"Why don't you let me decide what I want and what I need?" She stared at him, her playful attitude of a moment ago vanishing. "My father has made that mistake for too many years, and for too many years I've let him. I'm not about to let you jump into his shoes and decide what's best for me either." A tight smile pulled down the corners of her mouth, and the warm look in her eyes grew cold. "What I need is a man who is emotionally available to me and, unfortunately for us both, you're not. I know that. I'm attracted to you, but it's not all I want or need. All my life I've watched my father withhold himself from my mother, and I'm not about to step into that kind of relationship."

Jack followed Maggie to the door. "I'm fine now, Jack. Why don't you head back to work? Your services are needed more there than here now."

CHAPTER SIX

ON SATURDAY, Maggie's first day off since her father's phone message, she sat at the kitchen table and contemplated the cereal floating in her bowl.

The kitchen door burst open. Maggie jumped to her feet, knocking over a chair in the process. Ella stood in the doorway, clutching two bulging bags of groceries. She rushed to take a grocery bag from Ella, but it slipped through her hands and dropped to the floor with a dull thud.

"Hope that didn't have the eggs in it," Ella said, as Maggie retrieved the bag and placed it carefully on the counter.

"I'm sorry, Ella. You startled me."

"Startled you?" Ella looked at Maggie's pale face. "You're jumpy." Ella set her groceries on the counter. "What's wrong? I know we haven't known each other for very long, but you can talk to me if you need to." Ella motioned to the table, and Maggie sat. "It may not be any of my business, but is this about Jack?"

Maggie nodded and then shook her head. "Yes and no. It's more about my father's message from the other day. It's still bugging me. I keep expecting him to walk through the door and drag me, kicking and screaming, back home."

Ella snorted. "He can try, but he's not going to walk in here without looking down the barrel of my shotgun."

Maggie placed her hand on Ella's. "No one has ever offered to threaten my father before. That's so sweet of you. I really do appreciate it." She sniffed back a tear.

Ella laughed. "You just haven't been in Alaska long enough yet. Did you and Jack talk the other day?"

"Yes. I told him about my situation. My father."

"What did he say?"

"He reminded me that I gave him a commitment."

"That sounds like good advice."

"Coming from a man who can't let go of a commitment and expects me to honor it."

"What do you mean?" Ella asked, her green eyes intense.

"It means that Jack's still deeply connected to his deceased wife." She searched Ella's eyes, but found them unreadable. "I don't mean for that to sound harsh, but I'm attracted to Jack. That's no secret, and he knows it. But I can't let myself become involved with him, even if I wanted to, because he's emotionally unavailable."

"That's the dumbest thing I've ever heard."

"I'm sorry," Maggie said, and dropped her gaze, shamed at her admission.

"Not you. That idiot that calls himself a doctor. Listen. I've known Jack for a long time. Arlene was a wonderful woman, but she wouldn't have approved of Jack's inability to move on with his life."

"How did you know Arlene? Were you friends?"

"The best. She was my daughter."

Tears filled Maggie's eyes as she stared at Ella's face, the miles and years stamped on it. "I'm so sorry. I had no idea." Maggie shook her head and clutched her hands to her stomach as it cramped, feeling like a lump of clay had formed there. "I'm so ashamed. You've had such a devastating loss, and I'm complaining about my family and my social life."

"Don't go getting mushy on me, girl. I loved my daughter and mourned her death. But I let her go. Jack hasn't been able to do it. And he's not been interested in anyone since Arlene died. At least not until you showed up. I've seen the way he looks at you. He's struggling."

"If you want me to find another place to live, I will. Me having a relationship with Jack must be making you uncomfortable." Maggie twisted her fingers together.

"Nonsense. We made a bargain and, like Jack, I expect you to honor it. Unless you aren't happy here and want to go somewhere else."

"No. I love your home. I think of it as my home now, too, and I don't want to leave." Ella had put Maggie at ease and some of her tension waned.

"Good. 'Cos it's too damned hard to find another roommate on such short notice." Ella patted Maggie's hand again.

Relieved laughter bubbled from Maggie at the gesture, and she wiped the sheen of tears from her eyes.

"Enough talk of the past. What do you say we go fishing?" Ella asked.

"Fishing?" Lines from years of exposure to the salty sea air were engraved on Ella's tanned face. If Maggie hadn't known that Ella had fished for a living, she could have guessed.

"Yes. Like out in my boat on the ocean. That's usually where the fish are." Ella rose and started to put away the groceries. "I was planning on going today anyway. Why don't you come along?" She turned and assessed Maggie. "You don't get seasick, do you? 'Cos I'm not holding a bucket for you."

"I don't know. I haven't been in a boat since I was a kid."

"We'll pick up some Dramamine on the way, just in case."

"Great. This should be fun." Maggie helped put the groceries away, then changed her clothes.

An hour later Ella and Maggie unloaded a cooler of sandwiches and drinks from the car. With each woman grasping a handle, they carried the cooler to Ella's fishing boat. The older woman boarded first, and Maggie followed.

"Whew. That thing is heavy. Are you sure we need that much food for just the two of us?" Maggie asked as she flexed her hand, cramped from the weight of the cooler.

"Hello, there."

Maggie turned to find Jack standing behind her. "Jack? What are you doing here?"

"Going fishing." He shot an amused glance at Ella.

"Oh. Did I forget to mention that Jack was coming, too?" Ella asked as she took the wheel and started the engine.

"You might have neglected that tiny detail," Maggie said over the noise and gave her friend a sidelong look. If Jack could take it in his stride, so could she.

"Sorry. Getting old does take its toll on the brain cells. Must have slipped my mind," Ella said with a grin.

"I'll bet. Your mind gets more slippery every year," Jack said, and secured the cooler against the side of the boat with bungee cords.

"This is an obvious surprise. If you don't want me along, I can stay behind," Maggie said to Jack, not sure of how she felt about Ella's matchmaking.

The man couldn't have made her more uncomfortable had he stripped her naked right then and there. The look he threw her left her with little doubt that he wanted her. His gaze always brought a thrill to her that made her heartbeat a little strange, feeling the erratic beat in every cell of her body. But this look turned her knees to jelly and the little spot below her carotid pulse twitched. As if that spot had a memory and wanted Jack's lips on it again.

"You should come along," he said. "It's a great day for fishing."

"You're right," she said, and took a seat behind Ella to hide the quaking of her limbs.

"We're gonna go catch us some halibut. I know a great place," Ella said. "Earn your keep, Jack, and cast off the lines."

With years of expertise pumping through her veins, Ella guided the vessel out of the harbor and into the open sea. Maggie relaxed against the seat cushion and drew in a cleansing breath of fresh sea air. Pretending the wind whisked away all of her cares and problems, she watched the scenery go by. It was exotic in its unique-ness. Rough rock outcroppings the size of football fields thrust out of the sea, plunging upward in search of the sun. Seals dotted the formations in the lower plateaus, barking and bawling. Puffins, black and white diving birds with bright orange beaks, soared over the high spaces. Occasionally one landed here or there to check a nest of young ones or squawk at a rival.

The salt spray soothed Maggie's frayed nerves, and she remembered why she had chosen Alaska, aside from being far from her family. The wildness here spoke to a part of her soul that she had neglected since childhood. Somehow, some way, this land alongside the sea was already the home of her heart, and she knew she couldn't leave it.

"Look there," Ella said, and pointed off the starboard side. "A pod of orcas."

"I wonder how our whale made out," Maggie said. One glance at Jack, and she knew his thoughts ran along the same track as hers. How could they be so in tune, so alike in their thoughts, only having known each other for such a short time? Maggie wondered if something more, something unnamed, had motivated her flight to Alaska. Maybe more than her happiness was at stake.

"The paper reported that it swam off at high tide. It didn't wash up, so F and G believe it made it safely out to sea again," Jack said.

"I'm glad. I hope it made it back to its family safely," Maggie said and watched the pod.

Jack sat across the narrow aisle and watched her. Fewer than three feet separated them, but Maggie felt as if the entire width of the sea loomed between them. Regret burned like an ulcer in her stomach, and she wished for something to cool it. The memory of the kiss they'd shared the other night stole into her mind. Despite the cool air brushing over her skin, the burn of desire flushed her neck and face.

"Here," Jack said, and handed her a bottle of sunscreen. "Put this on. You're starting to turn red already."

Maggie took the bottle, grateful to have something to concentrate on other than Jack's mouth and how well he used it when he wasn't putting his foot in it.

Ella pulled the boat into a protected cove on one side of a rock island. "This is one of my favorite spots. Henry and I used to fish here all the time." She handed Maggie a saltwater fishing rod already rigged and ready to go.

"Was Henry your husband?" Maggie asked, as she tried to throw the baited hook overboard, but only succeeded in tangling the line.

"Yep. He was my man for most of my life." Ella threw her own rig out and settled down with a book to wait. "Met when we were ten. After he died, I never looked at a man the same way."

"Here, let me help you with that," Jack said, and untangled Maggie's line with a skill born of years of experience.

"Thanks. Ella didn't quite tell me what to do with this."

"You just want to drop it over the edge and let it sink. Halibut are flounder, and they linger on the bottom. It's like bringing up a barn door when you hook a big one." Jack tossed the bait overboard and handed Maggie her rod. Their hands bumped as they exchanged the pole. The blush that had started earlier deepened. Maggie refused to look at Jack, afraid that he'd see her emotions written on her face. Desire had no place in her life now. Not for Jack, not for anyone, and she wished it would go away. She remembered her one intimate experience with a man in the past that had hurt her so deeply and ended badly, and this one had disaster written all over it. To open herself up again would take courage she didn't know if she had.

The motion of the boat easing back and forth with the gentle waves lulled Maggie into a complacent mood. She watched Jack as he looked out to sea at a group of seagulls squabbling over some tasty treat they had found. She leaned over the edge of the boat, trying to see beneath the surface.

Jack glanced over to see Maggie looking down into the water. Everything was new and fresh to her, and she smiled as a salmon jumped close to the boat. Joy bubbled from her on a laugh that made Jack smile. Arlene had grown up fishing with Ella, but never went for pleasure. When they had been married she'd said she'd never go again. But now, watching Maggie claim the joy her life had been lacking, his heart cramped a little. He was lucky enough to be there, to share the experience with her, but only from a distance.

"Why didn't you tell me Ella was your mother-in-law?" she asked.

He stole a quick glance at Ella, who seemed to be engrossed in a romance novel and sat with her feet propped up on the rail. "It didn't seem relevant at the time."

"And later?"

"I didn't think it was important, that's all. I wasn't intentionally keeping anything from you."

She nodded, accepting his explanation, and watched as a seagull dove into the water with a splash.

"Does it matter all that much now that you know?"

"No. I don't suppose it does," Maggie said. The tip of his fishing rod moved, and it drew her attention. "Your rod's wiggling," she said.

"My what?"

At his bemused frown she pointed behind him. "Your rod?"

In seconds all three of them had fish on their lines.

"We must have hit a real bunch of them," Ella cried as she rigged up more rods and tossed the baited hooks into the water. "I told you this was a great spot!"

By the end of the day they had hauled in fourteen halibut, varying in size from twenty-five to eighty pounds, not huge by Alaskan standards but definitely keepers.

Exhausted, Maggie flopped like a rag doll in the bottom of the boat, surrounded by fish. "What are we going to do with all this fish? You don't have a freezer big enough to hold it all, do you, Ella?" she asked.

"Jack's got a deep-freeze we can put some in. We can give some to the clinic and sell the rest to a few restaurants in town. They always need fresh fish."

Ella dug out several long fillet knives and handed one to each of them. "Get to work," she said, and grabbed one of the fish to clean.

"We're going to clean them now?" Maggie asked, wide-eyed. "I've never cleaned anything so big in my life."

"Just watch me a few times. You'll get the hang of it," Jack said.

"Says you, who has surgical experience under his belt," Maggie complained with a small pout.

Jack just grinned. They worked together, cleaning the fish. "You want to clean these out at sea. If it's done in the house, you have to be careful. If you don't dispose of the leftovers properly, bears can be drawn to the scent at your house."

"Bears?" Maggie froze, her eyes wide. "Like *real* bears?"

"Yes, real Alaskan brown bears, or Kodiak bears. Remember that patient we had a week or so ago? He'd been cleaning fish at home and before he could remove the skins and leftovers, a Kodiak found him." Jack sighed and handed her another fillet. "Even cleaning up doesn't guarantee that a bear won't be attracted to the scent anyway. They can smell blood and fish from miles away."

"Wow. I had no idea."

"Bears are amazing animals. One of these days you'll see some around town. Before they go to den they will be looking in every Dumpster and back yard for any food they can find."

"From now on I'll be more careful taking out the trash." Maggie laughed.

The trio had had a fun but exhausting day. As they returned to Kodiak, Maggie started to shiver. Though the sun was still high in the evening sky, clouds had moved in, obscuring it, and the air cooled. Jack opened the seat cushion beneath him and pulled out a blanket. "Here, wrap up in this," he said, and handed a green one to Maggie.

"Thanks," she said, enveloping herself in the rough

wool. Jack moved across the aisle, covering the few feet that had separated them earlier, and sat next to Maggie, sharing his warmth with her.

"You did a good job out there," he said, and pulled her close against his side. "You're adapting quickly to the Alaskan lifestyle. Pretty soon you won't ever want to leave."

"I already don't want to leave," she said.

Jack glanced at Ella. Her attention stayed forward as she steered the boat. "Stay," he whispered. He tucked her head under his chin and wrapped his other arm around her.

Maggie sank against his warmth, easing into his side, grateful to share his body heat, and snuggled into the comforting warmth of his body. This was how she'd imagined sharing a relationship with a man. All those memories from the past began to vanish. Jack was healing her. Sharing something as simple as body heat with him felt like a gift, recharging her emotionally. But deep down she knew Jack's inner warmth wasn't available to her. Not now and maybe not ever. Risking her heart on him would just get her hurt. She didn't need that on top of everything else that had gone wrong in her life.

Maybe she wasn't cut out for relationships. Maybe a nice house plant she could talk to and an electric blanket for cold winter nights would be better.

CHAPTER SEVEN

MAGGIE returned to work on Monday to what she was coming to accept as Monday morning mayhem. Anyone who had developed any sort of condition over the weekend landed at the clinic doors bright and early.

People with coughs or summer colds, a weekend warrior who had stepped on a rusty nail, and a mom who had ignored her own fever too long arrived first.

The busier Maggie kept herself, assessing and triaging patients through the clinic, the less time she had to think about Jack and the pain of a relationship with him or the emptiness without him. As the long twelve-hour shift wound down, the staff started to relax around six p.m. The last patient to come through was Tom, the elderly patient who had been at the clinic a week or so ago.

"Hey, there, Tom. How are you today?" Maggie asked as she led him to a treatment room. As they walked side by side, she noted his ashen complexion and sweat-covered face. She grabbed a wheelchair and eased him into it.

"Whew," he said, panting. "That hall gets longer every time I come here," he said as they entered the treatment room.

"Lie down on the gurney and let me put some oxygen on you—that'll help."

For once Tom complied without argument as Maggie assisted him onto the stretcher. Maggie knew he was ill if he didn't have a smart comment to make about his health or the weather.

"Are you having chest pain?" Maggie asked, and placed electrode pads and connected him to the monitor. Adrenaline shot through her system like an Arctic fox after a hare. "Let me call for Jack." She pushed the code-blue alarm button on the wall and staff rushed to the room. When Jack entered the cubicle, he hurried to the side of his friend. Though he examined Tom, he grilled Maggie. "What are his vitals?"

"Pressure's 50 over palp. Sustained V-tach with an uncontrolled rate of 200." Maggie supplied the distressing information. "No chest pain, but he's shocky. I just put oxygen on him, and his saturation is poor at seventy per cent."

"Tom? Can you hear me?" Jack asked, and opened one of Tom's eyelids. "Stay with me, Tom. I need you to stay awake."

Without a word Tom's eyes rolled back, and he lost consciousness. Jack flashed a glance at Maggie and then looked at the monitor. He didn't disagree with her assessment. "We have to shock him out of this," he said, and Maggie handed him the paddles of the defibrillator while she hit the charge button. She was right there, anticipating his needs.

"Charging, 200 joules," she said, and watched the monitor for the signal. "Charged."

Jack placed the paddles on Tom's chest and squeezed

the buttons. Tom twitched. Jack looked at the flat line on the monitor and verified with a carotid check. "Dammit."

Amos started CPR compressions, and Randy gave Tom extra oxygen.

"Again," Jack instructed. A muscle in his jaw twitched.

Seconds later a buzz signaled full charge again.

"Charged," Maggie said in a voice loud enough to be heard over the chaos in the room.

"Again." This time Jack zapped 300 joules of electricity into Tom's chest, praying it was enough to shock the heart out of the lethal rhythm.

"He's got a rhythm now. Junctional, in the thirties," Maggie said, and Jack handed the defibrillator paddles to her. Thinking ahead to what Jack would need, she broke out more equipment, knowing what he'd want in a cardiac emergency.

"Get the external pacer on him and turn it up to eighty." As Jack turned, Maggie placed the pacer pads in his hands.

"Got it."

The silence in the room after the chaos was overwhelming. Everyone in the ER knew and loved Tom. He was a fixture in the community. Watching Jack study the monitor, Maggie could see the tension in his shoulders and the way he clamped his hand on the back of his neck. A muscle in his jaw twitched. She wished she could ease his distress, but she couldn't. None of them could. But together they were doing their best to save Tom.

An hour later, after Tom had been made as stable and

comfortable as possible, they moved him to the mini-ICU. If he survived the night, he would need a pace-maker, which would require a flight to Anchorage.

"Don't you want to send him tonight?" Maggie asked as they left the ICU. "I'll go with him."

"No. It's too risky. I need to call his family in case we can't find a living will. Or in case he doesn't wake up." Hands balled into fists as his sides, Jack paced the hallway outside the ICU. The ICU consisted of a two-room ward converted with extra equipment for the temporary management of critical patients. They either became stable enough to transport after the first twenty-four hours or they died. A dedicated ICU couldn't be justified under those conditions.

"Jack, why don't you go back to your office to rest or go home?" Maggie clasped his sleeve and slowed his frantic pace. Her heart ached for the pain she knew was his. New griefs often brought up old ones and made them fresh again.

"I can't. I've got to stay with Tom. If something happens to him, I'll never forgive myself for not being here."

"Go home for the night," Maggie insisted.

"Watch yourself, Maggie," he said, eyes narrowed. "You don't have the right to speak to me that way."

"I don't have the right? Being a nurse here gives me the right, whether you like it or not. It's my respon-sibility to remind you of when you're not being rational." Maggie took a deep breath. "Step away from him, give yourself time to settle down, and then go back in. At this rate you'll burn up all of your energy pacing the hallway and won't have anything left if Tom does need you later."

"I need to be left alone." Jack strode away from Maggie and left her standing in the hall alone.

The nerve of the woman. He knew what he needed and it certainly wasn't advice from her. Returning to his office, he was just about to shut the door when Amos walked in.

"How's Tom?" he asked, and dropped into a chair across from the desk.

Jack huffed out a stressed sigh and fell into his own chair.

"He needs an internal defibrillator with a pacemaker, which I can't do here. We've got the external one on him, but that's only a temporary measure at best. If he survives the night we'll fly him to Anchorage tomorrow for pacemaker placement." Rubbing both sides of his head with his hands, he let out a groan. "It's so frustrating that we can't do something as simple as a pacemaker here on the island. If only I had someone who wanted to live here who could run anesthesia. I just can't do it all."

"I'm sorry. I know Tom is a friend of yours, but he knew he needed a pacemaker two years ago. Remember when he came in here almost in the same condition he's in now? He's been living on borrowed time for that long. It was his choice, Jack. And he made it. You can't change that."

A long sigh escaped Jack as he recalled the incident. "Yeah. I know. Doesn't make it any easier to accept."

"Why don't you take off for the night and get some rest?" Amos suggested.

"Why is everyone telling me to go home?" Jack asked, unable to disguise the irritation in his voice.

"Is it because you're as grumpy as a Kodiak bear and look like an old boot?" Amos said, then waved away any response Jack might have made. "I'm sorry, Jack. I can't tell you what to do. But think about it. Take a few hours of rest then come back if you need to check on Tom." Amos left the office and closed the door behind him.

Jack tipped his head back against the leather chair and closed his eyes. Was he out of it? He'd just come back from vacation a few weeks ago, but now it felt like years had gone by since his trip. Rubbing his eyes, he tried to think of what more he could do for Tom.

Nothing. There was nothing he could do other than what he'd already done. But one more check on Tom wouldn't hurt.

With a hand weary from the day's work, Jack pushed open the door of the ICU and walked to Tom's bed. He took Tom's hand and held it. Tom squeezed Jack's hand and struggled to make eye contact. Sedation, fatigue and an ailing heart made it hard for him to focus.

"You look like you're resting OK," Jack said, as Tom struggled to focus on his doctor. Jack turned to the nurse, Gloria. "How's he doing?"

"He's about as stable as we can make him," she said, and double-checked the IV pumps.

"Good." He rubbed the back of his neck. "I'm wondering whether I should spend the night here or go home."

"Go home. We can deal with this guy. There's no reason for you to stay. I've got your pager number, and I'll call if anything changes."

Jack considered Gloria. "I swear there's a conspiracy to get me out of the hospital tonight," he grumbled.

"Hmm. I wonder why?" She pursed her lips and stared at him.

"OK, I give up. I'll go home. If there's any change—"

"I'll call you," she interrupted, and returned to the monitor station. "Promise."

Jack picked up his keys and locked his office. He may as well go home. But to what? An empty house? He didn't even have a dog or a cat to keep him company. His pace slowed as he thought of Maggie. Why not call her, invite her to dinner? She could keep him company for a while. Maybe he could get to know her better. Jack slammed the door of his Jeep and the direction of his thoughts came to a screeching halt.

No, she'd never accept, not after he'd walked away from her in the ICU. He had to remember that they'd been brought together by temporary circumstances and nothing else. He hadn't noticed anything special about her. Nothing at all. Aside from the way her smile made the outer corners of her eyes crinkle up. Or the way her eyes changed color with her moods. And speaking of moods, he'd never noticed how passionate her kisses had been and how they'd stirred feelings and sensations he'd almost forgotten about. But not quite. Remembering stirred something in him he'd thought long dead. Had hoped was long dead. Opening himself again would bring such pain. Not something he wanted ever again.

As Jack opened his front door, he looked around the house, as if seeing it for the first time. The log home was something he'd wanted since the first time he'd seen one years ago. Arlene had loved it from the moment she'd walked into it.

The smile that crossed his lips was brief and full of

sadness. Why did life have to dish out such terrible troubles? As he moved into the living room he picked up a photo of the two of them, taken a few years ago. They'd been on a trip to Hawaii then. So in love it had almost hurt. The pictures on the table progressed in a time line documenting Arlene's illness, her decline and the last picture taken days before her death. She'd changed so much. In the end she hadn't been the person she'd once been. But he'd still loved her. Still did.

Or did he? he wondered as he replaced the picture. Ella had yelled at him more than once to put the photos away, to quit picking at the festered wound in his heart. *Give it time to heal and get on with your life.* Her words still blistered his ears. She hadn't been back to his house since. But he couldn't put them away. Or at least he hadn't been able to at the time. Could he now?

Supper first, though. A man couldn't make decisions with hunger gnawing at him. Thirty minutes later, his appetite sated by a lunch meat sandwich and a bowl of canned soup, Jack brought a cardboard box from the garage. The box was from the last purchase of oil for his Jeep. It seemed disrespectful to be packing away pictures of his dead wife into a box that had been used for engine lubricant. But then again he'd been putting too much emphasis on the stupid things in life. Too much sentimentality. The time had come to start to live again. Without Arlene.

Jack fought back the acid clawing its way up his throat at the thought. He'd need an antacid before this night was over. Again and again, the same thing had happened when he'd tried to put Arlene behind him. He'd felt like he'd dishonored her and what they had meant to each other. Too many people had told him otherwise, and he'd pushed them away. Who was right and who was wrong no longer mattered.

He picked up the last photo and stared at it, seeing the reality of Arlene's death as if for the first time, the last time. In the photo Arlene's hair was thin, damaged by the chemo. Her color was sallow, and she looked like a shadow of herself. Days after the photo had been taken, she'd died. Wrapping the framed picture in last week's newspaper, he placed it in the box on top of the others. He folded the flaps of the box together and taped them shut. Returning to the garage, he placed the box up on a shelf, next to his socket set and wrenches.

As he reached to take the box down again, his pager went off. Dashing back into the house, he grabbed his phone and dialed the hospital.

"What's wrong?" he demanded.

"Tom's gone," Gloria said.

Jack heard the distress and tears in her voice. "What happened? Why didn't you call me sooner, dammit?" Jack dropped into a chair, the angry shot of adrenaline hissing through his system making his knees weak. "Why didn't you call me?" he whispered again.

"It happened too quick, Jack. One minute he was OK, the next he was gone. We tried to code him, but he was just gone. Tom knew it was his time and didn't fight it. You were the last one to see him, and I think he waited for you to say goodbye."

"I'm coming over there." Jack hung up the phone and strode from the house to the Jeep. Within ten minutes he'd parked his vehicle at the front of the hospital and rushed inside.

The ICU was silent. There was no noise in a place that was usually deafening from it. Tom lay in his bed, unmoving, as if just asleep. Jack would have believed that except for the waxy pallor of the man's skin. Seated next to the man on the bed, Jack took Tom's hand. It was still warm. Jack hung his head and shut his eyes.

Gloria came and drew the curtain around them, closing them off from the rest of the unit as Jack said goodbye to his friend.

Maggie didn't know what to do, what to think or how to behave. Jack had kept his distance from everyone at the clinic for two days, and tonight was Tom's funeral service. A small church service at six to be followed by drinks and revelry at Brownies pub.

Not quite what Maggie was used to but, given the relaxed attitude of Alaskans, she wasn't surprised. Tom had been a town leader and exceptional friend to one and all, though he'd never stood out as a wealthy man. He would be missed, but he would be upset if anyone mourned him overly long.

The clinic closed early for the night so that everyone could attend the church service. Maggie wore her best jeans and a light sweater.

For the service Ella wore her finest pair of camou-flage pants and a clean white shirt. Hiking boots replaced the fishing boots she usually wore. "You'd better go find Jack," Ella said to her.

"Why do I need to go find Jack? He's a big boy and can handle everything all by himself."

"If he was anyone but Jack you wouldn't hesitate to help or console him. But because he's Jack, you're being stubborn." Ella gave her a nudge toward the back door of the church. "It'll take hours to get out of here. That pastor hasn't seen this many full pews since the last funeral, and he's going to take advantage of it. Go down to the docks and see if Jack's there. That's where he goes when he needs to think." She turned away to wait in line with the rest. "I'll see you at the pub later."

Dismissed, Maggie left the church by the back door. The air was fresh and brisk enough to blow away any lingering sadness from the funeral. She'd only met Tom a few times, but after the service she felt like she knew a little more about him. Maggie enjoyed the short walk to the docks. She leaned against a rail and looked among the boat slips for Jack, but he wasn't there. Bouncing down the set of cement steps to the lower docks, she wondered where he had gotten to.

"What are you doing here?" Jack said from behind her. She almost lost her balance on the edge of the dock. He rose from a bench hidden by the steps. No wonder she hadn't seen him.

"Looking for you. What are you doing?" she asked. Jack started to wander away, and Maggie fell into step beside him.

"I'd say hiding from you, but you'd get mad at me if I did. And it wouldn't really be true."

"I'm glad you didn't say it, then," she said, and shoved her hands into her jeans pockets. "I've been worried about you."

"Why? I'm alive and well." The dullness of his eyes belied that statement.

"I'd say I don't think you are, but you'd just give me some lip about it, wouldn't you?" Maggie elbowed him in a playful way, hoping to jump-start him into having a conversation with her.

"You're probably right. But I wouldn't admit that to anyone." He shrugged and captured her gaze. "Except maybe you."

The wind lured strands of hair out from her tight braid. Loose wisps tickled her face. She reached up to tuck them behind her ear, and Jack captured her hand on its way back down. The gesture surprised her, but pleased her, too. Their pace slowed as they neared the end of the dock. Leaning against the rail, they watched the gentle waves, the boats coming and going with the tide. Maggie sighed, recapturing the contentment that had been lost to her for many years. Loving it here.

"Did you need something?" Jack asked.

She gave a short laugh. "I was just thinking how at home I am here. How right it feels to be standing on this dock in the wilds of Alaska. Kodiak is less cosmopolitan than Boston, but at the same time it feels more like home than home has ever been."

"So you're going to stay after all?" Jack held his shoulders tense.

Her gaze met his, held it, then released it. "I'm staying."

"I'm glad," Jack said, and sighed, his stance visibly relaxing.

"I'm sure Tom's death brings back bad memories of your wife and losing her."

"You're sure?" he asked, and bristled at her words. How many people said such stupid things at funerals? he wondered.

"Yep. I'm sure," she said, and faced him, holding his gaze, challenging him to give back what she was giving him.

With narrowed eyes he stared at her. "How can you be so sure?" Unable to stop himself, he stepped closer and pushed that stubborn lock of hair behind her ear. Again.

"I'm sure, because you're just not yourself."

"How so?" The open honesty in her face humbled him. God, she was beautiful. And she didn't even know it.

"You're withdrawn, short-tempered, and..." She snapped her fingers. "Oh, wait. That's how you *usually* are. I forgot," she said with a silly grin, but then sobered. "If you want to be alone, I'll go."

Those eyes. Surprise and desire sparkled in them. Nothing in the world could make him resist their spell right now. And he didn't want to. For once he didn't want to fight himself. Didn't want to ignore that hint of desire he felt every time he was with Maggie. Right now he wanted to give in and live right in this moment. He felt like that drunk in the ER, hypnotized by her presence.

"You've got a mouth on you, haven't you?" he asked. But he didn't care what came out of that mouth as long as he could press his lips against it and take a long, slow drink.

CHAPTER EIGHT

JACK moved into her, breathing in her unique fragrance of sandalwood and musk. With his hands cupping her face, he raised it to his and kissed her.

Breathless with anticipation, filled with need, Jack opened his mouth over her soft, wet lips and kissed her. Like a dying man, he held on to Maggie, needing her softness, her sweetness. He needed everything she was to keep him from dying right there on the docks.

Maggie parted her lips, opened her mouth to him and drew him to her, hooking her arms around his middle. The ragged breath she drew told him how affected she was. As her tongue tangled and danced with his, he knew he wanted her. Not just in a physical way, though that came raging out from behind the locked door in his heart.

After what seemed like an eternity, Jack pulled back, as breathless as Maggie.

Stunned by the kiss, Maggie searched his eyes. "Why did you do that?"

Unable to hold her gaze, he looked out to sea again, disturbed at how often he found himself desiring intimacy with her. "I don't know. Something comes over me when I'm near you." He sighed and dragged a hand through his hair. "I'm also getting tired of it. Half of the time I don't know what to think or feel when we're together, whether that's at work or in private. I want to touch you, to talk to you, to hear you laugh." He clutched the rail to keep from reaching out and dragging Maggie back into his arms. Each time it was harder to resist her. "Sorry for taking liberties with you. You don't deserve half a man coming on to you all the time. I can't give you what you need or what you want."

"You don't know what I want, Jack. You've never asked me. If you're half a man, it's because you choose to be. For some reason martyrdom is your way of dealing with the world and everyone in it. What happened to you that you'd rather stay alone by choice the rest of your life than take that step to share yourself with someone else?"

"My wife died, that's what happened. How can you ask that? You should be able to understand why I can't reach out." Anger frothed inside him, as if on the edge of a wave ready to crash.

"You do reach out, Jack. You just won't hold on." Maggie turned to walk away from him, but froze. She stared at the steps, where a man stood. He wore casual clothing, and his discomfort in them was obvious. Maggie took a step forward and pressed her hands to her face. Another step closer, then she launched herself at him, laughing and crying and spreading kisses over his face. Jack moved closer, determined to see who had motivated Maggie to spread her hugs and kisses so freely.

"Is it really you? What are you doing here?"

"It's me, little sister." He grinned.

After a boisterous hug, Jamie set Maggie down. "I can't believe you're here," she said. "Just look at you. I haven't seen you in jeans for years. Are you sure you're OK?"

"I can't believe I'm here either. My suits are in the rental car, so have no fear, I haven't gone totally casual on you."

Maggie turned to Jack with a breathtaking smile on her face, and he wished that he'd been the man to put it there. "Jamie, this is Jack Montgomery, my boss and medical director of the clinic where I work. Jack, my brother, Jamie Wellington."

"James," Maggie's brother corrected with a grin in his sister's direction. The men shook hands, but sized each other up as men did who both had some claim on the same woman.

"What are you doing here? Did Father send you?" Maggie asked with a hand clutched to her chest.

Jack detected the uncertainty in her voice. "I'll let the two of you catch up. Maggie, I'll see you another time. Nice to meet you, James," Jack said, and left the siblings alone. His time with Maggie was over for now.

"Yes, Father sent me to bring you back. But while I came this far away from home, I decided to stay for a few days, take some time off."

"You never take time off," Maggie said. "And I'm not going back." Maggie led them away from the dock and back toward town. "Where are you staying?" Jamie always required luxury accommodations wherever he went.

"The Kodiak Lodge was the best I could find."

Maggie nodded. "It's a lovely hotel."

"Yes, it is, and what do you mean, you're not coming back?"

"Exactly that. I've found my place here. For some reason the wilderness and the people here suit me. I've come to love it here much quicker than I ever would have thought. It's as if I was meant to be here, Jamie. I just had to figure out where I belonged in life, and this is it, not back east under Father's thumb."

"If you need to have a little fling, by all means do it, but, please, don't stay in a place like this." He looked around, not seeing the village the same way she did.

"I'm not having a fling," she said, but the heat of a blush filled her cheeks. "I'm staying."

"But Father has everything set up for you."

"Set up for him, you mean."

Jamie shrugged. "Perhaps. But it will further your career if you work with him on this, not against him. He could have you set up for life if you want."

"I can set myself up for life, and I intend to do it here."

"You'd give up your inheritance for this place?" Jamie asked, and looked around with distaste clearly written on his face.

"What's wrong with earning my own money and taking care of myself, instead of depending on someone else to do it for me? Neither you nor Father can take that away from me. I won't let you." Maggie crossed her hands over her chest and huffed out her breath. "I'm his daughter, not his possession. I'll make up my own mind what's right for me, and this is it."

Jamie looked in the direction that Jack had disappeared. "Does the good doctor come with the job? Is that what you're after?"

Maggie stopped and glared at her brother. "What do you mean?"

"I mean, is Jack the reason you're staying?" Blue eyes as clear as her own stared down at her.

"No. Jack's wife died, and he's never going to get involved with anyone."

"That's good. Less incentive for you to stay," Jamie said, and they resumed walking. The Kodiak Lodge was just a few yards away, and they gravitated toward it.

"Jamie, how can you say that? If this is what makes me happy, you should be more supportive of my decision. I'm no longer living the life Father has invented for me."

"Sorry. I've never been good at the mushy stuff. You know me, if there are numbers involved, I'm all over it." He sighed. "Will I be seeing you tomorrow?"

"Not unless you come to the clinic. I work twelve-hour shifts for the next three days, but if you come by around lunchtime I can try to break away to eat with you." Maggie turned and walked home, more determined than ever not to allow the men in her life to change her mind.

Alaskan weather was never predictable and varied as much as the people. Maggie watched out the window of the clinic as her last scheduled shift of the week drew to a close.

"Is it raining?" Catherine asked from behind her.

"Just a drizzle." Maggie turned to her co-worker. Catherine hadn't lost her baby yet, but she was still reluctant to talk about it to anyone other than Maggie. "Why don't you take off, Catherine? I think the weather is keeping everyone home. It's been slow all day, and I can handle the rest of the shift."

Catherine wrapped up the remains of her meal. "If you don't mind, I could use a little extra rest."

"I don't mind at all."

"Let me clear it with Jack first."

"Clear what?" the man in question asked as he entered the empty triage area.

"Is it OK if I go home early? We're pretty slow around here."

"Not any longer. Sorry, but you're going with me. You're next on the flight schedule, and we just received a transport call."

"What kind of transport?" Catherine asked.

"There's an injured man who needs to be flown out of his fish camp. Everyone else is stranded due to the weather, but it hasn't reached us yet. Catherine, you'll be flying with me. Sorry this has come up." He patted her shoulder.

"It's OK. I don't mind," she said, her eyes downcast.

"I need to go to the docks and get the plane ready for the trip. Can you come over to the plane slip in about an hour?"

"Sure. I'll need to get some equipment ready, too."

As soon as Jack had left, Catherine burst into tears. Without hesitation, Maggie pulled the woman into her arms and hugged her tight. "Shh. Don't worry, honey. You don't have to go."

"You heard Jack. It's my turn. We always rotate to make it fair to the staff, but I don't want to go. The flight could cause a miscarriage, and I'm almost through the most dangerous time with this one." Catherine sniffed and pulled back, trying to wipe away the moisture that flooded her eyes. "No. I'll go. It's just a transport, right? I'm sure it will be no big deal." The anguish in her eyes betrayed her words.

"It'll be OK. You'll see. Let's get that equipment together, and I'll help carry it."

Jack proceeded with the maintenance check of the medical transport float plane. The community had raised money and with the help of a private endowment had purchased it for the clinic. As a licensed pilot, Jack flew most of the local transports. He'd been flying in the turbulent and dangerous air over Alaska for ten years without mishap. He had no reason to believe this trip would be any different. Just as he completed the maintenance check footsteps on the dock alerted him to Catherine's arrival. "Catherine, I'll be right with you. We'll get going in a few minutes." Dragging himself out of the internal storage compartment, Jack stepped out onto the float. The welcoming smile faded from his lips.

Maggie stood on the dock, dressed in her flight suit, her arms filled with gear.

"What are you doing here?" he asked, confusion written on his face. "Where's Catherine?"

Maggie smiled and gnawed her lip. "Catherine and I switched places. She's going to work out the end of my shift, and I'll take her flight."

"Why?"

"I haven't taken enough flights since I've been here

to keep me happy, so we traded. It's no big deal, Jack." Maggie handed him equipment to stow. There would be enough room for the equipment, one patient on the stretcher, the nurse and pilot, and a small cooler of food, but nothing else. Every other speck of space was filled. Some of the equipment was permanent, built into the plane for monitoring patients and storage of supplies.

They finished loading the plane before Jack spoke again. "You should have let me know about the switch."

"You left the clinic too fast. Is it a problem to do the transport with me?"

"No," he said, but his eyes were wary and his jaw clenched.

"If you have difficulty working with me, Jack, you need to tell me. We can be professional about this, can't we?"

"We can. And we will." Dammit. Why did Maggie have to be the one to go with him? Life had been much simpler before Maggie Wellington had burst into his clinic and his life.

As Jack taxied the plane away from the dock, he watched for other airplanes and boat traffic and maneuvered the plane safely through. Maggie adjusted the headset so it fit her. It was the only way they could communicate during the flight. The engine was too loud for casual conversation.

"Are you receiving me?" he asked, and spared a quick glance in her direction.

"Yes." Maggie nodded. "Where is the camp?"

"About an hour away, if the weather holds."

"Think you can put up with me that long?" Maggie asked.

Jack turned to face her and that grin of hers.

"I can deal with you that long. How's your brother doing?"

"Oh, he's having more fun playing the stock market on the computer than coming out of the hotel." Maggie shook her head and sighed. "I've tried to get him to do some tours, but he won't budge. The market must be hot now."

"What does he do for a living? Even in casual clothing he looks like a money man."

"You're right. He buys struggling companies, chops them into pieces and sells them for profit. Not something I understand, in more than one way."

"Me neither." The engine whined. The speed of the plane forced Maggie back into her seat and she was thankful for the doorhandle to hold on to. After they were airborne they picked up their conversation.

"We're in the putting-things-back-together business, aren't we? I mean, people come in torn apart by a car accident or a bear or disease, and we try our best to keep them whole or make them whole again."

Jack considered her words and felt himself relax, intrigued that she could so easily read his thoughts, share his philosophy. In some ways Maggie had been born to be here in Alaska with him. She matched the vivid beautiful landscape. She didn't just agree with him because it was easy. They shared the same ideas, the same philosophy. Loving her would be easy for the right man. It just couldn't be him. "That's what we do. And you're very good at it. I haven't had much chance lately to let you know I've really appreciated your skills in the clinic. All I've heard is Maggie this and Maggie that, and how good Maggie is. You're not only good with tasks and anticipating what I need in a crisis, you're great with people, making them feel comfortable in situations that are out of their control."

"You're going to make me blush, Jack."

"Sorry," he said, and looked to see if it was true.

"Don't be sorry, keep it up. I like it."

Jack laughed, surprised at how good it felt to laugh with her. "Don't push your luck, Wellington. You're going to work for any compliments you get from me."

The giggle that escaped from her mouth crept into his ears and stayed there for him to remember.

As they approached the fish camp, they followed the river to the designated area. Thankfully Jack was familiar with the camps along the river. When he brought the plane down toward the surface of the river, Maggie gripped the instrument panel and clenched her eyes shut.

"Don't worry," Jack said with a laugh in her ear. "We're on floats. We won't sink."

"I hope you're right," she said, her voice a tight squeak. "This is my first float-plane landing."

"Any landing you can walk away from is a good one," he said as he taxied the plane to the dock of the remote cabin. A lone figure stood on the dock and waved to them.

"Dammit. That guy doesn't look hurt. If we've flown in here for a hangnail, I'm not going to be happy."

"Let's take a look and see before making judgments." Maggie patted him on the knee, and Jack's spurt of anger fizzled down to irritation. She was right again.

They got out and secured the plane to the floating dock. The boy waiting was a young teen and not the victim described by the rescue team. "Are you injured?" Jack asked.

"No, it's my grandfather," the boy said.

"Why don't you take us to him?" Jack asked, and shouldered one of the medical bags that Maggie handed to him. They looked at each other with identical concern.

No one had told them about a second person.

"What's your name?" Maggie asked.

"Abel Topsekok," he supplied as they hurried toward a small cabin. No trees grew in the area, but grasses grew in wild clumps, clinging to the ground with tenacious roots. Low bush plants were loaded with berries not yet ripe enough to be picked. Bears in the area would soon be after them.

Abel opened the door and led them to the cot where his grandfather lay on his side, covered by a heap of blankets.

Abel spoke to the man in a language that neither Jack nor Maggie understood.

The injured man opened his eyes and looked at Jack, nodded and closed his eyes again.

"Let me get some vitals on him," Maggie said, and placed a blood-pressure cuff on the patient's left arm.

"Abel, does your grandfather understand any English?" Jack asked as he took in the ample size of the patient. Though not tall, he was stout in the middle, likely from a traditional native diet, high in fat, required to survive the vicious winters in remote Alaska.

"Very little. He's a traditional man and has lived in

his village all of his life. He always said there was no reason for him to learn English when he had no reason to leave his village."

"I see." Jack knelt beside the bed and examined the gunshot wound on the man's left side. "How did this happen?"

"I tripped, and my gun went off." Abel bent his head and wiped his face on his shoulder. "I was hunting for rabbits," Abel said, tears choking his voice. "Is he bad?"

"Bad enough. He's going to need surgery for sure. Tell him we need his permission to take him to the clinic in Kodiak. And ask him if he has any allergies."

Abel and his grandfather exchanged a few sentences, and the patient nodded. "OK," he said with great effort.

"What's your grandfather's name?" Maggie asked.

"Elmer Topsekok," Abel said, and held on to his grandfather's hand.

"We should probably give him a little morphine to take the edge off of his pain," Maggie said.

"Go ahead. Two milligrams as soon as you get an IV hooked up." Maggie and Jack worked together. They packed the wound with gauze soaked in Betadine solution to prevent infection, started an IV for hydration, and made Elmer as comfortable and stable as possible without over-sedating him with morphine.

"Let's try to sit him up now," Jack said, and slid his arm behind the man's shoulders.

It took all three of them to get Elmer to his feet. Dizzy from loss of blood, he swayed and paled. "You're going to have to walk to the plane," Jack said. "We can't carry you."

Abel translated and pointed to the plane. Elmer

nodded and shuffled along, clutching his injured side, flanked by Maggie and Jack. Though it took only minutes for the awkward group to get to the plane, to Maggie it felt like hours. So many things could go wrong. She was just grateful that Jack was with her. They had to work together to save this man's life. "Once we get you inside you can lie down on the stretcher," Maggie said. Again, Abel translated.

"You realize that Abel's going to have to go along, don't you?" Maggie whispered to Jack.

"I know." A muscle in his jaw twitched. "We can try to squeeze him into a corner, but we'll be over the safe weight limit." Jack glanced at the men as they climbed into the plane. "Elmer looks like a solid guy and so does Abel."

Lightning split the sky and thunder echoed, still miles away. Despite the cool weather, Maggie started to sweat. But she climbed into the plane. She hooked up a blood transfusion to Elmer. His color had almost turned green during the walk to the plane, and the effort it had cost him to get into the plane was enormous. Blood seeped through the bandage they had applied against his wound. Maggie reinforced the dressing with more gauze padding. Removing it could start the blood flowing faster, so she left the original in place.

During the time it had taken them to stabilize Elmer, the storm that had kept the other planes grounded worked its way toward them, threatening, closer and harsher, just a few miles away now. Jack looked at the sky boiling with black clouds and slashed with lightning. "We'd better get moving."

They loaded the equipment and stowed it in the rear of the plane.

"How are we going to do this?" Maggie asked. Worry like she'd never known seared through her and burned like a hot coal in her gut.

"I don't know. We're going to be seriously over-weight with all of us in the plane," Jack said, his jaw aching. "We're not prepared for this. There's nothing else I can leave behind." He stood on the plane's float. Maggie stood on the dock.

"Leave me behind," she said, as a few fat drops of rain hit her in the face. As she looked overhead at the storm, something inside Maggie fused. Resolve, strength and courage mixed together, and she knew she could do it. She could remain behind without fear, and she took a step backward. "You'd better get going before that storm breaks and we're all stranded. Elmer won't tolerate much more blood loss. You can come back for me when the storm lets up." Her brave words ended when her voice cracked.

Jack leaped onto the dock beside Maggie and grabbed her arms, pulling her close. "This is not accept-able, Maggie. I can't leave you behind. *I won't.* You're not prepared to stay out here. This is real wilderness, not some pretend camp-out in the back yard."

"There's the camp that the men used. It's not the Ritz, but I'll be safe in it. And you'll come back for me as soon as the storm lets up, right?" She hoped that Jack couldn't feel the trembling vibrations in her limbs, the anxiety that shot through her system. "It'll be OK, Jack. I trust you. I trust you." She reached out and pressed her palm to his cheek, wanting to touch him again, feel his strength and bring some of it into her.

Jack huffed out a sigh of exasperation and raked his

hand through his hair. "How can you say that? This isn't an issue of trust, Maggie. You're safety is important to me, and I'm responsible—"

"Then be responsible and take the patient in." She blinked, breaking the intensity of his stare. "Then come back for me."

Jack dragged her into his arms and held on to her like he'd never let her go. A tremor rocked him and resonated through her. "I don't want to leave you behind. I can't."

"You have no choice, Jack. Elmer is in a critical condition and getting worse by the minute. He needs more medical attention than we can give him out here. Keep your focus where it belongs. Don't go getting emotional now." She pulled back and clutched his hands, searched his eyes. "This is what we do, remember? We fix things, broken people. Get into that plane, and go fix him."

"Maybe I can do some surgery in the cabin—"

"And use what for anesthesia? Two milligrams of morphine? Be realistic, Jack! I'm sure the worst thing that will happen to me is being bored. I have my jacket. We have a cooler of food I can keep, and I'll be fine," she insisted, hoping it was true. She had to be strong for him. And for herself. "I'll be...fine." Her voice cracked, and she swallowed the lump in her throat.

"God, Maggie. This isn't right. I don't want to leave you." Jack looked at her beautiful face, the intensity of her blue eyes, memorizing every nuance of her. Planting a desperate kiss on Maggie's trembling mouth, Jack clung to her, tasted her, desired her. Despite the tense situation, Jack kept his lips pressed to hers. Every second his lips moved over Maggie's was a second seared into his memory. But he needed to imprint her feel, her taste, her everything onto his soul. "I'll be back as soon as I can."

"Don't take any chances you don't have to," she said. "Be safe."

Jack stepped away from Maggie. "I'll be back," he said, but kept his eyes on Maggie as if seeing her for the first time.

Or the last.

He climbed into the plane and took his seat. Abel took Maggie's seat.

"Be safe, Jack," she said, and memorized his face. She reached her hand out, and he squeezed it.

"I'll come back for you," he said, reinforcing his commitment to her.

"I'll be waiting."

"It could be two days until the storm lets up enough for me to fly in again," he said. "It's a bad one."

Maggie could hear regret choking his voice as he shoved his headset on, and her throat closed, preventing her from responding to him. She nodded and withdrew from the plane.

Jack closed the door. The engine started and the propeller hesitated once, then spun as the motor caught. Maggie looked through the windshield at Jack. Grim-faced, he gave her a thumbs-up.

Maggie returned the gesture and watched as the plane taxied out into the swollen and choppy river. The plane bobbled over the waves, trying to pick up enough speed to take off, and Maggie held her breath, her heart thrumming in time with the prop. Soon, they were safely in the air. Jack banked the plane and flew over her, tipping the wings in both directions in final salute.

Rain now fell in a steady downpour, but Maggie stood on the dock until the plane had disappeared. She wiped away the rain mixed with tears from her face. She picked up the cooler from the dock and walked up the muddy path to the camp.

Once inside the small cabin, she set the cooler on the dirt floor and shrugged out of her wet coat. A dust-covered kerosene lantern sat in a corner. Obviously it wasn't used very much. Maggie looked around for another light source. A similar lantern with battery power sat in the center of a picnic table. A twist of the knob verified that the lantern was in usable order and she set it in the middle of the table.

Then the storm erupted with blinding lightning and deafening thunder. Maggie sat at the table with her hands folded up, praying that Jack had made it back before the worst of the storm hit.

Jack landed the plane in the inlet and slowly released his clenched, numb fingers from the wheel. If the transport had taken any longer he'd have lost the feeling in both hands. The ambulance crew waited on the dock. As soon as he cut the engine, the men moved to open the door of the plane.

"Is my grandfather going to be OK?" Abel asked.

Jack heard the crack of his voice, but didn't know if it was from emotion for his grandfather or fear of the storm. "We're going to do everything we can to make him better. After you're settled at the hospital, we'll try to contact your family in your village."

"My grandmother will want to hear from us by tomorrow."

"She'll be worried if she doesn't hear from you?" Jack asked.

"She'll be furious!" Abel exclaimed. "We're supposed to bring back fish for her to dry for the winter. If she doesn't get started now, they won't have enough to last."

"Your grandfather won't be ready to make the trip back to the village by then, and certainly won't be able to fish. But we'll make sure your family has enough food for the winter."

Only two hours had passed since Jack had returned to Kodiak, but it felt like two days. Getting the patient to the clinic and stable wasn't the problem. Waiting out the storm was killing him. To keep busy and be ready to take off when the storm let up, Jack filled the plane with food, his rifle, extra ammo, sleeping bags and other survival gear.

Lightning shattered the sky as the storm poured its worst down onto the island. After adjusting the radio to the weather channel, Jack listened to the forecast, hoping he would hear some good news. Another storm was coming on the heels of this one, but in between he might catch a break.

An unexpected knock on the door of the plane interrupted the weather report. Ella and James stood outside, wearing bright orange ponchos. Jack opened the door. "What are you two doing here?" he shouted.

"Are you going back for Maggie?" Ella yelled back.

"Yes."

"It's too dangerous for you to fly right now. You know that," Ella said. "Don't be an idiot, Jack. She's safe for a while, isn't she?"

"I can't leave her out there by herself," Jack said. Ella would understand why he had to go, why he needed to go. "I can't leave her."

"Bring my sister back. She's not up to this kind of situation. Nothing like this has ever happened to her before," James said, adding to the burden of guilt already weighing down Jack's heart.

"Nothing like this has ever happened to me either," Jack said. He slammed the door against the rain, wishing he could shut out his feelings as easily, but the rain continued, as did the trembling in his heart. Ella and James dashed away to the safety of the pub beside the dock.

Jack's hands clenched into fists, and he held them to his head, indecision clawing at his gut. Was he pushing himself beyond his abilities by going back into the storm for Maggie? He watched overhead as lightning dissected the sky in jagged flashes, like the wrath of some angry god.

Storms this severe weren't unusual in Alaska, and he'd braved many over the years, but he'd never intentionally flown into one. Jack pulled the hood of his jacket up over his head and got out of the plane. He entered the pub to wait with Ella and James. Maggie was safe at the camp for the moment. Killing himself to get back to her wouldn't help any of them. But it was killing him not to go.

Maggie ate a sandwich and drank a can of soda. The damp air seeped into her bones, chilling her. She moved to the bed. It was more like a wide cot, but it worked. When she sat down, the fragrance of dried grasses and herbs wafted around her and soothed her frayed nerves. Huddled against the wall with a blanket thrown over her lap, she tried to stay warm. Her thoughts, more than anything else, were the coldest part of her.

What if Jack didn't make it back? No one would know where she was. Would they? Would someone else come to rescue her? Could James organize a rescue mission? Ella would. Maggie's tension eased a bit at that thought. Ella could compete with the storm overhead for attention.

But as she thought of the danger Jack was going through to save that patient, a sheen of moisture blurred her vision. Bravery gave way to emotional exhaustion. She flopped onto the bed and fell into a restless, dream-filled sleep.

She dreamed of Jack and how strong he was. Bravery and courage were hard to come by these days and Jack had a strong dose of both. Sometime later she woke with a dreamy laugh as the Jack in her dream shook his jacket out and sprayed her with rainwater. In her dream she wiped away the moisture from her face.

But the water dripping on her face was real and it woke her fully. Blinking sleep and the dream away, she didn't know what she would do about a leaky roof. She just hoped it wouldn't collapse.

When she climbed from the bed, Jack stood beside it, and he was no dream.

"Oh, Jack! You're back!" she cried and flung herself into his arms.

Cold and wet, the man looked like he'd jumped into

the river fully clothed. But she didn't care. With a handful of his collar, she jerked his face down to hers and kissed him.

Jack had never tasted anything as precious as the kiss Maggie planted on him. Urgency drove him, and he plundered her mouth with his tongue, her warmth infusing him with a heat he'd all but forgotten. The relief that poured out of him was almost tangible, and he quivered. Maybe it was from nerves shot from the long day he'd had flying through the storm. Or maybe the rain had given him a chill. Or maybe it was just from having Maggie in his arms where he wanted her that fed the need pulsing through him.

With a gasp Maggie pulled away and framed his face with her hands. "I'm so glad to see you," she said, and her bottom lip quivered.

He stroked her mouth with his thumb and cupped the back of her head, bringing her close again for a hard, quick kiss. "I was going nuts. I had to come back. Thinking about you out here alone in the wilderness and this storm was more than I could take."

"You put yourself in danger for me. No one has ever done that. I've never been worth that to anyone." Tears welled in her eyes.

"You're worth it to me," Jack said, and took her mouth with his. Her muffled cry made him want to rip her clothing from her and make love to her right then and there. Knowing she wanted him filled him with power. He felt like a man again. She'd made him a man again.

"Maggie," he said, not knowing what to say or how to say it. But he needed her with every cell in his body.

"Take your coat off," she whispered, and helped him remove it.

"I'm probably getting you all wet. I'm sorry." Jack hung the coat on a peg by the door to dry and tried to quell the desire throbbing through him.

"I couldn't care less about the water. I just want to be held by you."

The look of need and desire in Maggie's eyes left him with no doubt that she wanted him.

"You shouldn't have come back until the storm eased," she said and stepped toward him.

As he stepped closer to her he removed the heavy cotton shirt that covered his T-shirt and dropped it on the table. "Come here," he said, and opened his arms.

CHAPTER NINE

MAGGIE eased into Jack's arms, and they clung together for a long time, drawing comfort and strength from each other. "I can't believe you're back, but I'm so glad you're here," Maggie said. Realizing he was shivering in her arms, she pulled back from him. "Did you bring more clothes? You're soaked."

"They're in the plane," he said, and pulled the slicker over his head. "I'll go get the supplies I brought and be right back."

When he'd left, Maggie dropped into one of the chairs, rocking back and forth with excitement, fear and overwhelming desire for him. Oh, God, how was she going to get through this night without flinging herself into Jack's arms? Oh, right. She'd done that already. Not that he'd seemed to mind, but they were supposed to be keeping it professional between them.

Minutes later Jack returned and dumped an armload of supplies just inside the door. "There's more to come," he said, and disappeared back into the rain.

Maggie watched for his return and opened the door for him. While Jack dealt with the survival gear, Maggie moved the food into the kitchen area. He spread a sleeping bag onto the first bed and tossed a bag onto the second one.

"How is Mr. Topsekok?" Maggie asked, as she watched Jack open the sleeping bags. She tried not to wonder if they would zip together into one.

"Much better. Giving him the transfusion when we did helped a lot. It's a good thing we took Abel with us, too," Jack said, and propped the rifle beside the door.

"Why is that?"

"He's diabetic and had a hypoglycemic episode."

"Is he OK now?" Maggie asked, relieved they hadn't left him behind.

"He's fine. Gave him some dextrose IV and took him to the diner. The kid ate like a horse." Jack laughed.

"I'm glad they're going to be OK." Maggie smiled, more at ease now that they were on a safe subject. "You did the right thing."

Jack ran a hand through his rain-soaked hair, shoving it back. He dug a towel out of a duffel bag. "I've been on such an adrenaline kick since I left here, I'm not sure I'll be able to sleep." He held out a hand that visibly quivered.

Maggie took the towel from his hands and directed him into one of the chairs. "Sit."

"Why?" he asked, but sat.

Maggie ignored the question and dried his hair with the hand towel. She rubbed his thick hair, squeezing excess moisture from it. With fingers that shook a little she fluffed the strands into order and draped the towel over his shoulder. "Why don't you change into dry clothes and try to relax?"

Maggie moved away as he opened a duffel bag of

clothing. With her back to Jack, she tried not to picture what he looked like.

Naked.

"Can you give me some help?" Jack said.

She heard him struggling with the clothing. "What kind of help?"

"My boots. They're stuck."

Maggie turned, and her mouth went dry. With no ability to control her hungry gaze, she took in Jack's state of undress all at once. Dark hair scattered over his bare chest and converged into a line that dropped low over his flat abdomen. The muscles of his chest outlined his anatomy better than any textbook could ever hope to illustrate. Lean but well defined, Jack stood and waited. His eyes were half-closed, and she couldn't read his expression.

Clamping down on her overcharged hormones, she knelt beside him and unlaced one of the heavy boots he wore. The water inside created suction that she worked hard to release. With a slurp it gave way and Maggie almost landed on her butt as it came off in her hands. After she'd removed the second boot, she moved away, afraid she'd betray the need that welled within her.

Emotionally available or not, she wanted Jack with her heart and her soul. She wanted to touch him, hold him, feel his skin beneath her fingers and against her, inside her. She thought back to her brother's words about having a fling. Could she do that with Jack? Could she open up to him when she knew he couldn't do the same for her? Could she just have sex with him and leave it at that? All her life she'd obeyed the rules and done what had been expected of her. When was she ever going to do something for herself? After that first disastrous relationship in college, she'd never been intimate with a man again. But Jack made her feel things that she shouldn't be feeling. Her heart pulsed, her mouth went dry and other parts of her ached for him.

Listening, she heard Jack remove the remainder of his clothing and the light rustle of dry fabric as he dressed again.

"You can turn around now. I'm dressed."

"OK." She turned, but didn't look at him, just fiddled with looking through the supplies. "You brought enough stuff to keep us going for a while," she said, amazed at how much he had brought.

"I didn't know how long we'd be here, so I brought plenty." He handed a backpack to her. "Ella sent some things for you."

Maggie took the bag and rummaged through it. She brought out a pair of sweatpants and shirt. "That woman is a gem," she said, and hugged the fresh clothing to her. A toothbrush and toothpaste, brush and a hair tie, socks and clean underwear. Maggie stepped to the sink and brushed her teeth, savoring the fresh clean taste.

"I'm going to try to sleep a while. It's been a long day. Goodnight, Maggie," Jack said, when she'd finished.

"Goodnight." Even though Maggie had just brushed her teeth, her mouth went dry at the thought of sleeping next to Jack. "Which bed do you want?"

"Doesn't matter," Jack said with a shrug.

"Why don't I keep the one I had, and you take the other?" she asked.

"Fine," he said, but didn't move away. He just stood there and stared at Maggie.

"What? Do I have toothpaste on my face or something?" she asked, and started to wipe her mouth.

Jack grabbed her arm before she could complete the motion.

"No. Don't do that."

Before she could think or act, Jack stepped up to her and took her mouth with his. Her breath caught in surprise. Opening her mouth to his, she welcomed the soft warmth of his tongue, satisfied by the touch, the intimacy of kissing him, and she met him stroke for stroke. Strong arms moved around her waist and pulled her tight against him. The fabric of his pants was no barrier and left her with little doubt that Jack desired her. At least physically. The dampness of his hair beneath her fingers reminded her of the storm outside. But it was nothing compared to the storm raging inside her.

Jagged bolts of desire, want and need shot through her. Beats of thunder from her heart echoed in her soul, and she knew it would never be just sex with Jack.

Jack released her lips and pressed his forehead against hers, his breath coming in quick gasps. "I want to look at you."

Maggie's hands moved to the buttons on her shirt, but then fear stopped them. Her lips clung to him, but otherwise she couldn't move.

Jack covered her hands with his, and they trembled as he released the first button on her shirt, and the second, and the third. "You are beautiful," he said as he pushed aside the fabric that kept her skin from his view. Maggie tipped her head back and he pressed his lips to her collar-bone, tasting the tender flesh there. She was as soft as she looked, and he traced the tip of his tongue upward, past the dip at the base of her neck and stopped to outline her ear. Her breath came in uneven shudders, as did his. Nibbling on the lobe of her ear, he knew he couldn't stop himself from exploring every inch of her body.

He felt like a drunk, and Maggie was his drink. "I need you, Maggie," he whispered in her ear. "I want to make love with you so badly it hurts," he said. The words sounded strange, forming in his brain. "I know I shouldn't want you the way I do, but I can't stop myself. Tomorrow I may hate myself, but tonight I'll hate myself more if I don't hold you." His hands traced the edges of the lace bra molded to her curves, and he was lost to her. "Will you let me?"

She looked up at him with her vulnerable big blue eyes. "I've only been with one man," she said softly, pausing to gauge his reaction. Her eyes were full of pain, full of remembered sorrow. "And it was a disaster. It devastated me." Jack stroked his hand down her face, brushing away her silent tears. Maggie looked deep into his eyes, offering herself to him. For the first time laying herself bare. "I want you to take away that old memory and give me a new one to keep with me," she whispered. "Make me forget, Jack. Please."

Jack sought her mouth with his and Maggie gave in to a kiss full of longing, regret, passion and need. She wanted him, she wanted this to go on for ever.

Jack dropped hot, open-mouthed kisses on her face and her neck and her ears as his hands cupped her head. He wanted to erase any bad memories from her past. He wanted to give her the experience she deserved. To show her how perfect this could be. Tunneling his hands into her hair, he held her close. He felt her tentatively brush his skin with her hands. Fingertips went up his spine to his neck, urged his arms up, and he tore off his shirt.

With his mouth on hers, he led her to the cot and laid her down on it, then covered her body with his, needing to touch every inch of her, breathe in her fragrance and keep it in his mind forever. A woman's curves and softness had never been as welcoming as hers were right now.

Licking and kissing her neck and moving downward, Jack sought out the lush fullness of her breasts with his mouth, following the contours and curves. His fingers dragged down the straps of her bra and moved to the back and released the clasp.

He clamped his mouth onto a rosy nipple and sucked it, flicking the tip of his tongue across the smooth skin until it puckered.

Maggie twisted, pressing more fully into him, and her hands gripped his arms, giving him unobstructed access to her breasts. "Jack," she sighed. "Oh, Jack." He reached for her other breast and filled his hands with her. Unable to resist, he licked the other soft, pink peak and watched as it responded to his touch.

Maggie's hands got busy. They roamed over his shoulders and arms and raked through his hair. Each touch, each breath, each sigh made him want her more.

Jack stripped off his jogging pants, but then sat on the edge of the bed, clutching the mattress in his hands. He hesitated, hating himself for wanting Maggie, disregarding his vows, until she knelt behind him. The feel of her breasts pressed against his back and her arms around his neck felt so right. So very right. But how could he make love with her?

How could he not?

"Let's take this slow, Jack. There's no reason to rush," she said, and held on to him, rocking him, the tips of her breasts teasing the skin on his back. He turned and looked at her.

Maggie's blue eyes were dewy with desire. Her hair, mussed from his hands, escaped its braid. Lips, swollen from his kisses, parted with her breathing.

"Sit back," he said, and Maggie moved back onto her heels. Jack turned toward her, and his glance roamed over her breasts, their fullness beckoning him to touch them again. With one finger he drew an imaginary line from her jaw, down her neck, over the bump of her collar-bone and lower until the curve of her breast interrupted the line. Turning his hand, he cupped her breast, then reached out for the other.

"Maggie," he whispered, and captured her gaze, trying to see into her soul. "I need you like I've never needed anyone in my life."

"I need you, too," she said. "If all you can give me is this one night, I'll take it." She drew him to her, then lay back on the bed. Jack's hands worked the fastening of her jeans and dragged them off her hips.

Now they were flesh to flesh, and Jack plundered her mouth, unable to get enough of the taste and the feel of her, wanting to crawl inside her. Tangled together like this, Jack couldn't think of anything else, except being with her. No past, no present, no future. Wanting to explore more of her body, his hand moved downward over the curve of her waist and hip to her soft woman's flesh. Delving inside, he almost lost control as he found how ready she was for him. "Maggie," he whispered, unable to create any other sensible thought.

"Come here," she said, and guided his body to hers and sought his mouth.

Hesitating at the edge of joining with her, a flash of sanity struck him. "I don't want to make you pregnant."

"I'm on the Pill for other reasons. I need you now."

Jack eased inside her moist flesh.

And almost exploded as her tender flesh gripped his. He grabbed her hips and gasped. "Don't move."

"What's wrong?" she asked, but stilled.

"Nothing. It's just been a long time for me, and I want to please you."

He blew out a breath, trying to control his body. But she felt so good and so right to him. Jack moved his hands up to cup her face and gave her a long, slow kiss, hoping to distract himself from how he slid so easily into her and how her body accepted him, how perfectly they fit together. Maggie drew her legs up, wrapped them around his hips, and he was gone.

Driving his body into hers after so many years of celibacy, he was unable to find the control he sought. But with Maggie control no longer seemed like something he needed.

He turned on his side and brought Maggie to hers. He drew her leg up over his hip.

"You humble me," he said, and stroked the inside of her thigh until she quivered. "I want to make you feel as incredible as you've made me feel."

She pressed her lips together with a moan, unable to speak as Jack stroked her, delved inside the folds, and moved upward to the most erotic spot of her body. The tiny pearl responded to the light strokes of his fingers, and Maggie pressed her face against his neck with a gasp of indrawn breath.

"Don't hide," he said. "I want to hear you." He stroked his tongue deep inside her mouth and mimicked the motions with his hand. Long fingers explored deeply in her body, while his thumb stroked elsewhere and took her to the edge.

Fingernails digging into his arms, Maggie cried out and clung to Jack. Her body pulsed around him, and his body roused again from her response. Turning her onto her back, he entered her while tremors still moved through her.

"Maggie," he whispered, as his body throbbed. Moments later he rocked into Maggie while she moved her hips with his. He crashed again, losing himself in Maggie.

Finally, the effects of the exhausting day overcame them. They curved together and slept while a soft rain danced on the roof.

CHAPTER TEN

MAGGIE shivered and pulled the blanket over her. Or
tried to. But there was no blanket, and Jack slept curved
into her back so she couldn't move without disturbing
him. One hand pillowed her head and the other rested
possessively on her hip, fingers splayed loose in sleep.
His breathing fell slow and deep.

Before Maggie could stop it, a chill shot through
her, and she shivered.

Jack stirred. "Cold?"

"A little."

Jack rose and got the other sleeping bag, unzipped
it and draped it over them. "I want to hold you again,"
Jack said, climbing in beside her. "Is that OK?"

Maggie turned to face him and settled with her head
on his shoulder. She closed her eyes. "Fine with me,"
she said, and sighed, more content than she'd ever been
in her life. Her old memory was nowhere to be found.

Jack kissed the top of her head. "You feel wonderful against me," he whispered. "Thank you."

Hours later, morning came with a burst of rain in
another storm on the heels of the first. Maggie woke to
the smell of fresh coffee.

She popped her head out from beneath the cocoon of the sleeping bags. She sniffed and her mouth watered at the fragrance. "Is that really coffee I smell or am I hallucinating?" she asked, and watched as Jack moved around the small eating area. The smile on his face made her heart flip at the simple gesture.

"Are you ready for some?" he asked, and brought a cup to her.

Greedily she took the mug from him and sipped the scalding brew. "Thanks. I need my coffee in the mornings before I can move."

"Did you sleep well?" he asked, and watched her face, looking for something, he wasn't sure what.

"I slept great. Better than I have in years," she said, and he was satisfied with that. "Must be the fresh air out here," she said.

He laughed and it felt good. "You're such a tease," he said, and stroked her cheek with his hand. "I love that about you. You try to keep a sense of humor in a tense situation."

"Do you think this is tense?" she questioned, worried that the atmosphere between them was changing.

"No, tense was the wrong word. Unusual…unusual for both of us."

She sipped at the cup again. "Unusual is right. I've never been stranded in a fish camp in the wilds of Alaska before." She smiled. Then she sat upright, her eyes concerned. "My brother will be worried about me."

"I relayed a radio message to him and to Ella that we're OK." He squinted out the small window. "This secondary storm is going to keep us grounded for at least another day."

"Seriously?"

"Yes. Is that a problem for you?" He sipped his coffee and sat on the edge of the bed beside her.

"No. It's just strange. It's like we're in a totally different world out here. Alone. Weathered in. Are we co-workers or lovers now?" She looked up at him, her gaze questioning.

"Or both?" he said, and curved his fingers beneath her chin. "Can't we just enjoy this time for now?"

"Is it the same for you?"

"Kind of strange, surreal, wonderful and frightening all at the same time?"

She nodded.

He rose and turned away, uncomfortable with the direction of the conversation. "Are you game to try something new today?"

"Uh, sure. What did you have in mind?" She rose and put on her sweatshirt and pants.

"Did you see the fish wheel down on the river?"

"Fish wheel? I never heard of one, so I don't know if I saw it or not."

"It's basically a large scoop for fishing on the river. It turns like a wheel on a mill, but instead of scooping water, it scoops up fish."

"It's hard to envision, but I'll try it." She tied her boots and stood.

"Abel was concerned about not getting enough fish for his grandmother to dry for winter. I thought maybe we could do some fishing and take the catch up to their village."

"That's a wonderful idea," she said.

"Not afraid to get a little wet, are you?" The grin that burst onto his face was something he couldn't control.

She grinned and grabbed one of the slickers. "Not me. I'm from Boston, remember?"

They trekked through the rain upriver about a hundred yards to the fish wheel. Maggie looked at the flimsy contraption and then at Jack, her eyes wide. "Are you nuts? I'm not getting on that thing," she stated, and rooted her feet where they were.

Jack turned to face her and laughed, enjoying her reaction. "It's not as bad as it looks. Once you get on, it's pretty sturdy."

"Yeah, right. Selling bridges now, too, Jack?" She crossed her arms.

Jack moved to step out onto the framework dock and bobbled before he balanced on the wooden platform. "See?"

"If you think I'm getting on that…that…" She waved her hand in the direction of the wheel.

"We're doing this for those less fortunate than ourselves, remember?"

Maggie narrowed her eyes and glared at him. "That's just mean." She watched as he worked to set up the wheel and maneuver it into position. And her resistance dissolved. Jack was willing to do this for the Topsekok family. What was her problem? A little rain? A little physical labor? If she fell in the river, she'd just get wet. She was already wet. "OK. But if I fall in and get eaten by wild Alaska salmon, you're responsible, buddy," she said. Maggie picked her way through the tall grass at the edge of the river and waited for Jack to help her onto the platform.

Grinning the whole way to her side, Jack held out his hand and brought her onto the platform. "Thank you," he said, and then released her hand.

Maggie wobbled, losing her balance immediately, and Jack reached for her. With his hands on her waist to steady her, she grabbed the supports and held on. Looking up at Jack, his face so close to hers, she wanted to reach under the hood of the slicker and drag his mouth to hers. Instead, she clutched the wooden side. "I'm OK now."

Out in the middle of the river, they fished, using the primitive wheel, which was surprisingly effective, to scoop the fish. They settled into a rhythm, with Jack using his muscle to work the wheel and Maggie piling the fish to the side. They talked little during this time, but worked as a team. After several hours out in the river, Jack moved the platform to the shore and secured it in place.

By the end of the day Maggie had a new respect for lox and bagels. They loaded the fish into heavy-duty trash bags and packed ice from the coolers around them to keep until morning.

"The rain has finally quit," Jack said as he observed the sky beginning to lighten from black to grey.

"I love the rain, but I'm happy to see the sun again, too," Maggie said, and rinsed her hands in the river. "Ugh. I'm sure I'll smell like fish for a week," she said, and wrinkled her nose at the odor that lingered on her hands.

"Try some of this. It'll get the smell off your hands," Jack said, and tossed her a white tube.

"Toothpaste? Will it make my hands minty fresh, too?"

"Smart ass," Jack said with a grin. "Just do it."

After a few minutes of scrubbing with a glob of the green gel, Maggie was amazed at how easily it removed the fish smell. "Now, what about the rest of me?" she said, looking down at her mud-spattered clothing.

A squeal of surprise erupted from her as Jack scooped her up into his arms. He carried her to the edge of the dock and dangled her over the river.

"I have the solution for that." A mischievous grin lit his face, and Maggie clutched his shoulders.

"Jack Montgomery! If you drop me, I'll report you to the medical board."

"For what?" He scoffed at her threat and dipped her once.

"Nurse abuse."

"Abuse? You really think this is abuse?" he asked, his voice husky. His eyes turned dark, and Maggie recognized the burst of desire that shone in their dark depths as it quivered through her.

"You didn't think it was abuse last night," he said.

"Last night was different." She watched his mouth as he spoke. She imagined those lips feasting again on her body.

Jack released her legs, and she stood on the dock beside him, swaying with the movement of the river. His free arm drifted down to rest on her hip. A frown crept over his face, and he took a step back from her, his playful mood suddenly gone. Shoving his hands into his jacket pockets, he turned to face the river.

"What's wrong?" she asked, but refrained from touching him, as she longed to do.

"Nothing." He sighed. "I was going to build a fire

and cook one of the salmon for dinner. I can heat some water for you to bathe if you like."

"That would be wonderful," she said, wondering at the abrupt change that had overtaken him. She hoped it wouldn't last. The lighter side of Dr. Jack Montgomery was very appealing but, oh, so fleeting.

"It'll take a while, so I'd better get started."

Maggie watched him walk away toward the camp and let him go. The storm had kept the mosquitoes away, but now, with the rain and wind settled, they descended on her, intent on getting at every inch of exposed skin they could find. After swatting without effect at them, she ran to the camp and darted through the door.

To find Jack undressed, down to his underwear. Maggie stopped and gaped at him. "What are you doing?"

"Washing?" he said, and lifted the cloth in his hand. The self-deprecating look in his eyes tweaked her heart. "I figured the colder the water, the better."

Tearing her gaze away would have been difficult, so she didn't. She took the cloth from his hand and dipped it in the frigid bathing water. Soap applied, she moved to his back. Jack shivered and tried to pull away from the chill water. "Woman, are you trying to freeze me?" he said, as waves of goose-flesh crossed his body.

Maggie smiled. "You're the one who wanted a cold bath." She scrubbed his back and returned the cloth to the water. She prepared it again and applied it to his chest, washing his pecs, abdominals and up to his arms, watching the goose-bumps skate across his skin.

"You don't know what kind of torture this is," he said, and closed his eyes.

"Yes, I do."

When Jack opened his eyes, playtime was over. He grabbed her arms and pulled her to him.

Cold and wet and half-naked, he'd never wanted a woman more than he had at that moment. Last night they'd come together with a passion born of fear. Tonight frustrated anger consumed him. Anger pushed him to the edge of reason, and he took Maggie's mouth with his, pouring all the sexual frustration of the last two years into the kiss. Jerking away from her, he leaned on the table and almost tipped it over. "God, Maggie. Do you have any idea how much I want to make love to you again right now?"

"No."

He looked at her, taking in the way she held his gaze, the firm line of her jaw and the swollen lips. She tried to control her breathing, but he knew those deep breaths weren't because she'd just run a marathon. "Oh, I think you do."

"Why don't you tell me?"

"I'm standing here almost naked, dousing myself in ice water to freeze my desire for you. It's not just my body that wants you, Maggie. It's my heart, my mind. But I can't. Every time I look at you, something pulls at me, and not just physically. Making love with you last night was beautiful, and I needed it more than you'll ever know. But for both our sakes it has to be the only time."

"Why? Why does it have to end?" she asked, and started toward him. "Can't you give us a chance?"

"Long before I met you, I made a commitment."

"You need to *be* committed if you think you're the only man who's lost a wife, a mate, a lover—"

"I lost my life," he snapped, and his voice cracked.

"You didn't. You have a life. You're just afraid to live it."

Slack-jawed, Jack stared at her.

"You're afraid that reaching out to someone could get you hurt again, and it probably will. Well, welcome to the real world, pal. It ain't easy, but it's the only one we've got."

She stormed out of the cabin and left him standing there, dripping wet and alone, his mind more confused than he would ever have anticipated.

He'd been confused before about women in the past, so the current situation didn't really surprise him. When he'd first discovered what a woman really was, that had scared him, intrigued him and eventually baffled him. But he'd been young with an unbreakable heart. Or so he'd thought. Until Arlene. Their relationship had been easy. Maybe too easy. And when she'd died, he'd died, too. At least, that's what he'd wanted to do, prayed for it every night for months. But too many people had needed him and his skills as a doctor for him to give in to the luxury of overwhelming grief. So he'd buried himself in his work until the weeks and months had passed. By the time the initial numbness had worn off, he'd been so deeply embedded in work that he hadn't been able to grieve.

Jack dried himself and changed into fresh clothing. Digging into the supplies, he pulled out a hunk of cheese and a bottle of wine. Tucking the bottle under his arm, he left the cabin. Maggie stood on the dock again, against the backdrop of the newly blue sky, skirted on the horizon by departing stormclouds.

Thankfully, the light breeze kept the mosquitoes away. Unable to think of anything to say, he stopped behind her.

"I've been watching the most amazing wildlife show, Jack."

The soft amazement in her voice tugged at his heart.

With her arm outstretched, she pointed across the river. "A mama bear with two cubs is fishing over there." Her finger moved to another area. "Loons have been swimming in that area, although I can't see them very well. Their voices really pull at my heart, they're so melancholy." Then she pointed to an area far down the river. "And I think a moose is out there, eating river grass."

"Alaska is an amazing place." That she felt about his home the same way he did just about dropped him to his knees.

She turned and noticed what he carried. "Offering tokens of your questionable affection?" she asked, with a gentle look in her eyes and a sad smile on her face.

"It's all I have."

"It's all you'll offer."

"Can we take this slice of time and enjoy it for what it is?"

"What is it, Jack?" She took a glass from his hand and tipped it, waiting for him to pour wine into it. "A chance to be lovers with no strings attached? Nobody except us knows it happened, so it can't be real, right?"

They sat on the dock and drank the wine. Jack pulled out a pocket knife and sliced cheese for her. He fed it to her and watched as she chewed, then sipped the wine with the cheese still in her mouth. On impulse, he leaned into her, took her lips with his and tasted the intoxicating flavors mingled in her mouth. The kiss was gentle, sweet and powerful.

Jack filled her glass again and drank from his, keeping his gaze on her, wishing things could be different between them. "This slice away from reality is all I can give you. It's up to you whether you'll take it. Can you be my lover for another day, then return to Kodiak, forget this happened, and go on with your life?"

"Go on with my life? You mean, as in dating other men, maybe sleeping with them?" She chewed her cheese and contemplated him with the fire of challenge in her eyes.

The thought of another man touching Maggie and enjoying the pleasures of her body the way he had last night filled him with rage, but he had no right to it. "There are no strings attached to this time." Though it killed him, he had to say it. A bite of cheese, a sip of wine, a pinch of guilt.

Maggie stood. "I'm going to go wash up. I'll see you in a bit."

She left him sitting there with the glass paused halfway to his mouth. The incessant, infuriating buzz of the mosquitoes reflected his mood.

He tried to be patient while he finished the glass of wine and wrapped up the cheese. Some impulsive part of his nature wanted to guzzle the rest of the bottle down so that he had an excuse to forget about his commitment. But if losing his wife to cancer hadn't made him a drunk, the prospect of spending another night with Maggie shouldn't make him one either.

About thirty minutes passed before Jack returned to

the cabin. As he pushed the door open, a sheen of sweat appeared on his palms and he wiped it away. How could something like this make him nervous? How could something like this *not* make him nervous?

He entered the dimly lit cabin to find Maggie watching him from the table. She had brushed and re-braided her hair, washed and changed clothing.

A checker set lay open in front of her. Challenge glittered in her eyes.

"What are you doing?" he asked, and set the glasses and wine down.

"Waiting for you."

"For?" He let the question hang.

"Strip checkers."

Jack laughed and almost choked. "Are you serious?"

"Yep. I won the strip checker championship my freshman year of college, I'll have you know. To this day that record stands."

Doubtful, but intrigued, Jack stepped closer. "Strip checkers championship? How many layers of clothing did you wear?"

"That's my secret."

He moved closer still. "And how many layers do you have on now?" he asked, watching as she dropped her gaze from his and fiddled with the edge of the checkerboard. Moving behind her, he bent down to kiss the side of her neck and watched as the tiny hairs stood to attention. She wasn't unaffected by him. "Maggie?"

"Yes?"

"Do you really want to play checkers?" he asked, and licked her neck, intent on driving her mad.

"Wh-what?" A shiver made her shoulders quake.

"Strip checkers? Remember that?"

"Oh, yes," she said. "It was the only thing I could find to entertain ourselves with."

"Really? No books?" He moved to the other side, still behind her, and nuzzled that side of her neck.

"Why don't you come out from there?" she asked.

He sat opposite her.

"Your move," she said, throwing down the gauntlet.

CHAPTER ELEVEN

SEVERAL games of checkers later Jack shivered in his Jockeys and glared at Maggie. "You weren't kidding, were you?"

"About what?" she asked, and raised a brow, mock innocently batting her eyelashes at him.

"About being a champion checkers player."

"No. But the strip part was slightly embellished," she admitted. "I used to beat the pants, no pun intended, off my brother. Made him mad, too. That was the part I liked best." She grinned and stacked the checkers for a new game.

"He was very concerned about your safety."

"What do you mean?"

"He and Ella came to see me before I left. I had to delay flying out for a while, and I sat in the pub with them." Jack reached for his shirt and put it on. "He's really a nice guy and loves you a lot."

"He's OK as brothers go. I think I'll keep him."

"My brother and I used to beat the hell out of each other."

"You have just one brother?"

"And a sister." He made a move on the checkerboard, but his heart was no longer in it.

"Where are they?"

"Seattle area. They get up here once in a while or I go down there." He shrugged. "They've asked me to move closer to them since Arlene died, but it seemed like too much trouble at the time."

"Would you like to move someday?" She countered his move and took a checker.

"Under the right circumstances I suppose I would, but I haven't given it much thought."

They finished the game, both subdued. At the end, when Maggie took his last checker, she looked at him. "You let me win that one."

"My heart isn't in it, I guess." Suddenly restless, he moved away from the table and pulled on the rest of his clothing.

"I can't, Jack," Maggie whispered, clutching her hands together in her lap.

"Can't what?" he asked and turned.

"Can't be your lover and walk away like nothing happened. Last night meant something to me, but if all you want is sex, then you're looking for it in the wrong person."

A flash of anger shot through him, and he moved closer to her, placed his hands on her shoulders. "Last night meant something to me, too. More than you'll ever know. You made me feel like a man again, Maggie. Something I haven't felt since Arlene died. I'll always be grateful to you for that."

"Grateful?" She shoved away from him, her eyes bright with anger or unshed tears. "I don't want thanks. That's not why I slept with you."

"Why did you?"

"Because I wanted to." She huffed out a breath and tried not to give in to the tears behind her eyes.

"That's it?" It wasn't quite the response he'd anticipated.

"Isn't wanting to make love with you enough?" she asked. "I care about you, and I wanted you. I was frightened about being here alone, but that wouldn't make me jump into just anyone's bed. Being with you made me feel precious, Jack. That's hard to let go of. The last time I let a man close to me he humiliated me and I swore off men. Until you." Her lopsided smile tugged at him. "You made me feel special, Jack."

"You are special, Maggie." He stepped closer still and tucked a strand of hair behind her ear. This time he didn't hesitate. Performing the gesture somehow felt right now, he'd done it so many times. "You're a very special woman. You're caring and compassionate, an excellent nurse. You're funny and beautiful, and I've come to admire you in the short time you've been here."

"But?"

"But nothing. It's all true."

"You just can't think about having a real relationship with me."

There it was and he hated to disappoint her. "No. I can't have a real relationship with *anyone*, not just you."

"Then you're an idiot, Jack." Anger sparked in her eyes, masking her pain. "Do you know what you're giving up?"

"A chance for more heartache if something happens to you, or our relationship doesn't work out." He shook his head. "No, thank you. I've had enough heartache to last me a lifetime."

"Coward."

Jack spun to face her. "After what I went through to come for you in the middle of that storm, you can stand there and call me a coward? I wasn't sure I was going to make it here, Maggie. The storm could have overpowered my plane, I could have been struck by lightning, or gotten lost, and you're calling me a coward?" He grabbed her by the shoulders, but she pushed away from him.

"That was the easy part, wasn't it? Risking your life was nothing. Risking your heart is too much for you. I'll bet making love with me, though physically enjoyable, was tougher for you than to fly into that storm."

Speechless, he stared at her. "You have some nerve when all you've done is run from Daddy all of your life," he said, lashing out at her.

"Thanks to you I've stopped running, and I'm facing my demons. Why don't you take your own medicine, Doctor?" She turned away from him, and he let her go. "I'm going to bed. Goodnight."

The glance she threw at him was cold. He deserved it because she was right, dammit. He sat on the bed and removed his boots, then lay on top of the sleeping bag, contemplating Maggie's words. She rustled around, getting comfortable on the other bed. He listened to her breathing, but it never became even or deep.

"Are you awake?" he whispered.

"Yes."

"I'm sorry. I didn't mean to hurt you."

"I know."

But as he listened to her muffled breathing, he could tell she was crying. He sat up and went to her. Drawing her resistant body up, he pulled her onto his lap and rocked her.

Jack kissed the top of her head and pressed his cheek to hers as she held on to him, loving the feel of her body against his. "I wish I could make your hurt go away."

"You're the one who's hurt me, but you're the only one who can make it go away." She sniffed and wiped her face with the heels of her hands.

"Isn't that how relationships work, no matter what kind?"

"I guess." She slid from his lap and faced the wall. "Sorry."

"Don't be." The comfort he offered was a legitimate excuse to hold her in his arms again. Probably for the last time. "Let's get some sleep. We're going to have a busy day tomorrow." He moved to the other bed.

"Goodnight, Jack."

He lay on top of the sleeping bag, contemplating a spider crawling from its corner to investigate the camp. That lasted for about half an hour before Jack got up and went outside. Maybe the sugar in the wine kept him from sleeping. Maybe sleeping in an unfamiliar place made him restless. Or maybe anticipation about returning to Kodiak tomorrow wouldn't let his brain turn off. In the past none of those things had ever affected his sleep. He glanced back at the cabin, remembering the way Maggie slept. What he wouldn't give to crawl into that sleeping bag with her and discover all the nuances of her body he'd missed last night.

He'd give anything, but would he give *up* anything

for her? Could he give up Arlene? Curling his hands into fists, he stared out at the river, calm again now that the storm had passed. Tied to the dock, the plane bobbed gently. They'd take off in it tomorrow and return to reality. That thought saddened him more than it ever had before. After being away, he'd always looked forward to going home, but not after this trip. This trip was different.

If he had his way, he'd stay at this primitive camp in the wilderness locked away with Maggie for ever. Out here he could forget and just live like the man he wanted to be. Back in Kodiak too many reminders of his past life with Arlene prevented him from moving on.

Maybe he should leave the island and start a new life somewhere else, as his family had often suggested. But he wasn't sufficiently motivated to uproot his life and start over. Starting over was for a generation younger than his.

A noise behind him made him turn quickly. Danger was never far away in Alaska. And there it was, staring him down.

Maggie stood on the dock behind him, wrapped in a spare blanket. She was the most dangerous and most beautiful woman he'd ever come across.

"Are you all right?" She blinked, her eyes soft and sleepy.

"Yes. Just getting some air."

"Oh. I thought maybe you couldn't sleep, like me."

"Having trouble?" he asked, and put an arm around her shoulders, unable to resist drawing her against his side.

"Yes. Returning to Kodiak is bothering me."

"Why?"

"I've enjoyed our time away, and I can't say I'm eager to go back." She shrugged. "Jamie's there. He'll ask questions about us. He's very perceptive."

"You don't have to defend yourself to anyone, not even your brother," he said, the idea irritating him.

She looked up at him, her big blue eyes captivating him. "Let's go back in. I'm cold."

Once inside she wrapped herself up in a blanket and crawled inside the sleeping bag. She huddled there, trying to stay warm and trying not to give in to the urge to call out to Jack, trying not to trade her convictions for physical need.

She knew he could satisfy her. He'd proved that last night. But the needs of her physical body didn't compare to the needs of her soul, her heart and her spirit. He'd proved that he wouldn't satisfy those needs.

Trying not to cry, she faced the wall and attempted to sleep.

When morning came, the smell of coffee hung heavy in the air. Jack was already up and had some of their gear packed in the plane.

"C'mon, Maggie. We're burning daylight, and we've got a lot to do." Jack jiggled her awake.

"What time is it?" she asked.

"Doesn't matter. The sun's up."

"The sun's up at midnight, too," she complained.

He passed a cup of coffee near her nose, rousing her from her sleepy state.

She sat up, reaching for the cup.

"We've got to get to Chinook Falls and deliver the fish. Then we return to Kodiak."

Memories of the last two days flooded her. She drew on the stout brew to give her strength to get through this one.

After a hurried breakfast and another cup of coffee, Maggie dressed and stowed her belongings in the plane. And then they were off.

Sunlight glinted off the surface of the water as they followed the river north to the tiny village of Chinook Falls. The trip took about half an hour by plane, but it would have taken the Topsekoks many hours to reach their camp by vehicle.

Jack landed the plane on a clear stretch of the river and taxied to the docks. An elderly man helped tie it up.

"Thanks for the help," Jack said, and shook hands with the man, then assisted Maggie from the plane.

"Any time. That's some plane you got there," the old-timer said, admiring the single-prop plane.

"It's a special medical transport plane. We're looking for the family of Elmer Topsekok—do you know them?"

"Sure. Out here everyone knows everyone or is related to them," he said. "You and the missus come with me, and I'll take you to Mrs. Topsekok. She don't speak no English, though." The man led the way through the village on bowed legs that had probably suffered a case of rickets. In this wilderness fresh fruit or a source of vitamin D were hard to come by, and many people suffered from nutritional diseases.

The man led Jack and Maggie to a frame house, knocked on the door and introduced the couple to Mrs. Topsekok in her own language.

"We have a load of fish for her. Her husband has been

injured, and he's been shipped to Anchorage for surgery. He'll be fine, but needs to spend some time there recovering. We brought the fish for her family because he couldn't bring it himself."

The man translated. Maggie could see a range of expressions and emotions flow over the woman's face. Shock and disbelief were followed by relief. She grabbed Jack, pulled him into a fierce hug, and did the same to Maggie. Rushing into the house, she returned with a sea-grass basket about the size of a small tissue box. It had a small lid on it and a blue and green design woven into it.

"She made this and wants to give it to you as a small gesture of thanks," the guide said.

Maggie took it in her hands, afraid she was going to crush the delicate basket. The skill needed to produce a product of this detail took decades to master.

"That's some gift. Some of her baskets are in the Smithsonian," the man said.

"Please, thank her for me. I will treasure this," Maggie said, and clutched the basket to her chest. Maggie leaned down to kiss the gnarled cheek of the woman and was rewarded with a pat on her face by a work-roughened hand.

After the fish were unloaded and the plane refueled, a boy of about ten years old with eyes as black as obsidian and hair to match raced to them. He tugged at Jack's sleeve. "Are you the doctor man?" he asked.

Jack bent down to match the boy's height. "Yes, I'm the doctor man. Do you need a doctor?"

"No, my grandpa does," the boy said, and started off down the street.

"Wait," Jack called. "I need my medicine bag." The boy waited impatiently as Jack retrieved a medical supply bag from the plane. He and Maggie trekked along as they were led to a house. From outside they could hear someone coughing inside. Maggie and Jack exchanged a concerned look and then entered the home.

"In here." The boy pointed to a small bedroom. "He's sick bad."

Jack knelt on the floor beside a man debilitated by emphysema, his barrel chest having changed over the years to accommodate the disease process. The man coughed deeply again and spat up blood.

"He might have TB," Maggie said, and grabbed face masks for them to put on.

"I know. Unfortunately, it's making a big comeback up here," Jack said, and reached for his stethoscope to listen to the man's lungs. Jack shook his head and didn't need to listen for long. "On top of that, he's got pneumonia."

"Is that bad?" the kid asked, his eyes wide as he watched Jack.

"What's your name?" Jack asked the boy.

"Amos George."

"Well, Amos, your grandpa is sick bad and should go to the hospital. We can have him flown to Anchorage and they'll take good care of him."

"Is there anyone else to help you?" Maggie asked, wondering if the boy was alone with his grandpa.

"My mom. But she works in the market sometimes."

"The store in the village?" Maggie asked.

"Tell her I'll call Anchorage and send a plane for him. We can't help him in Kodiak for what he's got," Jack said.

"OK," Amos said, looking frightened, his breath puffing through trembling lips. "Thank you."

As they left the house another woman approached them about an ill family member. Jack and Maggie made recommendations and left.

"This is astounding," Maggie said, her pace slowing as they neared the plane.

"What is?" Jack watched her.

"So many sick people and the total lack of medical care in the village. It's appalling." Maggie had never encountered such poor people who lived on the edge of society and on the edge of the wilderness. They couldn't just go to the next town for care. The next town was hundreds of miles away over impassable mountains.

"It's not something that people who live in remote areas have ever had or expect to have."

"But couldn't the state or the government do something about it?" The idea of having absolutely no medical care had never occurred to Maggie until now.

"Like what?"

"Like build a clinic for these people."

"And who do you propose will run it?"

"Surely someone would live here, wouldn't they?"

"Would you?" he asked.

Maggie looked around the village before answering. There were no trees. The landscape was barren and very different from Kodiak Island. The village consisted of two churches, a post office and a small market, with houses interspersed between them. There wasn't even a bar. A community center was the largest building in town. "I don't think I personally would, but what about…?" Maggie's voice trailed off.

"It's a whole different lifestyle up here, isn't it?" Jack watched her as she took it all in.

"Yes, it is."

"I can't even find an anesthesiologist full time for the Kodiak clinic. There's no way a doctor would live out here full time."

"But what about a locum, a PA or a nurse practitioner? There must be someone who could do it?"

Jack paused, considering her suggestion. "That we might be able to get, but there's no clinic for a locum to work out of at this point."

"Maybe we can work on getting them one." With that idea in mind, Maggie's attitude changed and determination stiffened her spine. "Let's go to the community center and see if there's anyone else who needs help right now."

Jack followed her, admiring her courage and willingness to help these people. But when winter set in, he knew she would not want to stay there. Her determination wouldn't last through the harsh months.

Jack and Maggie set out on the return trip to Kodiak after seeing a total of eighteen patients. They all needed medical care unavailable in the village.

Maggie concentrated on taking in the beauty of the scenery below to distract herself. Tundra rolled in gentle slopes, covered with bushes and grasses, but little in the way of real trees. The landscape seemed barren at first glance, but as she watched, the life within the barrenness peeked out here and there, determined to survive, no matter what the circumstances.

"Are you OK?" he asked.

"Fine. I was just wondering if I dreamed the last few days. It's difficult to think about going back to civilization again, isn't it? I hate leaving those people without proper care," she said, and clutched the sea-grass basket to her. She would treasure it always.

"Yes. But you weren't dreaming." He clasped her hand and held it a moment, needing that tempting connection with her again before returning both hands to the controls.

Facing the front again, Maggie closed her eyes and tried to prepare herself for their landing in the real world. But she couldn't get the images of the villagers out of her mind, how poor they were, how little they had. But they were happy. At least, they looked happy. With the money she was turning down from her inheritance, these people could really benefit. An idea came to her, but before she could thoroughly explore it, Jack interrupted her thoughts.

"We're going to be landing in a few minutes," he said.

Maggie blew out a nervous breath and watched Jack. "Here comes reality, ready or not."

CHAPTER TWELVE

WITHIN an hour of landing in Kodiak, they had become celebrities. At least, on a small scale. Many of the villagers and hospital staff arrived to welcome them back from their unexpected adventure. They were unceremoniously dragged to the pub for celebratory toasts to Maggie's courage when she'd stayed behind for the sake of a patient. Jack's bravery for flying into the storm to rescue Maggie was toasted, as was his equal stupidity for flying into the storm to rescue Maggie.

A newspaper reporter took photos of the couple and interviewed them for an article. Maggie was more interested in notifying the public of the poverty in Chinook Falls than in discussing her rescue. Hours later she dragged herself home, dropped her clothing at the door of the bathroom and drowned herself in the shower for half an hour. When she emerged in her bathrobe from the billows of steam, Ella was home.

The woman grabbed Maggie and pulled her into a fierce hug. "Girl, I'm so glad you're home safe," Ella said. "You two scared the wits out of me and half the town." There were actually tears in her eyes, though she quickly turned away from Maggie.

"I'm glad to be back, too. It was a wild couple of days. Seems like a week passed."

"You aren't kidding," Ella said. "Your brother and I sat in the pub, drinking all the way through the first storm. By the second one we had to go get something to eat, so we stayed at the diner most of the day."

Maggie gaped. "You and Jamie drank together?"

Ella nodded and led Maggie to the couch. "Sure did. That boy can hold his liquor, too."

"I'm amazed," Maggie said, shaking her head.

"That he can drink?"

"No. That he would drink in the pub. He's more a country club kind of guy."

"Well, he held his own at the pub. You'd think he'd been going there all his life. Didn't embarrass himself once."

"Wow." Maggie removed the towel from her head and finger-combed the long wet strands out while she chatted with Ella.

"So, how was your time with Jack?" Ella asked.

"It was OK, I guess." She moved and her long hair covered her face.

"You guess?"

Maggie sighed and pushed the hair back. "He's still deeply committed to Arlene and isn't letting go any time soon, if that's what you meant."

"It was." Ella sighed. "I was kind of hoping you two would come to an understanding while you were away."

"An understanding?" Maggie's mouth went dry and her heart paused.

"You know." Ella gave Maggie a saucy look and twitched her brows.

"Ella McGee," Maggie said in a haughty tone, but couldn't meet Ella's eyes. Feeling as if she'd just bitten into a fiery red pepper, Maggie's face flamed at Ella's innuendo. Unable to answer the woman without an outright lie, Maggie stood. "Don't get your hopes too high on that one," she said. "Excuse me, Ella, but I've got to dry my hair, and then I'm going to bed. I'm exhausted."

"Didn't get much sleep while you were gone?" Ella asked.

"No," Maggie admitted.

"Aha! Something did happen, didn't it?" Ella's eyes narrowed to slits as she studied Maggie.

"Wh-what do you mean?" Maggie stared wide-eyed and tried not to betray anything.

"If you didn't get much sleep, what were you doing when you were supposed to be sleeping?"

"We went fishing."

"Fishing? That's a new one." She snorted.

"No, really. We used the fish wheel on the river at the camp and flew a whole planeload of salmon to the patient's family up river. That whole village is so poor, it's appalling. No wonder they were worried about getting that fish home."

"Which village?" Ella asked.

"Chinook Falls."

Ella shook her head and clucked her tongue. "I know the place, and you're right. I wish we could help them out."

"Jack and I saw a bunch of patients while we were there, but they could all use additional medical care."

"Maybe we can do something for them here in

Kodiak. Have a fundraiser of some kind and send the proceeds to them."

"Do you think they would take an outright gift like that?" Maggie said. "Most people are too proud."

"Those people are just trying to survive." Ella paused a minute. "There used to be a cannery there that employed hundreds of people, but it closed down twenty years ago and the village almost died. Those folks are all that's left."

"That's so sad. I hope we can help them."

"Me, too."

Maggie yawned and stretched. "I've really got to get some sleep." She patted Ella's shoulder. "Thanks," she murmured as she drifted down the hall and shut her door.

Ella stared after her, wondering if all Maggie had said was true. She wanted her and Jack to get together. Maybe they just needed a little more help.

The next day was Jamie's last night in town, so he and Maggie shared a farewell dinner.

"You know what I'm going to do, don't you?" Jamie asked at the end of the meal.

"What do you mean? Do about what?"

"I'm going to spend the rest of our evening together trying to lure you back home into the fold of wealth, power and influence."

"You know those things mean little to me."

"I know, but Father doesn't. He's going to be all over me for not bringing you back, so I've got to at least be able to say I tried."

Maggie grinned, pleased he wasn't going to take

their father's side and make her choose between her family and her job, her new life. "I appreciate that."

"After seeing you here in this environment, I think you're right. You do fit in well." He sipped his wine. "But doesn't school appeal to you any longer?"

"No. I have my bachelor's degree and that's enough for me. At least for now." She looked down at her plate and toyed with the fork.

"If there's something you're interested in, why wait? You should apply to school right away. The longer you wait, the harder it will be to go back."

"I know. But I'm enjoying being away from a university setting for a change. This is hard to let go of for all the wonder of school again," Maggie said, sarcasm dripping from her words.

"Father would pay for you to return to school if you came home."

"I know. But this is something I want to do on my own." She leaned forward, hoping to pour some of her intensity into him. "I need to do this, for me."

"What is it?"

"CRNA school."

"What the heck is that?" he asked.

"Certified Registered Nurse Anesthetist school."

"Meaning?" Jamie's eyes registered only confusion.

"Meaning I could administer anesthesia for operations, conscious sedation for small procedures, and pain control for people with chronic pain. In a place like this, anesthesiologists are hard to find and keep. Having a skill like anesthesia would make me really marketable, and I could go anywhere, if I wanted to."

"But you want to stay in Alaska."

"Yes, though I couldn't go to school here. The closest school is in Seattle, so I'd have to go there."

Jamie looked around. The expression on his face reminded her of their father, and she waited for him to speak. "This place is so small…"

"You haven't seen small until you've been to the village Jack and I went to. They have nothing up there. Not even a fast-food restaurant."

Jeremy looked shocked.

"God, I know I couldn't live there." He shuddered. "No quality coffee around any given corner to satisfy my every whim? You're welcome to it." He flagged down the waiter. "A *latté* please. Do you want one, Maggie?"

"No. Plain coffee is fine. So, what are you going to tell Father when you get back?" Right now she didn't care. She'd grown in the last weeks and now she knew she was stronger than she'd ever been in her life. Even standing up to her father seemed like a challenge she could handle.

"I've already been emailing him, telling him about your adventures."

Maggie sat up straight. "What have you told him?"

Jamie smiled. "That you seem to have found your place in the world." He sat back and raised one eyebrow. "Possibly even found a love interest."

"Love interest?" The muscles in her throat contracted, and she almost choked.

"Yes. Of course, I had to tell him all about Dr. Montgomery so he could do a background check and make sure the man's not just after your money."

"Jamie! Jack couldn't care less about my money."

Maggie covered her face with her hands and groaned. "Please, tell me you didn't do that." The silence continued until Maggie looked up.

Jamie grinned. "Think I'd do that to you, little sister?"

She clutched his hand and squeezed. "You scared the life out of me. Had that been true, I would have been mortified if Jack had found out."

"Anyway, no worries from me. Of course, Father's going to be disappointed that you're not returning and may try to coerce you into coming home, but I'll try to intervene."

"You will?" Tears pricked Maggie's eyes. She and Jamie had been close growing up, but having him support her against their father's influence made her appreciate that relationship even more. "Thank you," she whispered. "It means a lot to me to stay here."

"I know. I can't promise he won't be on the phone to give you a royal piece of his mind, but you've got my support."

"You're a great brother."

"Now that I'm agreeing with you, you say that. Do you remember how many times we argued as kids, and you hated my very existence?"

"I'm your little sister. I was *supposed* to hate your very existence."

Jamie leaned back in his chair as their coffees arrived.

"Father's money doesn't appeal to me, but there is something he could do with it *for* me."

"What's that?"

"The village Jack and I visited needs a free clinic."

Jamie scoffed, nearly spewing his *latté*. "You know Father won't put money into something that he doesn't get a return on."

Maggie leaned forward, now fierce in her passion about the subject. "But he could name it after himself. And charitable donations are tax deductible. He knows that." She contemplated Jamie, wondering if he would go for the idea that had been forming in her mind since the trip to Chinook Falls. "And it would go a long way to show me he's willing to compromise with me."

"Compromise? Our father?" Jamie felt for her pulse. "Are you feeling all right?"

"Be serious," she said, and playfully slapped his hand.

"I am. And you are seriously delusional if you think he would go to that length to get into your good graces. He doesn't work that way. The world revolves around him, remember?"

"See what you can do. You make your living working business deals. See what you can do with this one." The waiter brought the check, and Jamie gave the man a credit card without looking at the bill.

They left the restaurant and stood outside in the midnight sun. "I don't know how you'll get used to this light thing," he said with a shake of his head.

"I want to, so I will."

"My flight is early in the morning, so I'll say goodbye tonight."

They embraced, and Maggie clung to him for just a moment, knowing it would be a long time until they saw each other again. "Thank you, Jamie. I appreciate you so much. And I love you, too."

Jamie pulled back and cleared his throat. "Yes. Well. I love you too, little sister." He kissed her cheek. "Take care of yourself, and try to stay out of trouble."

"I will. Be safe." Maggie turned and walked the few blocks home without incident, wondering if he would talk to their father on her behalf. In the meantime, she had a shift to work in the morning.

The next morning Maggie walked into chaos in the clinic. People ran back and forth to patient rooms. Call lights buzzed incessantly and the phone rang as soon as the secretary replaced it.

"What's going on?" she asked, and shoved her purse beneath the nurses' station.

"Gigantic case of food poisoning from a family reunion yesterday," one of the night shift nurses replied on her way to the utility room.

"Oh, man. That's so gross," Maggie said. But she jumped into the fray and carried spit buckets, bedpans and clean linen. None of the staff rested for hours. When Catherine passed by, Maggie took a bag of dirty linen from her. "This is too heavy for you! You need to go to the lounge and rest for a little while," Maggie said, and gave Catherine a friendly push in that direction.

"But—"

"I'll cover for you. It'll be fine. I'll come get you in fifteen minutes."

But that time came and went before Maggie realized that she'd forgotten Catherine and the woman hadn't returned. Maggie found Catherine curled up in a ball on the sofa in the lounge. "What's wrong?" She rushed to her friend's side.

"I'm losing the baby," she sobbed.

"Are you bleeding?"

"Just spots."

"Any cramping?" Maggie asked.

Catherine nodded. "A few. But this is how it always starts."

"If I remember correctly, it's not uncommon to have a little spotting in the first three months." She helped Catherine to sit up. "Now, go wash your face. You can sit and answer the phone or something." Maggie left the lounge and came face to face with Jack.

"Oh, hi, Jack."

"What's going on? Where are you and Catherine? We're busy as hell out there."

"I know. She'll be out in a minute. She needed a break, and I saw to it that she got one."

"*You* did? You're not the charge nurse today."

"No, I'm not. But that's not the point."

"What is the point?"

"I'm concerned that Catherine's not getting enough rest and is working too hard. Can we send her home for the rest of the day?"

"With the clinic full of sick patients? No way. We're trying to find more staff to come in." Jack frowned. "If Catherine's not pulling her weight, I'll have to have a chat with her."

"You will not," she said, and grabbed Jack by the sleeve. She led him to a remote area of the clinic, away from any eavesdroppers. "You will leave her alone. If something needs to be done, I'll do it for her."

"What's going on? Catherine's perfectly able to handle the work on her shift."

"She can't do any lifting, and she needs frequent rest periods." How much could she tell Jack without giving away Catherine's secret?

"What are you talking about? Is she ill?"

Maggie huffed out a sigh of resignation and closed her eyes for a second. She had to trust Jack with Catherine's secret. "She's pregnant, Jack. She's already had two miscarriages and is afraid she's losing this one. She's spotting."

Jack stepped back from Maggie. "Pregnant?"

"Yes."

"You're sure?"

"Yes. But she's spotting now and is quite upset. She needs to rest."

"Absolutely." He frowned. "Maybe I need to examine her."

"No. No one else but us knows she's pregnant, and until she gives us leave it's going to stay a secret."

He pulled a hand through his hair and sighed. "OK. But how are we going to cover her absence?"

"I can cover her patients until you can find another nurse to come in."

"Agreed."

But after another hour Jack hadn't found anyone else to come in. Everyone was out playing today. He gave Maggie the bad news. "I'm afraid we're going to be short-staffed for the rest of the shift."

"It's only eleven a.m."

"I know. It's going to be a long day. I'm sorry."

"What most of these people need is just IV fluids for hydration, Phenergan for the nausea, and let the bug run its course."

"That seems logical. Just what I would do. Good call."

"So unless something urgent comes in, that means you're relatively free, doesn't it?" Maggie asked, and looked Jack up and down his length with her sharp gaze.

"Sure, but—"

"Roll up your sleeves, Doctor. You're about to be demoted to nursing assistant."

"What? I can't possibly…" He stopped at the narrow-eyed look Maggie laid on him, and he swallowed.

"Are you too good to empty some spit buckets or haul laundry sacks?"

"No, but—"

"No buts. Get to work."

Maggie showed Jack a side of medicine he'd never really thought about. He'd always known someone did the dirty work. Now he was doing it. He emptied trash bins, changed linen bags when they overflowed and took the full ones to the laundry room. He even changed a few bedpans for those too infirm to get up and almost threw up himself, but he managed.

Maggie watched as he completed every task she assigned to him without complaint. And he did a thorough job of each chore. She approached Jack as warmth flowed in each pulse of her heart, though she tried to harden herself against softer emotions where he was concerned. "The shift's almost over, Jack, and everyone looks like they're going to make it. No signs of respiratory failure in any of them. Just the yucks. We can start discharging them to go home for the rest of their recovery."

"That sounds good." He wiped his forearm over his forehead and grinned.

"You did great today. I'm really proud of you," Maggie said. Against her better judgment she pulled him close for a quick hug.

"Careful. I'm a mess," he said, but his arms went around her.

"I don't care. Thank you," she said, and kissed his cheek. "Today would have been hell without you."

"You're welcome." Jack grinned at her pleasure in something so simple. But being part of a team meant doing things you weren't accustomed to when times were tough. He'd discovered that all over again today. Having Maggie lead him through the steps humbled him.

"Why don't you go wash up and get ready to sign discharge instruction sheets? I'll get them ready for those who are doing best." She started to walk away.

"Maggie?"

"Yes?"

"Thanks for asking me to help. It opened my eyes to a lot of things I've taken for granted."

"Really?" she asked with a sideways smile.

"Really."

"I'm glad I could help open your eyes about something, Jack." She just wished she could open his eyes to allowing himself to love again.

The stack of charts piled on the desk required completion before they could end the shift. But more than two hours later she was still at it, trying to get as many people out of the clinic and home as possible so that the night shift didn't have to take all the overflow.

"Why are you still here?" Jack asked, as he took a last walk through the clinic, amazed it was as clean and organized as it was after the hell that had occurred there today. That was thanks to Miss Maggie Wellington who had stepped up to the plate and hadn't run from trouble.

"There's too much to do yet for me to just go home."

"Isn't that why we have more than one shift, Maggie?" he asked. "Exhausting yourself won't do your patients any good."

"Yes, but—"

"But nothing. It's time for you to go home. Night shift can finish up. Besides, I know you haven't eaten anything since lunch and it's almost nine p.m."

"You're right. I could use something." Maggie patted her stomach, but as she made the gesture another thought occurred to her. "I wonder how Catherine's doing?"

"Why don't you call her?" Jack suggested, not liking the distress in Maggie's eyes.

"I could. But if she's asleep, I don't want to wake her up."

"That's considerate of you." He sat on the desk. "I know it's late, but do you want to get something to eat at the diner before you go home?"

"With you?" she asked.

"Yes."

"You buying?" Maggie grinned.

"Yes." Jack couldn't help but respond to that infectious grin.

"I'd love to."

They walked in silence to the diner, and Maggie tried to stifle a yawn. Jack noticed and grinned. "Tired, eh?"

"Yes. I haven't slept enough this week, and it's catching up with me."

They sat in a corner booth away from the stragglers.

"Ella was suspicious about us on the fish camp trip," Maggie whispered.

"Suspicious?"

"Maybe that's too strong of a word. She was more like hopeful."

"Really?"

"She wants us to get together."

"Maggie—"

She held up her hand to stop him. "I know. You don't have to tell me again. I told her there was no chance of that happening."

They finished the meal talking only about work, clinical issues and safe neutral topics. Maggie said nothing about wanting her father to open a clinic in Chinook Falls. Why bother? If her father didn't come through, no one would be disappointed except herself.

Jack's pager went off, and he answered the clinic's call on his cell phone. Thirty seconds into the call he hung up, tossed some money on the table and grabbed Maggie's arm.

"We've got to go. Catherine's losing the baby and she's hemorrhaging."

Maggie clutched Jack's hand as they raced back to the clinic. "Dammit, I knew I should have called her."

"Where is she?" Jack called, as they burst through the doors.

"Trauma three," Gloria said, and hurried after them.

Despite the long shift, Maggie ran to help her friend. She rushed to Catherine's side and clasped her friend's hand. "It's going to be OK, honey. Jack and I will take good care of you."

Catherine clutched Maggie's hand as if it were a lifeline. "I think I've already lost the baby. I passed some tissue, but I'm still bleeding heavily," she said, tears flooding her face.

"Jack's going to have to check you to see if you're still pregnant, and we'll run blood work, too."

"Don't worry right now about anything. Maggie and I are here with you," Jack said.

Maggie turned to him. She'd never heard him use such a soft, compassionate tone with anyone. An ache in her chest throbbed in response.

"Who's your doctor?" Jack asked.

"Sara McGuire. But she's on leave for two weeks."

"Is there someone on call for her?" Jack snapped on a pair of sterile gloves, and Maggie squirted lubricant into his hand.

"No. The other doctor she's with is on maternity leave and their practice is so small…" Catherine clutched her stomach. "Ouch."

Jack examined Catherine. "I'm sorry, but you were right. I can't feel the baby. You're still bleeding a lot and probably have some retained tissue that needs to come out. I'll set up your transport to Anchorage."

"No. Can't you do it here?" Distressed, Catherine came up onto her elbows.

"No. There's no one to run anesthesia, and I'm not a gynecologist. It's been years since I've done a D and C."

"Jack," Maggie interrupted. "I can keep her sedated.

Conscious sedation was something we did commonly at my last job, and I'm certified to administer it."

Jack frowned, and considered Maggie's statement. He started to shake his head. "I don't know if we can take the risk. What if something goes wrong?"

"It's not like you're going through her abdomen and need the higher-level anesthesia. But with a heart monitor, an IV and the right dosing of meds, I can keep her comfortable and out long enough for you to do the procedure."

"I can do it, but Catherine has to agree," Jack said.

"I agree. I agree. I'm in too much pain to make the flight for something you can do right here and now." She reached for Jack's hand. "Please, do this for me," she whispered. "I don't want to leave my home to have this done by strangers."

"Sign the consent, and I'll do it. Where's your husband?"

"Out on a fishing trip." Catherine's chin trembled and Maggie stroked Catherine's hair back from her face.

"It'll be OK. I promise," Maggie said, and offered what she hoped was a comforting smile. "Jack and I will take care of you."

"You're a good friend," Catherine whispered.

Minutes later everyone was ready.

"What's your plan?" Jack asked. Though he didn't outwardly betray it, Maggie knew he was nervous. The set of his jaw and the focus in his gaze told her.

"I start with small increments of Fentanyl for the pain and a few milligrams of Versed for amnesic effects, titrate to her response and keep her out." She turned to Catherine. "Do you have any allergies?" Maggie asked.

"No."

"Just listen to the sound of my voice and leave all your worries behind. Take a deep breath in and out," Maggie said, and injected the first micrograms of Fentanyl into the IV line. Maggie kept up a soothing verbal stream of nothing that Jack found as soothing as his patient. Catherine's eyes drooped, and Maggie kept her gaze on the heart monitor. After several minutes Catherine breathed slow and deep. "Night-time, Catherine." Maggie turned to Jack. "She's under."

"Good work," Jack said, his gaze lingering a moment on Maggie, wondering what he'd ever done without her.

CHAPTER THIRTEEN

AFTER the procedure Maggie eased up on the sedation and sat with Catherine, stroking her hair as the medication wore off. Near two a.m., Catherine stirred.

"Is it over?" she asked, and tried to focus on Maggie.

"All over, Sleeping Beauty," Maggie said, her heart aching for Catherine's loss.

"So much for that pregnancy."

"I know this is tough on you, but try to get some rest."

"I will." She squeezed Maggie's hand. "Thanks."

"You're welcome. I'll stay with you tonight, if you like," Maggie offered.

"Don't you work tomorrow?"

"Jack switched me with another nurse, so I'm off."

"I'll be OK. Go home and get some rest. Brittany is on tonight, and she'll look in on me."

"She's been in several times to check on you already. But I'll be back in the morning to see you."

"I'll be fine, and I can go home in the morning."

Jack pulled back the curtain and entered the cubicle. His hair stood on end in clumps, sleep wrinkles marred his face, and he shook his hand as if it had fallen asleep.

The man had never looked better to her. "How's our patient, Maggie?"

"Vitals are good, just a little bleeding, and she's roused nicely from the sedation without nausea or vomiting."

"You two make a great team," Catherine said.

Jack considered her words and looked at Maggie, his gaze never wavering. "You did a really good job with this."

"Thanks." A blush warmed her neck and crept into her face.

"She's great," Catherine said, without opening her eyes. "Give her a raise. A really big one."

Jack chuckled. "I'll think about it. We'll come back in the morning." Jack and Maggie left the room. "Want me to drive you home?"

"Yes. If you don't mind, I'd be grateful. It's been a long day."

In a few minutes they pulled up to Maggie's door. "I meant it when I said you did a great job back there," Jack said, his hands clutching the steering-wheel.

"I was shaking the whole time. I'm still shaking now." She held up a hand that visibly trembled.

"You never showed it. That's a sign of a real pro." He sighed and rubbed a hand over his face. "And I have to apologize to you."

Surprise lifted her brows. "For what?"

"For being an ass when we first met. I misjudged you based on your looks and your lack of field medicine." He took one of her hands in his. "But you have other fine skills that we need here."

"We?"

"Yes. The clinic." He cleared his throat and looked away, unable to speak aloud the feelings he had for her. Doing so would only get both of them hurt. "I'm releasing you from your probation."

"What do *you* need, Jack?"

"I've given up on my needs. They're irrelevant."

She faced him in the seat and turned a glare on him. "I disagree. If you're suffering from mental or emotional distress, I don't think you can be as good at your job as you could be. If you're happy, you'll be happier at your work, even if you hate it."

He grabbed her by the shoulders, all of the emotions he'd held back gnawing at his gut, clawing to get out. "You are the only one who has made me want to betray my vows. The only one."

"You're not betraying your vows by having a relationship with someone. Your wife is gone. You're not. Can't you see what's right in front of you, Jack?"

"What is right in front of me?" he asked, his words a husky whisper filled with electricity that sizzled over her.

"Me."

Jack buried his hands in her hair and kissed her. This was one of those long, slow, hot kisses, designed to rouse lustful desire. Jack's lips melted against hers and without any effort he eased her mouth open for his tongue to lure hers into a silken dance of desire. In no hurry, Jack dragged her across the seat and all the way onto his lap. Maggie lay across his chest and gave in to the magical sensations Jack Montgomery's mouth stirred. The glide of his lips across hers, the slow heat generated by his tongue made her want to make love to him with an ache, deep in her soul, that had never been satisfied by anyone except him.

He stroked her face, her neck and his hand roamed over her breasts as if memorizing their shape and how they fit in his hand. He lifted his head.

"Come home with me tonight," Jack whispered. "I want you to stay with me."

Maggie opened her eyes and stared at Jack's face, inches from her own. His eyes shone with desire for her. She was sure that her gaze reflected the same need, but that wasn't the only need she had for Jack. "I can't."

"You aren't working in the morning," he said. "No one will have to know you were at my place."

Maggie slid from his lap and returned to her seat with a sigh. "That's just it, Jack. It doesn't matter to me if anyone knows or not. Not that I'm going to shout from the rooftops, 'I slept with Jack Montgomery.' I'd know."

"Does anyone know?" he asked.

"No."

"Good. That's best."

"Best for who?" Maggie asked.

Jack raked his hair. "You want promises I can't give you, Maggie. You're asking too much of me."

"I don't want promises. There are no guarantees in life, and I wouldn't ask you for one. I'm only asking you for a chance. A chance to love you without restrictions." Maggie opened the door and stepped out. "I'm sorry." She closed the door of the Jeep and ran into the house.

Jack watched her go, slammed a fist against the steering-wheel, and cursed. He put the vehicle in gear and drove home. Restless despite the late hour and the grueling day they'd had, Jack couldn't sleep. Reaching for the refrigerator door, the kitchen light reflected off his wedding band. He closed the fridge. There was nothing in the damned thing anyway. Instead of trying to seek solace in food, Jack decided a cold shower would be better. It would douse the lust that had seized his body since Maggie Wellington had come to town.

Immersed in the shower, he contemplated the events of the day. The food-poisoning patients would all recover after a few more days of rest. Then Catherine came to mind. He knew she'd suffered through two miscarriages in the past, and this one wasn't going to be any easier for her emotionally, especially with her husband absent. But the spirit healed with time. He knew hers would.

Suddenly Jack frowned, realizing something. Maggie had known Catherine was pregnant. That must have been why they'd traded places at the last minute for the transport. That was Maggie, always putting other people's needs before her own, always there for a friend. Jack closed his eyes and rubbed his hands over his face. His ring scraped his forehead. "Ow," he said. That was the second time he'd noticed the band in just a few minutes. It usually stayed in the background, and he never noticed it.

Without thinking any more about it, he slipped the ring from his finger, reached out of the shower and placed it next to the sink. After he'd finished the shower he rinsed off with cold water. He almost leaped from his skin at the frigid temperature change. He looked down his body. Yep. That ought to work for a while.

Wrapped in a towel, he left the bathroom and entered the bedroom. So many of Arlene's things still lay around. Even the closet held her clothing and shoes he'd never gotten around to packing up.

Jack put on a pair of ratty sweat pants, T-shirt and well-worn trainers. A trip to the garage for a box, and he returned to the bedroom. One by one, he packed away Arlene's belongings. Since they'd had no children, there was no one to save them for. Perhaps Ella would want some of Arlene's collectibles. He'd call her tomorrow to see if she could come over and help.

Lying down on the bed, Jack tried again to sleep, but images of Maggie and their time together at the fish camp swamped his brain, refusing to leave him to the peace he sought.

In a bed across town, Maggie punched her pillow, lay with her head at the foot of the bed and drank hot chocolate, all in the hope of finding a few hours of sleep. Images of Jack kept her from it. Each time she drifted into a light doze she jolted awake, the feel of Jack's body against hers so real she thought he had come back to her.

She rose and took two Benadryl. The clinic prescribed the antihistamine to help people with insomnia without resorting to narcotics. Maggie prayed to the god of sleep to take her under for a few hours—she needed the sleep badly. In the meantime, she dug through her file folder and pulled out the paperwork for CRNA school. In the time it took for Maggie to fill out the first two pages of the application, the Benadryl started to take effect. With a satisfied stretch and a yawn she left the paperwork on the kitchen table and returned to her room. The rest of the references and her résumé could wait until morning.

* * *

Maggie didn't have to be at the hospital, but she wanted to beat Jack over there to check on Catherine. She pulled on a pair of denim shorts, a plain white T-shirt and an Alaska sweatshirt over the top. With her hair pulled into a high swinging ponytail and feet shoved into backless tennis shoes, she was ready. On the way out the door she tucked some money into her pocket and all but skipped to the clinic, refreshed and ready to see Catherine.

The place was quiet for a change. She pushed through the staff doors, looking for Catherine.

"Miss? Can I help you?" Kyle called out to her. "This area is restricted to staff only."

Maggie turned around with a laugh. "Kyle? It's me."

The man staggered and slapped a hand to his chest as he glanced her up and down. "Whoa, Maggie. You look *so-o* different out of uniform. I thought you were a tourist who'd gotten lost." He took her hand and kissed it, and she giggled. "Let me be the first to say thank you."

"For what?" she asked, puzzled.

"For wearing those shorts." He eyed her legs. "Those are a mighty fine set of limbs you got there. Ever use them to hike with?" he asked.

Jack watched the flirtation going on from the doorway. He clenched his jaw and narrowed his eyes. Somehow the pencil in his grip snapped, startling him. He took one step forward, then stopped. He had no claim on Maggie. How many times had he told her so? She could flirt with whomever she wanted. With a laugh she embraced Kyle, and Jack's control broke into pieces like the pencil.

The hell he didn't have any claim on her. Long strides carried him forward.

"Kyle, don't you have patients to check on?"

"I just checked—"

"Yeah. I saw what you were checking." He took Maggie by the arm. "Come with me." He marched her into his office and slammed the door behind them.

"What are you doing?" She jerked her arm from his grip. "You don't have any right to treat me this way."

"You were causing a distraction in the middle of the clinic," he said, and tossed the broken pencil pieces into the trash can.

"I came to check on Catherine."

"She's gone home already."

"Fine. Then I'll just go to her house." She started toward the door.

"Guess you can go back to Kyle now. Sorry I interrupted."

"What the hell are you talking about? Interrupted what?"

Jack crossed the room. "I saw you, Maggie. I saw how he looked at you. He has no right to look at you like that. No right to touch you like that." Jack's hands clenched into fists, and he longed to do something useful with them, like bash them into Kyle's face.

"Did you happen to notice how I looked at him?"

"What?" Jack shook his head, trying to clear the anger from it.

"I looked at him like I look at Jamie. Like a brother. There's nothing sexual between us, but that's none of your business, is it? And as you won't make it your business, leave me alone."

"Before you go, here's your paycheck." He reached into his desk and pulled out an envelope, then opened the door for her to leave.

Maggie took the envelope from him and tore it open. She frowned as she looked at her paycheck. "Jack, this is wrong. It's way too much money."

He took it from her, glanced at it and handed it back to her. "It's correct. Look at the hours worked."

Maggie read it again and frowned. "I still don't understand."

"You got time and a half for the transport and the time at the fish camp."

Maggie stared at him as if he'd lost his mind. "You paid me to have sex with you!"

Jack yanked her back into the office and slammed the door again. "No, I didn't pay you to have sex with me. You get time and a half for the transport until you return home again, however long that takes—that's the policy. We were gone for two days. And keep your voice down. Someone could hear you."

"So what? I'm through doing what people tell me to do because it's uncomfortable not to or because it's proper. I've had enough! I'll tell anyone I want that we had sex. In fact, I think I'll take an ad out in the newspaper. They even have pictures of us together so it should be easy." Maggie reached for the door.

But Jack was faster. He caught her by the arm and spun her around to face him. Without thinking, he smashed through the restraint that he'd kept around himself since he met Miss Maggie Wellington. His arms flashed out and brought her against him, molding her to his body, the fit more perfect than anything else in life.

"You are mine." With a growl, primitive sounding even to him, he captured her mouth with his. The taste of her was pure wild Alaska honey. She met his ferocity with her own, grinding her lips against his. She met the thrust of his tongue with hers. Her hands fisted in his hair, refusing to release her hold on him. Jack backed them against the wall of the office. He held Maggie there, plundering her mouth, memorizing every scent, texture and sound of her as he claimed her for himself.

He broke away from her mouth and seared kisses down her neck, irritated that clothing barred her skin from his. The reaction of his body was swift and fierce, straining against his zipper. If he could rip off Maggie's clothes, he'd take her there against the wall in his office, regardless of anyone who might hear them, and spend himself inside her until they were both drained and satisfied.

As if coming back into his body, his movements slowed, and he noticed Maggie's ragged breathing. He looked at her face, and he pulled back as he noticed tears. In that moment he knew without question that he loved her. How in God's name was he going to live with that? How was he going to live without it? For her sake, he had to let her go. With hands that trembled, he cupped her face.

Maggie hiccuped and tried to control her tears.

"I'm sorry. It won't happen again."

Looking miserable, Maggie pulled away from him and grabbed a tissue from a box on his desk. "God, Jack. Can't you see that I love you? It's written all over me every time we're together." She wiped her face.

"You think you love me," he said, her words twisting in his gut, more painful than any knife wound.

"You idiot. I know I love you. The sad part is that you won't meet me even halfway." She opened the door and looked at him, her eyes filled with sorrow and pain. "Goodbye, Jack. I'll give you my resignation by the end of the day." She turned down a hall away from the main clinic, Kyle and other potential witnesses.

By the time Jack had settled himself enough to go after Maggie, she'd disappeared. Without thought as to the consequences, he raced after her, assuming she'd have gone home. So many times he'd just entered Ella's house without knocking, but he hesitated now at the threshold. Should he just go in and have it out with Maggie or walk away from her for ever?

But as he went to knock on the door it opened, and Maggie stood before him. She reached out and took his hand in hers. "I'm sorry I yelled at you."

"Maggie…" He looked up at her and in that moment he knew he had to tell her he loved her and claim her for himself. How could he? Yet how could he not love the courage and humor and all the things that made her Maggie? He lifted his hand and gently stroked her cheek. "I can't help myself, Maggie, but I love you. God, help me, I do."

"Jack? You're just distraught. This isn't real, it's not true." She began to move away from him but his grip on her hand made her stay.

"No. You've at last managed to open my eyes all the way. I do love you, but—"

"Stop right there," she interrupted, and placed her fingers on his lips. "Say it again."

"I love you," Jack said. Yet inside sadness plagued him. What about Arlene?

"I know you've held yourself back. And I don't want you to give up anything for me."

"What do you mean?" He frowned, but hope flared to life in his heart.

"Your love is big enough for both Arlene and me. If you'll let me, I'd like to know her." She stroked his hair.

Jack clasped her against him as his vision blurred. "I'd like that." He took an unsteady breath and blew out all the doubts, the worries, and the guilt. "I do love you."

"I love you, too."

"I don't know what kind of future we can have, but I'll work on it with you." He stood and looked down at the table beside her. With a frown, he noticed the paperwork she had been working on. "What's this?"

"An application for school." She took the papers from his hands and stacked them to one side.

"School? You were going to leave without telling me?" He could hardly believe this was happening.

"Jack, sit down." Maggie frowned and tried to urge him into a chair.

"I don't need to sit down. I need some answers." His heart raced in his chest. Had he just been delusional a moment ago? "You can't leave."

"As usual, you're jumping to conclusions. A huge one this time. I'm *not leaving*," she said, and groaned through gritted teeth. "Now, sit down and listen to me for just a minute," she said, and shoved him into a chair.

"I *do* want to go to school. CRNA school. But it's going to take me a year to go through the process and get accepted. So I won't be going anywhere for a while."

Jack raked his fingers through his hair. "But you'll still leave, won't you?"

The sorrow in his eyes almost brought Maggie to her knees. "Yes."

"Well, I guess that's the end of it, isn't it?" he said, and stood. "I knew—"

"I'd hoped that you'd come with me." Maggie chewed on her lower lip, hesitation and vulnerability on her face.

Jack stopped at the door and turned. "Come with you?"

"Yes. To Seattle. That's where I'm going to school. Your family's there, and I had hoped that you would want to see them again, maybe make a home with me."

"Make a home with you?" Jack blinked as the blinders fell away from his eyes. For good.

"Yes. Then we could come back. You've talked endlessly about not having anyone to run anesthesia. After I graduate, I could do it. We could run the clinic together, Jack." She moved toward him, her steps slow, hesitant. "That is, if you want me. If you love me and want to make a life with me."

Before Maggie realized he had moved, Jack was holding her against him. "Of course I want you. I've spent the last few weeks trying not to, but I just can't be with you and not want you any longer. I don't care who knows any more. I love you, Maggie. I love you."

Her hands clutched his, and her eyes went wide. "You took off your ring," she whispered.

"I did. It was the right time." He kissed her hard, then drew back. "I want to make a place in my life for you if you'll have me. In my heart. All of it."

Tears flooded Maggie's eyes. "Jack." She breathed

his name. "I don't know what the future holds, but I want one with you in it. I love you. I've loved you since the trip to the fish camp. I know you had to leave me behind, and I loved you for coming back for me."

"I was so scared for you, but I didn't know why until now. You've made my life worth living again, Maggie. I'll be forever grateful to you for that." He smiled and his time it reached all the way to his eyes.

"Grateful?" Maggie stepped back as the smile dropped from her face and apprehension curled in her stomach.

"Yes. I believe it's important to thank people when they do good deeds."

"I've just bared my soul to you, and you're *grateful* to me? Oh, God. This is so humiliating." Maggie hung her head.

Jack placed his hands on her shoulders. "I am grateful, Maggie. Because it made me realize how much I love you and what an idiot I've been in not seeing how much you love me, too."

She looked up at him and met his gaze, seeing the truth in his words. "Would you put another ring on your hand?"

"Only if it's yours," he said, and kissed her.

EPILOGUE

MAGGIE shivered, but whether it was from nerves or the cold she couldn't tell. A wintry wind ruffled her full-length white coat. Matching boots warmed her feet beneath the ivory lace gown. Flowers didn't last long in the cold air, so Maggie carried a bundle of silk calla lilies.

Catherine fussed at her one more time, adjusting the wreath of flowers and cascade of ringlets dripping from Maggie's crown.

"It's been quite a year, hasn't it?" Catherine smiled. She was so pleased that Maggie had found the happiness she deserved.

"Yes, for us both." Maggie reached out to hug her friend and had to accommodate the woman's enlarged belly. Catherine's dreams were also coming true with a viable pregnancy.

"You are the most beautiful bride I've ever seen," Catherine whispered, and wiped tears from her eyes. "I cry at everything these days, but they are happy tears for you."

"Thank you," Maggie said, and looked away from her friend up at the bright blue sky. Winter was arrived, crisp and clear, providing six hours of brilliant sunshine. Today Maggie's special day seemed blessed with even more. It was welcome in the midst of a winter carnival.

"Are you ready?" Jamie asked as he fluffed his coat and stamped his feet, trying to stay warm.

"Yes."

"No doubts?"

"None whatsoever," Maggie said, and gave a smile to Jamie.

"Then, little sister, I think there's someone waiting for you."

"Take me to him," she said, and tucked her arm into the crook of his.

Jamie helped Maggie into the waiting dog sled and climbed in behind her. "Let's go, Ella," he said.

"You got it. Hike!" she called to the team of eight Alaskan sled dogs. They pulled together and the sled shot forward through the snow.

Ella mushed them through the village and past the church, too small to accommodate all the guests. Everyone who knew the couple wanted to offer good wishes for their future together.

The winter carnival had begun. Ice sculptures of mermaids, whales, fishermen and wolves were scattered around the area, giving an otherworldly ambiance to the day.

The small group arrived at a castle of ice that took center stage. Guests milled around, admiring the sculptures and drinking hot coffee, but everyone turned as the sled came to a stop.

Jamie jumped out and then offered Maggie his hand as she stepped out of the sled. "Ready?"

"Definitely." She nodded, smiling. From the entrance of the castle Jack stood only twenty feet away, the light in his eyes only for her.

The music began, and Maggie clutched Jamie's arm as they walked down the aisle of ice to her man. Jamie gave her over to Jack, who leaned down and whispered into her ear, "I love you, Maggie."

"No kissing before the pronouncement," the minister said with a grin.

"Then hurry, because I want to kiss her. A lot," Jack replied, and those close enough to hear chuckled.

Maggie and Jack recited their vows, binding their lives together.

After the ceremony the festivities moved indoors, and Jamie took Maggie aside. "Father sent a present," he said, and drew a long envelope from beneath his coat.

Maggie shook her head, trying not to let old emotions take hold. "I don't want his money," she said.

"Good, because you aren't getting it." He put the envelope into her hands. "This is the first installment for the free clinic you want to build."

Maggie clutched Jamie to her. "Oh! You did it. Thank you," she cried.

"This was all you, little sister. If you hadn't asked, it wouldn't have happened."

As Maggie wiped away a tear, Jack approached. "Jamie, why are you making my bride cry on our wedding day?"

She turned and smiled up at her new husband, handing him the envelope.

Jack quickly scanned the document and pulled Maggie into his arms. "You are an angel, my angel," he said.

"Yours and only yours," Maggie said, and kissed him.

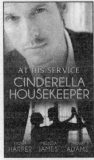

The World of Mills & Boon®

There's a Mills & Boon® series that's perfect for you. We publish ten series and, with new titles every month, you never have to wait long for your favourite to come along.

Blaze.

Scorching hot, sexy reads
4 new stories every month

By Request

Relive the romance with the best of the best
9 new stories every month

Cherish™

Romance to melt the heart every time
12 new stories every month

Desire™

Passionate and dramatic love stories
8 new stories every month

Visit us Online

Try something new with our Book Club offer
www.millsandboon.co.uk/freebookoffer

M&B/WORLD2